Praise for J.T. Ellison's
ALL THE PRETTY GIRLS

"J.T. Ellison's debut novel rocks.
Darkly compelling and thoroughly chilling, with rich
characterisation and a well-layered plot, *All the Pretty
Girls* is everything a great crime thriller should be."
—Allison Brennann,
New York Times best selling author of *Fear No Evil*

"Taylor Jackson is a fresh portrayal of a cop with a serial
killer to catch. Creepy thrills from start to finish."
—James O. Born, author of *Burn Zone*

"An impressive debut that is rich not just in suspense but
in the details. It's all gritty, grisly and a great read."
—M.J. Rose, international bestselling author of
The Reincarnationist

"*All the Pretty Girls* is a spellbinding suspense novel and
Tennessee has a new dark poet. J.T. Ellison's fast-paced,
clever plotting yields a page-turner *par excellence*.
A turbocharged thrill ride of a debut."
Julia Spencer-Fleming, Edgar Award finalist
and author of *All Mortal Flesh*

"Ellison hits the ground running with an electrifying
debut. *All the Pretty Girls* is a masterful thriller, shockingly
authentic and unputdownable. Fans of Sandford,
Cornwell and Reichs will relish every page."
—J.A. Konrath, author of *Dirty Martini*

J.T. ELLISON
ALL THE PRETTY GIRLS

MIRA

All the characters in this book have no existence outside the imagination
of the author, and have no relation whatsoever to anyone bearing the
same name or names. They are not even distantly inspired by any
individual known or unknown to the author, and all the incidents are
pure invention.

First published in Great Britain 2010.
MIRA Books, Eton House, 18-24 Paradise Road,
Richmond, Surrey, TW9 1SR

ISBN 978 0 7783 0390 9

60-0910

MIRA's policy is to use papers that are natural, renewable and
recyclable products and made from wood grown in sustainable forests.
The logging and manufacturing processes conform to the legal
environmental regulations of the country of origin.

Printed in Great Britain
by Clays Ltd, St Ives plc

J.T. Ellison is a thriller writer based in Nashville, Tennessee. Her short stories have appeared in *Demolition* magazine, *Flashing in the Gutters, Mouth Full of Bullets* and *Spinetingler* magazine. *All the Pretty Girls* is her first novel in the Taylor Jackson series. She is a weekly columnist at Murderati.com and is a founding member of Killer Year. Visit JTEllison.com for more information.

For Randy
and
my parents.
Love you more.

One

"No. Please don't." She whispered the words, a divine prayer. "No. Please don't." There they were again, bubbles forming at her lips, the words slipping out as if greased from her tongue.

Even in death, Jessica Ann Porter was unfailingly polite. She wasn't struggling, wasn't crying, just pleading with those luminescent chocolate eyes, as eager to please as a puppy. He tried to shake off the thought. He'd had a puppy once. It had licked his hand and gleefully scampered about his feet, begging to be played with. It wasn't his fault that the thing's bones were so fragile, that the roughhousing meant for a boy and his dog forced a sliver of rib into the little creature's heart. The light shone, then faded in the puppy's eyes as it died in the grass in his backyard. That same light in Jessica's eyes, her life leaching slowly from their cinnamon depths, died at this very moment.

He noted the signs of death dispassionately. Blue lips, cyanotic. The hemorrhaging in the sclera of the eyes, pinpoint pricks of crimson. The body seemed to cool immediately, though he knew it would take some time for the heat to fully dissipate. The vivacious yet shy eighteen-year-old was now nothing more than a piece of meat, soon to be consigned back to the earth. Ashes to ashes. Dust to dust. Blowfly to maggot. The life cycle complete once again.

He shook off the reverie. It was time to get to work. Glancing around, he spied his tool kit. He didn't remember kicking it over, perhaps his memory was failing him. Had the girl actually struggled? He didn't think so, but confusion sets in at the most important moments. He would have to consider that later, when he could give it his undivided thought. Only the radiant glow of her eyes at the moment of expiration remained for him now. He palmed the handsaw and lifted her limp hand.

No, please don't. Three little words, innocuous in their definitions. No great allegories, no ethical dilemmas. No, please don't. The words echoed through his brain as he sawed, their rhythm spurring his own. No, please don't. No, please don't. Back and forth, back and forth.

No, please don't. Hear these words, and dream of hell.

Two

Nashville was holding its collective breath on this warm summer night. After four stays of execution, the death watch had started again. Homicide lieutenant Taylor Jackson watched as the order was announced that the governor would not be issuing another stay, then snapped off the television and walked to the window of her tiny office in the Criminal Justice Center. The Nashville skyline spread before her in all its glory, continuously lit by blazing flashes of color. The high-end pyrotechnic delights were one of the largest displays in the nation. It was the Fourth of July. The quintessential American holiday. Hordes of people gathered in Riverfront Park to hear the Nashville Symphony Orchestra perform in concert with the brilliant flares of light. Things were drawing to a close now. Taylor could hear the strains of Tchaikovsky's *1812 Overture,* a Russian theme to celebrate America's independence. She jumped slightly with every cannon blast, perfectly coinciding with launched rockets.

The cheers depressed her. The whole holiday depressed her. As a child, she'd been wild for the fireworks, for the cotton-candy fun of youth and mindless celebration. As she grew older, she mourned that lost child, trying desperately to reach far within herself to recapture that innocence. She failed.

The sky was dark now. She could see the throngs of people heading back to whatever parking spots they had found, children skipping between tired parents, fluorescent bracelets and glow sticks arcing through the night. They would spirit these innocents home to bed with joy, soothed by the knowledge that they had satisfied their little ones, at least for the moment. Taylor wouldn't be that lucky. Any minute now, she'd be answering the phone, getting the call. Chance told her somewhere in her city a shooter was escaping into the night. Fireworks were perfect cover for gunfire. That's what she told herself, but there was another reason she'd stayed in her office this holiday night. Protecting her city was a mental ruse. She was waiting.

A memory rose, unbidden, unwanted. Trite in its way, yet the truth of the statement hit her to the core. "When I was a child, I spake as a child, I understood as a child, I thought as a child: but when I became a man, I put away childish things." Or became a woman. Her days of purity were behind her now.

Taking one last glance at the quickening night, she closed the blinds and sat heavily in her chair. Sighed. Ran her fingers through her long blond hair. Wondered why she was hanging out in the Homicide office when she could be enjoying the revelry. Why she was still committed to the job. Laid her head on her desk and waited for the phone to ring. Got back up and flipped the switch to the television.

The crowds were a pulsing mass at the Riverbend Maximum Security Prison. Police had cordoned off sections of the yard of the prison, one for the pro–death penalty activists, another comprised the usual peaceful subjects, a third penned in reporters. ACLU banners screamed injustice, the people holding them shouting obscenities at their fellow groupies. All the trappings necessary for an execution. No one was put to death without an attendant crowd, each jostling to have their opinion heard.

The young reporter from Channel Two was breathless, eyes flushed with excitement. There were no more options. The governor had denied the last stay two hours earlier. Tonight, at long last, Richard Curtis would pay the ultimate price for his crime.

As she watched, her eyes flicked to the wall clock, industrial numbers glowing on a white face: 11:59 p.m. An eerie silence overcame the crowd. It was time.

Taylor took a deep breath as the minute hand swept with a click into the 12:00 position. She didn't realize she was holding her breath until the hand snapped to 12:01 a.m. That was it, then. The drugs would have been administered. Richard Curtis would have a peaceful sleep, his heart's last beat recorded into the annals of history. It was too gentle a death, in Taylor's opinion. He should have been drawn and quartered, his entrails pulled from his body and burned on his stomach. That, perhaps, would give some justice. Not this carefully choreographed combination of drugs, slipping him serenely into the Grim Reaper's arms.

There, the announcement was made. Curtis was pronounced at 12:06 a.m., July 5. Dead and gone.

Taylor turned the television off. Perhaps now she would get the call to arms. Waiting patiently, she laid her head down on her desk and thought of a sunny child named Martha, the victim of a brutal kidnapping, rape and murder when she was only seven years old. It was Taylor's first case as a homicide detective. They'd found Martha within twenty-four hours of her disappearance, broken and battered in a sandy lot in North Nashville. Richard Curtis was captured several hours later. Martha's doll was on the bench seat of his truck. Her tears were lifted from the door handle. A long strand of her honey-blond hair was affixed to Curtis's boot. It was a slam-dunk case, Taylor's first taste of success, her first opportunity to prove herself. She had acquitted herself well. Now Curtis was dead as a result of all her hard work. She felt complete.

Taylor had stood vigil for seven years, awaiting this moment. In her mind, Martha was frozen in time, a seven-year-old little girl who would never grow up. She would be fourteen now. Justice had finally been served.

As if in deference to the death of one of their own, Nashville's criminals were silent on this night, finding better things to do than shoot one another for Taylor's benefit. She drifted between sleep and wakefulness, thinking about her life, and was relieved when the phone finally rang at 1:00 a.m.

A deep, gruff voice greeted her. "Meet me?" he asked.

"Give me an hour," she said, looking at her watch. She hung up and smiled for the first time all night.

Three

"I sure am glad we don't live in California."

Detectives Pete Fitzgerald, Lincoln Ross and Marcus Wade were killing time. Nashville's criminal element seemed to be taking a vacation. They hadn't had a murder to investigate in nearly two weeks. The city had been strangely quiet. Even the Fourth of July holiday had procured no deaths for their investigative skills. No one was scheduled for court, and their open cases were either resolved or held up by the crime lab. They had hit dead time.

The three men were crammed in their boss's office, watching TV. A perfectly acceptable pastime, especially since the department had inked a deal with the cable company. Ostensibly, the televisions were to be tuned to twenty-four-hour news networks, but the channels invariably got changed. Usually to accommodate the guilty habit of daytime soaps to which many of the detectives were addicted.

Today though, a car chase through the mean streets of Los Angeles had captured the three detectives' attention. Exciting, splashy. A kidnapping, a semiautomatic weapon at the ready, even a stolen red Jaguar. The car rolled through the various highways, rarely going under seventy miles an hour, captivating the news announcers that speculated breathlessly about whether the kidnap victim was in the vehicle or not. The homicide team cheered on their brothers in blue.

Fitz swept a beefy arm up and looked at his watch. The chase had been going on for nearly two hours now. "They put that spike strip down about five minutes ago. Wheels should start coming off here soon."

"There you go." Marcus pointed to the screen, where a large piece of tire had flown from the back wheel of the Jag, narrowly missing the pursuit car. His brown eyes were shining, excited. Fitz gave him a grin, the kid was just so young.

"You ever done a chase, Marcus?" he asked, leaning back, arms over his prodigious belly.

"No, but I have done all the training for it. I can drive, man, I can drive."

"Remind me not to give you the keys. It's over now." Lincoln Ross stood and stretched, brushing invisible wrinkles from his charcoal-gray Armani suit. "He starts running on rims, they can do a Pitt Maneuver and knock him out. See, there it is."

The pursuit car slipped up on the Jag like a black-and-white snake, then gently bumped the back right fender. In a textbook reaction, the driver of the Jag spun out, slamming into a guardrail, losing a fender, and came to rest facing traffic. In an instant, vehicles surrounded him, cops with long guns and sidearms pointed at him. No escape.

The TV anchors congratulated themselves on a story well covered, predicting it would be anywhere from five minutes to five hours before the standoff would be over. Promising not to break away from the coverage until there was a resolution, they brought in the experts, a former police officer and a hostage negotiator, for the requisite public speculation of the criminal's past. A producer somewhere in New York turned off the five-second delay a moment too soon, and the detectives stared as the door to the Jaguar opened. The suspect jumped out, dragging a woman out of the driver's-side door by the hair.

There was frantic movement on the ground, a quick tightening of the cordon around the kidnapper. The suspect looked up in the air, making sure the overhead helicopter had a moment to focus its long lens on his grinning face. He pulled the woman upright, lifted his arm and shot her in the head. He was gunned down before she hit the ground, the pandemonium obvious. The network went black for a heartbeat, then focused on the face of the shocked anchor. He looked green.

"Like I said, damn glad we don't live in California," Fitz grumbled.

The phone rang and he answered, listening carefully while jotting a few notes. "We're on it."

"What's up?" Marcus had leaned so far back in his chair that he threatened to tip over on his back.

"Body out in Bellevue. I'll go. I'll call Taylor from the car."

Lincoln and Marcus were up immediately. "We're

coming, too," Marcus said. "I know I don't want to sit around here anymore. Do you, Lincoln?"

"Hell, no."

They marched dutifully from the office, gathering suit jackets and keys on the way out. Lincoln grinned, happy at last for an excursion. "At least there won't be a car chase."

The day was stifling, humidity in the high nineties, a threat of rain on the horizon. Though it was full light, the sun was not shining. A thick miasma of haze blanketed the sky, turning the blue to gray. Nashville in the summer.

The crime scene was populated with sweating men and women. Their movements were sluggish, practiced, not at all urgent. Several wore masks to shelter their fragile sinuses from the smell. A decomposing body in ninety-degree heat could fell even the strongest professional.

They were assembled in a grassy field at the Highway 70 and Highway 70 South split, near the westernmost edge of Davidson County. The area was known as Bellevue, only fifteen minutes from downtown. Another couple of miles and Cheatham County would have the job. It was Metro Homicide who had gotten the call instead. Taylor had felt the same sense of boredom her detectives were experiencing, and was happy for the diversion.

She stood over the body, drinking in the scene. Her blond hair was pulled into a messy ponytail, her long body casting grotesque muted shadows in the high grass. She wore no mask, her nostrils pinched and white, her mouth open so she could breathe without inhaling death. A Jane Doe, young, brown hair massed beneath her swollen body. Brown eyes glinted dully from cracked eyelids. The bugs had done their duty, ingesting, laying eggs, repopulating their masses. A struggling white larva spilled from the girl's mouth.

Taylor nearly came undone, imagining that worm in her own mouth, and mistakenly took in a deep breath through her nose. She winced and turned away for a moment, watching the activity around her. Usually the death greeters would swarm like their own type of insect, but no one was in much of a hurry today. Fitz was ambling back toward the crime scene control area, he'd taken a cursory look at the body, covered his mouth and politely excused himself. She could see Marcus and Lincoln conferring in the distance, waves of heat shimmering around their bodies. Crime scene techs carried brown paper bags to their vehicles, patrol officers kept their backs to the body. The scene stirred, listless, the entire group indolent in the heat.

Except the man striding effortlessly toward her. He was a big man, dark haired, graceful. He wasn't one of hers.

He stopped in front of one of the patrol officers, flipped open a small leather identification case, speaking loud enough for Taylor to hear. "Special Agent John Baldwin. FBI."

The officer stepped aside to let Baldwin continue his trek toward Taylor. He slipped the case into his breast pocket, then came to her with his right hand outstretched. He winked as he took her hand. She felt the warm pad of flesh press her own for a brief instant. A concussive touch, she felt it all the way to her toes. She stood straighter. At nearly six feet, she generally towered over men. This one was taller by nearly five inches, and she had to look up to meet his eyes. They were the oddest shade of green, deeper than jade, lighter than emeralds. Cat eyes, she thought.

Her heart beat a little faster. Taylor's right hand went to her neck, an unconscious gesture. The four-inch scar was barely healed; she still looked as if she'd been garroted. A knife slash, compliments of a crazed suspect. A permanent souvenir from her last case. Gathering herself, she flipped her ponytail off her shoulder and gave Baldwin a brief but warm smile.

"What are you doing here? I didn't ask for FBI backup. It's just a murder." She paused for a moment, concerned by the expression on his angular face. She knew the look. "Please tell me it's just a murder?"

"I wish I could."

"Why the posturing?" Taylor looked over Baldwin's shoulder. There were few people on the scene who weren't familiar with John Baldwin. Her team—Fitz, Marcus and Lincoln—had worked with him before.

"I needed this to be an official consultation. I think I know who she is." He gestured almost carelessly at the body prostrate at their feet.

"Ah. Out of state, I'd guess. We haven't had any missing persons reported in the right time frame for this."

"Out of state. Right. Mississippi." The statement was absent, an afterthought. Baldwin was circling the body, taking in all the details. The bruises around the girl's neck were visible despite the decomposition. He made another circle, smiling to himself with a bizarre look of triumph. The body had no hands.

"I think this may be the work of our boy."

"Your boy?" Taylor's eyebrow went up an inch. "You know who did this?"

He ignored the question for a moment. "Is it okay to touch her?"

"Yes. The crime scene techs have finished with her for now, and we're waiting for the medical examiner to haul her out of here. I was just giving her one last look."

Baldwin reached into his pocket and pulled out a pair of thin white latex gloves. He squatted next to the body and reached for the girl's right stump, knocking a few maggots off in the process.

Taylor prompted him again. "Your boy, you say?"

"Mmm, hmm. I don't know his name, of course, but I recognize his work."

Taylor went down on one knee beside him. "He's done this before?" She spoke quietly. No personnel were within earshot, but just in case, she didn't want the leaks to start before she had a grip on what was happening. Habit.

"Twice, that I know of. Though he hasn't hit for a month. We've dubbed him the Southern Strangler, for lack of a better name. You know us feds, not an original thought between us." He tried for a smile, but it came out as a leer.

"Why haven't I heard of this…strangler?"

"You have. Remember the Alabama case a few months ago, in April? Pretty little college nursing student, disappeared from the U of A campus. We found her in—"

"Louisiana. I remember."

"Right. The second was last month, from Baton Rouge. Found her in Mississippi."

Taylor searched her memory for the details of the

case. It had been all over the national news networks, with correspondents broadcasting live from Baton Rouge, lamenting and glorifying the kidnapping. But no one had put the two together, as far as she knew. She told Baldwin that.

"The time frame was lengthy enough that the media didn't jump on the connection. And we kept a few things back. The hands, for one."

"Why, for God's sake? Aren't you guys supposed to get the word out so we small-town law enforcement types know we've got someone on the loose?" Her sarcasm missed its mark. Baldwin only nodded.

"The lubricant, too. We think there is consensual sex, he uses a lubricated condom. Whichever M.E. catches it should look for that."

Taylor shook her head, putting aside the strange reality that had marred her beautiful southern town. A serial killer, passing through her turf. Great. It wasn't something she was prepared to keep quiet.

"I already called Sam, she'll take good care of her." Dr. Samantha Owens Loughley was the chief medical examiner for the mid-state of Tennessee, and a friend. "You said you know who she is." She indicated the body with a jerk of her chin, eyes accusing.

"Her name is Jessica. Jessica Ann Porter. Jackson, Mississippi. She's only been gone three days."

Taylor looked down again. Three days? The decomp was more advanced than that. Baldwin read her thoughts.

"You know how this works. Heat's speeding up the process. Two weeks in this mess would be all it took to get her down to the bones. We're lucky we found her so quickly. Another week and it would have been hell to ID her in the field."

"Tell me more."

"There isn't a lot more to go on. He likes brunettes. Young brunettes. All three girls have brown eyes, are late teens to early twenties, and we don't have really good victimologies on them. None of them had risk behaviors, none of them had been seen with strangers, nothing. They just went poof. One day they were living their lives, the next, they were just gone. I've been working the periphery of the cases. I was kept informed but I didn't do the investigation myself. Now that we may have three victims, I'm probably getting involved full-time."

Taylor heard tires crunching on the gravel on the side of the road. The body, Jessica's body, she corrected herself, was only about ten yards from the roadside. The news van would be able to get a clear shot. Too clear. She waved to Marcus standing by his car, motioned to the van. She didn't need to say a word. He started signaling to them immediately, forcing them away from the scene. Taylor watched as he maneuvered them to a very discreet vantage point, one from which they wouldn't be able to view the body. She smiled to herself. Screw the newsies.

Baldwin had taken a notebook out of his back pocket and was writing furiously, scribbling notes as quickly as his mind could feed them through his fingers to his pen.

"Have you found…?" Baldwin's voice trailed off. A uniformed officer was waving frantically at Taylor. She eyed Baldwin for a moment, realizing he knew exactly what the fuss was about. He just shrugged and put out a hand in a "you first" gesture. She stared him down for a moment, then made her way to the gesticulating officer. The look of horror on his face was evident from twenty paces.

"You have something there, Officer?" Taylor didn't recognize him, he must have been fresh out of the academy.

"Yes, Lieutenant," he answered, Adam's apple bobbing. Taylor reached him and followed his pointing finger. In the grass, lying quietly, was a hand.

Taylor reared back, but Baldwin leaned over the hand with interest. She tried for glib.

"Well, Special Agent, since she's missing both hands, I'd say we should find another right around this area, shouldn't we?" The sinking feeling in the pit of her stomach belied the bravado in her statement. She had the distinct feeling there was more to the case than he had told her. He confirmed it in the next moment, the way he gazed at the wayward hand was a dead giveaway that there was more to this than met the eye. She dismissed the patrol officer with a flick of her hand. He scrambled away, visibly relieved.

"No, we won't." He gazed up at her, his green eyes troubled. "You can search for it if you want, but it won't be here."

"What the hell? He's taking the girl's hands off, leaving one in the field and taking one with him? Some sort of trophy?"

Baldwin nodded. "Definitely a trophy. There's just one problem."

For the briefest moment, the reality of what a psycho could do with a severed hand crowded her mind. She shoved the thought away. "What's the problem?"

"This isn't Jessica's hand."

Four

Baldwin excused himself to call in to Quantico, and Taylor signaled for Fitz to join her. He tromped through the field like a general commanding troops, his oversize belly leading his feet.

"What's the fed doin' here?" he asked, tone neutral. Taylor glanced at him, trying to gauge if there was anything more to the inquiry, but Fitz's face was closed, guarded. She decided it was just that, a question.

"Guess." Taylor shaded her eyes, watching Baldwin slink through the crime scene, an overgrown cougar smelling fresh blood.

"He's here to profile the killer because there's a pattern," Fitz answered, following Taylor's gaze. There would only be one reason for a profiler to be playing in their sandbox.

"Two before her. We have a possible ID at least. Jessica Ann Porter. From Mississippi. Where's Lincoln?"

"Back at the car with Marcus."

"He needs to work his magic on the computer. Tell him I want to have all the information the feds have on these murders. The first was the girl from Alabama, the coed that went missing and was found in Louisiana in April. The second one was taken from Baton Rouge in June and dumped in Mississippi. Have him pull all the particulars, and let's see what we have to work with. The feds held back information on the cases, including the fact that the killer is transporting a hand from the previous victim to the new dump site. I'm sure Baldwin will share all that he knows, but I want to have our own file going on this guy."

"You sure he'll give you everything?"

Taylor winked and gave Fitz a full-watt smile, her gray eyes flashing in the white air. "I'm sure."

Taylor was putting the finishing touches on a Bolognese sauce. She tasted, stirred in another spoonful of oregano, tasted again. Hmm. Garlic. Another clove went into the pot and she shut the lid, savoring the rich spiciness that wafted through the steam.

The light was failing outside, darkness rapidly approaching. She busied herself cutting up a fresh five-grain baguette, wrapping it in foil and setting it in the warming oven to toast. She took a sip of wine, a lovely Chianti from the Montepulciano region of Tuscany that she'd discovered with the help of the owner of her local wine store. She called the man Geppetto because of his resemblance to the cartoon version of Pinocchio's father. He was a kindly man with a droopy gray mustache and excellent taste in Super Tuscans. He loved the nickname, but allowed no one but Taylor to bestow it upon him. She smiled and took a deeper drink.

With nothing to do but wait for the sauce to finish cooking, she sat at the kitchen table, sipping wine and watching the lightning bugs hover over her deck. Her home was simple, a log cabin she'd bought for herself years earlier, cozy, tucked in the rolling hills of the Tennessee central basin. She had deer and rabbits, and had seen a fox with her kits trailing behind earlier in the year. Privacy, quiet, all the things an overworked homicide detective needed.

Her thoughts drifted, inevitably, to the earlier crime scene.

Sam had directed the scene, gotten Jessica's body ready for transport. The body, dehydrated and warm, had proved difficult to handle, and the transporter had lost his grip when they brought her up to the gurney. He dropped the head of the bag, and the flies had buzzed angrily. Taylor cursed the muggy weather—death wasn't easier in the cold, but it was more bearable.

What kind of killer were they dealing with? Consensual sex, then strangulation and mutilation, like a bad date gone horribly wrong. Taylor knew Baldwin's profile would fill in some of the answers.

Jessica Porter was being autopsied in the morning. Taylor would be there, a show of respect as well as an attempt to get ahead of Jessica's killer. Clues were always available—even the most fastidious killer left something of himself behind. The fact that this could be his third murder was upsetting, to say the least.

The missing hands bothered her. Death as a rule was never pretty. Taking the girl's hands was an obvious attempt to conceal her identity. Dropping her in a lonely field in ninety-degree heat would do the rest. But why in the world would he deliver the hand of the previous victim to the new crime scene?

Taylor was caught off guard when Baldwin explained the killer's signature. She'd asked the obvious question. Where is the other hand?

He'd given her a mirthless laugh. "That's the question we all want to figure out."

They could have easily missed it. Hell, they'd gotten lucky. The Realtor who was listing the land for sale had dropped by to put a new number on his sign. He was overwhelmed by the smell of rotting flesh, and had called the police when he found the body. Fate had been on their side this day. If it weren't for that they might have missed Jessica Porter for a few weeks, maybe more. Enough time for the heat and the bugs and the vermin to do their job, making it very difficult to identify the remains. The killer was no dummy.

But they'd found Jessica, and now they had a line on the killer. Taylor was wondering about the connection between Jackson, Mississippi and Nashville when she heard the front door open.

"How's my favorite debutante?"

She shot a nasty look toward the owner of the boisterously deep voice, which made him grin. Covering the few yards to her in three quick strides, he grabbed her and pulled her into a rough embrace. She nestled her nose in the hollow above his collarbone and sighed. He smelled good, fresh. There was no scent of lingering death, just soap and cedar. She nuzzled him once more, then pushed him away, hard. He stumbled back, putting up a hand like he could stop the torrent that was about to come.

J.T. Ellison

"Dammit, Baldwin, why didn't you tell me?"

"We're having pasta, I presume? It smells great."

Her look was murderous and he gave her a sheepish shrug. "What did you want me to do, Taylor? How was I supposed to know he was going to come to Nashville? The Porter girl went missing three days ago, and I didn't get the call right away. Next time I'll be sure to roll over and casually mention that a girl has been kidnapped in Mississippi, you might want to be on the lookout for her body here in town. Hell, Taylor, give me a break. I didn't have a clue where he'd be heading. I didn't even know it was the Strangler until I looked at her body."

He reached out as if to stroke her cheek, but she turned away and went to the stove. She busied herself stirring the sauce.

"C'mon, sweetie. If I thought I had a handle on this guy, I would have told you sooner. He hasn't been active for a month. In the wind, totally. We have so little to go on, things are being held together with a wing and a prayer. He doesn't give us a lot to work with. Missing hands and dead bodies."

Taylor turned back to face him. His green eyes were clouded with worry, the salt-and-pepper hair standing on end. She knew that he'd been running his hands through it, trying to make his mind work harder.

"Missing hands and dead bodies seem like an awful lot to me." She sounded peevish and felt idiotic. There was no reason to be mad at Baldwin, he was just doing his job. A job he wanted her to do with him. It looked as if they were going to have the chance to work together, just like he wanted.

"Are you setting up a task force?"

"It's me at the moment. I knew I could work with you on it, so I'm freelancing. There're two other guys working the old cases—Jerry Grimes and Thomas Petty, I'll share information with them, they'll share with me. You know how it is."

Baldwin had been acting in a consultant capacity, on loan from the FBI to Metro Nashville Homicide, for three months now. His help had proved invaluable to her cases. Of course, sharing a bed with him wasn't such a bad perk.

She gave him an appraising smile. "You work fast. Talked to Price, have you?"

He sat at the table, nodding. "Garrett Woods made the call." Woods was Baldwin's boss at the FBI, and friends with Mitchell Price, the head of the Criminal Investigations Division for Metro. Homicide was his responsibility.

Taylor turned back to the stove. "I'm hungry. We can talk about this later."

Baldwin smiled at her. "Who says we're going to talk?"

Taylor was in the shower when the call came. Baldwin knew better than to answer her phone. She was fiercely private and detested the idea of anyone confirming the fact that she and Baldwin were, well, involved would be the best way to put it. Very, very involved. It just wouldn't do to have her detectives questioning her motives or intentions, and she preferred to let them wonder at the nature of their personal relationship. If they knew she was sleeping full-time with a fed, they'd look at her differently. At least, that's what she told herself.

Her best friend was the only one she'd confided in. Sam Loughley thought she was crazy for trying to keep it hush-hush, tried to convince Taylor time and again that her team wouldn't be harassed in the least by Taylor's relationship with Baldwin, but Taylor liked to keep her work life and her private life separate.

She stepped out of the shower, toweled off and made her way to the answering machine. The message was brief. "Call in," the voice said, immediately recognizable as Fitz. It was late, and she was tired, but she dialed Fitz's cell and waited for him to answer.

"'Lo?"

"Fitz, it's Taylor. What's up?"

"Just thought you'd want a heads-up. We got a missing persons report about half an hour ago. Girl named Shauna Davidson, from Antioch. Don't know if it's anything, but she's been missing since yesterday. Never came home last night, so her mother says. She has been trying to reach her, but Shauna isn't answering her home or cell phone. The mother saw the news, heard the report about a dead girl in the field and thought it might be her girl. She completely freaked out. Problem is, the girl in the field isn't Shauna Davidson, and Shauna doesn't seem readily available."

Taylor felt her stomach sinking. "Is she brunette?"

She heard Fitz flipping pages. "Yep. Brown on brown, five-six, hundred forty pounds. Eighteen."

"Any more information on her? Where does she work? Maybe she showed up there?"

Fitz flipped another page. "Doesn't say. Kid like that, I'd bet some clothing store or waitress job. She's in Antioch, probably works at Hickory Hollow or something. I'll chase it down. I'm headed to her place now. Shouldn't be too hard to figure it out. There are officers on the scene, word over the radio is possible foul play. Could be the lock's busted on her door, could be more."

"Well, get out there and see what it looks like. Hopefully, she's just out of pocket."

"I'm on it. I'll call you if we need you."

"Thanks for letting me know. I'll see you in the morning unless something happens tonight."

She hung up the phone. The media would have a field day with this. It was one thing to keep murders and kidnappings from other states out of the news cycle. A murder and kidnapping in their own backyard, however, would be impossible to keep quiet. She checked her watch. Five to ten.

She grabbed a Diet Coke and went to the living room. Baldwin had fallen asleep on the couch, a thick case file clutched in his hands. She recognized the lettering—FBI Eyes Only. She stood looking at him for a moment, not wanting to wake him but knowing she should. He'd want to hear this. She shook his shoulder gently and he started.

"What's the matter?" He sat up abruptly, the folder falling from his hand. It spilled onto the carpet. Taylor saw crime scene photos, horrific images of death. Helping him gather the photos, she wondered what the hell they were doing. Dealing in death day after day. It was a thought she'd been having more and more often lately.

"Fitz just called, there's been a missing persons report filed on an eighteen-year-old girl named Shauna Davidson. He's headed to her place right now, he'll call if he needs me. I wanted to see if the newsies are carrying it."

The look of dread on Baldwin's face was enough to confirm her fears. It was likely that Shauna Davidson wouldn't be coming home tonight.

Taylor turned on the television and curled her legs under her on the couch. The lead story was the body found in Bellevue. They had full-blown coverage of the day's events in the field where they had discovered Jessica Porter's body. Nashville did so love its crime.

Taylor flipped through the other local channels, all of which were tackling the story.

"Shit. Shit, shit, shit, shit, shit."

Baldwin gave her a weak smile. "Looks like the cat's out of the bag."

Taylor flipped back to Channel Five. Whitney Connolly, their lead reporter, was at the scene. It looked like a three-ring circus—what were they hoping to find? Metro had cleared the scene, there was nothing left for them to see. But the b-roll from earlier was gold. The cameras were angled perfectly to catch the landscape of the field, the highway full of flashing blue lights and metro cruisers. Taylor flinched when she realized Channel Five had captured the crime scene techs losing their grip on the body bag as they placed it on the stretcher, the body being jolted—the photographer had gotten a close-up of the bottlenose flies scattering like a cloud of dust. Lovely.

Taylor's cell rang again—Fitz was requesting her presence at Shauna Davidson's apartment. So much for a quiet night. She hung up and pulled on her cowboy boots. Whitney Connolly, who had no more dirt to dish, was asking for anyone who had information regarding the body that had been found in Bellevue to call Metro

Police. Her report had been more thorough than the other channels', her words lingering with delight. Taylor sometimes thought that Connolly enjoyed her job a little too much. Reporting on death and disaster suited her well.

"Whitney Connolly is as tenacious as a pit bull. She's one of the few reporters that seem to enjoy taking on some of the local crime stories, wants to see them through." Baldwin spoke absently, giving credence to Taylor's silent opinion. She glanced at him, he was lost in thought, staring at the television screen.

"I went to school with her."

That caught his attention, and he turned to her. "A fellow debutante from Father Ryan?" he teased.

"Jesus, Baldwin. Yes, I suppose she must have been, she and her twin sister, Quinn. They were a year behind Sam and me. They would have been freshmen when you were a senior. I know you came into school late your senior year, but don't you remember them? That whole story…" She trailed off when Baldwin's phone rang.

He answered it brusquely. "Yes…? Yes, I've heard… No, I don't… I will… I agree… Okay… Tomorrow then." He hung up, then started pacing the living room.

"That was Garrett, making sure I'd heard about the missing girl. I'm officially being tasked full-time on this now, not just as a consultant. Figured that was going to happen."

Taylor gave him her sweetest smile as her own phone rang. She was already up, gun strapped to her side, ready to go. "Welcome to my nightmare. Let's go."

* * *

Taylor pulled up to the yellow tape that was strung across the parking lot to the Davidson girl's apartment building. She smiled as a young officer lifted the tape so she could drive through. Leaning out the window, she pointed to the car behind her.

"Let him through. He's with me." The officer nodded, and she watched in her rearview mirror as Baldwin maneuvered his car under the tape. She pulled up to the bevy of vehicles, turned the engine off and stepped into the night. Baldwin followed suit. She waited for him to join her, then they made their way through the maze of blue-and-white vehicles toward the building.

Fitz met them halfway up the stairs. He looked to be on his way down. Instead, he let them pass, then turned and followed them up, divulging information as they climbed.

"First officer on the scene knocked on the door, didn't hear or see any movement from inside. No signs of forced entry. The landlord gave him a copy of the key, so he proceeded to open the door. It was locked from the inside, but only the push button, not the dead bolt. The officer went in, looked around. Things didn't look out of place until he hit the bedroom. The bed's unmade, biologicals all over it. Crime scene kids are about finished with it. We've done a canvas, too, no one remembers seeing her last night or today. Doesn't look too good."

They'd reached the door to the apartment and ducked under more crime scene tape. There were only a few people left in the room. Taylor nodded to them as she assessed the scene.

Shauna Davidson lived well. The apartment was tastefully decorated with a modern flair. A flat-panel television took up one wall, surrounded by high-end stereo equipment. A tan leather sofa dominated the room, buttery soft fawn suede cushions piled high. A good place to relax. There were adjacent chairs in dark brown suede, and a slate coffee table that drew all the colors together. Not a thing was out of place, as far as Taylor could tell. Magazines were lined up with precision on the corner of the coffee table. There were no errant drinking glasses or cans, no used newspapers. Good taste and a neat freak. Interesting for a young girl.

To the right, Taylor could see a small kitchen and a short hallway that led off the living room. She followed the hall, seeing an unused guest room, an office and, finally, the master bedroom. Here, things were not so neat.

The bed's comforter was lying on the floor, the sheets a tangle at the foot of the bed. Blood soaked the mattress. Taylor looked to the crime scene tech standing deferentially to the left side of the bed, waiting for her.

"Do you have any Polaroids that show exactly how you found it?"

"Yes, ma'am. We tried to take the samples without disturbing the scene too much."

"You've put things back in order then? Matches the Polaroids?"

"Yes, ma'am, this is pretty close to how we found it. We came in, saw the blood, backed out and started taking pictures. Then we took all the samples. It's not as much as it looks, and the biologicals were desiccated. Been there for at least a day. Dusted the bed and side table for prints, came up with a few. We'll get it all into the system, let you know. Soon as you're ready we'll finish bagging and cart it out."

Taylor nodded her thanks and the young man left the room. She turned to Baldwin and Fitz. "Well?" she asked.

Baldwin took in the room, the blood. Taylor could see the signs of recognition on his face. She waited him out. He crept around the room, making notes, taking a few of his own pictures.

Taylor watched Fitz out of the corner of her eye, he was getting impatient. She was, too. "Baldwin, talk to us. What's up here?"

He closed his notebook, slung his camera over his shoulder. "It all looks familiar. This is similar to what I've seen in the other girls' apartments. The unmade bed, the blood. I think he charms them, gets them to invite him home and into their beds, then strangles them and cuts off their hands. Transports the body to wherever he's picked next." He shook his head. "Shauna Davidson. I don't know where we'll find her, but she makes number four. He's speeding things up."

Baldwin paced around the room. "See, there's no sign of forced entry. That's consistent with the other three girls. I think he picks them up somewhere, a bar, a library, who knows. They invite him back to their place. Maybe things get out of hand, maybe the sex starts out consensual, but just as quickly, they're dead. There's no real signs of a struggle. We haven't found any drugs in their system. I think he must tie them up." He circled to the head of the bed. "Hey, get your crime scene guys back in here."

Fitz disappeared and came back with one of the

crime scene techs. Baldwin motioned the man over and pointed to the headboard on the wrought-iron bed. "You missed something," he accused.

The tech turned red, realizing he had missed something. A pale fiber was attached to the frame of the headboard. He quickly collected it, apologizing. As he left, Baldwin clapped him on the back.

"Probably from a rope. We found it at the other scenes, as well. That's why there isn't much sign of a struggle. That he would tie them up fits. See, this kind of killer is excited by the helplessness. Anger, excitement, pleasure, they all come from the same place for this guy. He has a thing for their hands, which I haven't figured out yet. The fetishistic elements are all there, I don't think he's doing it to hide their identities. He's highly organized, plans in advance. The fact that he parts with any of his trophies is interesting. It's a clue, a trail of bread crumbs that he's leaving for us. He wants to sensationalize the killings. Taking the bodies over state lines, the mutilations, all were calculated efforts to make these crimes heinous and splashy. A surefire recipe to get the FBI involved. He wants us to know him. To be sure that it's him. He won't deviate from this pattern, it's become his signature. Now we just have to figure out who he is. VICAP doesn't have a match to this MO in their system. Other than the forensics, we don't have any other information to go on. Witness statements are thin to nonexistent. He's a real ghost, which is part of his plan." The Violent Criminal Apprehension Program would guide them to corresponding murders if the system had a match. Baldwin had been watching for a hit, a fruitless endeavor thus far.

He stopped pacing, a gleam in his eyes. "It's a challenge. He enjoys the fact that he has us stumped. We can't predict where he's headed next, it assures that we're on our toes. Mark my words. He's begging for us to try and find him."

Five

Whitney Connolly sat at her computer in her home office, tapping out e-mails to people around the country. It was her usual morning ritual. Regardless of the day, she got up from her lonely bed, ran to Starbucks for a latte, greeting people she knew and those she didn't with a humbled smile, returned home and turned on the computer. She had a vast network that she communicated with, and the mails were sorted by priority. Friends came first, because that category had the fewest mails to go through. And since they were generally the kindest of the lot, she entered the next grouping with a sense of peace. The fans. They came in all colors, shapes and sizes. Female and male, young and old. Pleasant and not so pleasant. The messages were hard to escape; the network broadcasted all reporters' e-mail addresses on the screen as they gave their reports and posted them next to their pictures on the station's Web site so they'd be accessible to the viewing public.

Whitney felt it was important to answer, thanking

those who had enjoyed her work the night before, being courteous to those who hadn't. Being the top reporter in the Nashville market had its upside, that was for sure. Inevitably she pissed some viewers off, and she felt a sense of responsibility to acknowledge their displeasure and attempt to set things straight. Community relations, and all that.

Today was a good morning though. She had forty fan mails and only five weren't happy with her performance. She read the comments carefully, disregarding the wackos with a simple "I'm sorry you weren't happy with the broadcast. I'll make every effort to correct the problem." She effusively thanked those that sent generous, loving comments and seriously answered questions from those who thought they knew better than she did about the world they lived in. That done, she took a long drink from her cooling latte and set to work on the next group. The important group. The one that really mattered. The tipsters.

Whitney had a vast network of people across the country who sent her information. She had been cultivating the group for years, adding legitimate and not-so-legitimate contacts as she went. She had aspirations, big ones. She knew she was one story away from making it. Being a ranking reporter in Nashville was a pretty good gig. Her station had the highest rating in the market, consistently achieving higher market share than the other network affiliates. She handled the beat during the week, sat in the anchor's chair on the weekend 10:00 p.m. newscast. But deep down, she felt she was better than even a full-time local anchor job. She'd been paying her dues for a while now, and at thirty-four, it was time she got picked up by one of the big dogs. She wanted New York. Not Atlanta, where they all looked the same and weren't allowed to express their own opinions. No, New York was the place to be, and she was one big story away from being there.

She had the looks, that was a given. Tall, leggy and blond, she had a perfect nose that hadn't been surgically altered, full lips that had only seen a little work and a pair of flawless breasts that had cost her a fortune. Fincly drawn eyebrows two shades darker than her hair arched over what she had been told were spectacular blue eyes. Yes, she had the looks all right. And the brains to go with them. Not to mention the ambition to get the job done. She just needed that one story on her reel that would blow them away.

As she scrolled through her mail, searching for the address that would make her a star, she allowed herself a brief respite by switching on the television to the very network she wanted to work for so badly.

The News Alert flashed red across the screen, and Whitney felt her pulse quicken. She was a consummate newswoman after all. What would it be now? A bombing overseas? A trial decided? A politician caught with a dead girl or a live boy? Bad news makes good news for a reporter, regardless of the cost to the public. As the anchor's concerned face filled the screen, she felt the warmth spread over her body. She leaned back in her supple leather chair and smiled. He had struck again.

Six

Taylor woke early and flipped on the television. Despite Baldwin's prediction that Shauna Davidson wouldn't be found anywhere in the local area, a search had been organized. The early news was broadcasting the shot—a line of men and women in blue cargo pants and T-shirts, clutching long poles, moving purposefully through an open area adjacent to Shauna's apartment complex. Comfortable that the investigation was proceeding appropriately, she showered, pulled on her jeans and boots, snapped on her holster and gun and set out for Jessica Porter's autopsy.

She rolled along the highway, darting between speeding eighteen-wheelers, absently noting the beauty of the day. Entranced by the blue skies, she opened her window only to be assaulted by the oily fumes of the highway. She wrinkled her nose and shut the window, thinking back to the conversation she'd had with Baldwin before they'd gone to bed. He was adamant that the Southern Strangler was escalating, positive that the evidence in Shauna Davidson's apartment would trace back to the other three murders. Baldwin had a bit of a sixth sense when it came to his cases, a trait that was highly appreciated and necessary in his line of work. Profiling was a bit like being a criminal yourself. He had a knack for understanding what was within the mind of the killers he hunted. It frightened Taylor sometimes, his intensity and single-mindedness, but he got results. She was hopeful that having him full-time on the case would mean a happy outcome for Shauna Davidson, but didn't really believe it. There was too much blood in the girl's bedroom.

His little debutante. She snorted. She hated it when he called her that, and he knew it. He just loved to stick that pin in a little bit every once in a while. Hell, she would give anything for that part of her past to go away. It wouldn't, though, no matter how hard she might try to pretend. Taylor came from a wealthy family, and had grown up in an affluent area of Nashville known as Forest Hills. She'd had all the little luxuries of a well-bred girl, including the debutante ball she'd reluctantly attended in order to be properly presented to Nashville society, New Year's Eve after her eighteenth birthday. She wondered briefly if Shauna Davidson had been privy to such pointless goings-ons, and quickly dismissed the thought.

It still made her laugh to remember the outright fury she'd caused her parents when she told them she was going to be a cop. Her parents felt she had a few socially acceptable options to choose from as a career. It was generally expected that college was the first destination, where she would meet her future husband who was headed to medical school or law school. Once they were established within his residency program or a junior partnership and were back settled in Nashville, she could devote herself to raising the children, being a leader in Junior League, and maybe open a little specialty shop or form a small charitable organization, of course only after the children were in school full-time.

A second but not as popular option was to aspire to a profession of her own—medicine, law, marketing—finding a husband during the course of these actions and immediately starting the marriage/baby track.

But Taylor was Taylor, and dismissed both options out of hand. She'd watched her mother's life: lunches, teas, commitments to charity work that allowed her group of wealthy friends to continue living in their sorority days, never aging, never losing the shallowness that permeated their lives. Taylor knew that they did good work, that their charities made a difference on some level, but couldn't stand the idea of doing it herself.

That just wasn't for her. Taylor wanted excitement, even danger. She wanted to live, to really experience life in reality, not never-never land. She needed something to allow her to be her normal, unpretentious self. Nashville wasn't a huge town, and due to her rebellion against her mother's well-born intentions for her, she knew people in all walks of life throughout the city. And cops. Lots of cops. She'd had a few run-ins with the law, and as a result not only charmed her way out of trouble but also established friendships with a number of officers, who strongly influenced her decision to join their ranks.

It was a perfect fit for Taylor. She could give back to

her city and not sell herself out in the process. And there was a sense of power, lurking around town, dealing with shady characters and criminals, that she really got off on. She was living in a real world, not one based on spun-sugar bullshit and cutthroat social climbing. Of course, the idealistic view Taylor had, wanting to be a protector, to take care of the people in her community, became crowded by the comprehension that while the cops took care of everyone, no one was there to take care of them. It was a difficult realization, and explained why so many cops had such complicated personal lives, from multiple divorces to illegal drug use, alcoholism and psychological problems and serious control issues. But Taylor still held on to her utopian view of the purpose of the force. She never wanted to go down the broken and tortured path she had seen many of her fellow cops follow, and believed she had the strength to keep herself in check.

So against her mother's wishes, she went to the University of Tennessee, received her B.A. in criminal justice and applied to the force as soon as she graduated. Accepted immediately, she went through the Police Academy, cementing relationships with the people she would make her career with. She was a popular student, though her training officer had a tendency to make things a little rough for her. She was young and pretty, and he was the type that didn't see the need to have women on the force. The dinosaurs were out there, for better or for worse. It didn't deter her, only made her stronger and more committed.

Her first dose of reality wasn't long in coming. Driving her squad car through downtown, keeping an eye out for trouble on Second Avenue, she received a message on her endlessly ringing computer screen that a stabbing had been called in from the projects. Taking off with lights flashing and siren blaring, she arrived to see a young black man sprawled on the ground in a grungy doorway. He was surrounded by wailing family and friends who were trying to stop the copious amounts of blood pouring from a gaping wound in his stomach. In desperation, they were trying to shove his intestines back into the yawning hole. It made no difference. He bled out at her feet. The EMTs arrived moments later, but too late to stop Taylor from losing a large part of her innocence on a dark street deep in the worst projects in town. She finished processing the crime scene and headed back to the station, and once in the locker room she noticed that the man's blood covered her boots. She could never describe the overwhelming emotion she felt then, but she quickly learned to put her feelings aside.

She nearly laughed at the memory of that young girl, shocked by a little blood on her shoes. She'd seen plenty since, enough to weaken the idealistic view she'd had as a rookie officer. Now, at thirty-five, she was the youngest female lieutenant on the force, headed a crack team of homicide detectives, and had seen more than enough blood, some of it from her own gun, some of it hers. Yes, the idealism was well and truly gone now.

She pulled up in front of the Forensic Medical Building on Gass Street, secure in the knowledge that she knew who she was, and was relatively happy with that person. Relatively.

Baldwin had suggested she apply to the Academy, go through the rigors to become an FBI agent, but she'd turned him down cold. She belonged to Nashville.

Dr. Sam Loughley, medical examiner and Taylor's best friend, was sewing closed the Y incision on Jessica Porter's limp chest as Taylor rolled into the autopsy suite.

"Wow, you were quick. Didn't know you would be done already."

Sam looked up and smiled through her plastic shield. "I'm not early, you're late. It's seven-thirty already. Tim, could you finish up here for me?"

"Sure, Doc, no problem." Sam handed off the tools to her assistant and walked toward the decontamination room, pulling off her smock and gloves as she went. Taylor followed dutifully.

It was only after Sam was cleaned up, they both had a cup of tea and were ensconced in Sam's office, that she would comment on the autopsy.

"She didn't take a terrible amount of abuse."

"I don't know, Sam, being strangled and having her hands cut off seems a bit excessive, don't you think?"

Sam nodded. "Well, of course it is. I just meant that she wasn't horribly abused, beaten or anything. The hands were done postmortem. The strangulation was manual, there was no evidence of rape. It wasn't as bad as some I've seen. She wasn't torn up, just had the characteristic bruising and tearing I'd associate with rough consensual sex. He used a lubricated condom, and I didn't retrieve anything that would qualify for DNA. I've taken all the samples and sent them to be run. Dr. John Baldwin, FBI agent extraordinaire, called early and told me to send all the trace and the blood work to the FBI lab. It'll go quicker that way."

Despite all efforts to the contrary, Nashville didn't have their own forensics laboratory to process elements from their crime scenes. Baldwin had just saved them both a major headache.

"So do you have any other info for me?"

"Not really, Taylor. The results won't be back for a couple of days. Cause of death was definitely manual strangulation. We'll just have to wait for the rest. Baldwin mentioned this was an ongoing case?"

"He seems to think this is the work of a serial killer the FBI has christened the Southern Strangler. Based on the transportation MO, this is his third kill." She drifted off for a moment. "I wonder what he does with their hands? Why he's leaving one behind at every scene?"

Sam grinned. "Probably an acrotomophiliac. You know, less is more."

Taylor wrinkled her brow. "What the hell does that mean? It doesn't sound good."

"Means he's sexually attracted to amputees."

"Aw, Sam, that's really—"

"Relax, it was just a joke. The hand that was recovered yesterday didn't have the level of decomposition I'd expect from one that had been excised a month ago, so I'm operating on the theory that it was frozen. Running all the tests on that one, too. C'mon, let's get out of here and get something to eat. I'm starving."

They went to breakfast, catching up, pointedly not talking about the case. Sam was pregnant, effusive with excitement and joy at the impending arrival of her first child. All of their conversations lately ultimately found their way back to the being inhabiting Sam's belly. When they finished the umpteenth round of baby-name options, Taylor dropped Sam off back at the medical examiner's office, then went to her own.

Lincoln had pulled together the information on the previous murders, trolling information that must have been supplemented by Baldwin at some point, since the crime scene photos were copies of originals with the FBI stamp in the lower right-hand corner. The files were on her desk, and she delved into them.

There was little more to be gleaned than what Baldwin had already shared with her. The first murder, Susan Palmer, had occurred April 27. She was reported missing, and when police went to her house, they found an almost exact replica of the scene Taylor had witnessed at Shauna Davidson's apartment. There was no sign of forced entry, the bedroom was the source of interest. Taylor gazed at the bed, stripped of sheets, bloodstains on either side of the mattress. The blood was ultimately matched to Susan Palmer, and there were fibers adhered to both the bed frame and the blood that came from a national brand of industrial-grade rope. The photos from the area Susan Palmer's body had been found were also eerily familiar. Long saw grass obscured her body in the first few shots. Close-up pictures of her handless arms had attendant blowups, detailing the wounds. She absently noted that the photographer was wasting his life working for the police, he was adept at making the scene come alive.

There was one inconsistency in the photos that caught her eye. She pulled out a magnifying glass and examined it. Tracing back through the report, she matched the numbered card to the line in the report. Number 38, unidentified vomit. Hmm. She tucked that tidbit away and went on.

She opened the next file, immediately drawn to a picture of the victim. Jeanette Lernier had a wide smile and laughing eyes. She looked like someone Taylor would have enjoyed sharing an off-color joke with. Her animation bled through the photograph. Finally breaking the trance, she read through the rest of the report. Mind-numbingly similar, down to the close-up shots of the bloody stumps.

She read through the witness statements. Jeanette's family and friends adored the girl, that much was certain. People not so close to the family made a few disparaging remarks, accusing the girl of fast living. One mentioned she thought Jeanette was having an affair with a coworker, but supplemental reports didn't address the issue. She made a mental note to ask Baldwin why.

Finished with her perusal, she set to work doing the paperwork detailing the case of Jessica Ann Porter. She compiled a comprehensive murder book, pulling together all the reports from the various officers attendant to the crime scene. It was boring work, tedious but necessary. Even if the FBI swooped in and completely wrestled the case away from her, she wanted her diligence noted.

She worked most of the day by herself. Lincoln and Marcus were both off, and Fitz was running the search for Shauna Davidson and gathering more information on the missing girl. At five o'clock, she decided to call it a day. She hadn't heard from Baldwin but assumed he'd show up sometime in the evening or during the night. She didn't need to be in his way right now, he'd have enough on his plate getting his own investigation under way. She brought the murder book with her, just in case.

Seven

Taylor felt the hand slowly sweeping up the back of her thigh. She stretched languorously, burrowing her face deeper in her pillow. The hand drew closer and closer to her panties and she took a deep breath of anticipation.

The shrill ring of the telephone brought her fully awake, as did the muttered curse of the man who belonged to the hand.

"Damn, who's calling this early?" growled Baldwin.

"If I had to guess, I'd say work. Generally, no one calls me this early in the morning unless someone's dead." She slapped his hand away playfully, for despite the ringing phone, his fingers had not veered off course. She reached across the bed and picked up the phone, glancing at the caller ID. She was right. "Lieutenant Jackson here."

"Taylor, it's Price."

Captain Mitchell Price didn't usually call her at home unless it was absolutely necessary. She struggled to sit up, smashing a pillow behind her back so she'd at least sound like she was up and awake.

"Good morning, Cap. What can I do for you?"

"We've got a situation that needs to be handled." It wasn't like him to be so gruff. She could only imagine what could be wrong to have him snapping at her. She glanced out the window and saw that it was raining softly.

"We've had another attack by the Rainman." She could hear the strain in the captain's voice. "It was his choice of victim that's got us involved. I need you to head over to Betsy Garrison's house."

"He raped the lead investigator of his case? Are you kidding me?"

Price sighed, and Taylor's heart reached out to him.

"He damn near killed her. She's been taken to Baptist, but the scene needs some control and the chief asked for you personally."

"Uh-oh, that can't be good."

The Metro Nashville Police Department had come under new management, and the rank and file weren't pleased with the choice.

"He wanted a ranking female on the case. You're the homicide lieutenant. If she dies it falls under our auspices anyway. Maybe he's using some foresight, or maybe he just wants to make it look good for the press. I don't know. Things have been crazy down here this morning. The B shift caught two project murders, and with that Shauna Davidson girl missing… Either way, if you can extricate yourself from whatever you're doing, I'd appreciate you getting over there and letting me know what's happening."

Taylor felt a brief moment of panic. Surely he didn't know what she had actually been up to. She weighed the thought, then decided no, he was just being funny. Price was like that. Half-misogynistic old-school cop, half-caring, sensitive police. She played along.

"You're making assumptions, Captain."

"I just figured you might be trying to have a life, Lieutenant. Now get over there and do me proud." He hung up the phone, leaving Taylor with an odd sense of satisfaction. She knew it had probably been Price's idea that she step into the case.

She set the phone back in its cradle and glanced across the room at Baldwin. His phone had rung but she hadn't noticed. As he talked quietly, a sense of dismay crossed his rugged features. That couldn't be good.

He gave her a half smile and said goodbye to whoever had decided to ruin *his* morning. He came back to the bed, sliding between the sheets and giving her a small kiss.

Taylor threaded her fingers in his dark hair, too long by Bureau standards and perfect by hers. Silver bled from his temples and it curled slightly at the nape of his neck. She slipped her hand down, rubbing his neck softly.

"Bad news, babe?" she asked.

"I have to go to Georgia. They've found Shauna Davidson."

And those four words stopped the gentleness of their morning.

Eight

Taylor was on full alert when she arrived at Betsy Garrison's home. Betsy lived in East Nashville, once the habitat of drug lords and crack whores. But the neighborhood was "coming back," as the residents liked to say. Hip new restaurants nestled in with Victorian homes, restored to within an inch of their former glory. Young professionals ruled the area, BMWs and Lexus SUVs gleaming in the driveways, ones bought with earned money rather than by illegal means. Trees soared into the sky with abandon, even the birds and squirrels had taken on a prosperous hue.

But the street where Betsy lived seemed to be in mourning on this rainy day. When Taylor rolled up in her black Xterra, she only recognized one other car parked strategically along the street, a beat-up Ford F-150 pickup. She sighed. No marked cars for this trip. You could say the police were undercover, protecting one of their own. There was no yellow crime scene tape blowing giddily in the breeze. No news vans lined the street. Word had been kept quiet, a need to know only, nothing broadcast over the air, all calls made to private phones and cells. An ambulance hadn't even made its way down the narrow streets. Betsy had been taken out her back door and stuffed into the waiting car of her partner in Sex Crimes to be transported to the hospital.

Taylor shook her head at the ratty truck. Fitz definitely needed new wheels. But he stubbornly refused, swearing to stand by his rust bucket until the bitter end. From the looks of it, the end wasn't far off. She pulled behind it, stepped carefully to the curb to avoid the puddle in the gutter, and snapped open her umbrella. She walked quickly up the driveway and around to the back door of the house. Fitz was standing there, the ever-present cigarette dangling from his lips. It was lit, and though Taylor felt a rush of annoyance at Fitz, who had quit smoking a number of times unsuccessfully, she immediately dug in her pocket for her own pack. Drawing up beside him, she lit her own and inhaled deeply. Only a slight tickle in her throat reminded her that the doctors would be royally ticked off if they knew she was smoking, but she dismissed the thought with a wave of her hand. Fitz caught the motion and grinned.

"Justifying your addiction to the noxious weed to your doctors in your head again?"

Taylor gave him an affectionate smile. Fitz just knew her too well. They'd worked together for several years, and despite the fact that she was nearly twenty years his junior and a woman to boot, he'd never had a problem with her being his boss. Just the opposite, he had been the one who'd stood by her promotion to lieutenant last year when many in the force did not. And he was one of the few who didn't mind the new chief, either, but that was Fitz. Always willing, near retirement and couldn't give a care to politics. Besides, the new chief had restructured the department in such a way that Fitz had gotten a promotion and pay raise, which did nothing but improve his mood. More to retire on, as he jovially put it. Now Homicide was set up so that Fitz was the sergeant and had six detectives working under him. He reported only to Taylor, and she, as the department lieutenant, reported only to Mitchell Price. It was a top-heavy hierarchy, but the people of Homicide had managed to come out unscathed and with more power than they had before. Price, being the captain, had control over all the CID, Criminal Investigations Division, and the lieutenants for each division reported to him and him alone. It gave him more authority but less oversight, so he depended heavily on his LTs to make all right in the world for him. He now reported directly to the chief, and the political headaches were worth it to him since he could keep his people out of the fray.

Taylor sucked on her cigarette and forced the thoughts of doctors' disapproving glares out of her head as she ran two long fingers along the scar on her throat. She gave Fitz a brief hug, tamped the half-smoked cigarette out on the sole of her cowboy boot and pocketed the butt. No sense disturbing the crime scene.

"So tell me what's happening. You got the background on Shauna Davidson for me, right?"

"I did. Wasn't a mall rat like I thought, she wasn't working. Taking some summer courses, but that's it. The idle rich…" He smiled at Taylor and she shot him the bird. He laughed and continued. "She'd been out with some friends after class. No one has a lot of details to share yet. We'll get it, don't worry."

"Okay then. We'll have to report all the information to Special Agent Baldwin, he's going to be working the case."

"Taylor, about Baldwin."

"What? What about him?"

He looked at her hard and she realized he knew exactly what type of housekeeping she and Baldwin were doing. Fitz had always been able to figure her out.

She blushed. "Yeah, whatever. Let's not worry about that right now. Let's focus on this for the moment, then we can go over all the information you got on Shauna Davidson. Let me ask you this. Is Betsy okay?"

Fitz took one last lung-numbing drag on his cigarette and extinguished it. He pulled out a pack of gum, politely offering it to Taylor. She pulled out a piece and looked at him, waiting. He took his time unwrapping the silvery stick, as if gathering his thoughts. She wondered if he was debating whether to listen to her admonition about discussing her personal life with Baldwin, but he was back in professional, not personal, investigator mode.

"I don't have the whole story, but I got a call right before you showed up. She's gonna make it, but they had to take her into surgery to clean something up, some kind of blood pooling in her eye cavity. He broke her cheekbone, Taylor. Beat the shit out of her."

"That's not his MO."

"Nope. He usually ties 'em up and does 'em, then takes off. But this one was personal. Tied her up, raped her, then beat the shit out of her. She managed to get an arm free after an hour of struggling and called her partner, Brian Post, to come get her and take her to the hospital. It wasn't until she was there that they called Price. Wanted to keep it as quiet as possible. We don't need the press crawling all over this one. *'The Rainman' strikes lead investigator.* They'd have a field day with it."

"Brave girl, keeping her cool like that."

"You can say that again. I talked to Post, he told me she was totally calm, cool and collected about the whole thing. Only got upset when they told her that they needed to go in and fix the, whaddaya call it…"

"Occipital orb?" Taylor interjected, making a good guess.

"Yeah, that's it. She was upset that she'd be out of it for a while and couldn't help with the investigation. Broken face and she wants back in immediately. Ballsy chick, that one."

Taylor agreed. She didn't think she could handle herself nearly as well in the same situation. She knew she hadn't when she'd been the one in the hospital.

"So what do they want us to do?"

"They want us to go through the house and do the crime scene. They don't even want the CSIs out here, that's how deep this is getting buried. So far, only you, Price, the chief, her partner and me know. They'd like to keep it that way."

"Do you have a crime scene kit with you? And a camera?"

He gestured to his feet, where a large case that looked like a tackle box sat. "Picked it up on my way over."

"Thank you for thinking ahead. Here's my question.

Don't you think the Rainman will get pissed if he doesn't see his handiwork on the news?"

"I think Betsy wants to deal with that later."

"Okay, I'm cool with that. But we need to get a statement from her regardless."

"Post already did that. When we're done here, we can head over to Baptist and pick it up, talk to her if she's out of surgery."

Taylor contemplated the back door, the lock obviously jimmied. They had a job to do, so they may as well get on with it.

"Let's do it."

They snapped on latex gloves, slipped soft booties over their own boots and started working the scene. Taylor started with the broken lock, dusting for fingerprints and thanking the awning above the door for keeping the handle dry. She lifted a decent print from the doorjamb, took pictures of everything and then they slowly worked their way inside.

The inside of Betsy's home looked like a small tornado had come through. The kitchen table was overturned, the glass top shattered. Blood sparkled on the shards, and a trail of blood left the kitchen. Taylor followed it, taking pictures, to the living room. Blood soaked a corner of the couch, a lamp was overturned, but the rest of the room didn't look too bad. Taylor could see rope lying on the floor in front of the couch.

"Let me run this by you. He comes in the back door, surprises her in the kitchen. Awful lot of blood. Did he break her nose, too?"

Fitz was nodding. "Yeah, got her good right in the face before she had a chance to do anything."

"Okay, so he smacks her in the kitchen, drags her into the living room and assaults her on the couch. When did he tie her up?"

"Just from what Post told me on the phone, he disabled her in the kitchen, and she woke up on the couch, trussed like a Christmas pig. When he finished raping her, he tied her legs."

"Looks like he looped the rope around the back of the couch." Taylor was working her way around the room, taking pictures. "See the trailing ends here? That must be where she got herself loose. Okay, let's finish up here."

They set about their work, processing the scene, collecting some of the meager evidence the rapist had left behind. They bagged the rope—he always brought his own, plain store-bought nylon rope sold in every hardware store in the country, so it was virtually untraceable. There was no other physical evidence they could find. They had the print from the door, but that too was part of his MO. They set the place to rights as they went. They worked quickly but thoroughly, and when they finished they shared a look. Poor Betsy. As brave a face as she may want to put on, she had been through hell.

Her suspected rapist, dubbed with the moniker "The Rainman," had been terrorizing the women of Nashville for five years. He'd earned his name because he only struck when it was raining. He'd attacked seven women, eight now, by forcing his way in their back doors, tying them up and raping them. Simple, straightforward crimes. He never spoke, wore a ski mask, always used a condom. His victims had been known to say that it seemed he was almost disinterested in what he was doing. Just tied them up, slipped on a condom, forced his way into their bodies and left through the back door. That was it, nothing more. He'd never hit a single one, just threatened them into compliance with a gun to the head or a knife to the side. He had a unique but relatively innocuous MO, one some experts classified as a gentleman rapist. Until today, none of his victims had been physically injured.

Taylor and Fitz finished up and made their way to the backyard. They smoked companionably in silence for a time, until Taylor felt the need to point out the obvious.

"Think it was a copycat?"

"I think we have to look at the possibility, given this new MO. We'll know soon enough. If that print on the back door was his, they'll be able to match it to the other rapes. What a kook. Leave the rope and your print behind. They've never gotten a hit off the print, he's obviously never been in trouble with the law. So how a does a law-abiding citizen suddenly turn into a rapist?"

"Fitz, if I knew the answer to that, I could probably hawk it to the daytime shows and make a million dollars. Let's get over to the hospital and see if Betsy's out of surgery yet."

Nine

Baldwin sat as far back in the cramped seat as his legs would allow and fastened his seat belt for the quick trip to Atlanta. As soon as the plane cleared ten thousand feet and the pilot finished greeting the passengers, he pulled out his laptop and opened his e-mail. The file for the missing girl appeared before him. Shauna Lyn Davidson.

The call had come from Jerry Grimes, the field agent that had been running the cases from Alabama and Louisiana. He'd been instructed to keep Baldwin up to speed on the cases, and he'd complied, albeit reluctantly at first. Handing off his case to the FBI's most celebrated profiler rubbed him the wrong way. But now, the note of panic in his voice was near the surface.

"Baldwin, they've definitely identified Shauna Davidson in Georgia. Her body is in a field off a rural exit, near Adairsville off I-75. Looks the same, body dumped in a field, strangled and she's missing her hands. What the hell is this guy up to?"

"Grimes, you've told them what to look for, right? They need to find it."

"Awww, shit, I know, I know. They're looking for the hand now. I'm on my way there, are you coming?"

The accusatory note was not lost on Baldwin, but he chose to ignore it.

"I'm on my way, man. Hang in there."

Baldwin glanced at his watch and saw it was too early to order a drink. This was supposed to be a beautiful, quiet day, spent in bed with the woman he loved. Not a day to go traipsing through death. Yet here he was, on a plane to Atlanta to hunt for the Strangler.

Being a profiler meant long hours in strange locales, but the longer he worked for the FBI, the more he was struck by the commonality of every situation. Madman kills innocent, then does it again. An MO is established, the FBI is consulted and Baldwin would be thrown on a plane. He'd chosen this life, this world. He had the rare ability to disengage, to be unaffected by the horrifying details of the cases. But it was starting to wear thin. He didn't know exactly what he should do—stay with the FBI or strike out on his own. He'd love to steal Taylor away from Metro, but he knew in his heart of hearts that wouldn't happen anytime soon.

He pushed those thoughts away. He needed to stay focused, and thinking about Taylor Jackson would derail even the strongest of men.

Local law enforcement in Alabama and Louisiana had done all the right things in processing their cases. The Alabama authorities worked closely with the Baton Rouge cops. They ran all the right tests, did the right investigation and still had no clue who had strangled eighteen-year-old Susan Palmer, cut off her hands and dumped her body in a field in Baton Rouge. The crimes seemed connected, there were definite similarities—manual strangulation and missing hands. But it was Jeanette Lernier's case that had drawn the FBI's attention. When she was examined in the field, the medical examiner had rolled her and found a hand underneath the lifeless body. Everyone assumed it was Jeanette's. When DNA showed the hand belonged to Susan Palmer, from Alabama, people had gotten interested. Grimes and his partner, Thomas Petty, had been called to give interagency cooperation and support to the local authorities. When nothing happened for a month, the hunt was scaled back, Grimes and Petty went back to other cases, and the murders went into the annals of cold crimes that permeate small-town law enforcement. Grimes still kept a finger in the case, doing interviews with friends and family, but Petty caught the disappearance of a nine-year-old boy and was pulled off to work that crime. Time marches on. New crimes are committed. The cases weren't forgotten, just relegated to the back burner.

The details of the two cases were kept quiet in the hopes that somewhere down the road an answer would surface. Two families buried only parts of their cherished daughters. Now two more families would be getting their daughters' incomplete bodies back for burial. He prayed it would end here.

Baldwin had been made aware of the crimes but hadn't been actively involved in the situation. The call this morning, the call to arms tasking him to the case, was going to change all that. The FBI would be able to claim complete jurisdiction if necessary because the kidnappings and murders crossed state lines, but so far the local police had cooperated and appeared to be a major help in their investigation, not a hindrance.

The original FBI team, Jerry Grimes and Thomas Petty, were smart, seasoned agents. When Jessica Porter had gone missing, her bedroom found full of blood, local law enforcement loaded the details of the case into VICAP. When the MO matched, Grimes and Petty were called in to help assess the scene. When they examined her apartment, they immediately thought of the Strangler. Grimes had called Baldwin and informed him of the case. He'd forwarded the information they had, which wasn't much. Baldwin pulled this thin folder out of his briefcase and started refreshing his memory. It was written in the dry, impersonal tone of a police report, one that allowed no emotion to creep in and destroy the officers' and agents' objectivity.

CASE OVERVIEW—JESSICA ANN PORTER
The victim is a Caucasian female age 18. She is 5 feet 4 inches tall and weighs 120 pounds, has long brown hair and brown eyes. She was born on April 27, 1986, in the city of Jackson, Mississippi. She has a strawberry birthmark on her left bicep, a belly-button ring with a small crystal ball and pierced ears. The victim disappeared while walking home from her job as a receptionist at a Jackson community hospital. The victim…

"Ah, hell," he muttered. "I can't do it like this." Too damn impersonal. Baldwin closed the file in front of him and thought back to the discussion he'd had with Grimes. The man had been pretty broken up, too broken up. He had phoned Baldwin as soon as they'd cleared out of the Porter girl's apartment, finished with the statements of family and friends. Baldwin mentally replayed the conversation. It was a knack he had, being able to tap into his brain and extract what he needed with total recall. Taylor sometimes hated him for it, she could never get away with anything. He smiled at the thought, then plugged into his mental database.

It had been a quiet night. For the past few months, Baldwin had been tasked to the Middle Tennessee Field Office, ostensibly working as a regional profiler. Baldwin had been working cases for the FBI's Behavioral Science Unit out of Quantico peripherally, consulting when needed. He wasn't exactly in retirement, but on a pseudo sabbatical, allowing him to be in Nashville with Taylor. The arrangement was working wonderfully until this phone call, the familiar voice booming in his ear.

"The esteemed Dr. John Baldwin, I presume?" The sharp bite of sarcasm wasn't lost on Baldwin, even some of the FBI's own field officers didn't like dealing with the profilers.

"It's Jerry Grimes. I'm down here in Mississippi on a case."

Baldwin remembered how his heart skipped a beat, revving in anticipation. His senses went on high alert. Grimes wasn't calling him of his own accord, he'd been instructed to do so by a higher-up. He had dropped the niceties as well.

"We've got a missing girl. Young, brunette. Has all the hallmarks of…"

"The Strangler," Baldwin said, dread mixing with adrenaline in his stomach.

"Now, how'd you go and do that, Baldwin?"

"Good guess."

"Damn right, good guess. Her name's Jessica Ann Porter. I'm sure you've seen the reports on the news?"

"Haven't been watching too much. She's dead, I presume, or else you wouldn't be calling me."

Grimes had gone silent for a moment, and then answered with a cracked voice. *"No, she's just missing. We've got some blood on the bedsheets but no real signs of a struggle. It's like she disappeared into thin air. No one saw her after she left work for the day."*

Baldwin fast-forwarded through the conversation to Grimes's description of the girl.

"She's a beautiful kid. She's got all this brown hair, got these big brown eyes, the kind that just shoot right through you. That's just from pictures. She was the damn homecoming queen, man. Getting ready to go back to college in the fall, wanted to be a nurse or doctor, something she could do that would help people. She volunteered at the homeless shelter in town and delivers meals to shut-ins. The kid's a saint, and no one we've talked to has had anything bad to say about her."

Baldwin remembered thinking, uh-oh, Jerry's taking this kind of personal.

Grimes continued. *"I knew something was hinky and I should probably give you a heads-up, just in case."*

There wasn't anything else Baldwin could do but hear the man out. Cases with kids got to every good investigator, and sometimes just talking it out was the best thing. They'd hung up with Baldwin promising to do a little research on the missing hands and what it could mean. Then Jessica Porter turned up in a field in Nashville, with what was presumably Jeanette Lernier's hand with her.

The phone had rung again early this morning. Baldwin saw the caller ID number and knew it was Jerry Grimes, calling about Shauna Davidson. He was right.

"We got another body, Baldwin. Pretty sure it's the girl missing from Nashville."

That call had put him on a plane. He ran it through his head, the cadence becoming a bit like a child's song.

Susan Palmer, Alabama. Found in Louisiana. Jeanette Lernier from Baton Rouge. Found dead in a field in Mississippi. Jessica Porter, Mississippi girl, found mutilated in a field in Nashville. Shauna Davidson, Georgia bound…

Though he'd gotten a row to himself, the woman in the aisle seat across from his gave him a strange look, half pity, half disgust. He must have been talking aloud. He gave her as reassuring a smile as he could, then fumbled all his folders back into his briefcase. As the pilot came over the radio to tell them they were cleared to land in Atlanta, he realized he was excited by the challenge.

Ten

Whitney Connolly dragged her eyes away from the television and returned her attention to her computer. Sure enough, the address was there, the message that she was hoping for had arrived. She wet her lips and ran the mouse over the message header. It was innocuous, like all the others. A Poem for S.W. was all it said. The return address was a garbled mass of letters and numbers—IM1855195C@yahoo.com. A generic address from a huge server. She'd asked a friend who was sometimes more than a friend to try to find out who the sender was, but he'd told her that the address bounced off several other servers, so in effect, it didn't exist. Whoever was sending her the messages was virtually untraceable, and obviously smart enough to cover his tracks. Whitney didn't worry about that though. When the time was right, her anonymous friend would reveal himself to her. They always did.

She opened the mail and found the following lines:

How can those terrified vague fingers push,
The feathered glory from her loosening thighs?
How can anybody, laid in that white rush,
But feel the strange heart beating where it lies?

P.S. From your backyard.

Mmmmmm, she thought. This one was a bit sexual. But of course, if he was murdering girls, why wouldn't he be writing sexual poetry? He seemed quite talented, at least in her mind.

She felt the goose bumps parade up and down her arms. Man, she was getting messages from the killer her FBI contact called the Southern Strangler. Why he had picked her, she didn't know. But she didn't want to go to the police just yet. After all, what would she say? "By the way, Officer, I've been communicating with the man who is responsible for murdering those poor girls." She didn't even know for sure that this guy was for real. She had nothing to go on, but all of that was going to change today.

She printed out the e-mail, then carefully archived it in three places to make sure she didn't lose it if her computer was to suddenly crash. She copied and pasted the verses into her notes and looked back at the three previous entries, starting with the first.

A perfect woman, nobly planned,
To warn, to comfort and command;
And yet a Spirit still, and bright
With something of an angelic light.

P.S. This was found at the crime scene.

She had made copious notes underneath the entry, trying to make sense of the poem. And what crime scene? She'd gone through nearly every crime in Nashville that she could find, badgered detectives, worked her sources. No one knew anything about a poem found at a crime scene. She chalked it up to a nutcase and filed it away. It was silly, a little love poem sent to her private e-mail address. She even imagined for a moment that it was from an anonymous lover, someone that she knew but didn't want to reveal himself to her.

But when she received the second e-mail, she realized that this wasn't a message meant for her.

> *A creature not too bright or good*
> *For human nature's daily food*
> *For transient sorrows, simple wiles*
> *Praise, blame, love, kisses, tears and smiles.*

> *P.S. This one was from LA.*

That had sent her scrambling. LA could be one of three things, Los Angeles, Louisiana or Lower Alabama, as Nashvillians jokingly referred to the Gulf Shores area. A quick search showed a young girl had been kidnapped from Baton Rouge, Louisiana. She did some checking, followed the case, and when the body of Jeanette Lernier was found, she attached the name to the poem in her files. But there had been nothing on the media coverage that said anything about messages or notes. She knew that all investigations left things out of the statements allowed to the media, if only to rule out the copious nut jobs who called and confessed to the crimes. Despite repeated probing, none of her sources had any inkling about the notes.

Then the third note had come, right on the heels of the word that a body was found in Nashville. This one was alarming.

A sudden blow: the great wings beating still
Above the staggering girl, her thighs caressed
By his dark webs, her nape caught in his bill,
He holds her helpless breast upon his breast.

P.S. Do you get it yet?

Chilling, yet she was oddly exhilarated by the words.

Now that the word was out, that the Southern Strangler was on the loose and had killed three girls, she understood that the messages left with the bodies must correspond to these notes. After realizing the pattern, she'd gone back and marked the first entry Susan Palmer, then corresponded the notes to the names of the dead. She wondered for a moment about why she would be getting these messages. But she threw that thought aside as quickly as she had it; what did it matter? She was going to get the scoop.

This new message made her blood race. She was going to be a star.

This fourth note could reference the missing Nashville girl, Shauna Davidson. She'd cover the story tonight—on the heels of the murder, the missing person's case would generate a lead story on the ten o'clock news.

Whitney realized she didn't have any information that would lead her, or the rest of the media, to believe that Shauna Davidson was anything but missing. With the last three girls, she only received the messages after the girls' bodies had been found. Maybe this one had been found dead and they weren't reporting it. But no, they wouldn't be holding that kind of information back.

P.S. From your backyard. That struck a chord in her immediately. *My backyard.* It wasn't meant in the literal sense. He was too elegant for that. The other postscripts referred to locations. Her backyard must mean her hometown. Nashville.

That meant that she, Whitney Connolly, and she alone, knew that Shauna Davidson was dead.

She headed for the shower. She'd take a little extra time putting herself together for tonight's broadcast. She felt certain the whole town would tune in for her and the biggest story in Nashville tonight.

Eleven

Jerry Grimes met Baldwin as he came out of security in Hartsfield International. Baldwin took in the gray hair, the white face, the slight pinching around the mouth and knew that Grimes was taking this latest disappearance hard. He stuck out his hand and gave him a smile, trying for cordiality.

"Grimes, you are getting grayer by the day."

Grimes looked vaguely alarmed for a moment, as if he hadn't realized that age was leaching the black out of his hair. Then he recovered and ran his hands through the silvery strands. "Well, at least I still have some. That's saying a lot in this job."

They walked out the doors to Grimes's waiting car. He had left the car on the curb in the departures area. FBI got special privileges at airports these days. A uniformed officer stared with frank curiosity as they climbed into the sedan. Grimes removed the FBI placard from the windshield of the car. Pulling away from the curb, he got down to business.

"Okay, here's the deal. Media has the story, the locals couldn't keep it quiet. They've found the hand, it's been sent to the medical examiner, as well. We'll head straight to the morgue in this little town, Adairsville. I want to hurry up and get there, so buckle your seat belt."

All that bravado, Baldwin thought. Oh well. The ride went quickly, their conversation desultory. Grimes had theories about the cases, and Baldwin heard him out, though each one was as implausible as the next. Satan worship seemed to be Grimes's favorite. He finally stopped talking and the car went silent, each man lost in his own thoughts.

They arrived within an hour. Miraculously, the traffic had been relatively light through downtown Atlanta, and they branched off onto I-75, finding the exit for Adairsville easily. Grimes shot the car off the exit, and as they drove west toward the center of town, he pointed out the crime scene. Not that Baldwin could have missed it. Media vans lined the right side of the divided highway, a makeshift tent lean-to the focus of all their cameras.

Baldwin shook his head at the media trucks. They may have been able to contain the stories in Alabama and Louisiana, but it didn't look like they were going to be able to do that anymore. He started mapping out a strategy to use the media for their own purposes.

Grimes dropped Baldwin in front of a small, anonymous office building, promising to return as soon as he'd arranged a place for them to stay. Baldwin understood, not many people wanted to attend an autopsy. A young man who looked to be barely out of his teens met him in the lobby of the building. Introducing himself as Arie, he showed Baldwin to the autopsy suite. Arie handed him a gown and gloves, then took a seat on a stool next to the table, a notebook in hand. Baldwin took the last few steps into the room and saw the dead girl.

Shauna Lyn Davidson had not gone gently into that good night.

Her body was stretched out on a stainless-steel slab, her head cradled in a hard plastic U. She had bruises on her face, on her body. A large chunk of hair was missing from the right side of her head. Her nose was misshapen, a lip split. All the signs pointed to a struggle. Shauna had been badly beaten, a departure from the previous murders. He had a brief second of wonder—a different MO could mean a different killer. Normally, Baldwin would look to the hands to see what kind of shape they were in. In this case, all he saw were bloodied stumps. Definitely the same suspect.

The coroner was a jovial man, at least ten years past retirement age. His face was red from exertion, his hair white and straggly, his pants two sizes too small for his waist. He didn't look like he missed too many meals. He stripped off a glove and stuck out his hand. Baldwin took it, surprised at the strength of his handshake.

"I'm Doc Allen. Sorry you had to come all this way. We're ready to do the examination if you are. Already started, actually, just waiting on you to cut. All set? Good. Arie, you'll transcribe?"

The spotty boy nodded in response. It was time to do homage to the dead.

Autopsies were Baldwin's least favorite activity. But he stuck it out, listening with half an ear to Doc Allen prattle on. Only every third or fourth sentence had something to do with the body he was working on.

"So, I hear you're from up Tennessee way. Like it up there? I had a visit once, saw the Grand Ole Opry, oh, lookie there, hyoid's fractured. Strong hands to do that. Anyway, went to the Opry, saw that Marty Stuart guy. Didn't have any idea how little bitty he was, doesn't surprise me though. Lots of these folks are shorter in person. Definite saw marks on the ulna and radius, I'm thinking a straight-edged blade, maybe even a scalpel. Disarticulated right above the radiocarpal joint. So we went to this place called the Loveless Café…"

Baldwin tuned him out. He needed the background information on Shauna. Try to piece together a reason that she'd become the Strangler's fourth victim.

Doc Allen was finishing up now. Shauna's brain had been removed, ready to be fixed in formalin. The cause of death was apparent. The beating she'd taken was pretty bad, but she had been strangled so severely that her hyoid bone had snapped in two. That took a great deal of pressure to do. Baldwin imagined the killer, angry, excited, pressing harder and harder while Shauna struggled beneath him. Watching the life slowly drain from her eyes, enjoying the show. Baldwin was getting pissed off at this guy. Good.

Doc Allen seemed to want to keep talking, but Baldwin pointed to the other table, where a small item was covered by what he could swear was a simple store-bought handkerchief. Lord save me from small-time operations, he thought. The doctor bustled to the table and whipped the fabric back with a flourish, like a waiter removing the cover from a dinner dish.

"Here's your hand. Well, it's not yours, of course. Word on the street is you've got a wackjob moving body parts. I assume it belongs to your vic up in Nashville? Or was it Mississippi? I can't keep up with all your killers these days, much less the poor victims. Did I tell you about the time—"

"Dr. Allen, I hate to interrupt, but I'd appreciate it if you could get this hand printed and DNA samples drawn. We won't know if this hand belongs to the previous victim or not until we have the comparisons run. I don't mean to rush you, but I need to get out to the scene where Shauna's body was found, and I'd like to do it before it gets dark. Thanks so much."

He turned away, ignoring the good doctor's grumbling, and ran a hand through his hair. He'd give anything to be out of here as quickly as possible. There was nothing more to be learned.

Grimes and Baldwin made their way back to the site where Shauna's body had been found. The sun was setting, the media had moved off and they had the field to themselves. Baldwin stalked around, looking for anything that might give him a sense of the man who'd been here before, carelessly dropping Shauna's lifeless body in this anonymous grave. There was nothing.

That wasn't the right way to think of it. This killer wasn't careless, he was exceptionally deliberate. So far, every move was so precise it felt almost scripted to Baldwin, choreographed. But it was done to seem careless, like the bodies were just thrown away like so much trash.

He made his way back under the crime scene tape.

Two handless dead girls in quick succession was enough to upset his normal equilibrium. It had been a while since he'd worked a gruesome case. He was getting soft. Scratch that. He'd allowed himself to get soft.

They made their way to a roadside motel, ready to pack it in for the night. Grimes had suggested dinner, but Baldwin was exhausted. He demurred, agreed to breakfast in the morning, and they went their separate ways. Baldwin just wanted a shower, some sleep and a fresh perspective on the day's events. This killer was moving fast, and he had no idea how to get ahead of him.

He made several pages of notes, detailing some of his initial thoughts on the killer. There was forethought, though he was moving quickly, he wasn't in spree mode just yet. Baldwin wished there was a definitive way he could decide what would happen next, and contented himself with a second, thorough read of all the files. A picture was forming in his head—a view into the killings, into the psyche of the man responsible. He finally packed it in, hoping for a few solid hours of sleep.

Baldwin dreamed of wolves dressed in sheep's clothing, and woke intrigued. What an odd dream to have. He showered, shaved, placed a quick call to Taylor and made his way from the room. As he shut the door behind himself, he saw Grimes hustling toward him, beckoning with one hand. Baldwin went to him, eyebrows raised. "What's up?"

"Missing persons report. From a neighboring town. Noble."

Wolves dressed in sheep's clothing, indeed.

Twelve

Grimes was talking a mile a minute. "We're headed to where Marni Fischer was last seen. Let me give you her particulars. She doesn't match in with the earlier girls, but there are some commonalities.

"Marni's twenty-eight years old, five-ten, a hundred thirty pounds, with medium-length dark blond hair and brown eyes. She's originally from Orlando. This kid has a real story, one of those success things they profile all the time on TV. Her parents died in a car accident when she was only three years old. Her aunt raised her, but the aunt died when Marni was sixteen. She entered the University of Central Florida when she was seventeen on a full scholarship. Graduated at twenty-one with dual degrees in microbiology and chemistry. Immediately started at the Medical College of Georgia, she graduated there when she was twenty-five and started her residency. She's a third-year resident in the OB/GYN program."

Baldwin was eyeing Grimes. The background certainly fit the profile of the other girls. Grimes saw the look.

"Yep, she's a doctor. Another medical link. You think this guy is a psycho doctor out for revenge?"

Baldwin was shaking his head. "I don't know, Grimes. I'm not getting a sense of who this guy is. It's too early to summarize his motives based solely on the victimologies. Tell me the rest of it."

"Okay. She goes for her off-campus rotation at Noble Community Hospital in Noble. One of the doctors that she knows from the medical college suggested it would be a good place for her to get some experience with the poorer women who can't afford regular health and prenatal care."

He stopped for a moment. "By the way, she's engaged to be married. Guy named Greg Talbot. Fourth-year resident in the OB/GYN program. Their plan is to move to a small town somewhere in the rural South and provide prenatal care, as well as delivering babies for poorer women who don't have access to great health care."

Grimes had delivered this latest tidbit with a sly smile. Baldwin knew what Grimes was thinking. The fiancé was a perfect place to start. But he didn't comment, he wasn't going to leap to any conclusions, not this early. Grimes took the hint and continued with the story.

"Okay, where was I? Oh yeah, so Marni was supposed to go to her friend Sharon Baker's house in Augusta when she got off work at the community hospital. Her rotation was finished for the month, and they were going to celebrate. She was due in Augusta by seven o'clock. It's about a two-hour drive from Noble to Augusta. When Marni didn't show up at Sharon's house, she tried to call her on the cell phone, which said it was out of range. Sharon started worrying;

it wasn't like Marni to not check in if she was going to be late. She finally called Greg the fiancé, who was supposed to be in Atlanta for the weekend with some friends. He got in the car the second he got her call, drove up to Augusta, and on Sunday morning, they started looking for Marni. Traced the route she would have taken back to Noble, checking all the rest stops and gas stations along the way. No sign of anything amiss at her house. When they made it back to Noble, they went to the hospital and found her car in the parking lot. Her keys were under the car, her purse and cell phone on the front seat. They called the Noble police, who had the foresight to call us, and here we are."

Baldwin looked out the window, watching the massive mounds of kudzu as they drifted past. His mind was churning, trying to put it all together. The pattern was clear. Take a girl, then dump her in another city. Take another from that town. In which new town would they find Marni Fischer?

Alabama to Louisiana. Louisiana to Mississippi. Mississippi to Tennessee. Tennessee to Georgia. And Georgia to… "Hey, Grimes, do you have a map here in the car?"

"Yeah, should be one under your seat. I bought a Southeast map when I drove out from Virginia." Baldwin reached under the seat and pulled out the map. He flipped through until he found the page showing all the southeastern states. Let's see. Huntsville, Baton Rouge, Jackson, Nashville, Noble. Would he go back one state west to Alabama, in some kind of convoluted circle? Or move two states over to North Carolina? Baldwin shook his head, that wasn't the right way to look at it. He folded the map and placed it under the seat. No, he was going to have to examine the commonalities of the victims if they hoped to get ahead of this twisted mind.

"Grimes, talk me through the girls' profiles. Pretend I haven't heard anything about them. Start from scratch." Baldwin dug in his briefcase and brought out a notepad. Opening to a fresh sheet, he waited.

"Okay, anything you want. I'll start with Susan Palmer. Quiet girl, according to her family. She'd just graduated from nursing school, gotten a job at the Huntsville Community Hospital. She was a bit mousy, not a beauty like Jessica Porter. She lived in an apartment above their garage, mother has some sort of debilitating illness and Susan liked to be close by. They had a full-time nurse, but it was a woman and she was cleared immediately. No father, he died when Susan was young. It was just her and her mother. She was found by a canal in an old section of Baton Rouge, not a great part of town. No reason for her to be there, that's why we assumed he transported her, rather than her going to Baton Rouge, then getting killed. The M.E.'s report showed hesitation marks in the cut on her right arm. Said it looked like he was trying to get up the nerve to get the hand off. The left didn't have anything but the saw marks." Grimes cleared his throat, looking out the window as if he'd conjured the autopsy scene right there in the kudzu-choked hillside.

"It was weird. No one can remember her leaving after work, she didn't have a lot of friends at the hospital. Came in, did her thing and went home. We haven't figured out how she came across our boy's radar. She kept her nose clean and didn't make any waves."

"Invisible," Baldwin murmured.

"What's that? Invisible? Yeah, I guess you could say that. A safe choice then. But Jeanette Lernier, now, she wasn't invisible. Brash, daring, vivacious, all those words were used to describe her. She had a paid internship with some marketing company in Baton Rouge, trying to get some experience between college and graduate school. She had boyfriends, girlfriends, too, if you know what I mean, and was a regular on Baton Rouge's social circuit. There was word that she'd just had an affair with some big muckety-muck at the company she worked for, was very upset that things hadn't worked out. Came from a good family, had two brothers and a sister who are still in complete shock. It was like she was the life of the family and when she was gone, they died right along with her.

"Really sad case, if you think about it. She had everything going for her, but she ends up dead on the side of the road. Honestly, if we hadn't found Susan Palmer's hand at the scene, there's a good chance we wouldn't have connected the crimes. Even though the MO was the same, they just seemed so different. At least to me."

"I can understand that. But it definitely is the same killer."

"So tell me this. Why did he take a month off? Seems like he was on a roll, then quit."

"That's an excellent question. I'm getting a better sense of our suspect, but I'd like to know the exact why behind these killings, too. There must be some motivation… Anyway, keep going. Jessica Porter."

"Jessica Ann Porter, eighteen years old, five-four, hundred twenty pounds. Born in Jackson, shared an apartment with a friend. She was really trying to be independent. Her parents were dead set against the idea, but she charmed them into it. Tina and Steve Porter. Dad's a mechanic, Mom's a teacher. Down-home American family. She's got two brothers, Joseph, sixteen, and James, thirteen. They're pretty broken up—they worshiped her.

"She was attending the University of Mississippi, studying for premed or nursing, she hadn't decided which. She was working as a receptionist in the Mississippi Community Hospital so she could get a taste of being around medical personnel. I told you she was volunteering at the local homeless shelter and delivering meals, what's it called…?"

"Meals at Home?"

"Yeah, that's it. Meals at Home. She did that two nights a week. In the meantime, she lives with this sweet kid named Amanda Potter. They've been neighbors and best friends their whole lives. She was the one that told me about the hair."

"Grimes, I want to hear everything, even if you duplicate information you think you've given me before, okay?"

Grimes was gripping the steering wheel so hard his knuckles were turning white. "Yeah, I know. Sorry. Where was I?"

"At her hair."

"Right. So her friend Amanda tells me that Jessica has this long curly brown hair that everybody would kill to have, but she hates it, so she straightens it. She also told me that they've done a little experimenting, with alcohol and such. But Jessica never really liked it, so she's not a big party girl. She smokes on the sly, her parents don't know about that. She's just this smiley, sweet, soft-spoken girl with a head full of smarts. Seemed pretty grounded to me. Her buddy told me that she thought Jessica was a little naive, especially when it came to the boys. She's definitely a virgin. Or was, until this asshole got a hold of her."

"Okay, that's good. Tell me about how she disappeared."

"She was walking home from work, wearing green scrubs like all the staff. It's a pretty small hospital, they cater more to the indigents and poorer folk who don't have stellar health care. So anyway, her usual routine was to walk home, change clothes and go to the gym. Amanda indicated Jessica was pretty insecure about her body, that she spent a lot of time working out. Of course, Amanda thought Jessica was perfect, but you know how young girls are. Never believe in themselves the way their friends do. At least that's what I get from my daughter. You don't have any kids, do you?"

"No, I don't. Please, go on."

"Okay, okay, don't get so touchy. She left the hospital at five-fifteen and never made it home. Parents reported her missing around nine that night, and they put out the alert and started the search. Didn't make a difference. She had to have been long gone by then."

"Why do you say that?"

"Because when you found her in Nashville, she'd been dead for a while. Three days from snatch to find. The M.E. said she'd been dead at least twenty-four hours."

"Any idea where he held her? I'm assuming he didn't stay in the apartment with her the whole time?"

"Nope. Roommate came home, found the blood but

no Jessica. We checked as many motels as we could along the route from Jackson to Nashville, showed her picture around. Hell, man, there's tons of motels, hotels, bed-and-breakfasts along the route. Too many to cover in this short a time frame. Plus, he may be local. Have his own place to keep them."

Baldwin thought for a moment. "I'd be inclined to disagree with that theory. This guy has a plan. I can't imagine that he's picking a random motel to do his business. He certainly has a familiarity with each area, but he can't be local to them all." He grew silent, wondering. The killer had already covered five states. He'd have to have the geographical forensics team do a workup, see if there was an equidistant point that the killer might be working from. He made a note in his book.

"Let me make a call, I want to hear all the information the Nashville police have gathered about Shauna Davidson."

He dialed Taylor's cell phone, happy when she answered on the first ring. "It's Agent Baldwin," he said, trying to sound officious.

"Hi, Special Agent." Her tone was teasing, playful, and he realized she must be alone. He wished he were there with her.

"I'm going to put you on speakerphone. I'm in a car with Special Agent Jerry Grimes, he's been working the Alabama and Louisiana cases. He'll need to hear this information, too. You've got the background on Shauna Davidson?"

Taylor's voice rang true on the speaker, crisp and professional.

"We do have her background. Here you go. Twenty-one, five-six, hundred forty pounds, brown on brown. Attended Middle Tennessee State University, studying premed. Parents are Carol and Roger Davidson, both of them are accountants. Pretty well off, which explains the apartment being so nice. She was an only child, a bit spoiled according to her friends. She ran with a group of girls—they call themselves the Posse. Names are Megan, Kimber and Tiffany. They do everything together. They were all out together the night Shauna disappeared.

"They were barhopping, got a little drunk and went on the make. They went into a bar called Jungle Jim's for their last stop. Megan and Kimber were talking to a couple of guys and trying to get them to buy some drinks. Tiffany had separated from the group when they got there. Her boyfriend showed up and was all kinds of put out, saw her dancing with another guy. She was drunk, he was pissed. She sat with him and got engrossed in their conversation. Shauna was with Kimber and Megan while they were talking to the boys. Apparently she didn't think things were going anywhere, and when one of the boys made a pass at her, she blew him off. According to Megan, Shauna made the loser sign at him, you know, put her hand up to her forehead in an L, which made Kimber and Megan laugh. Kimber pointed out that Shauna wasn't an angel, but she was pretty picky about who she'd fool around with. And that's the last they remember seeing her.

"They're all feeling horribly guilty about it. They were really drunk, and no one was paying a lot of attention. Megan and Kimber saw Tiffany leave with her boyfriend, and when they were ready to go, they didn't see Shauna and assumed she'd gotten a ride with Tiffany."

"Did anyone see her leave the bar?"

"Well, a bouncer thinks he remembers seeing her leave alone. Says he saw her walking north on Front Street, which would be the way she would go if she was walking home. But that's it. Until she showed up in Georgia, that is. Same guy?"

"Same guy. We found a hand that we think belongs to Jessica Porter at the scene. It's being processed. But we have a problem."

"Don't tell me."

"Another girl's gone missing. A doctor from Noble, Georgia. We're headed that way to get some more information. Keep close to the phone, okay? We should have some more information for you soon."

"Okay, thanks for letting me know. Talk to you later."

Baldwin clicked the phone off. "Let's talk some more about the crime scenes. What kind of evidence did you find at the scenes where the bodies were recovered?"

"Nada. Nothing. Zip. They were lying on their backs with their arms kinda stretched out, legs crossed at the ankle. But there's nothing to indicate they hadn't been just dumped there. We don't even have tire prints. Just some loose trash that the techs collected from the scenes. Cans, bottles, papers, that kind of thing. Did you get any of that from your Nashville site?"

Baldwin took a deep breath. "No, nothing evidentiary at all. Just Jessica's body and what's presumably Jeanette Lernier's hand. We'll have to wait for DNA to match it absolutely…"

"Just like here in Georgia. Man, this is totally fucked up."

"He's not giving us much to go on, is he? And now we have Marni Fischer missing. She's been gone how long?"

"Since yesterday after her shift ended, around five."

"If he's holding them for three days, that gives us until tomorrow night, right?"

"Yeah. And this guy uses the interstates. So he could be anywhere by now."

Baldwin looked at the file in his lap. Marni Marie Fischer, age twenty-eight. A beautiful face stared at him with laughing eyes. He perused her features, noting the differences between this new missing girl and the ones before. She was older, he saw that immediately. The first three girls had been in their late teens. And Marni had dark blond hair. All of the previous victims were brunette. He found himself saying a quick prayer that maybe Marni Fischer was simply missing, not the latest victim of the Southern Strangler.

Grimes's phone rang, and he picked it up, listening intently to the person on the other line. He hung up and shook his head as if trying to clear the cobwebs, then dragged his eyes back to Baldwin. "Okay then, let me fill you in on what they've got. A whole bunch of nothing, to be succinct. Sheriff wants us to meet him over at the hospital now. They want to tow Marni's car to the impound lot, but they kindly agreed to wait for us. I know you like to look at your scenes in situ."

Baldwin nodded at him. "Great, that will be a big help."

"He's also bringing photos of the scene so you can see exactly how they found it."

"Then let's hope there's something that will give us an idea of where he's taken her." Baldwin slid lower in the seat, chewing his bottom lip. He had a bad feeling that they weren't going to find anything that would let them save Marni Fischer.

Thirteen

Taylor and Fitz pulled up to Baptist Hospital's emergency entrance and parked. Making their way through the emergency-room throng was an adventure. Taylor counted six patients that had blood streaming from various places along their bodies. The fluorescent lights made the blood look orange. She swallowed back a moment of distaste. The last time she had come through these doors was on a stretcher, her own blood threatening to spill onto the linoleum floor.

Her last major case popped into her mind—it was always there, just below the surface.

She and Baldwin had met on that case four months prior. He'd been in town on a sabbatical, Metro had needed the help of a profiler. A mutually beneficial relationship ensued, one that pushed Taylor and Baldwin into long hours and tense situations. Being thrown together, two strong personalities in conflict, there had been an inevitable attraction. They had been on the trail of an armed suspect. In the end, cornered, the desperate suspect had gotten into a face-off with Taylor, and lost.

But it wasn't without a price.

Even all these months later she could see the knife swinging at her, feel it bite into her flesh. She'd killed the man, but not before he left her a permanent souvenir, a wicked slash across her jugular.

Her hand went to her throat. She wouldn't have it any other way—she and Baldwin made a good team. When she nearly died, he'd been right at her side, and hadn't left. Still, being back in this emergency room gave her the chills. She tossed the thoughts away.

"Fitz, where would she be?"

"Probably up in surgery. Chief asked the E.R. doc to put her down as Jane Doe so the media wouldn't get their hands on the story. Let's see if it worked." He went over to the information desk, badged the receptionist and asked for Jane Doe's whereabouts. He turned to Taylor with a smile and pointed toward the elevator, then lumbered away before the receptionist could get too interested. The subterfuge was working so far.

Taylor joined him, and they rode up to the surgical floor in silence. The antiseptic smell leaked into the elevator before the doors opened. Taylor was assaulted with a memory of time served in the hospital. She was sorry that Betsy would have to experience the other side of policing—recovering from assault. It happened, not to everyone, but often enough. The elevator doors opened before she could fully relive her pain, and they went to the nurses' station.

"You have a Jane Doe up here?" Taylor asked, trying to look noncommittal. The woman looked right back at her and Taylor immediately saw that everyone knew Betsy Garrison was Jane Doe. But the nurse played along.

"She's just back from recovery. The doctor is with her now. Down the left hall, she's in 320."

They thanked her and walked toward the room. Taking a look inside, they could see two men, one the doctor in his green scrubs, the other Brian Post, Betsy's partner. He looked stricken, but after a moment he laughed and sat down next to the hospital bed. Taylor knocked softly on the door. They looked up and beckoned her and Fitz in.

Betsy Garrison, the tough, feisty head of the Nashville Metro Sex Crimes Unit, was sitting up in the hospital bed, a huge white bandage covering the left side of her head. She looked beaten up and tired but gave as genuine a smile as she could muster.

"Taylor, Fitz, c'mon in. Join the party."

Taylor took up residence on the opposite side of the bed from Post, who was scowling possessively at Betsy. That's interesting, she noted. Looks like Post has more than professional concern for his partner.

She leaned over and gingerly gave Betsy a hug. Fitz leaned against the door to the bathroom, looking distinctly uncomfortable. He was an old-fashioned kind of guy, didn't like to see ladies in distress. Betsy picked up on it immediately. Her voice croaked as she spoke, still rough from the anesthesia.

"Fitz, I see that your chivalrous sense of justice is piqued. Why don't you take Brian here and get him a cup of coffee. He's been mothering the hell out of me."

Fitz didn't have to be told twice. He crooked a finger at Post, who reluctantly rose. With a brief kiss on the one unbandaged piece of Betsy's forehead that was still visible, Post followed Fitz out of the room.

Taylor settled in and gave Betsy an expectant look. They'd known each other for several years, had actually been on patrol together. They were as good friends as two female cops could be, and had a great deal of respect for each other.

Betsy jumped in first. "It looks worse than it is. Broke my nose and the cheekbone. But they got everything fixed up, and I'll look better than before. That sweet doctor did my nose while I was under. No more bump!"

Taylor gave her a small smile. "You're keeping up a brave face. How are you really?"

Betsy deflated slightly, trying for a smile and grimacing instead. "I hurt like hell. I'm embarrassed as hell. I feel like an idiot. My own suspect rapes me? I mean really, if that got out on the force, I'd have to resign. None of the guys could ever look at me the same again. As it is, Brian's just about to die having to see me like this."

"But Brian's got more than a professional duty to you, am I right?"

Betsy shifted uncomfortably, the starchy sheets crackling at the movement.

"Caught me. We've been dating for six months or so. He's a great guy. I know they always say not to date anyone you work with…" She trailed off, eyes sliding away.

Before the horrible case that nearly cost Taylor her life, she had been caught up in the shooting of one of their homicide detectives. The fact that she had slept with him wasn't well known. Taylor looked into Betsy's eyes, wondering if the female in her had picked up on the long-dead affair. Deciding there was nothing to her statement, she brushed the comment aside.

"Now, tell me what happened last night."

A little light died in Betsy's eyes, but she answered. "I had fallen asleep on the couch. I woke up when I heard a noise outside. Went into the kitchen to see what it was, and there he was. The Rainman, in his black ski mask, dripping all over my kitchen floor. I tried to handle it, you know?"

"Where was your weapon?"

"Oh, of course, it was upstairs in my safe. I'm really careful with it—my sister brings her kids over unannounced all the time. Don't want there to be any accidents.

"So I tried to talk to him. Ask him what he was doing in my house. He didn't say a word, just flew across the kitchen like he was shot out of a cannon. Punched me in the face hard enough to knock me out. When I came to, he was finished and leaving. I wasn't even awake when he raped me. I don't know if that's good or bad, but I'm glad I don't remember it, at least for now. Add insult to injury, you know?"

Taylor did know. And thanked her lucky stars.

"So what was weird to me was that he was in and out in like twenty minutes. I noticed it was three-fifteen when I heard the noise. When I woke up, it was, like, three-forty, and he was long gone. That didn't give him a lot of time to enjoy himself, you know?"

Taylor got up and walked to the window. "But he never lingers at a scene, right? The other women he's raped say he's rather dispassionate. Did you get that sense?"

"Before or after he punched me?"

"Ah. Point taken."

"Taylor, you and I know this guy isn't about sex. He's just some strange little man that feels he needs to make a point. There's never been any violence before now."

"Do you think he's going to keep at it?"

"I honestly don't know."

"Let me ask you this. How do you know it's the Rainman?"

"Oh, they didn't tell you? Rape kit came away with DNA."

"You've never gotten DNA before, have you? That's great news."

Betsy shook her head gingerly, grimacing at the pain. "We have gotten DNA in the other rapes. He uses a condom, but he's sloppy—when he takes it off, he always leaves a drop or two behind. We've been keeping that tidbit quiet because we can't get the damn Tennessee Bureau of Investigation to run any of the newer samples through CODIS in a timely manner. At least not anytime soon."

The TBI's CODIS database was backlogged for a year or more at a time. The Combined DNA Index database was so popular that their lab was overwhelmed with the number of samples to get into the system. Maybe this would bump the cases up the ladder.

Betsy continued. "They ran it a couple of years ago, after the 2002 rapes. There wasn't a match, but the database was in its infancy around here then. The samples from 2004 are up there, they just haven't been processed. If he's in the system, we'll find him. It's just a matter of doing it before we all die of old age."

Taylor shook her head. "We've got to get our own lab. Maybe because it's you, they'll give it a push."

"Jesus, God no, we can't let them know. Taylor, please, you have to find another way."

"I know. I'm going to do everything that I can to keep you insulated from this." She rolled her neck to stretch the kinks out. She was tired all of a sudden. That was never a good sign. As much as her mind knew she was a hundred percent, her body liked to think otherwise.

Betsy continued her analysis. "The Rainman takes the condom with him, right? But we do have the spermicide. The lab has the chemical signature and we have a brand. Matched it to each rape." Betsy gave her a little smile that said, "See, we haven't fallen down on the job completely in Sex Crimes."

Taylor noticed Betsy's eyes starting to droop, and decided to ask what was on her mind. "You think he knows who you are?"

"Oh, yeah. We gave a press conference a couple of weeks ago, after the last rape. So he knows I'm on the case. What he doesn't know is we're getting close."

"Or maybe he does, and he wanted you to back off. Why do you think you're getting close?"

The spark came back to her eyes. Betsy leaned back into the pillows, looking smug. "The last victim thinks she recognizes him."

Fourteen

When Baldwin and Grimes arrived in the community-hospital parking lot, Baldwin could see a passel of men standing in the northeast corner. Waves of heat shimmered off the black asphalt. Grimes pulled up a few slots away and got out, went immediately to a large dark-skinned man with commanding shoulders and a shaved head. He held himself ramrod straight, and Baldwin pegged him as military from twenty feet away. He followed in Grimes's path and stuck out his hand for the requisite introductions and posturing. To his surprise, the sheriff flashed him a big smile. He was younger than he initially looked, and Baldwin breathed a sigh of relief. Sometimes the locals just weren't thrilled to have the FBI involved in their cases, and sometimes they were.

"Sheriff Terrence Pascoe," the man rumbled. "You must be John Baldwin. I read your white paper on anger-excitation killers in the *Law Enforcement Bulletin* last year. Great stuff. It's good to have you. Sorry about the heat."

"Thank you, Sheriff. Not much better in Nashville this time of year. Agent Grimes told me you wanted to tow the car. I appreciate you holding off for me."

"Not a problem. The locks are popped." He handed a manila folder to Baldwin. "Here're the crime scene photos. Nothing much different, 'cept we pulled the keys out from under the car to process. We've been holding her cell phone in case any calls come into it." He held up a bag with the phone. "Already dusted it, so I've just kept it on my person until I turn it in to Evidence. We didn't get anything off it but her prints. Same for the car. No prints other than her and the fiancé, which isn't surprising. We've talked to him and let him go back home. He's praying she makes a call to him. Straight shooter, I highly doubt he was involved in this."

Noble may have been a small, poor town, but they had a first-class sheriff. Baldwin gave him a nod of gratitude, took the file and glanced at the high-resolution crime scene photos inside. The sheriff was right; other than the keys being under the car, the tableau was identical.

Baldwin pulled gloves out of his pocket and eased himself into the small BMW. He was thankful they'd left the door open, it must have been well past 120 degrees in the car. He felt around the seats, noting the lack of typical accumulation usually present when a woman spends a lot of time in her car. It was very clean, perfectly organized and told a clear story about Marni Fischer.

She kept herself in shape. There was a gym bag on the back seat. Baldwin rifled through it—Lycra shorts, wicking T-shirt, socks and high-end running shoes. A brush, hair dryer, small soap-and-shampoo containers completed the bag. There were medical textbooks stacked in the seat next to the gym bag. The console held lipstick, hair bands and classic Ray-Ban aviator sunglasses. Typical stuff.

Baldwin worked his way through the car, not finding anything out of place. When he opened the glove box, a piece of paper fluttered to the floor. He picked it up carefully by the edges and gave the sheriff a questioning look. "You guys see this?"

"Hasn't been printed, if that's what you're asking. I read it, it's just a poem. Figured her boyfriend gave it to her."

Baldwin stepped out of the car and looked carefully at the note. It was a poem. A love poem. Typed on a piece of white paper with nothing else on it. He wasn't surprised the sheriff hadn't thought twice about it; in normal circumstances, no one would. But Baldwin was a profiler, and his sirens went off as he read the lines.

> *Being so caught up,*
> *So mastered by the brute blood of the air,*
> *Did she put on his knowledge with his power*
> *Before the indifferent beak could let her drop?*

"Yeats," he murmured. Grimes and the sheriff looked at him closely.

"You really think a poem could make any difference in this case?" Grimes was shifting from foot to foot, anxious, realizing they may have their first break and it wasn't because of him.

"Grimes, did you find any poems at any of the other scenes?"

"Not where we found the bodies. I don't know if anyone checked the victim's effects. Shit!"

He pulled out his cell phone and punched in a number. "Thomas, it's Grimes." Baldwin recognized whom Grimes had called. Thomas Petty was Grimes's partner and had handled the start of the investigation. He had been on-site for two of the murders, present at the death scenes.

Grimes was pacing in circles. "You're still in Alabama, working that missing-boy case, right? Do you have some sharp contacts that can do something for us? Good, here's what we need. You need to get in touch with the police in Alabama, Louisiana and Mississippi. Have them go back through all the girls' effects. If they need to call the families, go out and visit the houses, do it. Have them look for a piece of paper with a poem on it. That's right, poetry. Make sure they look in the girls' cars, too." He cleared his throat, his voice sounded jumpy and anxious. Baldwin could read his face—had he missed the most important clue in their case? "Especially the glove boxes. Call me back as soon as you can."

He hung up and shook his head. "You really think this is from the killer?"

Baldwin nodded. "This guy's playing games. Surely he wouldn't leave us hanging with nothing to go on. The hand exchange is one clue. Let's see if this is another." He took out his notebook and copied the verses, though he knew the poem by heart. It was one of the most intriguing he knew. He handed the paper off to the sheriff. "Could you get this printed for me, please?"

"Absolutely. I'm sorry we missed it."

"I may be wrong. But it just seems too out of place to be Marni's."

"Why?" asked Grimes, looking uncharacteristically perplexed.

"A girl that structured... A stray piece of paper may not be unusual in your typical car, but I can't imagine she'd leave this lying around loose in her glove box. All of her information is separated into envelopes, there're no stray receipts or mess." He glanced at Grimes. Granted, the man wasn't a profiler, but it didn't take a genius to see that Marni Fischer was a control freak. "Nothing else was out of place."

The sheriff retrieved a sleeve of plastic from the crime scene kit in his trunk and slid the note into it, then handed it off to one of his deputies. The man fairly ran to his car and took off.

"We'll know quick. I've got a good guy in my lab who can find anything if it's there to find."

"I appreciate it." Baldwin shielded his eyes and gazed at the hospital. So far the only thing linking most of these girls was their chosen or intended profession. If there were other notes, then they might have something.

"There was no sign of foul play at Marni's home?" Baldwin asked.

"Not a thing. I know about the other cases, that they were taken from their houses. This one looks like she was taken right here, just as she was getting into her car. There's another bee for your bonnet. Is there anything else? I need to get this scene cleared and get started on a rural search. I know you think this guy's going to take her out of state, but I need to make sure." Sheriff Pascoe was ready to go, to get his part of the investigation under way. There was nothing more they could do here. Baldwin shook his hand and thanked him for all his help.

He and Grimes went back to town in silence. Grimes parked at the motel and they walked in the strong sunshine to get food and to go over their next moves. Grimes looked rough, unshaven and red-eyed. He was taking every aspect of this case to heart. If Baldwin were to evaluate him from a psychological perspective, he'd say Grimes was teetering on the edge.

They went to Jo's Diner, a local establishment worn with age. The entire restaurant could have fit in the lobby of their motel. Pictures of locals plastered the walls, some fresh and new, some so old and grainy that the black-and-white images merely suggested their occupant's features. The walls were yellowed from years of nicotine, and the formerly white lace drapes drooped gray and unhappy over smeary windows. Baldwin and Grimes got looks from tired men who appeared to have grown into the stools at the counter. The smell was intoxicating, and Baldwin realized he was starved.

They sat at a metal table covered by stained and cracked Formica laminate. A huge woman with shoulder-length braids pranced over. Baldwin couldn't believe how lightly she moved considering her bulk. Her waitress uniform was spotless, and *Lurene* was stitched in fancy black embroidery above her ample left breast. She slapped down two cups, filled them with strong black coffee and gave the men a look.

"Good morning," Baldwin said. "We'd like—"

"Let me guess, sugar. The works." She yelled back

over her shoulder to a rheumy-eyed black man with grizzled hair who could be seen in the kitchen. "Eugene, two full plates." She turned back to them.

"You just let me know if you need anything else after that." She chuckled, a deep throaty laugh that brought a smile to Baldwin's face. She gave him a dazzling smile of her own and stepped back to the counter. Every eye in the place was trained on her, and she knew it. She may have been a big woman, but she exuded sensuality.

Baldwin turned back to Grimes, amused to see the look of appreciation in his eyes.

"That's some woman, huh?" He enjoyed the blush that spread over Grimes's cheeks.

Their waitress returned with two plates groaning with food. Pancakes, scrambled eggs, bacon, sausage and a bowl of grits filled platters big enough for ten men. To top it off, soda biscuits paraded off the edges of the plates.

Baldwin couldn't hold back a laugh. "This *is* the works, isn't it?"

"It is, sugar, and you leave anything behind, I'll have your hiney. You two look like you could use a good meal." She placed the plates with a flourish, pulled an assortment of jams from her apron pocket, reached behind her and refilled their coffee, all without her gaze leaving Baldwin's eyes. Her braids clicked softly as she moved about, getting them settled. He sensed she wanted more, so he sat silent, not making a move toward his plate. He was right.

"Sugar, you here about that sweet young doctor that went missing?"

"Yes, ma'am, we are." Grimes looked at Baldwin, excitement and hope brightening his eyes. Ma'aming a waitress was the universal signal that meant "Please, tell me everything you know." She obliged.

"You know, she came in here all the time. Had a thing for my Eugene's pancakes. Said they were the best she ever tasted." She raised a disapproving eyebrow. "You're not tasting yours."

Baldwin tucked his fork into the fluffy mound and steered a bit to his mouth. It was heaven. Marni wasn't off the mark as far as Eugene's pancakes were concerned. He told Lurene so.

She nodded gravely. "He's got a secret, won't tell me a thing. We've been running this place for twenty years, and he still won't tell me what he does to 'em."

Grimes had watched this exchange absently while shoveling food into his mouth. He tried to croak out a question, but Lurene gave him a stern look.

"Don't talk with your mouth full." Grimes covered his mouth sheepishly, sending Baldwin a mental message instead. *Get her to talk,* his eyes implored. This could be the best information we get.

"Lurene, you said Marni Fischer came in here often. When's the last time you saw her?"

"Friday morning. She always comes in before work on Friday, says it's her treat for the week. Boy, that girl sure could put away some food. Always had what you're havin', finished the whole plate and usually asked for more biscuits. They're my own recipe, you know."

Baldwin took the hint and demolished a biscuit. He was amazed, he'd never had anything quite so good. Having grown up in the South, that was saying something. He gave Lurene the compliment and she practically purred. Baldwin imagined Eugene must have his hands full.

"So you say you saw Marni on Friday. She didn't stop in Saturday?"

"Nope, sugar, she didn't."

"Any chance you had a stranger in here on Friday? A man, maybe?"

She pursed her lips and thought hard, air leaking out the small O where her lips weren't entirely closed in a tinny little whistle. "Honey, we have strangers in here all the time. There was a boy in here, cute kid I hadn't seen before. But he was just a kid. Maybe seventeen, eighteen. He wasn't legal, I'll tell you that. Figured he was in here while his momma had an appointment or somethin'."

"What did he look like?" Eighteen was younger than Baldwin expected the killer to be, but it wouldn't hurt to ask.

"Handsome boy, dark hair, like yours. Don't really remember much about his features. Just a good-looking kid. Came in, ate and left, he was only here about twenty minutes, tops. Didn't linger like you men." She winked at him. "I'm sorry for that girl, I liked her a lot. You finish your breakfast now, y'hear?" She topped off their coffee and left them to their thoughts. They finished as much of the food as they could, and Grimes wisely mopped up the remainder of his eggs with the last biscuit. They got up and went to pay, but Lurene waved them off.

"You just find that girl, okay?"

"We'll do our best, ma'am. Thank you for a wonderful breakfast." Baldwin surreptitiously slipped a twenty-dollar bill under a saltshaker on the counter and they made their way out onto the quiet street.

They sat in Baldwin's hotel room, waiting. At least, Baldwin sat. Thinking about how young his killer could actually be. A kid, that wouldn't fit. This guy was too organized, too mobile to be that young. He needed his own place, his own wheels and a lot of cash to circulate himself around the Southeast. Naw, that didn't work.

Grimes paced a few feet away. A member of his team had called a few minutes earlier. Shauna Davidson's apartment had been searched and a poem found in her desk drawer. Baldwin read and reread the lines Grimes gave him.

How can those terrified vague fingers push,
The feathered glory from her loosening thighs?
How can anybody, laid in that white rush,
But feel the strange heart beating where it lies?

This was not good at all. Baldwin closed his eyes to shut out the sight of Grimes's relentless pacing. He could still hear the man's shoes passing through the industrial-grade carpet—*swoosh, swoosh, swoosh, swoosh.*

As Grimes made his latest turn, his phone rang. He looked at Baldwin. "Finally." He snapped the phone open. "Grimes." He listened, then motioned for a pen and pad to write on. He scribbled furiously, nodding and uh-huhing for a few minutes, then hung up and looked at Baldwin.

"I really fucked up, didn't I?"

Grimes's admission of the mistake was surprising. An undercurrent of animosity had plagued their relationship from the beginning, yet here he was, ready to confess all his sins, to be absolved by the one man he didn't want in the investigation. Desperate times call for desperate measures. Baldwin couldn't justify the blunder, but he could understand it.

"Grimes, you've been dealing with three separate law enforcement agencies in three states. Countless people, high-stress situations. Anyone could have missed it."

"But you didn't," he said miserably. "See, I haven't really been on my 'A' game with this. I've been having some trouble at home, been thinking about retiring. Turn in the badge, get a real life." The melancholy in his tone was alarming. "I should take myself off the case. I could have blown the whole thing. I might have been able to save one of those girls."

Baldwin clapped a hand on the man's shoulder. "Hey, I didn't find the note in Nashville attached to Shauna Davidson's murder." He waited until Grimes met his eyes. "Listen, I need you to keep your head in the game. Yeah, it was a miss. A big miss. But we need to move forward now, okay? I want you on this case. Read me what they found."

Grimes nodded, swallowing hard.

Jesus, Baldwin thought. Just what I need.

Grimes shook his head, cleared his throat, tried to gain an element of dignity and control. "All right. Let's see how you do with these."

"More poetry?" Baldwin felt his heart beating just a little harder. His instinct was right.

"Yep. The notes have been there all along. Each girl had one in their personal effects. According to Petty, Lernier's and Palmer's were in their gym bags, Jessica Porter's was in her date book. We just didn't see it. God, how could we have missed this? They've been collected, they've already been printed, but nothing showed. Jesus, I've blown the whole case." Grimes was back off on his "woe is me" tangent, and Baldwin was getting impatient.

"Grimes. The poems?"

"Yeah, yeah, let me read them off to you. Ready?"

"Okay, shoot."

"This was in Susan Palmer's car." He read the verses aloud.

> *"A perfect woman, nobly planned,*
> *To warn, to comfort and command;*
> *And yet a Spirit still, and bright*
> *With something of an angelic light."*

Baldwin scribbled and nodded, murmuring to himself. "Wordsworth. Okay, who's next?"

"Jeanette Lernier. Here we go.

> *"A creature not too bright or good*
> *For human nature's daily food*
> *For transient sorrows, simple wiles*
> *Praise, blame, love, kisses, tears and smiles."*

Baldwin smiled. "Another stanza from the same poem. What was found in Jessica's dayrunner?"

Grimes flipped the page of his notebook. "Jessica, Jessica... Here.

"A sudden blow: the great wings beating still
Above the staggering girl, her thighs caressed
By his dark webs, her nape caught in his bill,
He holds her helpless breast upon his breast."

"Same poem?" Grimes asked.

"No, that's one's Yeats. Excellent poet, Yeats." He reached for Grimes's notebook. "Let me see that." Grimes handed it over and Baldwin read the lines again.

"Jessica's, Shauna's and Marni's poems are from 'Leda and the Swan,' William Butler Yeats. Jeanette's and Susan's are from a William Wordsworth poem, 'She Was a Phantom of Delight.' Our killer knows some of the classics."

Grimes scratched his head. "Apparently you do, too. But what does it mean?"

"See, that's the problem. It means something different to different people. What I'm concerned about is this stanza of Marni's poem. *Being so caught up, so mastered by the brute blood of the air... indifferent beak...* When he started, with Susan and Jeanette and Jessica, he worked hard. He stalked them, took his time, seduced them. Now he's picking up speed, moving too fast to get involved emotionally with his victims. These girls are a means to an end now, not an object worthy of worship and desire.

"And if he's become indifferent to their plight, then we're going to see an escalation in violence. 'Leda and the Swan' is classically recognized as a rape poem, a violent poem. Marni has drawn the mention of blood, I wouldn't be surprised if she didn't have some sort of brutality done to her that's more severe than was done to any of the other girls. But I'm just guessing, Jerry."

Grimes had his hands shoved deep in his pockets, his head bowed. "I wouldn't have known all that. Wasn't much good with that stuff in school."

Baldwin drew in a breath. "I think we'd better go regroup. Give you some time to get yourself back together. And give me some time to think about this."

Fifteen

He looked at his watch. It was time. He'd been sitting in silence in the rest stop, waiting for the right moment. The highways had quieted, the light of dawn still two hours away. He'd been driving all night, and had reached his destination right on time. Just enough time to sit back and reflect for a few moments. It was perfect. It was all *perfect.*

He looked over his shoulder into the back seat of the car. Luminous brown eyes glared back at him. She wasn't cowed, not this one. She was a fighter. Well, we'll see how she feels when she's under me, when she feels the breath leave her. He felt himself harden and licked his lips.

Half an hour later, the defiant eyes no longer burning a hole through his brain, he put the car into drive and slid, silent as a shark, toward the on-ramp.

Sixteen

Taylor walked across the steaming parking lot at the Criminal Justice Center in Nashville, mentally planning her day. She shielded her eyes against the sun, gazing at the office building she called home. The CJC was a squat, nondescript building that housed the main units of the Criminal Investigations Division, as well as the administrative headquarters for the Metro Nashville Police Department. In the reorganization, a number of offices moved out of the headquarters building and into various sector offices. The chief had killed the five sector divisions and cut them into three: South, West and North. Detectives that were originally slated to work in departments like Homicide and Robbery were now housed in the sector offices as general detectives. Taylor's team of homicide detectives had gotten to stay in the old headquarters and worked on homicides that had an element of ambiguity to them. If there wasn't a suspect, there was no evidence or the job just looked too tough, Taylor's team got the case. It meant a lot less busywork for them. The rest of the detectives scattered across the mid-state region pulled up the slack, covering basic plainclothes duties.

The Strangler case was spinning out of control, the media was screaming for answers. Cable news had seized upon the story and was creating a panic, updating every half hour, pointing out the failures on the part of law enforcement in all five states. Jessica Porter was lying in the morgue in Nashville, and Shauna Davidson's parents were begging for their daughter's body to be returned to them for burial. That part of the case was out of her hands. The FBI was working with, cooperating fully with, local law enforcement agencies, but in essence, they had taken the case from them. She let Price deal with the politics of the situation, duking out the jurisdictional issues. And no one could deny that the Feebs had access to better labs and more timely results; at least the forensics would be handled quickly and thoroughly.

She made her way up the back steps, stepping around the industrial ashtray that crowded the landing. She felt a brief pang of addiction and desire but soldiered on, slipping her access card through the slot. The door opened with a hiss and she entered the bland linoleum hallway. Following the green-striped arrow, she made her way to the Homicide office.

It was quiet this morning. Granted, most of the weekly departmental meetings were going on, so none of the brass was around. She wondered briefly if anyone had found out about Betsy, but dismissed it. That wasn't her job right now. Her job was to look over the Rainman case.

As she passed the Homicide office, she felt a moment of bitterness toward Baldwin. Her most interesting murder in weeks had been slipped right out from under her, another tasty case whisked away into FBI jurisdiction. She understood, but she couldn't stop the sense of disappointment. Not that a serial rapist was anything to sneeze at. On the contrary, the Rainman had proved so elusive over the past few years that she welcomed the chance to look at the files, see if she could find anything that the other detectives had missed.

But she wished, for a brief moment, that she was out on the road, tracking the Southern Strangler.

She walked through the overcrowded Homicide office. Even though a number of detectives from each of the three shifts had been moved to other offices, discarded junk remained. There were still sixteen tiny workstations packed into the room, but carpenters had begun reassembling the cubicles to make the spaces larger and more open. They'd end up with ten or so workstations: a little more private and a lot less cramped. She couldn't wait for things to be done.

With the reorganization, Taylor had moved up in the world. She'd taken over Captain Price's office when he'd moved to the second floor to be with the rest of the administrative corps. The desk, the chairs and, more important, the door, were now hers. She'd offered to share with Fitz, allowing him some privacy when she wasn't around, but he'd turned her down. He liked being out with the troops. Though she was a scant few feet away, she understood. The separation was palpable, and was taking some time to get used to. She still started when anyone knocked on the door frame. She rarely shut the door, it seemed only fair that she have the same lack of privacy that her detectives had.

The normally bustling office was peacefully silent. She knew two of her detectives, Marcus Wade and Lincoln Ross, were in court this morning. She'd sent Fitz home to get some sleep. The rest of the night shifts had gone home. She had the place to herself.

She was used to solitary time, almost always welcomed it. With Baldwin around, that was changing. He spent a lot of time working from her home. His technical transfer to Nashville's field office as the mid-state profiler meant he could curtail his travel, make his own hours, participate in cases that interested him. If a major case popped, like the Strangler, he was pulled in to work it. He was still the FBI's leading behavioralist, albeit one in semiretirement.

They weren't officially living together, but he'd taken over her home office, and she was secretly pleased with the messy decor. She felt like she belonged to someone for the first time, and if that meant he messed up her office, so be it. He also messed up the kitchen, but she'd forgive him just about anything if he cooked dinner. So many nights she came home tired and unwilling to put out that extra effort.

Since the "incident," as she liked to call it—it was nicer than blurting out "when I got my throat cut"—she found herself more tired than usual. The doctors said that was normal. The gash in her throat had severed an artery; her blood loss had been exponential. "You nearly died," they said. "Give yourself a break," they said. "The body doesn't bounce back that easily." It had taken three months before her voice had returned to normal.

Always a bit throaty, she was now downright husky, which Baldwin loved. He teased that she would make a great late-night radio announcer, or a phone-sex operator. She ignored his jibes, and worked hard on her rehab. There was a time when they thought she'd never be able to speak again, but she'd astounded them with a croak three days after her last surgery. Through hard work and dedication, she'd gotten herself back in shape and was stronger every day.

Amazing how her near miss with death had cemented their relationship. For the longest time, Taylor worried that he'd stayed out of pity. Now she knew better.

Smiling to herself, she went down the hall to the Sex Crimes office. The room wasn't empty, but all the detectives seemed preoccupied. She knew that Brian Post had told everyone that Betsy had been in a car accident and was in the hospital. This was the most plausible excuse anyone could come up with, and it masked her injuries wonderfully. He'd mentioned that Lieutenant Jackson from Homicide was going to look over the Rainman files while Betsy was laid up, and when she entered, she got a couple of friendly waves. Waving back, she walked over to Betsy's desk, where some kind soul had already pulled the files and bound them with a rubber band for easy transport.

She grabbed them and scooted out before anyone wanted to get into a big discussion, and went back to her office. The hallways were coming to life, uniforms and plainclothes men and women started drifting by in clumps of two or three. As she walked back to Homicide, the spirit came back into the building. She sighed. It had been nice to have the place so quiet.

She went into her office, switched on the lights and closed the door. She wanted some privacy to go through these reports. Seven women brutalized, not counting Betsy. Regardless of their lack of physical injury, emotionally they'd be scarred for life. She wanted to give them some respect.

She sat at her desk, took a deep breath and opened the casebook. An antiseptic summary greeted her. No conclusions, just the facts. She started to read, and was soon lost in the reports.

Taylor jumped when she heard the knock at her door. She laid a sheet of notebook paper strategically across the open files on the Rainman, just in case it was someone she didn't trust to know what she was doing, and yelled, "Come on in."

The door opened and Lincoln Ross stood there, filling up the entrance with his broad shoulders and beautiful Armani suit. Lincoln was a clotheshorse, plain and simple. He was also one of the most talented computer detectives that existed. He could track a fly down if it landed anywhere in cyberspace.

He gave her a gap-toothed grin, deep dimples forming in his mocha skin. "Whatcha working on, LT?"

"A new, well, an old case but new to us that's been dropped in our laps. Where's Marcus?"

"Getting a soda, he'll be here in a second. What's the case?"

"Let's wait for him, I don't want to go through it twice. How was court?"

"Excellent. Nailed the bastard. He's never going to practice again, unless they give out medical licenses in jail." Lincoln and Marcus had been working the alleged accidental death of a Belle Meade matron for a couple of months. Instinct told them it was a homicide, but the scene was set to look like a very convincing suicide. They'd been right. The husband of the victim had slipped a lethal cocktail of cyanide in his wife's drink before he put the gun in her hand and pulled the trigger. Lincoln had cracked the case before the medical examiner when he found a draft copy of the suicide note that had been deleted from the husband's computer.

Lincoln was still on a high. "Convicted him for first degree. They had that poor jury sequestered out for two weeks, but they came in with the verdict first thing this morning."

Taylor nodded her thanks. "Good job. Hey, Marcus." Marcus Wade strolled into the room looking like the cat that licked the cream off the canary.

"You look quite pleased with yourself." Taylor couldn't help but smile. Marcus was young and handsome and got such a charge out of catching the bad guys. So many cops simply didn't care, they just wanted to close a case. Marcus and Lincoln took a lot of pride in their capabilities, and Taylor was glad for it. It kept them motivated.

"I'm just the greatest homicide detective that ever lived," he bragged. "Next to you, of course, Loot." He winked and she blew him a kiss. Lincoln coughed into his hand, the muffled explosion sounded suspiciously like "bullshit."

"You're right, you are fantastic. So are you, Linc. Come on in and shut the door." They looked at her skeptically but did as she asked. They got seated in the not-so-comfortable chairs across from her desk. Lincoln pushed the door closed with his foot. With the three of them in the room and the door latched, it felt more like being in a cell. Though the office afforded more privacy, the room was tiny. Taylor filled them in.

"We're going to be working on a new case. You're both familiar with the Rainman?"

Lincoln's eyes grew wide. "The rapist? Did he kill someone?"

"No, he didn't. But he raped Betsy Garrison last night."

She waited for that news to sink in. Lincoln opened his mouth, then closed it with a brief shake of his head. Marcus spoke first.

"I assume you want this kept quiet?"

"Got it in one, puppy. We need to keep Betsy's name out of it at all costs. She doesn't want the people in her unit to know she's been raped. She got beat up pretty badly, too, and Brian Post's been informing people she had a car accident. Bless her heart, she's okay about the rape. I was at the hospital talking to her and she really was holding up well. Better than I would be."

"Did she have any information that we can go on?" Marcus had already switched into investigator mode.

"Fitz and I processed the scene, and we got a whole lotta nothing. There was a print on the back door that I lifted, and we need to see if that matches up with the prints on file from his past rapes. There's good and bad news, too. They have DNA, from *all* the rapes. They haven't released it to the public, or any of us for that matter, because TBI can't get the more recent rapes into CODIS. We've got DNA from Betsy, and the spermicide that was found in her PERK matches the condom brand he's been using. We've got the rope, but it's the same generic kind he's been using all along.

"Here's what I want. Both of you look at this like it's never happened before. New rapist on the street. Brand-new case. We have no usable evidence, no leads. Just find out who he is for me. Start here." She handed them both a copy of the summary sheet.

While identifying information was scarce, the Rainman had an incredibly unique pattern that was baffling the police. He only raped in months that ended in the letter Y—January, February, May and July. He only struck when it was raining, sometimes even in violent thunderstorms. Every attack came on the third Thursday of the month. And he'd only done two rapes a year. He'd struck twice in 2000, 2002 and 2004.

"This is the name and address of his last victim. She thinks she may have an idea of who he is."

"You're kidding?" they both chimed.

"No, I'm not. Betsy spoke with her after the latest rape, said she was really reluctant to relive the crime and give decent information. Problem is, she couldn't identify him. Doesn't know his name, can't remember where she knew him from. It's more like something about him seemed familiar to her. So go talk to her and see if you can jog her memory."

Marcus was reading the summary sheet. "There are a couple of major discrepancies here. He didn't hit on a Thursday, for one. We'll have to wait on the DNA—Taylor, are you sure we don't have a copycat?"

"I'm not sure of anything. Betsy seems positive that this was the Rainman. But you're right to question that. Get the print run. That should tell you pretty quick if it's him or not. Criminals break their patterns. Trust the evidence, it won't lead you astray."

"Okay, LT. We'll let you know." Marcus stood and stretched.

"Yeah, no problem, boss. We're on it." Lincoln gave her another crooked smile and they left her office, talking to each other quietly about the next steps they'd take.

Okay, she thought, one down. The nice thing about management, she got to give more orders. She smiled to herself. She would be right there with them, she just had one thing she needed to do first.

She picked up the phone and dialed her doctor's phone number from memory. The constant tests and checkups were past tiresome. Some of the medication she had been taking after the accident had wreaked havoc on her liver, so the doctors had taken her off the medicine but insisted on monthly checks of her liver function. A cheery voice answered the phone. "Dr. Gregory's office!"

"Shelby, it's Taylor Jackson. I wanted to get my test results."

The cheer kicked up a notch. "Oh, Taylor. Hi! Dr. Gregory was just about to call you. Hold on a second while I get him to pick up the phone."

Taylor stared at the watermark in the corner of the ceiling. She really needed to put a call into maintenance to see if they could replace that tile. It drove her nuts. As she started fiddling with a pencil, Dr. Gregory's baritone practically forced its way through the phone.

"How's my favorite cop?"

"I'm fine, Doc. Tell me you have good news and I don't have to get stuck anymore."

The doctor was quiet for a second, then cleared his throat. Taylor's heart sank. Dammit, she'd done everything they'd told her, and she felt fine. Well, as fine as she could, considering everything she'd been through.

"Please, Dr. Gregory, I thought everything would be okay by now." She heard the whine in her voice and straightened in her chair. She sounded like a petulant eight-year-old.

"No, no, Taylor, your liver function is completely back to normal. Are you feeling okay otherwise?"

"Well, yeah. A little tired maybe, but that's nothing new."

He breathed a slight laugh into the phone. "Well, honey, you're probably going to feel that way for a while."

As he continued talking, Taylor felt the world spin.

Seventeen

The sun leaked into the room, its wavering light barely brightening the small square space where Whitney Connolly was working furiously at her computer. She'd broken protocol this morning, skimming through her e-mails but not bothering to answer them. The only one that mattered, the only one she opened, was from her mysterious friend with the untraceable Yahoo account. The note was simple:

> *Being so caught up,*
> *So mastered by the brute blood of the air,*
> *Did she put on his knowledge with his power*
> *Before the indifferent beak could let her drop?*

There was no postscript. She didn't need them now. She appreciated that he recognized that she'd figured it out. How he knew was beyond her, but that didn't matter.

After seeing that note, knowing what must have

happened, Whitney got to work. Another girl was dead. So she was doing research. Any good journalist would, right? If she was getting messages from the Southern Strangler, she needed to have background. She needed to build the elements of the case, just like a cop would do. She had to start thinking about her reel, make everything come together so that when she broke the story and had the first interview with this guy, everything was in place. Why else would he be sending her messages, unless he planned on talking to her?

She flew through cyberspace, fingers clicking on the keyboard. She decided on Court TV's ultrainformative Web site on serial killers. Plugging in the search criteria, she sat back, waiting for the answers to be spit out at her. She wanted to see incidences of killers using poems at crime scenes.

She stopped for a second. There hadn't been anything on the news about the notes. She was assuming they'd been found at the crime scenes. At least, that's what her source in Louisiana said. The poem was in Lernier's gym bag, but no one thought anything about it. She'd heard, through that same source, that the FBI now had the notes, that they saw the significance of them. That just meant she had to work harder and faster.

Shauna Davidson had been found in Georgia, but her crime scene was still here in Nashville. Whitney placed a call, just trying to confirm that there was a note in Shauna's effects, and was shut down entirely. No one was talking to her. That in and of itself confirmed it for her—she was tight with her source in Metro's police, and if he wouldn't talk to her, things must really be heating up.

She went back to the computer. The search results were varied and numerous—apparently lots of serial killers liked to use poetry. Some wrote their own, some copied others. Some sliced famous authors into their own works. She bookmarked an article about the BTK killer in Wichita, Kansas, for good measure. At the very least, maybe something about Bind Torture and Kill would jump out at her.

She sat back and thought for a minute. At the very least, maybe she could find out if the poems were originals or copies. She bookmarked the site and pulled up Google, typing a line in from Susan Palmer's poem. *A perfect woman, nobly planned,* she typed, and hit enter. Bingo.

Apparently, the Southern Strangler wasn't creative after all. The poem was written by William Wordsworth. 4,950 hits on the search engine. From a poem called "She Was a Phantom of Delight." Well, how apropos.

Whitney realized she was on the right track. She did the same thing for Jeanette Lernier's note. *For a creature not so bright and good.* Whoa, that had 304,000 hits. She pulled up the poem and realized that both notes were simply stanzas from the same poem. She printed it, whipping the paper out of the printer almost before it was through and read aloud.

"She was a Phantom of delight
When first she gleamed upon my sight;
A lovely Apparition, sent
To be a moment's ornament;
Her eyes as stars of Twilight fair;

Like Twilight's, too, her dusky hair;
But all things else about her drawn
From May-time and the cheerful Dawn;
A dancing Shape, an Image gay,
To haunt, to startle and waylay.

"I saw her upon nearer view,
A Spirit, yet a Woman, too!
Her household motions light and free,
And steps of virgin-liberty;
A countenance in which did meet
Sweet records, promises as sweet;
A Creature not too bright or good
For human nature's daily food,
For transient sorrows, simple wiles,
Praise, blame, love, kisses, tears and smiles.

"And now I see with eye serene
The very pulse of the machine;
A Being breathing thoughtful breath,
A Traveller between life and death;
The reason firm, the temperate will,
Endurance, foresight, strength and skill;
A perfect Woman, nobly planned,
To warn, to comfort and command;
And yet a Spirit still, and bright
With something of angelic light."

She finished and thought hard for a moment. Some-thing wasn't right. Reading through it again, she realized she wasn't seeing the lines from the latest poem she'd received. She followed the same process. The author of the poem fragment in the newest note was William Butler Yeats. She printed it out and read it aloud.

> *"Leda and the Swan*
> *A sudden blow: the great wings beating still*
> *Above the staggering girl, her thighs caressed*
> *By his dark webs, her nape caught in his bill,*
> *He holds her helpless breast upon his breast.*
>
> *"How can those terrified vague fingers push*
> *The feathered glory from her loosening thighs?*
> *How can anybody, laid in that white rush,*
> *But feel the strange heart beating where it lies?*
>
> *"A shudder in the loins, engenders there*
> *The broken wall, the burning roof and tower*
> *And Agamemnon dead.*
>
> *"Being so caught up,*
> *So mastered by the brute blood of the air,*
> *Did she put on his knowledge with his power*
> *Before the indifferent beak could let her drop?"*

And that poem covered Jessica Porter, Shauna Davidson and the latest missing, yet to be found but in all probability very dead, Marni Fischer. Wow, that was pretty impressive imagery. But Whitney wasn't the expert in literature.

She walked back to her desk and sat hard in the supple leather, making the chair squeak in protest. No, Whitney was no English major. That was her twin sister,

Quinn. Her identical twin. Ashleigh Quinn Connolly Buckley, to be exact. Married to Jonathan "Jake" Buckley III, she was the perfect Belle Meade housewife. A Junior League hostess extraordinaire. Mother to two of the most adorable children on earth, the twins, Jillian and Jake Junior.

Whitney felt a quick stab of regret. She hadn't called the twins in a couple of weeks. She may try to stay out of her sister's perfectly groomed hair, but the kids were another matter. Quinn couldn't be more Whitney's opposite if she tried. They'd heard the same thing growing up all their lives, especially since their teenage years. That's when they really came into their identities.

Their mother had always used their full names, in conversation, addressing them, discussing them. Sarah Whitney and Ashleigh Quinn went to school today. Sarah Whitney and Ashleigh Quinn are going to camp this summer. Sarah Whitney and Ashleigh Quinn, get down here right now. Finally, Sarah Whitney rebelled, insisting that she be called just plain Whitney. Ashleigh Quinn had concurred, going with her more esoteric moniker, Quinn. It had taken several months of arguments, but the girls had prevailed. They became Whitney and Quinn, and their personalities diverged along with their names.

One thought led to another and Whitney realized she hadn't heard from her little brother in a while, either. Reese Connolly was so far off her radar most of the time that she forgot he existed. That's how she always wanted it. Who said families had to be close?

Tamping down a moment of frustration, Whitney

went to her stainless-steel refrigerator and pulled out a can of sugar-free Red Bull. Coffee and more caffeine, the secret to her figure. She jokingly called it the model diet. Cracking open the can, she stood at the sink, staring out the kitchen window at the huge birch tree in her backyard. A male cardinal parked his red feathers on the bird feeder, chirping contently while he ate his breakfast. Two squirrels barked at each other in a game of chase, and the breeze lightly shuffled leaves from the tree onto her deck. The Virginia creeper that was slowly strangling the bark from the tree reminded her of her past.

Whitney had never quite recovered after her parents' deaths. In an instant, all the comfort and stability she had known was gone. The Connollys were returning from an evening at the Tennessee Performing Arts Center, a drive they'd taken innumerable times. In a brutal collision, two loving, vivacious, happy people were stolen from their family by a drunk driver. Though it had been eight years, time hadn't lessened her sense of loss.

The uneasy peace their parents had provided between the siblings never fully recovered. The three children split their parents' fortune, but the rift between them grew with each passing year.

Whitney struck out on her own, throwing herself into her work, building her career. It fell to Quinn to mother Reese, shepherding him through his final year of high school, then getting him settled at Vanderbilt. Quinn had met Jake Buckley by then, and was getting pretty hot and heavy with him, but Jake was a good guy. Waiting for Quinn's little brother to get out of the house so they could marry wasn't a big problem for him. Quinn's money would cement his place in the world.

The unwelcome thought of Reese made Whitney's stomach turn. Even all these years later, she still resented him. Reese had always been an exceptional child, gifted in ways Whitney would never be. He was brilliantly smart and driven. He entered Vanderbilt when he was fifteen, finished his undergraduate coursework in two years and started in their medical school program. Now Reese was finishing his final year of residency in psychiatry.

Whitney thought back to the last time she'd seen him. It wasn't a planned meeting, they'd just run into each other at Quinn's home. He'd been talking about going to some godforsaken country in South America to work with a group operating on poor people. What lofty aspirations the boy had. Yet Quinn had been all dewy eyed about it, such an amazing opportunity, he's so young, blah, blah, blah. Grudges could last a lifetime, Whitney knew that better than anyone. Quinn understood. She didn't approve, she just understood.

Maybe she should give her sister a call. She looked at the clock. Surely Quinn was finished with tennis or dropping the twins at school or whatever it was she did in the mornings with all of her and Jake's money.

Taking one last look at the birch tree, she shook off the past.

She picked up the phone and speed dialed her sister's cell phone. The voice mail answered instead, requesting in Quinn's perfectly cultured southern accent that she leave a message. Whitney hung up without saying a word, instantly relieved. She'd just try again later.

Slamming the empty can into the sink, she walked back to her office. She wheeled her chair back to the desk and pulled out her file on the Southern Strangler. Maybe she could get some more work done on the background story. She was theorizing on many of the killer's attributes, working off research that she had gathered over the years on serial kidnappers and killers.

She worked quietly, the hour passing quickly. Closing the file, she stretched and decided it would be a good idea to hit Starbucks for another coffee. She always asked for Starbucks cards as presents, she lived off their espresso. She walked to the living room, gathering her purse, when something on the television screen caught her eye.

A News Alert was flashing across the screen. They'd found Marni Fischer.

She sat and turned up the volume. The anchor was intoning that Marni Fischer's body had been found off Highway 81 in Roanoke, Virginia. Roanoke. Something niggled at the back of Whitney's mind. She ran back into her office and pulled the file out again, reading the names of the cities involved.

"Huntsville, Baton Rouge, Jackson, Nashville, Noble, Roanoke. Huntsville, Baton Rouge, Jackson, Nashville, Noble, Roanoke."

Her heart was starting to beat just a little faster. Hands shaking, she pulled out the notes again, copies of the poems she had printed from her e-mail. She read through them, her breath coming in little gasps. Read them again. And again. Then it hit her. She knew who the Southern Strangler was.

She dropped the files and grabbed her cell phone out of her purse. Journalistic creed be damned. Screw the anchor job in New York. She had to warn her sister.

Eighteen

Taylor sat back in her chair, her hands entwined in her long blond hair. Sunlight glinted through the slats of the Venetian blinds behind her, the window one more small concession to her rising credibility in the world. The words of the doctor slapped through her brain like a pinball. Pregnant. Pregnant. Pregnant.

She ran the conversation with Dr. Gregory over and over in her head, as if she could rearrange the words, realign their meaning.

"That's impossible. I'm not late. I haven't ever been late. I think I'd know if I was late. And I'm on the Pill. Trust me, it's not something I forget about. So you have to be wrong."

"Taylor, these things happen. The tests are very sensitive, they can detect pregnancy hormones almost immediately. What you need to do is relax. I'm going to prescribe a prenatal vitamin for you and I want you taking one milligram of folic acid every day. No drinking, of course. And I don't suppose I have to tell you no smoking?"

Taylor felt like throwing up. Psychosomatic, she told herself. She couldn't have morning sickness just because the doctor told her she was pregnant.

"I'm telling you, Doc, this just can't be. I never—"

"It can, and it is," he said gently. "Now, I want you to make an appointment with your OB/GYN, and she can go over all of the additional information with you." His voice had quieted even more. "This is a blessing, Taylor. With the damage done to your body, you should be jumping for joy that it happened so soon. It's going to be fine, I promise. I have to run now, but I'll talk to you soon, okay?"

He'd hung up as soon as she whispered okay back to him. She stared at the phone receiver, then tossed it across the room like it was a snake that tried to bite her. Damn. It wasn't that she didn't want to have a baby. Just not now. At least, not until she knew if Baldwin was into that kind of stuff. They had been too busy doing what it took to make a kid rather than talking about the consequences. Consequences. Hell, she sounded like a thirteen-year-old in an after-school movie. What in the name of God was she going to do?

She picked up her cell phone and dialed Baldwin's number. As soon as she hit Send, she hit End and put the phone down on the desk in front of her.

The tears started to come, and she felt even worse. As a woman in her mid-thirties, she should be thrilled at the mere thought of a healthy child. Nearly everyone she knew had at least one child in the stable. The ones who didn't were desperately trying—innocuous prescription bottles of Clomid suddenly appearing on the bathroom vanity, the fervent prayers that the little stick would turn pink and the bleeding wouldn't begin. Then that heart-stopping moment when it did. The shots of Ovidrel, once daily, the woman bent in half in front of the mirror making sure her man is sticking her right. The prayers again that the maturation of the follicle would kick out that magic egg. The basal thermometers, the ovulation kits, tired husbands jacking off into plastic cups, their despair and embarrassment nearly as bad as their wives' desire for offspring. The in vitro fertilization, the bank accounts dwindling, all in that desperate search for something permanent of themselves to be left on this earth. Most of these women had spent years trying not to get pregnant; suddenly finding themselves unable to fulfill that one promise of womanhood was more than they could take.

The level of guilt Taylor felt rose appreciably. She wasn't trying to get pregnant. She didn't want to be pregnant. Hell, she and Baldwin were just finding each other. How would that fragile union support another life? They had never spoken of children. Their lives didn't seem to have room for that kind of future right now.

A knock on her door startled her. She quickly wiped away the tears, cleared her throat, mussed her hair and said, "Come in."

The door opened and ADA Julia Page stepped into the room. Glancing over her shoulder, she shut the door behind her, then leaned back against it. She looked Taylor up and down.

"Bad time?"

"No, not at all. I was just…" Taylor shrugged as her

voice trailed off. No need to explain herself. Julia wouldn't be interested in the details.

Julia Page was one of the assistant district attorneys representing Davidson County. Smart as a whip and about as tall as a dandelion, she looked more like a Pomeranian fluffed out for Westminster than the cut-throat attorney that she was. Her light brown curls framed her face, making her seem innocent and pure, a tactic that had snowed many a criminal. They got on the stand and saw her sweet blue eyes and cupid-bow lips and just knew that this sweet young thing was no threat. How wrong they were.

"Good, because we need to talk." Page stayed standing, keeping her eye level with Taylor's sitting form. "I think we have a problem."

Taylor groaned. If ADA Page was visiting with a "problem," it must be a doozy. A headache began to take hold behind her right eye. She reached into her top drawer and drew out a bottle of Excedrin, popped the top, then shook three out into her hand. She put them in her mouth and chased them with a swig of tepid Diet Coke. A thought hit her hard as she swallowed—caffeine. She probably shouldn't be having either the pills or the soda. She shook the thought off.

"What's wrong then, Page?"

Page took a deep breath and practically spit out the words. "Terrence Norton."

"What did the little turd do now?"

"He just walked out of Judge Hamilton's court a free man."

That caught Taylor's attention. "What do you mean, a free man? We have him dead to rights on murder one."

"Had," Page corrected. "Had him dead to rights. Jury acquitted him in forty-five fucking minutes. Forty-five fucking minutes, Taylor. All the evidence, the testimony, hell, the witnesses, none of that seemed to matter. We lost this trial, and it's a huge mess. You heard about the projects shooting a few days ago?"

Taylor nodded. "East Homicide caught it, they had the shooter in custody by the end of the night."

"Well, the vic was going to be a witness against Terrence in this trial. A few weeks ago, he changed his mind and his testimony, decided that he didn't see what he thought he saw. Refused to testify. We dropped him from the list, we had other witnesses. It smells like a hit, just in case he changed his mind again. The shooter is from Atlanta. He's claiming he was in town to see a friend who lived at the apartment next door to the witness. Says he and his 'friend' had an argument over the price of a package of heroin, the kid was lingering and was shot accidentally. That's just too damn convenient for me."

"I agree. There's more there. So Terrence is running drugs out of Atlanta now?"

Page snorted. "Right now, Terrence could be walking on the moon. He's really managed to build a reputation for himself. Did you know he's moving around town with four bodyguards when he's not in the lockup? That smacks of drugs to me, no pun intended. We don't have anything on it though."

"And the trial fell apart?"

"Yeah. His *peers* didn't think we substantiated our facts. That's a quote from the jury foreman, by the way. He's out on the courthouse steps, talking to

Channel fucking Four about it. And every other station that will listen."

"Can't you throw a gag order at them, or something?"

"No. Trial's over, they're free to say what they want. Terrence walked out of there like Michael Jackson, to the cheers of his fans. We have a serious problem here, Taylor. A really fucking serious problem."

Energy spent, Page flopped in the chair, head down. "We had him. I absolutely can't believe they acquitted him. This is the third time in the past few months. We have a serious problem," she repeated. Page was talking to her chest now, and Taylor could feel the waves of frustration rolling off her like a desert breeze.

Terrence Norton was a nobody from nowhere. Just another kid from the projects who had himself a rap sheet a mile long, assault, burglary, rape, murder, drugs. He got around the criminal scene, and with each arrest, his street cred went a little higher. With each acquittal, he became stronger, more important in the community. He was becoming a legend, and that was the most perilous thing a young criminal in Nashville could be. If he'd gotten strong enough to be bringing in drugs from out of town, he was more dangerous than they realized.

Taylor understood why Page had come to her. Fitz had developed a sort of rapport with Terrence after his best friend was murdered by another bad guy in the projects. Fitz had been trying to get Terrence to admit that the thug, known as Little Man Graft, had shot Terrence's friend. In the course of making the case, Terrence had been busted for shooting a homeless man.

When he'd been brought in, Terrence immediately asked for Fitz, offering to turn on Little Man for some consideration on this latest shooting charge. His testimony had secured Little Man a cell on death row.

Fitz had worked a deal with the punk, knowing full well that the officers on the scene of the homeless shooting had recovered a gun that matched the description of what Terrence had been carrying. Fingerprint analysis proved Terrence handled the gun, and the ballistics matched the gun to the bullets that killed the homeless man. Still, this jury had seen fit to let him off the hook. Page was right. They did have a problem.

Taylor eyed the woman. "What do you think is going on?"

Page looked her straight in the eye. "Take your pick. Jury tampering, witness intimidation, a corrupt judge."

Taylor laughed. "Yeah, right. Terrence Norton has gotten to Judge Hamilton. The man's an icon in this town. He's put away more criminals than you or I have ever met. There's no way Hamilton's involved."

"You don't think?" Page was staring harder, and Taylor felt a qualm in her stomach. Taylor's own father had been convicted of interfering with the election of a federal judge, and had done time for it. Taylor wasn't quite sure what Page's glare was insinuating. Judges were bought with money. Terrence Norton didn't have enough to get to a judge. Not yet.

"No, I don't think." Taylor returned the stare, her gray eyes steely. "Jury tampering and witness intimidation I can buy. But not Judge Hamilton. And I think you'd be wise to stay away from that train of thought. ADAs have gone down for much less."

Page stood up, huffing. "What are you saying, Taylor? That you'll report me for having doubts about why one of our most notorious criminals manages to walk out of court every damn time we arrest him, despite hard-core evidence?"

"Sit down. You know I'm not saying that. Jesus, Page, I think you'd know me better than that by now."

Page was still puffed up, spoiling for a fight. "I'm coming to you because I trust you, Taylor. If there's anyone in this town that I can believe in to see that this gets made right, it's you. You're not exactly the squeamish kind, you know?"

Taylor dropped Page's gaze, rolling her neck to relieve the tension. Not squeamish. Page was right about that. Taylor had killed, and more than once. She'd fought her way out of bad situations before, with force when necessary, and had the scars to prove it. She wasn't a violent woman by any means. No screaming fights, no broken glass, no beatings by a man. Yet the edge of mayhem lurked in the recesses of her mind, waiting. What female in any kind of law enforcement didn't have some inkling of brutality bred in her? She fingered her neck and said softly, "Julia, sit down. Let's talk."

The fight went out of the ADA and she sat back down, suddenly looking like a vulnerable law student seeking quarter for a perceived transgression. She fiddled with a curl over her ear, and Taylor realized how young she really was. It was easy to forget how young they both were. Seeing death and destruction every day, living in the world of crime, made them older than their years.

"I think we'd do right to look at the jury and witness angles, rather than at Judge Hamilton. Terrence has a much better shot at intimidating the people of the community who come into contact with him or his thugs than he does a criminal-court judge." Page started to say something, but Taylor held up a hand. "Now, I didn't say I wouldn't look into Hamilton. I just think it's much more likely that Terrence is screwing with the people he has ready access to, that's all."

Mollified, Page nodded.

Taylor continued. "Okay then, here's what I'll do. You trust Pete Fitzgerald, right? My sergeant?"

"Of course I do. Fitz helped make this case against Terrence. From what I hear, he has some kind of relationship going with Terrence. A mutual-distrust society. I have no worries about him."

"Then I'll assign Fitz to you. I'll make sure he's up to speed on the situation, and send him over this afternoon. You guys come up with a plan for investigating this. And that's all, Page. I don't want to hear anything more from you about Hamilton. I'll handle that side by myself. We can't have you getting fired, now, can we?"

Taylor stood, indicating the conversation was over. Page stood as well, looked up at Taylor and raised an eyebrow. "I'm out on a limb here, Taylor. Don't let me drop." She reached for the doorknob and flung open the door. A flash of fresh air infiltrated the office. As Taylor watched the ADA's retreating back, she reveled in the air, trying to use it to wash herself clean. A baby and a corrupt judicial system. What more could she ask for?

There was only one thing for her to do. She placed a call to Sam, asking her to meet for dinner. Taylor needed a friend right now.

Taylor stepped from the CJC offices absently, lost in her own problems. If she'd just taken a moment, taken one quick glance out the door before she stepped into the dusky night, her life might have been a little easier. Instead, she was hit with a vicious onslaught.

"Lieutenant Jackson," a shrill voice cried out. Taylor's head snapped up. A news crew from the local CBS affiliate had taken up residence in the CJC parking lot, looking to ambush her as she left the building. They'd succeeded.

"Lieutenant, we'd like a comment from you on the Rainman case. Is it true that your suspect raped and beat Detective Betsy Garrison of the Sex Crimes Unit?"

Taylor was caught completely off guard. She paused, mind scrambling. Shit fire on a hell brick. How did they find out? She gathered herself, standing tall.

"Is it true, Lieutenant?"

Taylor searched the young girl's face, trying to place her.

"I don't believe we've met."

"Edith Conrad, Channel Five News. It's my first day," she added proudly. "Is it true then? Detective Garrison is the latest victim of the notorious serial rapist, the Rainman? The same serial rapist that has been terrorizing Nashville's women has gone so far as to assault a member of Nashville law enforcement."

"You can stop proselytizing, Edith. I have no comment on the Rainman investigation. It is an ongoing investigation conducted by the Metro Nashville Sex Crimes

Unit. We don't comment on ongoing investigations. Since it's your first day, I'll let that transgression pass." She strode past the camera, purposely staring at a point five feet to the left.

"Lieutenant," the girl called out to her back. "I'll be broadcasting the information on the ten o'clock newscast. I just want to be sure I have the background correct."

Taylor ignored her, continued walking across the parking lot.

"Lieutenant, it's also come to our attention that there is DNA evidence in the case. Are you sure you don't want to comment?"

Taylor swung around. "Where did you get that information?"

Edith smiled coyly. "A well-placed source. Are you willing to confirm or deny the information? Because we both know I'm right on the money with this one."

Taylor stared at her briefly. The girl was petite, blond and thrilled with herself. Taylor did the only thing she knew to do.

"No comment." She crossed the street in a hurry, heard the girl's delighted voice behind her. "Did you get that?' she asked her photographer. "Please tell me you got all of that."

"Fuck," Taylor spat. She reached her truck, climbed in, and drove off before she opened her cell phone. She speed dialed Mitchell Price's number. He answered on the first ring.

"Price, it's Taylor. We have a problem. Channel Five has the Garrison rape."

The string of expletives would have done any sailor

proud. When Price finally calmed down, Taylor relayed the entire incident with the reporter.

"What do you want me to do?" she asked.

"I don't want you to do anything," he replied. "I'll get on the horn, see how we can spin it. Dammit, Taylor, you were supposed to keep this quiet."

"C'mon, Cap, I have. Only Marcus and Lincoln have the information. The leak came from somewhere else. The hospital, maybe, or the lab. It was a long shot that we were going to be able to keep this quiet."

"The press isn't supposed to give the names of rape victims on air or in print without their prior authorization. So hopefully they won't name Betsy personally. If they do, we'll light them up like a Christmas tree."

"It's the kid's first day, so I can't give you an estimate on the amount of integrity she has. But you'd best find a way to quash the story."

"We won't be able to quash it entirely, but I'll make sure they don't use her name. Dammit!"

"Sorry, Cap. All I can tell you is it didn't come from me or mine. Good luck with it."

"Not a word about it, Lieutenant. Hear me? Make sure there's nothing but a 'no comment' coming out of our side of the building."

"Gotcha. I'll talk to you tomorrow." She hung up, desolate. Nothing was going her way today.

Nineteen

Taylor rolled into the parking lot at her favorite watering hole lost in thought. She shoved the worries about Betsy Garrison and the leak from her mind for the moment. There was nothing she could do if the press had the information. Better to let Price deal with it. She had enough worries of her own. Her conversation with ADA Page was fresh in her mind, and she had taken the drive from downtown to Bellevue to think it through. Unfortunately, she had no answers.

She was greeted warmly as she entered the bar. It was smoky and dark but situated in a large, almost cavernous space. Big-screen plasma televisions were positioned over the bar, affording sports fans multiple views and coverage of all their favorite pastimes. Regulars nursed whiskey in the corners of the huge U-shaped bar, pushing quarters into the gambling trivia machines as if they'd get some money back. A few college-age coeds giggled at a table, throwing glances over their shoulders to see who was watching them. Ads for the latest beer

hung from banners and were backlit with neon lights.
It was a happy place.

Before Taylor was fully seated on her favorite high-
legged chair, a chilled glass of Guinness appeared in
front of her. She'd taken a liking to Baldwin's beloved
beverage, and had ordered it so many times that the
bartenders didn't bother to ask what she wanted. She
gazed at it longingly. She had the presence of mind to
know that she shouldn't drink, but the release she
would get from numbing herself begged her for a ride.
She rationalized; she'd had at least three beers last
night. If she hadn't talked to her doctor today, hadn't
gotten the news, she would have had at least three
more tonight. Perhaps she could just pretend that this
wasn't happening and have it anyway. It sounded like
a good idea. The glass almost magically appeared at
her lips and she gulped greedily, as if she hadn't had
liquids in weeks. The second pint went down smoother
than the first.

Sam blew into the room like a thunderstorm, all
heads turning as she wound her way through the bar.
Taylor almost laughed. Sam was beautiful, dark hair
sleeked into a high ponytail, pieces falling magically
around her face as if planned by a master stylist. Even
after a long day cutting up Nashville's dead, she looked
as fresh as if she'd just stepped from the shower. As she
enveloped her best friend in a hug, Taylor smelled the
blissful scent of baby powder. She almost choked on it.

Sam looked her over, and Taylor saw realization
dawn in her eyes. Taylor had gotten a good drunk on
one or two times in the past, and she knew Sam could
read the signs that she was headed that way like they

were plastered in neon on her forehead. Good friend that she was, she just smiled.

"What's the emergency, sunshine? Hi, Kat." She grinned at the bartender, a dusky-skinned half-Korean woman who looked almost Hawaiian. "Can I have some water? And get some for our friend here." She turned to Taylor. "What's wrong?" she asked bluntly, the smile gone.

Taylor took a deep breath, at a loss. Sam's belly had reached her first; she was barely three months along and already beginning to show. How she had managed to get pregnant on her honeymoon was usually a great source of amusement for Taylor. Now it was simply depressing.

"I honestly don't know where to begin. The Rainman case, you're familiar with it?"

"Yeah. Why're you worrying about it, that's Sex Crimes's case, right?"

"I've been helping with it. And it's going to hit the news tonight. Another victim, and I'm afraid they're going to name names. That's all I'm going to say about it, okay?"

Sam nodded. She was savvy to the inner workings of investigations.

"Then there's Julia Page, all in a dither about a case she lost today. Thinks there's jury tampering, dropped that in my lap this afternoon. Not to mention all the crap Baldwin's going through with the Southern Strangler. Do I need more to be upset about?"

"Give me a break, Taylor. That's all in a day's work to you. Now, what's really going on?"

Taylor looked at her sharply. Typical, she couldn't pull one over on Sam. Might as well get it off her chest. She took a deep breath. "I talked to the doctor today."

"Oh no, honey. Is your liver not showing the right levels?"

Taylor barked a laugh, drinking deeply of her draught. "No, the liver's just fine. There's a whole new problem." She tried to look Sam in the eye and failed. She knew Sam would understand. Taylor wasn't ready for a child. She and Sam had talked about it many times in the past, especially once Sam herself had gotten pregnant. But the immediacy of having to share the news was pressing on her like an anvil. She decided she'd best be out with it before she chickened out.

"I'm pregnant," she whispered.

Sam didn't miss a beat. "So you're sitting here trying to get in your cups. Excellent way to manage the stress, Taylor."

Taylor started shaking her head back and forth, a pendulum of distress. "Noo, that's not it at all. I'm…"

"You're at a complete loss. You're not ready to have a baby. You haven't told Baldwin because you don't know how he's going to react. You don't know what to think, how to behave, what to do. That about sum it up?"

Taylor gave her a dirty look. "Well, leprosy cases are on the rise, too. Besides, you're supposed to be encouraging me here. Not—"

"Not what? What do you want me to do? You're a big girl. You can make decisions for yourself. Did you want me to toss the beer over the railing and lecture you? I'll do it if you want. But I don't think that's why you wanted to talk to me. So get drunk and talk."

Taylor leaned back in her chair. Shit. That was the problem with good friends. They wouldn't condemn, wouldn't fly off the handle. She realized she was spoiling for a fight, much like Julia Page in her office earlier. As she fought back a snapping reply, she saw Sam motioning to Kat. A pack of fresh Camel Lights appeared at her elbow. Sam broke open the pack, pulled out a cigarette, held it out to Taylor and lit a match.

"Here, why don't you have a smoke while you're at it. Get it all out of your system now, girl, because tomorrow things have to change. For now, just…shit." The match had burnt down far enough to burn Sam's finger. She tossed the pack of matches on the bar and stuck her finger in her mouth.

Free ride. That's exactly what Taylor had been praying Sam would give her. Sam was a doctor, she knew the risks. If she said it was okay, then it was. She lit the cigarette, drew in deeply and blew blue smoke into the air, mindful to direct the noxious stream away from Sam's delicate state.

Sam spoke more softly this time. "Sweetie, I know you're so freaked out right now you can't see straight. Let's just ride this out. It's going to be okay."

Taylor let the tears start to fall.

Twenty

Whitney was driving in a panic. She'd tried Quinn at home, on her cell phone, at the country club for the remainder of the day yesterday and well into this morning. There was no answer at home or on the cell, and the country club staff hadn't seen her since Monday after she'd finished her morning workout on the tennis courts. Whitney had continued to hit Redial throughout the evening, finally getting desperate when she reached the answering machine at Quinn's home for the eighth time this morning. She left a message, telling her sister she was on her way over and to wait for her if she came home. If she got the message, she was to call immediately. She left the same message on Quinn's cell phone, realizing she was starting to sound slightly hysterical. She needed to get a grip on herself. She might be wrong. It wasn't out of the realm of possibility that it was just a coincidence. But she needed to tell her sister face-to-face so they could work it out together. They may not have been close, but Whitney did love her, and would do anything to protect Quinn.

The station had called, too, wanting her to come in and cover some new angle on the serial rapist that was breaking, but even that had to wait. Imagine, she was putting her own career on hold. She'd deal with that later. First, she *had* to see Quinn.

She forced her brand-new BMW X5 through the meandering traffic on Highway 70. This stretch of road, over Nine Mile Hill from Bellevue into the West Meade area, always lagged. All the locals knew that a speed trap waited to catch drivers as they blew over the hill faster than the forty-five-mile-an-hour speed limit allowed. She weaved, and touched her brakes as she came through the yellow flashing lights in front of St. Henry's, warning her to slow down to fifteen miles an hour so she wouldn't run over any lingering school-children. She slowed to sixty-five, then punched the gas as she passed through the intersection. She saw a crosswalk monitor shaking a fist in the air in her rearview mirror, but didn't slow.

The SUV gleamed in the sunlight, briefly blinding other drivers as it flashed past, narrowly missing bumpers and side mirrors. Horns blared, fingers were thrown, but Whitney ignored the danger she was putting herself and the other drivers in. The West Meade split at Highway 70 and Highway 100 was congested as usual, the awkward traffic pattern begging for an accident of mammoth proportions, but she caught all the lights. She found the short stretch of open road where Highway 70 briefly became the Memphis–Bristol Highway that indicated the wealth of the land had just increased tenfold. The sign for the Belle Meade Mansion flashed by in a blur of white and she realized she'd missed her turn onto Leake Avenue. No matter, she could get to Quinn's house through the main entrance to Belle Meade. The railroad tracks flashed by on her left and suddenly she was on top of the entrance.

She knew she was going too fast as she tried to take the right turn. She braked hard, and the X5 slid into a 90-degree turn onto Belle Meade Boulevard. As the Beemer tried to obey its master and turn on a dime, Whitney lost control. The SUV weaved precariously, flashing across the turning lane right into the two bronze Thoroughbreds that graced the entrance into the Belle Meade enclave.

The life-sized metal horses bucked into the air and crashed onto the street behind her. The impact didn't stop her SUV, which continued across the median into the oncoming traffic on the Boulevard. Drivers swerved to miss her, but one car stayed its course. Whitney's BMW plowed into and over the Audi station wagon, crushing the car and its three occupants.

In her panic, she'd neglected to fasten her seat belt. Without the restraint to hold her in place, the impact hurled Whitney through the windshield as if she were a missile. Her left foot caught in the wiper blade, and her broken, bloody body splayed on the shiny hood, mingling with the splat of a couple of lovebugs, all three joined forever in death.

Twenty-One

Baldwin had just arrived at the airport, checked his bag at the curb and was heading inside to grab a cup of coffee before his plane returned to Nashville, when his cell phone rang. He looked at the number and smiled. Taylor had tried to call him late last night, or early this morning, seeing as the time code on the message was 3:30 a.m. She hadn't left a message. He must have slept through the ring. He hated missing her calls, and wondered why she had tried him in the middle of the night. Sometimes it got to the point that they spoke to each other's voice mail for a whole day, trying to match up.

"Hi, sweetheart. Everything okay?"

Taylor's voice was a little shaky, but she sounded all right to him. "I'm fine. When are you coming home?"

"I'm at the airport now, my flight leaves in half an hour."

"Good. I, uh, we, uh—"

Baldwin heard a beep in his ear, glanced at the display and interrupted her. "Hold on a sec, Grimes is calling my other line." He hit the flash button. "Hey, Grimes."

"Baldwin, you haven't gotten on the plane yet, have you?"

"Oh, no."

"Oh, yeah. And the media is broadcasting the story already."

"Wait a second, would you? I need to get off the other line." He clicked over. "Taylor, I have to go. Let me call you right back." He hung up before he heard an answer and switched back to Grimes.

"Where is she?"

"They found her body off Highway 81 right outside of Roanoke, Virginia. The guy who found her called his girlfriend and told her to call the local Fox affiliate before he called the police. Wanted his fifteen minutes of fame. And before you ask, no, he doesn't look good for the crime. But we need to get up there ASAP. I've got a plane chartered here at the private airstrip. Go grab a cab and have them run you to this terminal, okay?"

The stress in Grimes's voice was palpable. Baldwin started walking toward the exit with purpose, firing questions as he made his way through the throng of people.

"What else do you know?"

"Other than the national news has already picked it up before we're on the scene? Well, she was strangled, I know that for sure. But the highway patrol officer I talked to down there wasn't the friendliest cuss in the world. This isn't going to be like Noble. So that's the extent of it."

Baldwin reached the curb and entered a waiting taxi,

instructing the driver and talking to Grimes at the same time. "Okay, I'm in a cab and should be over there in five minutes. We'll talk on the plane."

He clicked off, then punched in the speed-dial number for Taylor. She picked up before the first ring had ended.

"Thanks for hanging up on me." She sounded pissed and Baldwin grimaced. He hadn't meant to be rude, and told her that.

"I know you didn't. What did Grimes want?"

"Marni Fischer's body has been found in Roanoke. I'm on my way over to the jet so I can catch a ride up there. I don't think I'll be home tonight after all, honey. I'm sorry." He was genuinely distressed, he hated spending too much time away from her.

"Uhhh, that's okay. Just give me a call when you get some free time. I'm sorry, babe, I know you didn't want it to end up like this."

"No, but I was expecting it. Time frame was right. You were about to ask me something earlier."

"Oh, that's okay, it can wait. I have to go anyway, I'm meeting Sam. Just call me later, okay?"

"I will, sweetheart. Love you," he said almost absently. Once he'd determined Taylor was fine and needed nothing from him, his head had gone immediately back to the case. He hung up and shoved the phone back into its holster.

Roanoke, Virginia. The killer started in Alabama, went to Louisiana, Mississippi, Tennessee, then Georgia and now had ended up in Virginia. He flipped open his phone and made a quick call back to Quantico. His boss, Garrett Woods, answered on the first ring.

"Baldwin, are you on your way to Virginia?"

"Yes, I'm pulling up to the private terminal in Atlanta right now, Grimes has a plane ready to go. Do me a favor, would you? Put the locations of the dump sites and kidnapping sites into the geographical database, see what it spits out. I want to see if this guy is flying by the seat of his pants or if he might be following some sort of geographical pattern. Have them try to find central locations he could be working out of, and put in the assumption that he's not from any of the areas that he's been working in."

"You got it. Anything else?"

"I'll call you from Virginia. Until I get on the ground I want to hold off making any more judgments."

"Okay then, but get back to me later and let me know what you think."

"Will do, Garrett. Thanks." He clicked off just as the taxi pulled up in front of the private air terminal. He jumped into the cab, juggling his cell phone and briefcase. His cell rang again, an unfamiliar number with a Georgia area code. He got settled in the cab and answered on the third ring.

"John Baldwin."

"Dr. Baldwin, this is Sheriff Pascoe. I've gotten the report back from the lab on the note found in Marni Fischer's car. There weren't any discernible prints, just a couple of smudges. Could be from the victim, but I can't guarantee that. There just wasn't enough to go on."

"Well, it was a long shot. He's not making a lot of mistakes, there's no reason for him to start now. Particular and precise, that's our boy. Thank you, Sheriff. I appreciate you working so quickly on that."

"You'll keep me up-to-date on what happens, right?"

"Absolutely. You have my number, feel free to call anytime. I have to run, I'm at the airport now. You take care."

He shut the phone, overpaid the cabbie and made his way through the glass double doors. Grimes was standing in the middle of the large room and looked relieved when he saw Baldwin.

"We're wheels up as soon as you get on the plane. You ready to go?"

"Let's do it," Baldwin said.

Twenty-Two

Taylor was as hungover as she had ever been. She vaguely recalled the night before, crying into her beer, and later in the evening, Crown Royal. That had been a mistake, she hated whisky. It tasted like firewood soaked in grain alcohol, like she was chewing on wood chips. She'd thrown up almost as soon as she finished it. That's when Sam had decided Kat should follow them home in Taylor's truck. The ride was short, and Sam had poured Taylor into the bed. She woke with a headache, feeling nauseous, a gnawing certainty that something was wrong momentarily obscuring her thoughts. Then she remembered, and felt sick again.

After her brief chat with Baldwin, she'd managed a shower and set off for work, dark-lensed Maui Jims on in an attempt to shield her eyes from an overly bright sun. When had the sun become so powerful, started giving off midafternoon light so early in the morning? She was sure that it had never glowed with such a vengeance.

She opened the door of her Xterra and got in, grimacing. She sat back in the seat, turned her XM radio on, flipped to Lucy, her favorite alternative-rock station, turned the volume to a bearable level and lost herself in the music.

She'd tried many times to figure the exact moment she'd fallen in love with Baldwin. It was his vulnerability that had attracted her in the first place. She had sensed the emptiness in him the moment she'd met him, felt it reflect in her own heart. Was it love at first sight? Was it the first time they'd touched, a casual grazing of the hands? She'd been drawn to his tortured soul, searching for her own forgiveness as she tried to help him achieve his.

She shook herself out of the reverie, her headache starting to lessen. Baldwin. He was her man now. She wished he were here with her. He would placate her with his strong hands, lift the hair on the back of her neck, murmur in her ear as he caressed her body. And she would let him. But now, so early into their happiness, she was going to blow the whole thing. Her hand went to her forehead as a wave of nausea pulsed through her. Shit.

She turned the engine over and put the truck in gear. Driving toward West End, she tried to focus on the news she had received and failed. Things felt different this morning, but she chalked that up to her killer hangover. She glanced in the mirror and gave herself a lopsided smile. She'd figure her life out later. When her head didn't feel like it was going to explode.

She made her way through the traffic in West End and drove into the outskirts of Belle Meade. She had promised, before she was totally gone, to meet Sam at Starbucks this morning.

Taylor pulled into the lot and parked her truck. Making her way past the high-school girls in their green plaid skirts, white socks and Birkenstocks that populated the outdoor seating area, she made it to the door. An older gentleman balancing a tray of coffees kindly held the door for her with his butt. Her southern training kicked in and she gave him one of her best smiles as she passed. He grinned back a little sheepishly. Taylor with a full-watt smile on her face could bring the best of men to their knees. She spotted Sam in a cozy corner with overstuffed chairs and a small glass table loaded with drinks, cinnamon buns, a slice of iced lemon pound cake and a lonely bran muffin. Taylor snickered back a laugh. Sam's pregnancy was getting the better of her, she was wolfing down every sweet in sight.

"There she is, the woman every man wants and every woman wants to be. Sit yourself down here before your latte gets cold, girl."

"I don't envy anyone my position today. I feel like shit."

"Yeah, you're looking a little rough around the edges. Nice shades, though."

Taylor reached over and gave Sam a hug. She searched her friend's face hard, wondering if there was more from last night that she didn't remember. Sam didn't seem perturbed, so Taylor relaxed and sank gratefully into an overstuffed green velvet chair.

She started to reach for her latte, and heard sirens. They were getting louder by the minute, and she chided herself for wondering if they meant she would have to be making a call to a scene.

"Hear that? Hope it's nothing major."

"Yeah, probably a Belle Meade housewife with a hangnail." They both hooted out a laugh, it was just too easy to make fun of Nashville's elite community, to pretend that they didn't come from that enclave of Nashville society. When they stopped guffawing, Taylor realized that Sam was about to explode with some kind of news. She knew right away what it was going to be.

"Went to the doc this morning for the ultrasound."

"Ooooh, could they tell what we're having?" Sam's excitement was catching, they'd been waiting for the ultrasound to find out the sex of the baby. Simon hadn't wanted to know, but Sam's relentless begging had finally won him over.

"Well, in a way. There's a fifty-fifty chance we're having a little girl." Taylor started grinning, wondering immediately if she would turn out to be the tomboy her mother was. She almost missed Sam's next sentence.

"And there's a good chance we're also having a boy."

Taylor stopped, waiting for the words to sink in. "Twins? Twins! Oh my God, Sam, you really don't waste any time, do you? Instant family! Is Simon about to die?"

"He is, but he's happy. He says at least now we can stop worrying about the perfect names. Call them One and Two and be done with it. I told him it sounded like he was naming petrie dishes, but he just laughed." Simon Loughley owned the only forensics lab in town, Private Match. It was just that, private and very discreet. Also very expensive. Metro Nashville had used their services in the past on tough or expedient cases.

Sam continued prattling on, to Taylor's amusement. She knew Sam wanted to be a mother, and couldn't be more pleased that she was having two at once. It was too early for the doctors to be certain of the sex, but the second heartbeat had been exceptionally strong. Taylor could also see the fright behind Sam's eyes. Caring for two newborns would be a much different challenge than just one at a time. But she knew Sam would be a great mother. She wondered if she would, then pushed the thought aside.

"…So I told the doctor that it serves me right, using Depo-Provera all those years. When the eggs realized they could finally get out, they all crowded to the door. It's weird, I can just feel that they are brother and sister."

Taylor leaned into Sam, giving her a soft hug. "It's going to be wonderful, honey. We're going to have a ball!"

Sam looked at her, eyes searching for some confirmation that Taylor had laid the devils to rest about her own situation. With perfect timing, Taylor's cell rang, giving her an excuse to look away. She flipped the phone open and chose a point well over Sam's left shoulder to look at.

"Taylor Jackson." She immediately started shifting in her chair. "Hello, Dr. Gregory. No, I'm fine." She was silent for a moment. Then a moment more. "Are you sure?" The lightness that infused her voice made Sam look at her sharply. Taylor's grin reached from one side of the room to the other. "Thank you. No, really. Thank you."

She hung up the phone, biting her lip.

"Good news?" Sam asked.

Taylor settled back in her chair. "Apparently his nurse Shelby mixed up some of the test results. A woman with the *last* name Taylor is pregnant. I'm not."

"I thought that might be the case. You didn't have the look."

"And you didn't tell me that? I could have used a little doubt last night." Taylor didn't quite know whether to laugh or cry. But the relief she felt was overwhelming. The time just wasn't right for her and Baldwin. Maybe, well, who knew?

Sam, in her ever-placating way, reached out a hand and patted Taylor's arm. She didn't need to say a word.

After a long moment, Taylor started to speak, but just as she opened her mouth, Sam's pager went off. She unhooked it from her purse strap, looked at the readout and grabbed her cell phone. Punching in a few numbers, she quickly became the medical examiner instead of an excited expectant mom. She hung up, shaking her head. "Damn, I've got to go. Fatal car wreck at the entrance to Belle Meade Boulevard. That's what all the sirens were about. Wanna come along?"

"Sure, why not. I'm waiting for Lincoln and Marcus to call me anyway."

The two women got up quickly, tossing trash in silver containers at the door, and made their way to their respective cars. Sam called out, "Follow me," then disappeared into her new silver BMW 330Ci, a wedding present from Simon.

The accident scene was as gruesome as the copious sirens had foretold. Sheets covered victims, blood leaked onto the warming pavement, glass and bits of automotive wonders were scattered carelessly about. A child's doll lay forsaken in the middle of the street under a plate of shattered tempered glass.

Taylor marveled at Sam's ability to shake off her normal life for her work. She was barking orders, looking under sheets, moving through the mayhem like a swan through a shimmering lake. As a medical examiner, it was her job to deal with carnage and mayhem, but she was so smooth and seamless that everything seemed under control the minute she got to a scene. Taylor just sat on the hood of a patrol car and tried to stay out of the way. This wasn't her case, and there were enough people milling about that she didn't need to get in the way.

Sam came over to her, her face a bit ashen.

"You okay?" Taylor asked with concern.

Sam shook her head and shrugged. "I am, but this is one nasty wreck. Woman in the X5 ran over the Audi over there like a tank. Killed the occupants instantly. Driver's license says the mom's name is Tina Young. They're IDing the kids by the names on their backpacks—Meredith and Jason. Elementary-school age. It's pretty nasty, took the mom's head right off. At least I can tell the rest of the family it was quick, I doubt she had a second to know what hit her."

"Who's the chick from the X5? And what is it about Beemers in this town? Am I really the only person who doesn't have one?"

"You finished? Good. The X5's driver was Whitney Connolly. No seat belt, sailed right over the air bag and through the windshield."

Taylor felt the shock go through her like a bolt of lightning. "Whitney Connolly, the reporter from Channel Five?"

"Yeah."

"Oh, Sam. This place is going to be crawling with news trucks. What can I do?"

"Just try to distract them while I get her taken care of, okay? If anyone from Channel Five rolls up, they're bound to recognize her SUV."

"Do you want no comment, or do you want me to confirm that it was her?"

Sam looked at the scene for a moment. "You might as well realize her identity, but only to the Channel Five folks. They need to know right away anyway. Just use your discretion." She walked back to the scene, moving quickly to get yellow tarps over the bodies.

Taylor walked back across the street. Uniformed officers had already closed the road. No one was going to get through but the news trucks. And they were bearing down already. Taylor was relieved to see that the first one was Channel Five, then remembered that they had the Rainman story. Oh well, they'd better stay clear of that with her. At the very least they could have a quick confab and get things straightened out. She waved them down and directed them to the side of the road.

She recognized the reporter and her cameraman. Thankfully, it wasn't tiny Edith, but this particular reporter had covered many of her scenes in the past and had been just as obnoxious. She knew she'd have to hit quickly to keep them from rushing off and ignoring her. She motioned for the driver to open his window and slipped her head into the van.

"Tommy, Stacy, good to see you."

"When's the last time you've been happy to see us on a scene, Lieutenant? And why are you here? I thought this was just a car accident." Stacy Harper was a bottle blonde with square tortoiseshell glasses and a distinctly Yankee accent. She had been poached from Channel Two the year before. She knew Nashville, but Taylor felt she was a bit too whiney. Rumor had it she was dating one of the Tennessee Titans football players, which wouldn't surprise many. She had that perfect overbite that drove men wild.

"It is a car accident, but I need to tell you something."

Stacy and her cameraman were getting impatient, ready to pull out the camera and start shooting some b-roll for Stacy's package. The more raw footage they could compile, the better.

"What, Lieutenant? We need to start getting some shots of this scene so it can make the midday report. Hey, you want to comment on the Rainman?"

"Drop it, Stacy. Focus. Whitney Connolly was in the accident. Her X5 hit another car, killing all three people in it."

Stacy's eyes lit up for a moment. Immediacy was the name of the media game, and there was nothing like a scandal to boost the noontime ratings. "So you're arresting her for vehicular manslaughter? Was she drunk? I have to call my producer, he's going to flip." She started to pull out her phone but caught Taylor's eye and stopped. Realization dawned on her face.

"Oh, you've got to be kidding. She's not..."

"Yes, she is. So I think you do need to call your producer. We're only telling you so you can talk to the station and get moving on whatever it is you need to do."

Tommy and Stacy shared a long look. It was going to

be a very complicated day. They swung into action, getting into the back of the van and starting to make calls.

Taylor stepped away from the van just as Channel Four's van pulled up. She could see another satellite truck coming down from West End. She signaled a "hurry up" to Stacy and Tommy and started back toward the Channel Four van.

When they pulled to a stop, Taylor could tell they knew what was going on. Laura McPherson, the pretty brunette with what Taylor thought was one of the higher IQs in the field, stepped out of the van and came right for her. Taylor braced herself for the onslaught.

"Is it true that Whitney Connolly was killed in the accident?"

It never ceased to amaze her how quickly news could spread through Nashville. Taylor's mouth started forming a "no comment" when Laura shot out her hand, palm up.

"We're not going to do any film, so you can relax. We heard that Whitney was killed as well as three others. Someone on the scene called me to put in the tip, said she thought she recognized Whitney before they covered her up."

Taylor sized Laura up. Young, smart, as ambitious as any other reporter, yet the girl had never burned her before. She was one of the few, and though Taylor knew better than to think it would never happen, she respected that the woman hadn't ever misquoted her or screwed up a report. Taylor knew the rest of the force felt the same way. It was common knowledge who could be trusted and who needed to get the runaround on details. Laura had always done a nice job working the angles and hadn't left anyone out to dry. Integrity in a reporter. Taylor almost laughed.

"All right, but just because it's you. Whitney Connolly *is* dead. What are you going to do now?"

Laura gave her a look. "Talk to my producer, of course. Whitney was an icon here, we'll want to put together some of her best work to honor her with. I wouldn't worry about the rest of us, everyone will be keeping their cameras off. Respect for your fellow journalist, you know?"

"Why aren't you guys like that with everything?"

"C'mon, Lieutenant, you know how it is. We certainly don't want to offend any of the viewers. Besides, it's just not right to capitalize on her death, you know? I kind of admired her."

With that, Laura disappeared back into the news truck. Others were pulling up, the whole contingent of ABC, CBS, NBC and Fox local affiliates were in attendance, but there wasn't any activity from them. No satellites going up, no cables being unrolled, no copy being written. They were all huddled together, allegiances to individual stations forgotten, grieving the loss of one of their own. An unscheduled funeral cortege on West End. That's how we do it, she thought. When one of our cops goes down, that's how we handle it. All the animosity is forgotten, all the hate and fear is gone. We all grieve together. Most of the time. It had never occurred to her that the media would react in the same way.

Thank God, at least none of them were clamoring for information on the Rainman. They were too shocked to think clearly, for once. Taylor left them and walked back across the street toward Sam. She thought her friend still looked a little pale and could only imagine what she herself looked like. The first rush of adrenaline had passed, the hangover was back with a vengeance and she was very tired. As she reached Sam, she went to put an arm around her, then drew back when she saw the smear of blood on her sleeve.

"You've got some blood on you."

Sam looked down in surprise. "Hmm, clumsy of me. Oh well, it'll come out. How's everything with the newsies?"

"They're all standing down. No photos, no film. They're pretty shook up, most are just trying to decide how best to lead the show without upsetting the whole city. Actually not being vultures, which is nice. You don't need to worry about a thing."

Sam gave her a smile. "Thanks, T, you're the greatest. I've got to get to the morgue. You all set?"

"Yeah. I'm going to head in to the office. Take some aspirin. Get caught up on some things. Hope the boys have solved all my cases so I can put my head on my desk and sleep for an hour."

"All the men in the world, and so little time. Tell Baldwin I said hi." Sam gave her arm a squeeze and walked away.

Twenty-Three

Baldwin stood in the glaring sunlight, shielding his eyes and watching the panoply of activity around the body. Each person at a crime scene had a specific task, yet it looked like ants at a picnic, chaotic and busy. The similarity to the previous crime scenes was disconcerting, and he tucked the thought away to be brought back out later. He ducked under the yellow tape and worked his way to the periphery of the activity. Marni Fischer was certainly getting the best attention a body could get.

He made his way to her, slipping on his Ray-Bans so he wouldn't have to squint. Mesmerized by what had been a beautiful young woman, he squatted for a closer look, swatting flies away from his face. Marni Fischer was naked, lying on her back, arms spread out to either side. Her arms ended at the wrist, her hands no longer in their proper place. That's where the similarities ended. He'd been right on the money. The killer was escalating, the violence increasing.

His eyes traveled to what had been her face; knife

slashes had rent channels over an inch deep in a cris-scross pattern from her forehead to her chin. The deep cuts were borne of rage. Baldwin wondered what she'd done to piss him off.

He made a mental note to check the sexual activity—seduction had been the previous MO, that might be different here, too.

Her legs were demurely crossed at the knee, a gold chain nestled incongruously around the fragile bones of her right ankle. It struck Baldwin that it looked more like a shackle than purposeful decoration.

Another, smaller zone had been created a few yards from Marni's body. A pale hand, palm up in supplication, was nestled in the long grass. They were getting more adept at finding the hand of the last victim, at least. The local cops knew what to look for; they found it rather quickly. Why had the killer started leaving the hands away from the body? Just another item to add to his ever-growing list of quirks, the elements that made up the psyche of a murderer.

A breeze kicked up, and Baldwin was surprised to see a bank of black clouds approaching from the west, crawling furiously over the mountains. He wondered how long he'd been standing, staring. Better get a move on before it started to rain. The beauty of a southeastern summer afternoon, a thunderstorm was bound to crop up.

He turned and looked back at Grimes. The man wasn't going to make it. He'd been going downhill steadily since they'd gotten the call that Marni had been found. Right now he was trying to avoid the klieg light of a news truck instead of accompanying Baldwin to peruse the corpse. He was going to have to find a way for Grimes to get some rest, but while this killer was on the loose, that wasn't likely to happen any time soon.

Giving Marni Fischer one last lingering look, he started to walk to Grimes, but a voice rang out behind him.

"Can we move her now, Agent?" The voice was tinged with sarcasm. Baldwin looked toward the source, a beefy young sergeant with red hair, freckles and large hands that were balled into fists. Locals upset that their turf was being trampled on by the FBI. He could understand their frustration. FBI swoops in, literally, to steal their case right from under them. Just like he'd done to Taylor. He turned and signaled to Grimes, an implied question in the wave, and Grimes shook his head. Baldwin felt a tap on his shoulder. It was actually more of a punch, and he turned to see the redheaded sergeant standing belligerently next to him, his hands now restored to their proper place, holding the man's hips to his legs.

He moved a few feet away and rubbed his hand vigorously through his thick hair, making it stick out in all directions. He felt the frustration rise in him. A local sergeant copping attitude was going to give him a headache. He could hear the whapping drone of news helicopters above, looking for purchase with their long-lens cameras, bleating moment-to-moment information back to their anchors.

"I asked you if we could move her." It wasn't a statement but a challenge.

"Tell me something, Sergeant," Baldwin said quietly. The man glared at him as if Baldwin had murdered the girl at their feet.

"Was she posed, or was she dropped here?"

The man scratched his head. "Weel, it's pretty obvious that she was posed. Don't they teach you that kind of stuff where you come from, Mr. F BEE EYE agent?"

Baldwin gave the man a rueful smile. "Have you ever seen a body tossed out of a car, Sergeant?"

"Of course I have. Seen plenty. They tumble out and land on their backs, arms out in a crosslike position, and their legs... Oh."

"'Oh' is right. Take another look."

The sergeant took his time, walking widdershins around the body, sucking industriously on a toothpick that had magically appeared in the corner of his mouth. He made another pass, then spat, careful to turn away from the girl.

"Weel, I'd say there was a pretty good chance that she may have been tossed out of a car."

"And have you found any tire tracks to support that theory?" Baldwin gazed at the young man expectantly.

"There weren't any that we could see when we pulled up, no, sir."

Baldwin noted the "sir" and decided to stop hassling the kid. "So there's a good chance that the killer parked on the road, then carried her out here and posed her, rather than dumping her out of the car right at this spot and speeding away?"

The sergeant looked up at him with squinted eyes. "You were just playing with me, weren't you?"

"No, son, I never play when death is involved. I just wanted you to stop and think about another option. There is never anything obvious at a murder scene." He saw Grimes wave. It was time to get her to the morgue.

"Call in your folks. You can move her now. Besides, it's going to rain."

He turned his back and walked away from the dead girl. Maybe he'd taught the young sergeant a lesson. Especially in a situation as dicey as this one was shaping up to be, never make assumptions. He pulled his cell phone out of its waist clip and punched a number on speed dial. A voice on the other end barked "What?" in a semblance of a greeting.

"Garrett, it's Baldwin. I'm out here in Roanoke."

"Same guy?"

"Looks that way."

Baldwin felt rather than heard the great sigh that whistled through the phone. He empathized; when he'd first gazed upon the dead girl, he felt like all the wind had been knocked out of him.

"Do you have anything from the geographic profile yet?"

"No, it hasn't finished running. I was looking at the map myself, I think you're onto something. Problem with this software is it takes at least eight points to be accurate. So whatever it coughs out is going to be incomplete at best. I'd plan on working without it."

"Right. Well, if it spits anything out, let me know. It's better than nothing, which is what we have right now. He's definitely escalating, Garrett. Took her hands like the others, but cut her face up pretty good. If this was a generic killer, I'd say he was buying himself some time so we don't get an ID so quickly, but thanks to the media everyone in the country knows Marni Fischer is missing. He's not trying to mislead us, not taking their hands so we can't ID the bodies. He's collecting them.

I don't know, Garrett, something feels all wrong about this. It's definitely contrived, he's posed her like the others, but I'm not getting a handle on the why of this case. Moving too fast, traveling through this many states, I don't know if we're going to catch him in the act. He's building up to something, and he'll let us know what that is when he's damn good and ready. How many more will he take before he gets to that point?"

He sighed and ran his hands through his hair again. He'd have a Mohawk going by the end of the afternoon.

"Then Baldwin, I suggest you get five steps ahead of where we are now."

"I'm doing the best I can. I'm going to go in with her, be there while they do the autopsy. I need to see—"

Garrett cut him off. "I know. Go on."

Baldwin put the phone in his pocket and leaned against a sheriff's cruiser. He steepled his fingers in front of his mouth and blew out a sigh. In the midst of all this, he missed Taylor. She had saved him from himself, from the world of death and dying. She'd saved his soul, which was more important to his continued living than a heartbeat would ever be. Just the thought of her made him smile. A moment alone with her would make everything better. It always did. He imagined her puttering around the kitchen in Nashville, tossing out comments over her shoulder while she put together dinner. He saw her smile, her teasing gray eyes, one slightly darker than the other, those full lips, the honey-blond hair cascading down her back. He thought of the night he'd made love to her for the first time, and was embarrassed to feel himself harden. He shifted around so he was facing the cruiser and put his head in his hands. God, just the idea of her excited him, filled him with a longing that was almost painful. It was the inconsequential things that got to him. Her throaty laugh, that husky voice. The body that wouldn't quit. The silky skin on the back of her neck, leading into the scar that nearly took her life slashing across her throat. He ached for her, for her touch, a kiss, her voice, anything that would draw him away from this desolate field and into her warm embrace. It never ceased to amaze him how closely linked sex and death were. He supposed that was why men killed for love.

He looked around, taking in the leaves turning up in anticipation of the rain, the pollen that attached itself to every inanimate object in sight. The sun was getting dusky, the storm was moving in, clouds darkening the sky, and he was surrounded by flashing lights and the smell of death. Voices shouted around him, impatient, testy. Yet crickets chirped, unfazed by the threat of rain, making the scene feel like a big camping trip. He asked himself for the hundredth time what he was doing. Out chasing another killer when he could be home, warm in Taylor's embrace, protected from the reality of his life. He should quit for good, he knew it. Taylor had healed his heart, but killers still roamed his mind. He just wanted to go home, but he hauled himself off the cruiser. He needed to get to the morgue and witness the autopsy. No more time for love in his heart. He hardened it, turned off his inner psyche and approached Grimes.

"Hey, you ready to go to the M.E.'s office? They said they'd do the autopsy pronto for us."

"Baldwin, you go on ahead. I'm going to stay out here with the crime scene people, see if we can find anything, something useful before the rain washes away any evidence."

Baldwin nodded and looked for the red-haired sergeant. Within an hour, he found himself gloved and smocked.

He opened his mouth to speak but was cut off by the medical examiner, a kind young doctor named Rusty Sampson.

"Aha."

"Aha what, Doc?"

"She fought him, hard. See the bruises on her forearms? Defensive wounds, no doubt. She's got a knot on her head, too—may find a subdural hematoma when we get to the brain. She got knocked pretty good, that might have put her out. And there's a hyoid fracture. Could see the bruising around her neck pretty well out in that field, but here it is."

"He strangle her before or after he cut her up?"

"There was some clotting in the knife slashes on her face, so I'd have to say it was perimortem. But her hands were definitely cut off after she was dead. Not that that helps, he really tore the poor thing up."

"Was she raped?"

"I don't know if I can say 'rape' definitively, but look what I found in her." He held up a petrie dish with a small clear fragment of what looked like translucent skin in the center.

"Part of a rubber. It's torn off the rolled edge. Got lost inside her. Doesn't look to have semen on it, though of course we'll get it sent for testing. She had some lateral bruising, too. I'm not much for speculation, but it could be he lost it and had to go searching, you know? They aren't as strong as they look, a fingernail could rip it easily."

"I wonder…" Baldwin stepped away, his eyes unfocusing. Could the killer have realized the condom had slipped off, and that's why he punished Marni's body so severely? It was a possibility. He could have been desperate to retrieve the condom quickly and unable to find it. A simple issue for a normal couple. For a killer trying to hide his identity, a whole different matter. A failure of any kind would be enough to set him off. Another rung up the escalation ladder.

"Care to give me an estimate on time of death?"

"Well, the buffet line had been open for a day at least."

Baldwin shook his head. "Haven't heard that one before. Buffet line? Where do you guys come up with this stuff?"

"Think I heard that one on *Law and Order.* But in all seriousness, she'd been dead at least eighteen to twenty-four hours when you found her. Maggots in the wrist area, plenty in her other orifices, some hatchlings from the blowflies. It was hot out there and they got moving quickly. Add the sun and you've got yourself a virtual party."

"She'd only been missing for two days." Baldwin didn't add the rest of his thought. He hadn't wasted a lot of time before he killed her. This one he'd grabbed, killed, taken for a drive and dumped. He's got another jump on us. "Anything else?"

"Naw. I'll get more after tox comes back."

"Okay. Thanks, Doc. Let me know if there's anything else good."

Another one down, he thought as he left. Better go find Grimes, get him filled in.

Twenty-Four

Metro had drawn ranks around Betsy Garrison. The buzz was nearing epic proportions. Many officers still didn't know the identity of the latest Rainman victim, but almost all of them knew it had been someone on the force, and Betsy's name had come up more than once. After repeated threats, the media had agreed not to release Betsy's identity to the public, but they were having a grand time with their reports. The national cable outlets had gotten on board, as well; all the majors were carrying the story. Speculation was rampant, true-crime aficionados were calling for interviews and the entire department was bogged down. The Rainman was getting as much attention as he could ever possibly want, and Metro was paying the price.

With implicit instructions to step up the pace of the investigation, Lincoln Ross and Marcus Wade were chasing down leads and rumors as fast as they came. The most important was interviewing the previous

Rainman victim, the one who had intimated to Betsy that she knew who her attacker was.

Lincoln pulled the unmarked up in front of a small, 1940s bungalow. The paint was peeling, the window screens were torn, the yard dusty and grassless.

In this neighborhood, where the houses started selling in the high 800s, this home was one of the few bungalows left. The trend in Nashville real estate was to buy up the smaller homes on the pricey land, then raze the house and build a monstrosity. Value-added real estate, and it was an overwhelmingly popular choice.

Marcus looked around and voiced Lincoln's thought. "She doesn't really fit the profile of the others, does she?"

Lincoln shook his head silently, still staring at the house. Six of the victims lived in beautiful, well-maintained homes in gated communities. Even Betsy Garrison's house was in a trendy, up and coming neighborhood. It was part of the fear-mongering done by the Rainman—if he could slip in past the guards and wrought iron, he could get anywhere. He seemed to prefer his victims to be a little upscale. This woman, judging solely on the appearance of her squalid home, was not his typical catch.

They got out of the car just as an overweight beagle came tearing around from the back of the house. Sounding more vicious than he possibly was, he barreled up to Lincoln, baying like a full-grown blood-hound. His wagging tail betrayed his fierceness, and when Lincoln reached a hand down, the dog became all puppy. He quit barking and started whimpering in pleasure, thrilled to be getting some attention.

A voice screeched out the front screen door. "Wally. Waallleeee! Stop that racket now."

Lincoln and Marcus looked at each other. Lincoln shrugged, gave the dog one last pat and walked to the sagging gray porch. The steps squeaked in protest as he walked up them. The slight scent of marijuana wafted to his nose. He rapped hard on the screen door.

"Metro police," he announced with authority. He heard Marcus guffaw in the background, ignored him and knocked again. There was rattling from inside the house, then a tired-looking woman with stringy brown hair appeared at the door. Her eyes were bloodshot, but she didn't show any other obvious signs of intoxication.

"Yeah? Whaddaya want?"

Lincoln put on his polite face. "Lucy Johnson?"

"I didn't do anything wrong."

"We're here to talk to you about the incident you reported. The, uh, rape." Lincoln looked to Marcus for support, but Marcus was very busy scratching Wally's belly. Lincoln pursed his lips and turned back. There was a reason he was in homicide, a reason why he loved computers. He dealt with the dead, the inanimate, better than the living.

Lucy Johnson screwed up her face as if she was about to burst into tears. Lincoln looked at Marcus, beseeching him to come rescue him. Marcus left the dog and came to the door.

"Ms. Johnson, we just need—"

"Miss."

"Excuse me?"

"It's Miss Johnson." The threat of tears past, she smiled winningly at Marcus. He glanced at Lincoln out of the corner of his eye. Maybe she just didn't like big black men in designer suits. He stepped around Lincoln and motioned at the door.

"Can we come in, Miss Johnson?"

She threw a quick, desperate look over her shoulder. "Naw, let's do it outside. This place is a mess." She banged open the screen door, and Lincoln jumped out of the way before it came into contact with his suit. Marcus covered a laugh by clearing his throat.

In the daylight, Lucy Johnson didn't look quite as rough as she had in the shadows. Her hair was a day past fresh, but she had short shorts and long legs, attributes she wasn't past using to get on the good side of the detectives. She slipped her feet into a pair of ratty plastic flip-flops and walked out into the yard, swishing her hips for maximum effect. The beagle cowered for a moment, then went to his mistress, tongue lolling out the side of his mouth.

Marcus raised an eyebrow at Lincoln, who shook his head slightly. She'd responded better to Marcus, let him take the interview. Lincoln folded his arms across his chest and braced his legs so he wouldn't have to lean on the weathered porch column for support. Marcus followed the woman into the scraggly yard.

"I done told that Sex Crimes girl everything that happened. Didn't think she believed me," she said.

"Why's that?"

"She just had that look about her, you know? Like she was better than everybody else. Where's she, anyway?"

"Detective Garrison was in a car accident, ma'am. We're picking up the slack while she recovers."

Lucy shielded her eyes from the sun and looked away quickly. "She hurt bad?"

"She'll be fine, ma'am. I'll tell her you asked after her. Now, we were hoping to get a little more information from you about your case. Detective Garrison mentioned you may be able to identify your attacker."

Lucy toed a clump of dead grass. "Well, yeah, I might've told her that."

"Does that mean you can identify him, or you can't?" Marcus felt rather than saw Lincoln shift on the porch. This was going to be a waste of time.

Lucy paused for a moment, as if deciding whether to tell the truth or not. Marcus was reminded of a kid caught in the candy store, debating whether to admit she had the candy in her pocket or deny its existence till her dying breath. Conscience apparently won.

"It's not that I can identify him, exactly. It's just that something about him seemed really…familiar." She drew the word out slowly, like it had never been tried before, like she wasn't quite sure of its pronunciation.

Marcus rubbed his chin, trying to look thoughtful. "Okay, I can understand that. You don't want to finger the wrong man. Perfectly acceptable. How about this. Tell me where he seems familiar from."

"Well…everywhere. It's like he's always around, ya know? All the places I go to. The gas station for coffee, the gym, the grocery."

"Do you think he's stalking you?"

"Naw. He doesn't realize I recognize him. It's just that I seem to run into him everywhere I go. It's the arms. It was the only thing I could see, you know. His face was covered, his hair was covered, but he had these arms, and they were all strong and ropy and he held me down so hard. It's the arms that I keep seeing." There was a catch in her throat, but her eyes were dry.

"Ma'am, do you know his name?"

She shook her head, miserable, trying not to cry. "No."

"Anything about him? The way he smelled? A certain phrase he may have used?"

Lucy shook her head. "No, no, nothing like that."

"But you still think you know who it is."

"No, I didn't say that. I don't *know* who he is. But I recognize the car he's in," she added, a sly grin on her face.

Marcus gave a hopeful glance to Lincoln, who had also gone on alert. This could be a huge break. Imagine, they could solve the Rainman case in one day while the Sex Crimes Unit had been trying for years.

Marcus stepped a bit closer, put a hand on her arm. She didn't jerk away, just stared at his hand like she'd never been touched before. Marcus had an inkling that she had, just not in such a gentle way. She looked up at him, looked him straight in the eye.

"It's an unmarked car. The man who raped me is a cop."

Twenty-Five

Christina Dale woke leisurely, cloudy and warm. She clung to the last vestiges of the dream, images from her childhood, a park, or no, was it her backyard? It was green and warm, and she could smell a hint of onion in the freshly mown grass. The sky was as blue as a robin's egg, clear and heavy, with puffy white clouds floating by. She felt content, it was the best kind of dream, the one where you wake up and just know it's going to be a wonderful day. A languid smile moved across her face, and as she began to swim into focus, the images drifted, blown away on the winds of her mind.

She started to roll over and realized her body wasn't following her brain's command. That was weird. She must still be drunk from last night. That happened sometimes, she was still drunk when she woke up. Especially when they did those dumb drugs the college kids liked so much. The roofies always made her boneless the next day.

She tried to reach down and massage some feeling

back into her legs. Her eyes flew open and she knew something was dreadfully wrong. There was rope tied around her arms and legs. She came fully awake, panicking, adrenaline rushing through her body and bringing everything into focus. The rope cut bitterly across her ribs, her arms were stretched above her head, painfully pulling her shoulders from their sockets. She tried to wriggle but only succeeded in drawing the ropes tighter, nearly cutting off her breath.

"Oh my God," she moaned. It all came back to her. The lazy grin, the shock of black hair that fell across his forehead, those intense cobalt cat eyes. Her mother warned her time and time again that she was too open, too trusting, that if she kept on sleeping with every Tom, Dick and Harry she met around that she could end up hurt or dead. But who wouldn't respond to the gorgeous creature of a man that she had stumbled out of the bar with?

She stared around the room, trying to piece together how she'd ended up in what was obviously a mess. Had things gone too far last night? Had she asked to be tied up? She'd done it before, a small-town girl trying out new things without any repercussion. Maybe the man—Lord, what was his name—had simply passed out after they'd fooled around. She looked to either side and only saw the empty loneliness of a motel room, stark white walls, a cheesy landscape in oranges and yellows hanging above a cut-rate TV. She was alone.

Suddenly she heard the toilet flush and relaxed. A shadow moved along the wall and he popped into view. It was him all right, tousled and naked, looking even sexier than she had remembered.

"Mornin', darlin'. You wanna get me out of this and we can pick up where we left off?"

He smiled and moved no closer, just stood watching her like a feral cat in heat.

"Seriously, get me untied. This is starting to hurt." She realized even before she saw the knife that he had no intention of letting her go. Ever. She opened her mouth to scream but he was on her, slapping a piece of duct tape over her mouth so all she could hear was her own hysterical cries, muffled and caught in her throat.

As her mystery man dragged the tip of the knife slowly across her face, his cheerful grin disappeared, and he spoke only one word, the last Christina would ever hear.

"Bye."

Twenty-Six

Taylor was back in her office, waiting for Lincoln and Marcus to return from interviewing the previous alleged victim of the Rainman. She had missed a call from Baldwin, which left her moody. She wanted to talk with him, but he was up to his ears in dead girls.

As she fiddled with a few reports that needed to be completed, Fitz rolled in, with Marcus and Lincoln on his heels. He got to the office door first.

"Everything okay?" he asked gruffly.

Taylor gave him a startled look. "Everything's fine. Why?"

"You're just looking a little ill, that's all. You're not catching something, are you?"

Taylor waved his concern away. "Had a long night. I'm fine, really."

"Ready to go over what the kids got on the Rainman?"

She nodded. "Yeah, let's do it. But let's go into the conference room, I don't feel like crowding in here." She led them to the room down the hall, then locked the door behind herself so they wouldn't be interrupted at an inopportune moment.

"Okay, give it to me. Marcus and Lincoln, you first."

Lincoln leaned back in his chair and flipped a file open in his lap. "We talked with the last victim of the Rainman, Lucy Johnson. She was victim number seven, and had told Betsy she thought she recognized the guy, right? Well, after thinking on it for a few days, she wasn't totally sure she even wanted to point a finger. Marcus charmed her right out of her panties, so to speak, convinced her that it would be the right thing to do. Here's where the problem is. She thinks it's a guy that works out at her gym. She also sees him around town a lot, the Mapco when she goes for gas, Publix when she's shopping. So he's local to the area. Too local."

Taylor nodded. "Think she's legit?"

Lincoln shook his head. "We know he's been working a specific geographical area. He went pretty far out of it to get to Betsy in East Nashville. All the other rapes occurred out in the west and south parts of town, Bellevue, Forest Hills, Franklin and Brentwood."

"Where does Lucy Johnson live?" Taylor interrupted.

"That south part of Davidson County off Highway 100 that straddles Williamson County."

"And what gym does she use?"

"She goes to the YMCA at Maryland Farms." Lincoln was pulling more notes from his file. "At least three of the other victims work out at that gym. So that's a connection between them. I guess I can understand why Betsy got excited when Ms. Johnson told her that she thought it was a guy from her gym."

"Well, that's great, but did she identify him?"

Marcus gave a half smile. "Well, that's the problem. She's a treadmill and bike, he's apparently into the free weights. She didn't see his face anyway, so there's no ID to go on. She recognizes his arms."

Taylor looked at the file, flipping back through the witness statements. "Free weights? I thought he was supposed to have a slight build?" she asked.

"Slight, not tall, but muscular and strong. That's what Lucy Johnson said."

Fitz had been quiet throughout the exchange. "Can she pick him out of a lineup?" That was Fitz, taking it down to brass tacks.

"It's not a face that she remembers. It's the arms, the body, the way he walks. She also said she hasn't seen him at the gym in a while. So unless we pull their records and go through all of the ID cards, then get all of their arms in a lineup, there's no way to go this route."

Taylor chewed her lip. "I thought you said she recognized him from around town, running errands and the like."

Marcus glanced at Lincoln and they shared a silent look.

"C'mon, guys, spit it out. There's something more to her statement. What is it?"

Lincoln gave Marcus the barest of nods. "When she sees him around town it's not in gym clothes. She thinks he's driving an undercover. She thinks he's one of ours."

Taylor set the file on the desk and raised an eyebrow. "Undercover, like one of our detectives undercover? Or just plainclothes?"

"She doesn't know. She doesn't seem to know a lot

of things, but she's certain she saw him get into one of the white Caprices. She recognized the way a cop in Mapco walked, thinks he works out at her gym and that he showed up at her door and raped her. It's a little thin."

"Does she know the cop's name?"

"No, but she gave a really blasé description of him. Jarhead it sounds like. I don't know, Taylor, I can't imagine we could make an arrest based on how someone walked. And this Lucy Johnson didn't seem screwed in too tight, if you know what I mean. It could be that she's just seeing phantoms. Rape can be very traumatic."

"Thank you for the lesson, Marcus." Taylor gave him a smile. "But I'm not willing to overlook anything right now. Let's talk to Betsy and find out what she thinks. Could you handle that? I think she's being released today, you could run over to her house. And boys, I'm sure I don't need to remind you to look over your shoulders. We don't want the press camped on her doorstep, you know?"

"Sure, LT, no problem." Marcus sat back in his chair. "Wonder why he only hits when it rains?"

Taylor waited to see if anyone would answer, then chimed in. "Because the rain washes away his sins. Not to mention the evidence."

All three men looked at her, nodding slowly. Well, that made sense.

As Marcus and Lincoln left to go speak with Betsy Garrison, Taylor signaled for Fitz to stay behind.

"What's up?" he asked, twiddling a pencil between his meaty fingers.

"Julia Page came to see me. Seems she's a little

worried about our friend Terrence Norton's ability to beat each and every rap he's fallen for."

"Yeah, I heard about the reluctant witness getting shot by some runner out of Atlanta. Guy had an outstanding warrant, too—he's cooling his heels here while Atlanta scrambles to get him back. They want him bad, think he's a bagman for one of their biggest dealers. They want to play let's make a deal with him, and soon. You know how these guys seem to disappear into the earth as soon as their bosses get threatened."

"Yeah. Page seems to think it all goes deeper than that. She thinks he was brought in to silence the witness just in case he changed his mind about testifying. Thinks Terrence set it up."

"Anything's possible. Little shit like Terrence, he could have it in him. I didn't think he'd gotten quite to that level, but…"

"Would you be willing to look into it for me? See just how strong Terrence has gotten? Page would love to get him for tampering, intimidation, anything that could take him down."

Fitz stood and stretched, his ample belly reaching for the sky. "Sure, I'll get with her, talk to a couple of confidential informants. See what the word on the street is. I gotta tell you, he's starting to insulate himself pretty well. May be a bigger mess than we expect."

"Uninsulate him for me. The drug and gang scene is strong enough here, we don't need another player in the mix. Deal with Vice, whoever you need to talk to. But keep it quiet." She chewed on her pencil for a moment. "Page thinks the seeds of corruption may go even deeper. All the way to the bench."

Fitz guffawed. "I wouldn't worry my pretty head about that. Terrence doesn't have that much pull. Besides, Hamilton was ticked as hell at Page because the jury acquitted Terrence this time. I heard he was really hot for her ass, and not in a good way."

"Yeah, that's what I figured. Just pursue the witness/jury angle with Page, see if you can turn anything up. Keep your ear to the ground, work a couple of sources, see what shakes loose."

"You got it, sugar. Rather be dealing with a criminal I can understand anyway. Drug dealers, pimps, the regular Nashville nasties. I hate this serial killer shit."

Taylor was gathering up her things, trying to tidy up, when her phone rang.

"Lieutenant Jackson."

"Taylor, it's Mitchell. I need you to do me a favor."

"Since you're my boss, anything you ask me to do is actually considered a direct order."

Her smart-ass remarks usually made him laugh, and this was no exception. "While I appreciate that you're my subordinate, I have a feeling you're running the whole show regardless. I understand you were at the accident scene this morning where Whitney Connolly lost her life?"

"I was. Sam and I were having coffee around the corner, so I tagged along. Why, is something wrong?"

"No, nothing's wrong exactly. But I need you to head over to Quinn Buckley's home. She's Whitney Connolly's sister."

"I know who she is, boss. I went to school with them

for a couple of years. They transferred in after their 'incident.' Besides, I don't think there's a person in Nashville who doesn't know who Quinn and Whitney are."

"Yeah, well, it's been a long time, and those girls went through a terrible ordeal. And now Whitney's been killed, and it's been a big shock from what I hear. Not just a sister, but an identical twin. Apparently Quinn Buckley is taking the news very hard, which is to be expected. I've heard twins have some bizarre connection to each other that normal siblings don't have. Anyway, I'm getting off track. She told the officers that went to inform her of the accident that Whitney had been trying to reach her. 'Frantically' was the word she used. I thought you could head over there and see what 'frantic' means in Belle Meade."

"I'm happy to. I haven't been slumming in a while now. What's the status of their case, anyway? Did the guy ever get paroled?"

"Nope. He's still in and will be for quite a while. So I don't think this has anything to do with their past, just their present. But if you would go over and find out for me, I'd appreciate it."

"Will do."

"Where are you with the rapes?"

"Lincoln and Marcus interviewed the victim who thought she knew him. She's wobbly, I'm not sure if she's going to be the best source of information. But the boys told me something interesting. She's saying it was a cop."

There was silence from the other side of the receiver. "Do you think that's the case? Could that be where the leak came from? If it's one of our own, he could have leaked it himself."

"That's damn fine speculating, Cap, but I think it's

a little too soon to make those kinds of assumptions. I'm still convinced the leak came from outside this building. Lincoln and Marcus are chasing it down, I just sent them to talk to Betsy. We'll figure it out, I promise."

They hung up and Taylor finished gathering her things. She went out the back door, pausing at the top of the stairs where cigarette butts stuck like porcupine quills from an orange bucket of sand. She took a deep breath and kept walking, but stopped twenty paces away and dug in her pocket for her Camel Lights. Flicking a cheap, store-bought lighter, she took a drag. She rationalized for the millionth time. As soon as this case is over, I'll quit for good.

She went to the car, rolled the window down and put the stick in gear. Blowing smoke out the window, she took off down to Broadway, then turned right and headed toward West End.

She hadn't thought about the Connolly case in a long time. It had happened when she was only thirteen, and at the time, her parents had sheltered her a bit from it, not wanting to scare her. But she'd worked the rumor mill like every other kid in town, and while they may have had the story straight, no one knew all the details.

The Connolly girls disappeared one afternoon on their way home from school. They were attending Harpeth Hall, the exclusive all girls' prep school in Belle Meade. The school was close to their home, and they usually walked or rode their bikes back and forth to school in their little uniforms. So safe was the neighborhood, no one gave it a second thought. Their parents finally called the police that evening when the twins didn't come home. In the age before Amber Alerts and twenty-four-hour-a-day news coverage, the news hadn't gotten too far. Taylor never really remembered seeing it on television or in the paper, just hearing about it from friends. The girls disappeared, but were found a few days later. They'd escaped from their kidnapper, a strange man named Nathan Chase. According to the official accounts, they were just fine when they got home. The rumor mill, on the other hand, was moving in high gear.

The appearance of the Connolly sisters at Father Ryan, Taylor and Sam's high-school alma mater, had caused only a minor stir; the genteel students and their well-mannered parents had seen to it that the girls were welcomed with open arms and never bothered by the stories from their past. At least that was the surface impression. In reality, the whispers and stares were done discreetly, the stories told quietly behind closed Junior League doors, the privileged teens murmuring during cheerleader practice and football games. The walls of Belle Meade Country Club oozed the story, wiping themselves quickly if any member of the Connolly family appeared.

But the Connolly girls were readily accepted, invited to all the right parties, dating the best and brightest boys, making excellent marks and never failing to fit in. Or so it appeared. Their scandal, instead of hurting them, made them.

The summer skies were darkening with a typical afternoon storm. Taylor opened the sunroof, catching a breath of cool air that preceded the storm. Crossing Interstate 40, traffic was slow and aimless. Passing through the quiet streets of West End, she finally came to the intersection of Harding Road and White Bridge Road. The Starbucks date she'd shared with Sam seemed like days ago, not just this morning. She'd managed to put aside all the emotions from her two-day roller-coaster ride during the afternoon, but seeing the Starbucks brought the news, or non-news, back in a flash. Talk about dodging a bullet.

She supposed she'd have to tell Baldwin about the false alarm, share the near miss with him in as light-hearted a manner as she could. God knows she didn't want anything to screw with their relationship. Things were good. She was content. She loved him, he loved her. End of story. She didn't want the same things many women craved. A great man, a wonderful bedmate, relative companionship. That was enough for her. Certainly, her plan didn't have room for two point five kids and a dog. She'd never been married, hadn't ever come close. Before Baldwin, she'd always taken her physical pleasure where she could, avoiding all emotional entanglements. Discreet, short-lived affairs on her terms. Sex, not love. Funny, she'd never realized how lonely she had been.

She slowed as she came up on the entrance to Belle Meade. The accident had been cleaned up and the road was back open, but there was still glass scattered carelessly in the roadway and the grass of the median. Cars whizzed through the intersection without a care in the world, their drivers oblivious to the four lives that were lost in this very spot. A shiver of apprehension rippled through her, and she put the window up, blaming the feeling on the breeze billowing forth from the gray skies. She turned left and began making her way along the sedate and gracious boulevard.

She ignored the side street that led to the home she grew up in.

The drive for Quinn Buckley's mansion appeared. She turned into the entranceway and came to a black wrought-iron gate with a small box standing at window level to her left. She opened the window and stuck her head out.

"Taylor Jackson to see Mrs. Buckley, please."

There was no verbal acknowledgment, but after a few moments the massive gate creaked open. As Taylor maneuvered her car through the gates onto a narrow path, a deciduous forest swallowed her, beckoning and forbidding. The drive meandered through the woods for a few hundred feet. As she rounded a curve, the estate sprang into view. Even by Belle Meade standards, the property was massive. The plantation-style house was a white two-story washed-brick colonial with substantial columns forming a protected area that had been made into an elegant front porch. Four stone chimneys danced toward the sky. East and west wings abutted the main residence, and Taylor could see a separate five-car garage with a transom covered in ivy that led into the east wing. The west meandered into the woods, the architect finding natural beauty within his design. Black shutters blinked mournfully and the air seemed heavier as Taylor drove closer, as if the house itself was grieving.

She parked in front of a fountain reminiscent of the Italian Renaissance, taking in the care and nurturing that had gone into the landscaping around the front of the house. The place reeked of money. Taylor rang the bell and waited. Walked up and down the steps. Just as she started to get impatient, the ornate double doors to the main house swung open and Quinn Buckley appeared.

Taylor hadn't seen Quinn in a very long time. If she had spent any time paying attention to the upscale magazines of Nashville, she would have recognized Quinn Buckley for herself in an instant. But all she could see was Quinn's sister's face. Whitney Connolly floated at Taylor and she had to shake her head slightly to realize that it wasn't her. As she climbed the stairs to the front door and Quinn came into clear focus, she could see some of the minute differences between the two women. Quinn wasn't as curvy as Whitney, her mouth, though generous, wasn't as full and pouty. Taylor caught herself wondering just how much plastic surgery Whitney Connolly had undergone over the years.

Quinn Buckley had the look of her sister, that was for sure. But where Whitney Connolly had come across the television screen as well put together, Quinn Buckley oozed class and money. In her low-slung jeans and cowboy boots, Taylor felt slightly frumpy, an L.L. Bean figure next to a Lladró figurine. Noting Quinn's perfectly highlighted coif, she instinctively reached to smooth her own ponytailed blond hair, then caught herself, straightened to her full five foot eleven and strode purposefully the rest of the way up the stairs to the door.

Quinn extended a small, well-manicured hand to Taylor as she reached the top of the steps. "Lieutenant Jackson?"

Even her voice was different from Whitney's. It was softer, slightly higher pitched and definitely had more of a southern flavor to it. How two women could be so much alike and yet so different was amazing.

Taylor took Quinn's hand and nodded. "I am. How have you been, Mrs. Buckley? I don't think we've seen each other in several years. I'm so sorry we have to meet again under these circumstances. I was a fan of your sister."

Quinn's face closed for an instant, then she smiled graciously. "Of course. Please, won't you come in?" She turned and led the way into an oversize foyer with dual staircases creeping up either wall. Taylor felt a quick pang. Her parents' home had been set up just the same, and she remembered sliding down the curved balustrades. Quinn caught her staring and gave her a questioning look.

"Reminds me of…well, never mind." Taylor had gotten that look before, and it caused a moment of heat to flare up in her chest. Like she'd never been inside a fancy home. Please. She almost burst out laughing at the slightly imperious look Quinn was giving her. Among her former peers and their parents, Taylor always got the same reaction. Her parents had money, and yet she'd chosen police work instead of the privileged life that Quinn Buckley had obviously built for herself. Some of them just couldn't understand that money didn't mean anything to her.

"Yes, I see. Would you mind following me? I thought we could talk in the study." Quinn turned to her left and entered a huge, beautifully appointed room. The rich scent of leather tickled Taylor's nose, and she caught the fleeting tang of lemon oil. As she got farther in the room, she nearly gasped aloud. A study, my foot. This was one of the most beautiful libraries she had ever seen. Wall-to-wall bookshelves, warm furniture, oh, she could get lost in here for years. It didn't have the coldness and sterility Taylor had sensed from the rest of the first floor. This was a comfort room, a getaway room. Someplace to literally let down your hair and get cozy. She looked at Quinn and noted her lips twitching in amusement.

"I assume you're a reader?" Quinn walked over to one of the walnut shelves and plucked a book at random. "I am, too. Whitney was once, but she stopped enjoying it when she was in her teens. Me, I can't think of a better way to spend an afternoon than curled up in a chair losing myself in a good book."

"I'm the same way, but I don't have such a wonderful place to do it. This room is amazing."

Quinn gave her the first genuine smile Taylor had seen. "It's mine. I encourage the rest of the family to allow me my privacy when I'm in here. It's my own little escape from the rest of the world."

She sounded so weary that Taylor felt sorry for her. She'd just lost her sister, and here was Taylor, scoping out the room like a kid in a candy store. She got herself back under rein and turned to Quinn, her features carefully aligned to project the appropriate amount of grief and professional concern. She wondered briefly why Quinn would bring the police into her sanctuary—it seemed out of character. Quinn didn't strike her as the chummy type.

"I truly am sorry about Whitney. My captain told me you mentioned she'd been trying to get a hold of you?"

Quinn sank into a chair, pulling up her feet and curling them under her, like a cat. "Trying is understating it a bit. She must have called twenty, twenty-five times in the past day. My cell phone, my home phone, she left messages at the country club."

Ah, Taylor thought. Belle Meade Country Club. The social denizen's favorite Nashville campground.

"If you don't mind me asking, where were you?"

Quinn gave her an unreadable look, then stood and walked around the room, touching things as if to reassure herself that they were still among her possessions. "I was just…out and about, getting ready for dinner, running errands. Nothing special. I have a great many responsibilities, and I have a tendency to run around quite a bit. Sometimes I forget to charge my cell phone, sometimes I forget to check my answering machine. And Jake was in town, so I certainly wasn't going to answer the phone. My husband is out of town quite a bit and I try to make time for him when he's here. So we had a nice dinner, and went to bed early. This morning I went out for a walk and didn't bring my phone with me. By the time I got back and noticed that all the calls I'd received were from Whitney, it was too late. She'd already been in the accident."

Quinn's voice caught and she turned to the French doors. Taylor gave her a moment to compose herself, then asked a question.

"Mrs. Buckley, were you and your sister close? Did you talk every day, once a week?"

Quinn had recovered her composure. "No, Lieutenant, we weren't terribly close. Strange for identical twins, but we just grew apart as we got older." There was a gleam in her eye, either tears or a memory, and Taylor made a mental note to find out why they'd grown apart. "I'm sorry, Lieutenant, I'm being horribly rude.

Can I get you a drink? Coffee? Tea? I think I'll have a Diet Coke, if that's okay with you."

"Soda would be wonderful, thank you."

Quinn turned to the desk and picked up a small crystal bell. Taylor almost laughed aloud, it just seemed so incredibly pretentious. Quinn rang the bell and a moment later a young woman with flowing black hair and liquid brown eyes came into the room.

"*Sì*, Signora Quinn?"

Quinn gave her a warm smile that belied the master/servant nature of their relationship. "Gabrielle, *possiamo avere due Coca Lights, per favore? Grazie.*"

Gabrielle disappeared and Quinn turned back to Taylor. "She's wonderful. Italian girl, family's from Florence. She wanted to come and work in the States to improve her English and take a few classes, we needed someone to look after the twins and handle a few things around the house. She's acting as their au pair officially. They just love her. They can speak Italian better than I can now. Not that I'm fluent."

This explanation came out fast and furious. Taylor got the feeling that Quinn was hiding something. Interesting.

And twins? Taylor knew Quinn had children, but she hadn't thought to ask how many, boys or girls. Sometimes such pleasantries borne of politeness slipped her by. Quinn gracefully answered the unspoken question.

"The twins, Jillian and Jake Junior, are at school right now. They're nearly four and are so wonderfully bright. I've been blessed."

"School? That young?"

"Well, it's never too early to get them started. They attend a prekindergarten three days a week. Do you have any children, Lieutenant?"

The sudden shift threw Taylor for a loop. How was she supposed to answer that? Let's see, two days ago I was told I was pregnant, yesterday I found out I wasn't. I didn't tell my lover, so I have to have a long conversation with him after he finishes chasing a serial killer through the Southeast. She nearly laughed aloud before recovering and answering as truthfully as she could. "I don't yet, but my best friend is having twins. They just found out. Do you remember Sam Owens? It's Sam Loughley now, she was in my class." Good job, Taylor, she congratulated herself. Deflection is the name of the game.

"I do remember Samantha. She's the medical examiner now. That must be interesting. Well, that's wonderful. Children are such a joy. Jake and I were so thrilled when we found out… Oh, Lieutenant, I shouldn't be taking up your time with this. It won't help get my sister back."

Gabrielle interrupted, bearing their drinks on a silver tray with tall crystal glasses filled with ice. *"Grazie con tanto, Gabrielle. Lascili prego sulla tabella."* The girl set the drinks on a marble-topped table and left the room.

Quinn went to the tray, grabbed the soda can and ignored the glasses. Taylor raised an eyebrow and followed suit. The move seemed a bit informal from a very formal woman. Maybe Quinn Buckley wasn't quite as high-strung as she first appeared.

They went to the chairs in front of the fireplace, a conversation grouping that put them in face-to-face contact. Taylor sat and pulled out her notebook.

"Okay, Mrs. Buckley, can you tell me what Whitney was so upset about?"

"It would be easier to let you hear it for yourself." She reached behind her and hit a button. Taylor realized the answering machine sat on the desk behind them.

Aha. That's why we're meeting in Quinn's sanctuary.

"You said *my* answering machine earlier, Mrs. Buckley. You have more than one?"

"Oh, we've got a voice mail system for the family. This is for my private line." There was no other explanation.

The machine whirred for a moment, then clicked into play mode. A voice filled the room.

"Quinn? Quinn, are you there? Dammit, pick up the phone. I have to talk to you. I'm coming over, this just can't wait. If you get this message, wait for me at the house. And Quinn? For God's sake, be careful."

The voice was filled with hysteria, and Taylor felt a shudder go down her spine.

"Were all the messages like this, Mrs. Buckley?" she asked.

"Yes, for the most part. She never said what was so damn important that she'd wreck her car in her rush to get here. It would have been easier if she'd let me know what the problem was. And what I'm supposed to be careful about. Lord, that woman doesn't usually over-react like this."

She fiddled with the gold braid attached to an upholstered throw pillow.

"I was hoping you could look into things for me, Lieutenant. Perhaps examine some of the stories she was working on, see if something came up in one of them that could affect my family or me in some manner." She cleared her throat. "Perhaps Whitney came across something that may be...embarrassing? Other than that, I just don't know what to tell you."

Taylor was silent for a moment. "Mrs. Buckley..."

"Call me Quinn. We're of an age, after all. Mrs. Buckley always makes me think of Jake's mother."

Taylor nodded. "Quinn, you mentioned your husband travels quite a bit. May I ask what he does?"

"My, you really are out of the loop, aren't you, Lieutenant?"

"Taylor, please. Out of the loop?"

"Well, your father, Win? He's friends with Jake."

Ah, Win Jackson. That was something she didn't feel like dealing with right now. "My father and I aren't close. So tell me, what does Jake do?"

"He's the senior vice president of Health Partners. Your father is on the board of directors for the company."

"Oh," Taylor said in a small voice. Like that was supposed to mean something to her. Quinn must have caught her confused look, because she continued to explain.

"Health Partners is the leading small community–based hospital company in the country. Jake has to travel to all of their sites constantly to make sure everything is going well. They have holdings all over the Southeast and a few in the Northeast as well. They're growing bigger and Jake's job is to make sure they grow in the appropriate places." Quinn sounded bored, like she was reading a description off the back of an annual report. Even her eyes had taken on a bit of a glaze. Taylor surmised that

Quinn wasn't very interested in her husband's job, despite the obvious trappings and advantages the job gave. They certainly weren't lacking for money.

"Okay, that's good. I tell you what. I'm sure you want to go through your sister's things. I'll accompany you over there and have a look around. Does that sound good?"

"That would be fine. When would be convenient for you?"

Taylor noticed that the moment Quinn had started speaking of her husband all the warmth and sparkle had gone out of her voice. And now talking about her sister was bringing it all home.

"Anytime is fine with me. Would you like to go now?"

"I'd prefer tomorrow morning. I have some arrangements to see to, and I haven't been able to reach our younger brother, Reese. He is in Guatemala doing a mission trip with several other doctors from Vanderbilt. He's the youngest resident to ever go on one of their trips. They spend two weeks doing surgeries on cleft palates, joints, all the procedures these poor people have absolutely no access to. Reese will be doing some pre-op and post-op counseling. Anyway, that's neither here nor there. He's not due back for another week. I'll try to get word to him, but he told me before he left that there wasn't a solid line of communication. He'll want to have a hand in everything."

Taylor handed her one of her cards and said, "Anytime tomorrow morning is fine with me. Just give me a call and I'll meet you there."

With that they wrapped things up with a few niceties and Taylor made a hasty retreat. Something was very sad about Quinn Buckley, and it wasn't only that her twin sister had just died.

Back in her car, she decided she might have time to head over to Betsy Garrison's house. She dialed the number, and Brian Post answered.

"Hey, Post, can I come on over? I wanted to check on Betsy, see how she's doing. Maybe talk about the case for a moment."

"You know what, Taylor, it might be best if we gave it a day. She's starting to come off all the drugs and really grasp what happened and she's pretty pissed off. Having the story out on the air isn't helping matters. I don't want her to have to go through it with other people around, you know what I mean?"

"Of course. That's no problem. Have her call me when she's ready to talk. Meantime, do you want to be brought up-to-date?"

"I already spoke with Lincoln and Marcus. They brought me up to speed. I guess we have to start looking at one of our own, huh?"

"Well, there are lots of police uniforms in the mid-state. Maybe it's one of theirs."

"That would be great," he said a bit sarcastically. "Tell you what, I'll give your boys a shout in the morning and we can decide where to go from there."

"Sounds good. Give Betsy my best. Sounds like she's lucky to have you around."

"Will do, Taylor. Thanks."

Twenty-Seven

Baldwin got the call in his stifling hotel room nearly a full minute before the News Alert flashed on the TV screen.

"It's Grimes. We've got another one missing."

"Are you kidding me? It hasn't even been twenty-four hours." Baldwin was wide awake now. "Who is it?"

"Local girl, Christina Dale. Didn't show up for work this morning. This whole town is on alert because we've been here tending to Marni, and when she didn't show up they immediately called it in. And one more thing. We've got a leak."

Baldwin saw a flash out of the corner of his eye. He looked to the TV. Sure enough, the News Alert came up, a picture of a pretty brunette staring out from the screen. "We have a leak" was an understatement, and he told that to Grimes.

"I know, I know. I can't figure out who it is, either. No one that I'm giving information to, that's for sure.

Regardless, we need to get moving on this new victim. How soon can you meet me?"

"Let me grab a shower, say, fifteen minutes in the lobby?"

"Okay, I'll see you." Grimes hung up and Baldwin sat on the edge of the lumpy bed shaking his head. Too fast. Too fast. This guy was on fire, and they weren't any closer to finding out what was happening. They needed to kick it into high gear. He got up and walked to the bathroom, stripping off his boxers as he went. Oh, who was he kidding? They needed a break. They needed a big break.

"We got a break," Grimes whispered to Baldwin as he walked up to him in the lobby. Grimes was looking a bit better today, not rested but there was a glimmer in his eyes. "We got a break," he said again, low, and put his hand on Baldwin's back as if to propel him toward the front door.

Baldwin waited until they were outside and turned to him. "Let me guess. There was a DNA hit on the piece of condom."

Grimes looked vaguely disappointed. "No, there was nothing of use there. They recovered epithelial cells, but they were from a female. It's a wash, unfortunately."

"Damn," Baldwin huffed. "That was our best shot so far."

"You'll change your mind after you hear this. We had an anonymous call that Christina Dale was seen at a motel last night. Cheap-ass place, just a couple of miles up the road. We're gonna go in and check the room, she might still be there. We've got dogs meeting us, too…if she's gone, we might be able to track her scent." They got into the car and Grimes was buckling, shifting and steering at the same time. "Break, man, that's what we needed, a break."

"Yeah, no kidding. This is good, Grimes." Baldwin was skeptical that they'd find the girl in a cheap motel room with all the evidence they needed to catch the killer. But he was willing to try anything once. His thoughts drifted. It seemed a little unlikely that the Strangler had simply decided to grab a motel room for the night to kill his latest victim. Baldwin mentally slapped himself. You don't know she's dead, man. But if she was, and he left something behind for them, well, that would be nice. A motel room would be a blessing and a curse for them. Too many remnants to process, but something might pop out.

Grimes was still muttering under his breath as they pulled into the horseshoe-shaped drive of a budget motel that had seen better days. Paint peeled off the walls, a dirty gray that might have been white fifty years before. The Vacancy sign flashed, and Baldwin wondered if it had ever been turned off. There were cars piling up in the parking lot and Baldwin wanted the first crack at the room.

"Stall them," he said to Grimes as he jumped out of the car. He walked quickly to the office and shut the door behind him. A fan poured warm air through the room, making it sweltering. A man with one tooth sticking out from what seemed like his lower lip stared him down. Baldwin flashed his FBI badge and hoped it would impress. It didn't.

"We got a call that Christina Dale was seen here last night. Can you tell me what room she was in?"

The man stared at him, belligerence creeping up in his eyes, then dampening down like he'd stepped into a cold mental shower.

"Yuaa, she was here. Didn't see with who. Came in all drunk and stupid like she always does. Gave her the key to the room on the end. She didn't bring it back yet this mornin'. What's all this about?"

"Have you been in the room?"

"Ain't but the one key. I tolds ya she didn't bring it back this mornin'. What's all this? Did Christina do somethin' stupid, get herself in trouble with the law?" The leathery bald head and absence of teeth gave the man a shrunken look, as if a headhunter had stolen in during the night and worked his magic on the man's head, shrinking it down to portable size. Baldwin was almost staring but stopped himself.

"And you are…?"

"Call me Ishmael," the man cackled. Baldwin stared at him until he finally stopped laughing and said, "It's Jones."

"Mr. Jones, did you see who she came with? Was it a man?"

"What, you think she's one of those lesbos? 'Course it was a man. Practically a different man every night, seemed to me." He sucked his tooth, the noise making Baldwin's spine crawl.

"Mr. Jones, is there any chance you remember the particular man she was with last night?"

Jones sighed. "Prolly some young, good-lookin' feller. She seemed to like them damn black Irish, brought 'em around more often than not."

"Dark-haired men, you mean?"

"Black as coal. 'Course, I don't see much. I don't go spying on my folks."

"Of course you don't." Lying sack of shit. Baldwin was ready to pull that tooth right out of the man's mouth. "Were they in Christina's car?"

"Nope. Don't say as I know what kind it were, either. Just long and dark, that's all. Mebbe silver. Never was much of a car man. Like me those tits and ass though."

Baldwin watched the fan for a moment, biting his lip. If he were as old and wizened, he'd be bad-tempered, too.

"Anything else you can remember, Mr. Jones? Did you see what time the car left?"

"Can't say that I did. I sleep there in that back room over yonder, expect people to ring the bell if they needs me. I don't recall anyone ringing the bell after Christina came through. What'd she do?"

"I don't know, sir. Thank you for all your help, though. Mind if we break down the door if it's locked?"

"I don't give a rat's patooty what you do, so long as you pay for it. But them doors are kinda flimsy, won't take much to get it open."

"Okay, Mr. Jones. Why don't you stay in here while we go get that door opened." He left before the man had a chance to ask any more questions or get any ideas, and walked quickly back to Grimes. The old man hustled after him, stood in the doorway to the motel office and stared at the commotion.

"Room three. No keys, we'll have to take the door. The guy in there, the manager, didn't seem too concerned, just wanted to know if Christina did something to get herself into trouble. Saw her come in with someone driving a 'long car.' Was he the one that called it in?"

"I don't know who called it in, they just said it was an anonymous caller. I got the call from the sheriff's office, they'd gotten a call from their news station here in town."

Baldwin appraised the man. Sloppy work, Grimes, very sloppy work. He should know every detail of the events that led them to this motel. He was getting wound too tight. "We better be careful in case someone is jerking our chain. Let's just go up and knock first."

They made their way to the door and did just that. There was no answer. Baldwin turned the knob; it was locked from the inside. He signaled to a deputy who held a battering ram. The door wouldn't take much abuse, it looked rickety as hell. The man stepped up, swung once and the door burst open.

Baldwin looked inside and was assaulted with a strong coppery smell. He held up his hand to signal that he didn't want anyone else coming in the room, then flashed his Maglite through the door. The sight was grim.

He could see almost immediately that there was no one in the room. It was a small area, just large enough for a bed and a desk, the latter taken up with a battered old television. A door led off to the right and Baldwin could see the reflection of a toilet and tub in the mirror. He could see blood on the unmade bed, enough blood that his mind told him the story. If this was Christina Dale's last-known resting place, she was most likely no longer with this world.

He looked back out into the parking lot at the expectant faces and shook his head to signal that she wasn't in the room. He signaled to Grimes. "I need gloves and boots, and a crime scene tech to start collecting evidence. Do you have a camera in the car? We need to get some pictures of this." Grimes went to the car and came back with a digital camera.

"You can use this for now. The tech should have his own, but I always carry this in a pinch." He also handed Baldwin gloves and booties to cover his shoes, then put his own on. They were ready to see what had happened in the indifferent little room.

Baldwin took one step inside and felt the energy, a palpable mass that nearly took his breath away. Maybe because this was the first mobile killing site they had found, there was a different power to this crime scene—a deeper sense of evil. He hoped they would be able to learn more about their killer, and his anticipation ran high. Many of the other members of Behavioral Science didn't feel the necessity of physically being at a crime scene. They were meant to draw conclusions about personality types, not process an event off the ground. Baldwin had always felt differently. He found that being at the scene gave him an honest taste of the killer. Being in the same room helped him understand on a far deeper level what actually happened. Seeing the blood firsthand, tasting that coppery tang in the back of his throat, his eyes assailed by red, his olfactory senses working overdrive, gave him an overwhelming ability to know what the killer was thinking at the time he committed his crime.

He shone the flashlight throughout the room, and then focused on the light switch at the door. He didn't want to run the risk of destroying a possible print, so he decided to leave the light off and make do with his Maglite. He swept the beam back to the bed. The sheets were soaked with blood. He flashed the light around the walls—there was blood spray and droplets everywhere. The spray, the copious blood—he'd changed his pattern, without a doubt. Christina had been alive while she was separated from her hands. Intuition told him that she was dead.

The light took in the rest of the room. Something on top of the TV caught Baldwin's eye. Carefully picking his way to the television, he read the note aloud without picking it up.

> *"She half enclosed me with her arms*
> *She pressed me with a weak embrace;*
> *And bending back her head, looked up,*
> *And gazed upon my face.*
> *'Twas partly love, and partly fear,*
> *And partly 'twas a bashful art,*
> *That I might rather feel, than see,*
> *The swelling of her heart."*

"My, he does love the classics," Baldwin remarked, sliding the note into a plastic sleeve. "That one's Coleridge. It's called 'Love.'" He glanced at Grimes and nodded, looking around the little room for any other signs. He saw none, so he backed carefully into the dusty courtyard. The rest would be up to the crime scene techs. He hoped they were good.

"I wonder if he had feelings for her," Grimes asked.

"No, Grimes. He doesn't have feelings that can be equated to love. She's a pawn in his game. That's all. The poems mean something to him. I don't know if they're supposed to mean anything to us. Let's get this room processed, we need to see if we have anything that can link Christina Dale to the rest of the girls."

They stepped into the clearing in the parking lot.

Jones was holding court in the door to the office, a few locals had stepped onto the porch to exchange gossip with him. Lights were flashing, people were starting to crowd around. A deputy that Baldwin recognized from yesterday's crime scene with Marni Fischer started winding yellow tape around anything he could find that would help form a barrier between the public and the law enforcement officials that were processing the scene.

As Baldwin watched the parade of action, a black SUV pulled up and he breathed a sigh of relief. Grimes hadn't lost it completely, and had called in their own forensic team. The locals wouldn't be allowed to touch anything, only the FBI would be handling evidence. There was just no sense in messing around.

The dogs were next. They piled out of a dingy white pickup truck, a man in overalls and a John Deere cap herding them. There were two bloodhounds and a bluetick hound. Good trackers.

A deputy from the sheriff's office had gone to Christina Dale's home to check on her whereabouts when they'd first gotten the call that she hadn't shown up for work. When she wasn't to be found, the heads-up deputy grabbed a couple of pieces of her clothing. Knowing it was most likely futile, Baldwin watched as the dogs were given the clothing to smell. The handler stuck something cream colored under their noses and they whined and howled, straining on their leads, ready to go. The handler gave his commands and they were off. They ran about twenty yards to the east, baying, then slowed back to a walk, sniffing the ground, working in circles, growing more confused by the minute. The handler looked at Baldwin and shrugged. He must have put her in a car. Not a big surprise.

Baldwin looked around and felt the scene, despite the confusion, was out of his hands. It was time to find out more about the latest victim.

Twenty-Eight

The man was sweating. He was tired. It was hard work, getting a body in the right spot. But he was finished now, and he stepped back to admire his handiwork, rubbing his eyes with the sleeve of his shirt. Soon, he thought. Soon, it will be done and you will have everything you always dreamed of. You will have the world at your feet and I will be there with you. He smiled to himself and got back in the car. He had things to do.

He chuckled. "And miles to go before I sleep. Oh yes, miles to go before I sleep."

Twenty-Nine

Whitney Connolly's home was in a stately neighborhood in Bellevue, an area jokingly referred to as West Belle Meade. Trees lined the streets, the homes were mostly two-story brick with large yards. Children played in the streets and backyards oblivious to the cares of the world; the sun shone its blessings on their cavorting.

Taylor drove slowly through the neighborhood, wondering if she should look at buying here. It was obviously filled with kids and the homes were gracious and large, much more space than she already had. She'd toyed with the idea of selling the cabin once or twice in the past. With Baldwin around, things were getting a little cramped. Maybe that was the key. Break all her own rules. Buy a house, move in together and let people get over it when they found out she was dating a fed. Hell, her team was discovering her secret and none of them seemed to have any issues with it. Maybe she was the problem; her own prejudices were getting in the way. There was no law on the books against having a boyfriend, after all.

She'd counted it up last night. They'd been together for four months—just enough time for the newness to begin wearing off. He'd never officially moved in with her, just stopped going to his own house. She'd never encouraged him to leave. They'd fallen into a pattern while she was rehabbing—he'd bring home dinner, they'd talk about their cases, they'd end up in bed. Idyllic. Nothing easier to ruin a good relationship than having to talk about it. She knew he felt it, too, there was no reason to go chasing after it.

A woman with a yellow Lab walked by and gave her a friendly wave. Taylor sighed and allowed herself a moment of reverie before she pulled herself back into the here and now. There was plenty of time for dreams later.

She took a left turn and wound deeper into the neighborhood, pulling to a stop in front of a large red-brick house with white columns. Quinn Buckley stood on the porch, her arms wrapped around her body as if she was cold, her pretty face pinched and drawn. She looked terribly tired and uncomfortable. Of course, this house was a far cry from the palatial mansion Quinn was accustomed to, maybe she just felt out of her element.

Taylor chided herself silently. Now, *that* wasn't a very nice thing to think. The woman just lost her sister, give her the benefit of the doubt. She got out of the car and walked across the grass to the front steps. She saw that Quinn had already picked up two copies of the *Tennessean* and was holding them in her left hand. She held them up, shaking the papers slightly, the plastic covers rustling in her hand.

"I guess I have to cancel her subscription. I guess I'm going to have to do a lot of things around here." Quinn gave her a small smile that didn't make it all the way to her cool blue eyes.

Taylor nodded. "It's always hard to get things settled after someone passes. Is there anyone else who can help you? Did Whitney have a boyfriend, someone who was familiar with her everyday things?"

Quinn laughed, a bitter sound. "No, Whitney didn't have time for a boyfriend. She didn't have time for anyone but herself. I'm sorry, Lieutenant, but my sister was one of the most selfish people you could ever meet. Everything revolved around her and her plans, her dreams. She couldn't be bothered with anyone else." She turned and stuck a key in the lock. "She left it under the mat for the cleaning lady. She told me that a while ago, I assumed it would still be there and it was. Here we go."

The oak door swung open and Taylor was assailed by the smell of furniture polish and Clorox. Her heart sank. "Did the cleaning lady just come?" she asked Quinn.

"I believe she came once a week, but I'm not sure which day. Usually midweek, I think. Is that a problem?"

"No, not necessarily a problem. If I was investigating a crime here, it would be, but since this was ruled an accident, it shouldn't make a difference. But if there was something here that your sister was basing her panicky phone calls to you on, I would want to see it. But maybe we're grasping at straws. It doesn't mean that there's anything tangible. Let's just look around."

Quinn nodded and led the way through the foyer. The house was beautifully decorated to within an inch of its life. Parquet floors led to a spacious kitchen filled with the latest trends—black granite counters with an Italian-stone backsplash, whitewashed cabinets and stainless-steel appliances. An office area and breakfast nook split the kitchen from a large living room. Mullioned windows ran the length of the house along the back, and natural light flooded from the fenced-in backyard. Everything had a place, not a thing was disturbed. It was very homey, yet there was an antiseptic quality to it all. As if a decorator had decided what Whitney would like rather than Whitney herself deciding. Taylor supposed that if she was as busy as Whitney had obviously been, then she might have someone else do the decorating too.

Taylor moved slowly through the downstairs of the house. The maid had been thorough, there was nothing amiss. Damn, that just made things more difficult. As she turned to go into the living room, a briefcase and a laptop computer caught her eye. The brand-new computer was sitting on the desk of a built-in set of shelves, and the briefcase sat at the foot of the chair. Taylor carefully opened the briefcase but saw nothing that excited her. Whitney didn't bring a lot of paperwork home.

She pulled out the chair and sat in front of the computer. She opened the top and was rewarded with a full screen of e-mails. Whitney Connolly hadn't logged out of her computer when she took off like a bat out of hell for her sister's house. Taylor scanned the e-mails. She saw that several had come in today, the dates were current and the e-mails were still bolded, indicating they hadn't been read. She noticed that a few of the messages had red flags next to them. She'd seen Sam do the same thing with her e-mails, she got so many that she had to identify which ones she wanted to pay attention to first. Taylor wasn't as picky; she just didn't spend that much time online to have to devise organizational codes for her e-mail.

She started looking at the red-flagged entries, trying to see if something jumped out at her. She noticed there were a few that had already been opened but still had the red flag next to them. She turned to Quinn.

"Do I have your permission to go through Whitney's e-mails?"

"Of course, do anything you need. I'm going to go out on the back deck for a little air, if you don't mind." Quinn stepped out the French doors and turned her back to Taylor. Just as well, she thought. She wouldn't want some impersonal stranger to go through all of her things if she keeled over unexpectedly.

She started looking closer at the previously flagged e-mails and matching them to unread flagged mail. There were a couple that were self-explanatory, alerts from news organizations and the like. But there was one address she saw several times, the subject line always reading "A poem for S.W." She took a chance and opened the newest mail from that address.

The window opened and there were just a few lines on the page. Taylor read them aloud:

> *"She half enclosed me with her arms*
> *She pressed me with a weak embrace;*
> *And bending back her head, looked up,*
> *And gazed upon my face.*

'Twas partly love, and partly fear,
And partly 'twas a bashful art,
That I might rather feel, than see,
The swelling of her heart."

She closed the e-mail, feeling like a spy. And Quinn thought her sister didn't have a boyfriend. She scrolled through the list and saw that there were five more e-mails from the mystery man—IM1855195C@yahoo.com. She opened them and glanced through hurriedly. Each held a fragment of poetry like the first had. She wished Baldwin would send her anonymous love poems.

She went through the rest of the mail but didn't see anything that leaped out at her. It was time to let Whitney's sister take a crack at it.

"Quinn?" Taylor called over her shoulder, and Quinn came in from the deck.

Taylor pointed to the e-mails. "I've been through here and haven't seen anything that seems terribly out of place. She seems to get a number of e-mails from the same people. Would you like to take a look and see if anything strikes you?"

"I don't think that's necessary, Lieutenant. My sister's e-mail is just not something I'm interested in. And I can hardly think any of it would have to do with me."

"Well, have a quick look anyway. I did find some love poems that had been sent to her. I thought you said she didn't have a boyfriend." Taylor's voice was only slightly accusing. She wondered if there was any chance that Quinn knew anything substantive about her sister's life.

"Love poems? Let me see." Quinn leaned over the desk and Taylor pulled up the latest message. Quinn read the lines and got a strange look on her face. Taylor noticed.

"Something strike you as odd about this?"

Quinn's face took on a soft countenance, and her eyes got moist. "It's nothing, really."

Taylor wasn't going to let that go; the look on Quinn's face told her that there was something about the poem. "I think there may be something here. There're several more. Are you sure they don't mean anything to you?"

Taylor looked at Quinn, who was trying to look away. Taylor could see that her shoulders were shaking slightly, and she was amazed to see a tear fall down Quinn's lovely face.

"What's wrong?" she asked softly. "Is this getting to you?"

Quinn laughed out a sob. "No, it's nothing like that. I loved my sister, and I'm sick at heart that she's dead. But the poems, that's got nothing to do with it. My husband used to send me poems. He doesn't anymore." She turned away and gathered herself by walking through the kitchen, grabbing a paper towel, splashing some water on it and holding it to her face. When she turned back to Taylor, her eyes were shining but she was back in control.

"Silly of me, to think of Jake in the middle of all this. I guess seeing that Whitney has an admirer made me wish that Jake felt like that about me still." And with that, she left the room. Taylor could hear her rummaging around but decided to leave her alone for a while.

Taylor swept through the rest of the house, looking for anything that would give them a clue as to why Whitney Connolly was in such desperate straits to reach her sister. If only the maid hadn't wiped away any obvious intent by straightening and cleaning. If there were papers left out, notes or the like, there was no way to know. Then she had a thought.

"Quinn?" she called out. "Have the officers from the accident scene given you any of Whitney's personal effects?"

Quinn came back into the kitchen. "No, I'm supposed to go to the morgue and pick them up. They said there were a few things in the car… Oh, now that was dumb of me, wasn't it? We should have gone to get her things before we came all the way out here."

Taylor stifled a laugh, as if Bellevue, a scant five minutes farther out from downtown than Belle Meade, was on the other side of the universe. "It's really no trouble. We can head over there now if you'd like. I think we need to go through and see if anything in her stuff gives us a better idea than what we've gotten here."

"That's fine. I can write you a release and you can go through the information on your own, if that's okay?"

Taylor studied her for a moment. "I can do that, but you may want to be there." She hesitated, then decided it would be dumb not to ask. "Quinn, you don't think this has anything to do with Nathan Chase, do you?"

Quinn's face drained of color. "Oh dear God, you don't think he's…? Could he have gotten in touch with Whitney somehow?"

"Well, I don't know. Has he ever reached out to you or your sister before?"

Quinn started pacing, a pale manicured hand clasped to her throat. She looked as if she might shatter into a million pieces all over the foyer.

"No, we've had no contact from him. It was part of his sentence. And he's still in jail, I know, because I check every so often to make sure he's not getting out. He's not due for parole for another fifteen years."

Taylor digested that for a moment. Kidnapping was one thing, but Chase had been sentenced to at least thirty years. She made a mental note to look up the case and find out what exactly he'd been sentenced for. It probably wasn't germane to this case, but it wouldn't hurt to have the whole story.

"Okay, Quinn. I'll go and sort through Whitney's things. If I find anything of note, I'll let you know."

"Thank you. Tell me, when will her body be released? I need to start making plans for the memorial."

"Just give the M.E.'s office a call. They'll be able to give you all of that information. It'll be soon, I promise."

As they made their way toward the door, they didn't hear the chime go off on the computer to announce that Whitney had another new e-mail.

Thirty

Christina Louise Dale, better known as Christy to her family and friends, was a sad case. Nineteen years old, petite and brunette, Christy was always hustling, always looking for a way to get it done. She didn't have the money to go to college nor the grades to get a scholarship, so she worked hard and associated with the college students around Roanoke as often as possible. She was autodidactic, and when she mentioned that, most of the college kids didn't even know what it meant. On one hand, it was outrageous that she could be so much smarter than the rest of them and still not have a chance to go to school with them. But on the other hand, she secretly gloated, knowing that no matter what, she was better than all of them.

She continued her quest to educate herself and read everything she could in her spare time. She landed herself a job that would afford her the opportunities that had been denied to her so far in her short life. The parent company of her small community hospital had a program to give scholarships to those needy employees who demonstrated a will and a dedication to getting a higher education, but only in the medical field. That was fine with her. She could always do her time with the company and then branch out when she got a little older.

Christy bided her time. She was a diligent employee, even if the things she did outside of work were a little questionable. Admittedly, she drank too much. She drank too much and smoked too much. And oftentimes she did a few drugs that probably weren't the most legal things in the world. Nothing hard-core, but the soft stuff, the campus drugs. That way she felt she was experiencing the same things that all nineteen-year-old college girls experience. The booze, the drugs, the boys. Oh yes, the boys. She really liked the boys. But that wasn't exactly a bad thing, at least in her mind. She was in control of her body, she had the last word in everything she did. The fact that she might have sex on a given night with a guy that never asked for her number wasn't a problem. If she wanted to see him again, she could find a way to do it.

So maybe she dressed a little provocatively. Maybe she drank too much, slept around a little too much. What difference did that make?

Baldwin knew all of this, and more, so when he stared down at Christy's lifeless body, tossed off the edge of the road in Asheville, North Carolina, he couldn't help but wonder if poor Christy had any idea of the danger she was putting herself in, over and over, having sex with strange men, riding off in cars that didn't belong to her and, most importantly, taking a stranger back to the motel that she used when she didn't want her mom to know she was out fooling around.

But Christy's mother had known. She knew everything her daughter did, and either didn't care enough to do anything about it, or just didn't believe she could make a difference. When Baldwin had sat down with her, mere hours after they knew Christy's body had been taken from room 3 at the Happy Roads Inn, Charlie Dale didn't seem surprised.

Charlie Dale smoked continuously throughout their interview. Baldwin thought he would choke in the dim air of her trailer, and wondered if there had ever been an open window in the place. It was stacked with laundry, washed or unwashed was anyone's guess, trash, full ashtrays and dirt, layer upon layer of dirt. Charlie wasn't much of a housekeeper, and told Baldwin that. He'd smiled and pretended things were fine, which he assumed Charlie had been doing for at least a decade.

She didn't have a lot of nice things to say about her daughter. Christy had been a surprise in her mother's life, a surprise that had come along when Charlie was fifteen and madly in love with a boy from uptown Roanoke. When she found herself pregnant, she never heard from him again. It had been her and Christy all along, she told Baldwin. And that girl was never going to amount to anything, the way she ran around, whoring and drinking. Just 'cause it was good enough for her mama didn't mean it was good enough for her. I always wanted something better for Christy, she told Baldwin, but I never knew how to get it for her.

As Baldwin gazed down at Christy, he felt a sadness

that was as much sorrow for the girl's death as it was for the raw deal she'd gotten in her short life.

When they'd gotten the call that a body had been found in Asheville, North Carolina, Baldwin hadn't even blinked. The killer wasn't thinking too far ahead. Now that they were hot on his trail, he was grabbing, killing and dumping, and he'd really gotten on a tear. Christy hadn't even been missing a day, and now Baldwin stood over her battered body, looking at the knife wounds in her chest, the bloody wrists, wondering where her hand would show up. Marni Fischer's neatly manicured hand was a few feet away. Baldwin calculated. Where were the rest of the girls' hands?

His careful, methodical serial killer had escalated into a vicious spree maniac. At first glance, the killer was trying to draw them in, a heavy spider in a silken web of intent. But as each thread unraveled, each victim killed quicker than the last, the web tore. A sophisticated, organized killer could last for years off one kill. This one was decompensating at a rate Baldwin hadn't seen for a decade.

The change was fascinating from an empirical standpoint. It was Baldwin's talent, the ability to separate the victims and their lives from the crimes being committed. Psychologically, it was a simple issue. The killer's message wasn't getting through. This was frustrating him, and in turn, he was taking chances, not as worried about possible consequences. His endgame had started.

Forensics had a field day in the motel room. It was obvious that Christy had been repeatedly stabbed, and that blood added to the cast-off spray from the arterial cuts in her wrists created a gory miasma for the techs to comb through. The room hadn't been wiped down, so there were many fingerprints, almost too many to take exemplars from, considering the number of people who had been through that room. Baldwin assumed the killer was wearing gloves, they hadn't gotten a fingerprint from any of the scenes that they could place him at.

For the first time, they'd found a minute amount of semen mixed in with the blood on the bedsheets. In a regular case, that would have been cause for celebration. Because there had been no evidence collected from the earlier event with the ripped condom, there was nothing to compare with this DNA. Another telltale sign that the killer was on the edge, losing control. He was getting sloppy.

Baldwin had instructed the techs to file the DNA into the CODIS system, hoping for a match from deep within the bowels of the database, but he wasn't holding his breath. Something about these kills felt fresh to him. His profile stated that these were the man's first significant crimes, that his earlier record would be minor, if there was one at all. As he delved further into the case and the pace of the murders increased, the more on target his original assessment seemed. Not finding a match would reinforce at least one element of the profile.

Baldwin had asked Grimes to send men in to the bar Christy frequented, to find out if anyone remembered seeing her talking to someone or, better yet, leaving with someone. But Grimes had reported that no one saw anything out of the ordinary. One bartender had gone so far as to joke that keeping up with the men Christy was seen talking to would take an entire police force. His humor wasn't appreciated, and he quickly apologized and let them know that seriously, she could have been with anyone, no one paid attention to a crazy girl flirting her way through a few hours of drinks.

On a lark, Baldwin had asked Grimes to see if anyone remembered a young, dark-haired man, but that got a laugh. They were in a college bar; at least half the patrons fit that description. No one in particular had stood out to the bartender.

They just didn't have a lot to go on. Baldwin signaled that they needed to get Christy's body out of the brush and onto a gurney so she could be unceremoniously cut open and slid into a refrigerated drawer in the Asheville morgue, while Baldwin twiddled his thumbs and looked stupid, not having any idea how to stop this mercurial killer.

It was time to take a room, have a drink and try to sort all of this out. Preferably over the phone with Taylor. He'd realized lately that just talking to her cleared his mind, and his mind needed a lot of clearing now. He needed a strategy session, he needed to lay it all out and see what he was missing. Because he was missing something huge, and that wasn't going to get this killer stopped any time soon.

He watched through squinted eyes as Christina Dale was loaded into a bag, placed onto a stretcher, then set gently on a gurney that was slid into the open back doors of the M.E.'s cream-colored van. The trees seemed very green, the haze off the mountains very purple, the summer air surprisingly crisp and clean and only slightly mottled with the smell of death. Everything here seemed larger than life, realer than real, and it made Baldwin's head ache. Mountains always did that to him.

Baldwin came out of the shower and flipped on the television set. His hotel room was too hot, so he sat on the edge of the bed in his towel and watched the local news. The lead story was about Christina Dale's body being found. The reporter went through the details, which were sketchy, as Baldwin had made sure that not a lot of information was getting out. She traced the killer's moves over the past weeks, and she finished with a warning to all of the young women of Asheville.

"All women in the Asheville area are warned not to stay alone, and to keep your doors and windows locked. If you go out, please find someone to go with you. Don't speak with anyone you don't know, and carry pepper spray. We can't emphasize enough that you have to be on your guard. Keep your cell phone charged and handy. Don't get into cars with strangers. Everyone needs to be aware."

It was a good warning, nothing that any woman didn't hear on any given day, but given with such vehemence that it should give one or two women pause. Unfortunately, there was nothing in particular they could tell the women of Asheville to actually keep them safe.

He flipped the TV off and pulled out his files. He spread them on the bed in chronological order and started to go through them, beginning with Susan Palmer. There were definite similarities to the victims. Each had dark hair and eyes, they were between eighteen and twenty-eight. Body types were comparable; they were all strong and athletic. And they all worked in the medical field to some degree. Was he dealing with a deranged doctor who'd gone over the edge? That was as good a theory as any he'd had so far.

He was beginning to feel impotent. This killer was moving fast, and though there was a distinct pattern to his motions, there was no way to predict what city he would hit next. All they could do was catch him. And they weren't getting any closer to that goal, either.

He'd had cases like this before, that the killer's actions overrode the police investigation. He was more accustomed to the kind of killer that took his time. Patterns generally were established over weeks and months, not in days. This guy was on a frenzied killing spree, and spree killers were the most dangerous. But they almost always tripped up, and were caught quickly. They certainly didn't go from state to state taking women and depositing their bodies minus their hands in other states.

His escalation was actually a good thing. At this pace, he was bound to screw up. No killer was that smart. Leaving his DNA behind was the first of what Baldwin hoped would be many mistakes.

Baldwin's cell phone rang as the number to the FBI tip line appeared on the screen. He shut the TV off and glanced at the caller ID. It was Taylor.

"Hi, sweetheart," he said gently.

"Baldwin, are you okay? I've been following all of this on the news, you must be exhausted."

"Yeah, well, crime waits for no man. This situation just goes from bad to worse. Every time we catch up with him, he takes off again. I can't find a single predictor of where he's going to go next."

"Do you want to run it through with me? Maybe a fresh set of eyes, well, ears will help."

"Yeah, that might be a good idea. But first, is everything okay there? How's your rape case?"

He heard her get quiet, a moment of time in which he could almost hear the thoughts flowing through her brain over the phone. When she answered, he thought she sounded a bit discouraged.

"Things are fine. Have you seen the news? National media's picked up the Rainman story. Just their cup of tea, a real mystery. And who doesn't love a serial rapist? To top it all off, we have a victim who thinks the rapist is a cop, which isn't going over well. Oh, did you hear about Whitney Connolly?"

"Honey, I've been up to my ears here. Whitney Connolly from Channel Five? What happened?"

"She was in a car accident yesterday. Killed her and three others. It was pretty bad. I went to the scene with Sam before we knew it was Whitney. It's been awful, you can't turn on the news without seeing tributes to her. I've been working with her sister, Quinn Buckley, to try and find out if there was anything of a more sensitive nature that she was dealing with. She died on her way over to Quinn's house to warn her about something. We just haven't come up with what. I've been going through her personal effects all day, first at her house, then the things that they took out of her car after the accident. I'm not coming up with a lot."

"Well, she always seemed kind of flighty."

"John Baldwin, are you telling me you dated her? What little secrets are you hiding? I thought you said you didn't know them." Taylor hadn't known Baldwin at Father Ryan, either, but he knew her. It was impossible for anyone not to know Taylor Jackson—her ability to befriend students in all walks and her devil-may-care attitude had made her stand out.

"I didn't date her. We never even spoke. I'm just saying she seemed a little flighty. And I've always wondered what the real deal was with that kidnapping."

"Good segue. I mentioned the kidnapper's name to Quinn, to see if there was a chance Whitney's fears had to do with him. She mentioned he was still incarcerated and not up for parole for another fifteen years. I wanted to see what the deal was, so I pulled the file. Nathan Chase is in jail for more than just kidnapping. Sexual assault, sexual battery, aggravated rape and sodomy. Those girls went through a little more than just a kidnapping. I don't know how they kept it all so secret."

"I remember it was kept pretty quiet. And they had a lot of influence and power on their side. Peter Connolly, that's their dad, was a pretty high-powered attorney, if I remember correctly. They had the protection of being juveniles, too. Wasn't there some innuendo when they transferred to Father Ryan?"

"Well, sure, but nothing came of it. The staff kept a pretty tight rein on anyone who joked around about the incident, and it just faded away. I think it was easier for them to be in a new environment, no one really paid too much attention. Of course I know now that they must have been going through hell."

"So Whitney was trying to get to Quinn when she had the accident? And you haven't found anything?"

"No, I haven't. There was nothing in her car other than her cell phone and purse. No files, no notes, nothing."

"Did anyone check the memo function of her phone? I do that sometimes if I'm out driving and don't want to stop to record my thoughts."

Taylor started laughing. "You're brilliant, you know that? I better go check and see if there's anything on it, I bet you a million no one thought to check. Let me get to work on that, and I'll call you back."

"You should probably go to bed, sweetie, it's nearly midnight. I'm sure the phone can wait until tomorrow. You need to keep your strength up. Go to bed."

He was amazed when Taylor didn't argue with him, just told him that sounded like a good idea and she'd talk to him in the morning.

They said their I love yous, hung up and Baldwin went back to his files. He spread the pictures of each girl out on the bed and stood over them, staring into their accusing eyes. He went over the facts in his head. Their obvious connection was the link to the medical field. Maybe their killer had been molested by a pretty brunette nurse when he was little. He stopped himself from rolling his eyes. It could be as simple as that.

He decided to reorganize the files. It would be easier to spot similarities and differences if they all resided in one file with subfiles in it. Where they liked to eat, where they liked to work out, where they were employed, all the information was culled and put into new piles. Baldwin went back to the work pile. What if he looked at employer instead of industry?

Okay, he thought. Susan Palmer had just gotten a job at the Huntsville Community Hospital. Jeanette Lernier was an intern with a marketing company. Jessica Porter worked as a receptionist at the Mississippi Community

Hospital in Jackson. Shauna Davidson was working… damn, it didn't say. Only that she was premed at MTSU. Marni Fischer was a resident, working at Noble Community Hospital. Christy was a receptionist at Roanoke Community Hospital.

Baldwin flipped open his phone and called Grimes. The voice mail came on and he left a message. "Grimes, it's Baldwin. Did you get a work history for Shauna Davidson? It's not in the file. Call me as soon as you get this, okay?"

He hung up and paced around the room. Jeanette Lernier didn't fit the profile, she was in marketing. All the other girls worked at a local hospital. Shauna was premed. Community hospital. Community hospital. Hmm.

Time to make a leap. He opened his phone again, dialing the 800 information number. When the operator came on he asked for the number for a community hospital in Jackson, Mississippi. There was a pause, and the woman came back to him. She had a listing for a Jackson Community Hospital. He'd been operating under the assumption the community hospital was just a designator, not the name of the place. Well, damn. He thanked her and hung up, fumbling open his laptop and plugging "Jackson Community Hospital" into the Google search engine. Sure enough, it popped up.

He read through the site and saw a link at the bottom. It was called "About Health Partners", and as he opened it his cell rang. Grimes had finally gotten back to him.

"Shauna Davidson had been taking some summer courses, mostly in microbiology and immunology. She had to spend a few weeks doing practical applications. That's it."

"But Grimes, where did she do the practical work?"

"At the local hospital. Nashville Community Hospital. Why, Baldwin, you got something?"

"I'll let you know." He hung up, gave his attention back to the Web site and clicked on the Health Partners link.

He entered a sophisticated and accessible Web portal. Someone had spent a lot of time and effort to make it pop. It quickly became apparent that Health Partners was the parent company of the community hospital organizations. He went through all of the information, gleaning names and sites. The company had hospitals in several states, all up and down the eastern seaboard and throughout the Southeast. That was a bust. If the killer was focusing on hospitals this company owned, they would have to put out alerts from Florida to Delaware.

Baldwin closed the laptop, deflated. That had to be the link, and yet it only served to widen the field, not narrow it.

He dialed Grimes's number again, and again got voice mail. Damn, was the man sleeping already? He'd just talked to him and told him he'd call him back. Baldwin looked at the clock. It was 2:00 a.m. He'd been trolling through the Web for a couple of hours. Well, yes, Grimes probably was sleeping. This could wait until morning. The best he could do was have a background check done on all employees of the community hospitals in the cities where the girls were taken and hope that some aberration jumped out at him. There had to be something else.

Baldwin decided he'd better get some sleep. Maybe something would come to him in his dreams.

Thirty-One

Noelle Pazia stopped pedaling, rested her foot on the gravel and coughed for what felt like an eternity. She'd been coughing like this for a week, and the student health center, realizing she needed more than they could provide, had finally sent her in for chest X-rays. She suffered from asthma, and used an inhaler, but it wasn't touching this nasty cough. So she'd pedaled her mountain bike down to the Asheville Community Hospital, sat for two hours, gotten her X-ray and cycled back toward campus. Not that cycling was great for her cold or bronchitis or pneumonia or whatever sickness she had that made her feel so horrible. She could hear her father now, in his heavy Italian accent, "Noelle, you knowa you shouldn't be riding that crazy bike up and down those hills when you sick. You're smarter than that, *cara.*" Yes, she was, but she didn't have a car, nor did she feel like begging a ride off of one of her friends.

As she coughed and tried to catch her breath, she wished that she was back home in D.C., sitting at a table in the back of her parents' restaurant, watching her father, Giovanni, put the finishing touches on a fragrant pot of pasta e faglioli, a traditional pasta-and-bean soup that Noelle always craved when she wasn't feeling well. When she was growing up, her father would take one look at her pale face and start for the kitchen. No doctors, no drugs, just a big pot of *zuppa* to make her feel better. The remedy almost always worked. The one time she remembered it didn't was when she contracted the chicken pox from a Romanian boy who lived down the street and came to play in her backyard. The soup didn't help then.

But she wasn't anywhere near home. She was on the side of a road in North Carolina, sick with the croup and not a bowl of soup in sight. She needed to get back to campus and get to her study group in the library. Even sick, she felt the responsibility of schoolwork, and wouldn't miss the group. Most everyone had this crud anyway, so she didn't need to worry about giving it to anyone. There was a lot of work to be done now that she was fully into her major coursework, and if that meant she had to put off bed for a few more hours, that's just what she would do. She pushed her damp bangs out of her eyes, swung her leg back over the bike and started pedaling.

Thinking about her father's soup brought back more memories. As she rode, she remembered the compromise that she'd come to with her father. Giovanni was a stern man, hardworking and strict. He'd emigrated the family to America from a small mountain town in Italy called Sestriere so his six children could attend American colleges. Noelle was his youngest child, the last to go to college. She wanted to go to Colorado and study climatology, to go skiing and mountain biking in the biggest mountains in the country. Giovanni thought that Colorado was too far away. So they'd come to a deal after Noelle found the Department of Atmospheric Sciences at the University of North Carolina—Asheville. It gave her the mountains, and it gave Giovanni the peace of mind that she was only a few hours from home instead of three days' drive.

For the quiet, serious Noelle, UNC–Asheville was a dream come true. She loved her department heads, her roommate and the environment of the campus. She'd joined the cycling club and had made many friends. She'd even found a group of Catholic students that went to the church off campus, and she joined them as often as she could. Now, her sophomore year, she felt right at home. She had a lot of attention from the boys on campus, too. She was five-six, a hundred twenty pounds of lean muscle, shiny brown hair and soulful ethnic brown eyes, and she got quite a bit of attention from the opposite sex. But she was her father's daughter, and shunned formal dating because it was his wish. It didn't bother her, she had a lot of work to do for school and dating wasn't the most important thing on her plate.

She pedaled back through the gates to the university, rode through campus and pulled up to her dorm, West Ridge Hall. Securing her bike in the rack, she chained it and went inside. Wheezing as she walked the hall to her room, she wondered if she should cancel her attendance at the study group for her climatology class. She came to her door, unlocked it and went inside. She and her roommate kept the blinds up; their room afforded a beautiful panorama of the mountains, and they both enjoyed lying in bed gazing at the view. Noelle put her backpack down on the floor and stretched out on her twin-size bed.

Oh, that felt good. Too good. She knew she needed to get up and get going. Being sick was no excuse for missing that study group. So she managed to get herself up, slip on a jacket, grab her books and make her way out of her cozy room toward the library.

Ramsey Library stood in the center of campus, and the walk felt good. Physical activity had always been Noelle's cure when she didn't feel well, so a short walk to the library wasn't going to hurt. She walked along the quiet pathways, waving at people she knew, and went into the library to her study group.

They worked for a couple of hours, and Noelle was starting to feel pretty crappy. Just as they decided to take a break, her cell phone rang. Noelle excused herself and made her way to the side entrance of the library. She hated talking on her phone in a group setting, she found it rude when people talked on phones in restaurants and grocery stores. So she was mindful of the other students in the library, and she needed some air anyway.

It was a friend from the cycling club, asking if she wanted to go biking in the morning. As much as she wanted to, she turned the offer down, until she was done with her antibiotics, it just wouldn't be smart to push herself too hard. They chatted for a while as Noelle walked out of the library and sat on the steps. It was getting full dark, and as she hung up the phone, she thought she saw a shadow on the side of the building. She shook it off, there were so many people on campus, anyone could be walking around the corner of the building. Regardless, she decided it would be a good idea to go inside. She'd heard about that poor girl from Virginia, and as she moved toward the door, the hairs on the back of her neck stood up. She glanced behind her and saw that the shadow had become a man, but she laughed when she realized it was just another student. He was certainly too young and too handsome to be anything but. She gave him a smile and held the door for him.

He smiled back, and that was the last thing Noelle remembered.

Thirty-Two

Taylor woke up with a sense of purpose. Showered, dressed and fed, she grabbed the *Tennessean* from her front step and plopped down on the couch. Lee Mayfield, a crime reporter who Taylor didn't get along with, had the byline for the Rainman lead. She read through the article, scoffing. As usual, Mayfield had the details wrong. It wasn't just the police who couldn't stand her, her fellow reporters got fed up with her, too. She was infamous for showing up at the end of a press conference, or after shootings had wrapped at a scene, and getting her stories from the other media on the scene rather than doing her own work.

Taylor didn't bother finishing the article, or the paper, for that matter. Disgusted, she threw the paper on the floor and turned to business she had some control over. Whitney Connolly's cell phone. Scrolling through the options, she found memo and hit playback. Whitney's voice floated through the air, running down a to-do list. The last item was interesting, and Taylor replayed it several times.

"Need to talk to Quinn about the notes."

That was it. No clues, no other directions. It didn't even sound like this was important. Was she talking about the e-mails?

Taylor picked up the phone and called Quinn Buckley. Quinn answered on the first ring.

"Quinn? It's Taylor Jackson. I have been going through Whitney's personal effects that were in her car, and I have your sister's cell phone here. There's a recorded memo on the cell phone, I want to play it for you and get your impressions. Okay, I'm going to play it now."

She held the cell phone up to her own portable phone and replayed the memo. Whitney's voice rang out like a shot. Taylor couldn't help but get goose bumps, she didn't usually commune with the dead. That was Sam's job. She lifted the receiver back to her ear and heard Quinn crying softly.

"Oh damn, Quinn, I'm sorry, I should have warned you it was going to be her voice."

"No, that's okay," Quinn sniffled through the phone. "I just wasn't prepared to hear her voice again, like that. Was there nothing else?"

Taylor shook her head though no one was there to see it. "No, Quinn, there wasn't anything else. Do you know what notes she's talking about?"

"Who knows with Whitney? I was getting us both some note cards, maybe that's what she meant. She must have changed her mind about the style, or something. I had so hoped there would be something more."

"I don't know what to tell you, but I'll keep working on it. I'm sorry."

"No, Taylor, you're doing your best. I appreciate your help. They're going to release Whitney's body today. I think we'll be having the memorial next week, as soon as I can get in touch with my husband and little brother and make arrangements for the service. They're both out of town. I would appreciate it if you would come."

"Of course. Just leave me a message as to time and place, and I'll be there."

They hung up and Taylor felt terrible. Here the woman's sister was dead, her husband was perpetually out of town on business and she couldn't even contact her younger brother to help make the funeral arrangements. For a privileged life, it seemed very lonely.

Taylor decided the best thing she could do was get into the office. She brushed her still-wet hair into a ponytail, grabbed a Diet Coke and her keys.

The phone rang just as she was getting ready to walk out the door. She set her things down and answered it. Baldwin's voice boomed through the line as if he were in the next room, and she felt an overwhelming loneliness. Silly, she chided herself, he would be home soon.

"Hi, honey. Everything okay up there in North Carolina?"

"Well, no one's gone missing this morning, so I guess we're making improvements. I can't predict this one, Taylor, and it's driving me crazy."

"Then sit down and write me a love poem," she teased. "That should get your mind off things and back to where it belongs."

The comment was greeted with silence. Taylor wasn't hurt exactly, but she felt stung, usually Baldwin would coo right back at her. But before she could say anything, he spoke.

"What made you say that?"

"Well, I'm sorry, hon, I was just joking around. They've been on my mind since I saw them at Whitney Connolly's house. She had a boyfriend or admirer that was sending her love poems in her e-mails, and I read a couple while I was going through her stuff. It's no big deal."

But Taylor could feel the intensity coming off Baldwin through the phone. "Taylor, do you remember what the poems were? Anything in particular about them?"

"No, I didn't pay that close attention. Why, Baldwin, what's going on?"

"We haven't released this to the press, okay, so I need you to keep it very quiet. The killer is leaving the victims poems. Love poems, classics by Wordsworth, Coleridge, Yeats. You have to get me the poems off Whitney Connolly's computer."

"At the crime scenes? I don't recall anything like that at Shauna Davidson's apartment."

"One of Grimes's men found it in her desk drawer. They are completely innocuous, unless you know what to look for, the notes are easily missed."

"Jesus, Baldwin, if you'd told me I could have given you all of this yesterday. It didn't even register, I only glanced at a couple of them. Crap."

Taylor's head felt like it was going to spin off into space. She loved it, that rush of adrenaline that came when you got the big break. Things were making a little sense now. The notes.

"Baldwin, Whitney was trying desperately to reach her sister yesterday, remember? Her memo on her cell phone that you suggested I check? There was a message there that she needed to talk to Quinn about the notes. We thought it was something benign, like note cards. Maybe we were wrong. What do you think?"

"I don't want to jump to any conclusions. But I want you to get a hold of those poems and read them to me, let me see if they're a match to what we're getting at the scenes. The killer may be a fan of Whitney Connolly's, who knows. Can you get to that computer?"

"Yeah, let me call Quinn Buckley and get permission to go into Whitney's house again. I'll call you as soon as I have them in front of me."

Baldwin flipped on the news, trying to gauge public opinion on their handling of the case. The murders were the lead story, the sensational nature of the slayings, the fact that all the victims had a medical tie-in, the speed at which the killer was progressing. Everyone was baffled, desperate for answers. Gun sales were on the rise, and locksmiths were doing a brisk business all along the southeast corridor. Great, nothing worked better for an investigation than instilling fear in the public. And where were they getting all that information? Only a select few knew about the medical tie-in, the leak was high up on the food chain. He would have to deal with that sooner rather than later.

Baldwin sat incredulous on the bed for a few moments. Then a thought hit him. He opened up his computer and went to the Health Partners Web portal. He had glossed over a lot of the information last night, but something was tickling his conscience. He navigated the site until he found a section that was entitled

Contact Us. He clicked it open, and there it was. The home office of Health Partners was in Nashville.

He started scrolling through but couldn't find any more information. The company must have a listing of officers and executives, he just wasn't finding it online. No matter, that was something a quick phone call could provide.

He dialed the number that Health Partners had listed in their contact information. A pleasant southern voice answered, but Baldwin quickly realized it was voice mail. Damn, he was hoping to get a secretary. The voice gave him the option of hitting zero to speak to a live person, and he did just that. Muzak drifted out from his earpiece and he rolled his eyes. There was just something so wrong about hearing synthesized Aerosmith. "Dude (Looks Like A Lady)" just didn't work in the dulcet tones of elevator music.

After a few minutes, the music stopped and a real voice came on the line.

"Health Partners. Can I help you?"

He cleared his throat and gave a brisk no-nonsense answer. "Yes, you can. This is Special Agent John Baldwin with the Federal Bureau of Investigation. I need to get an organizational chart of your company."

"Sir, is there a problem?"

Great, he managed to get someone that wasn't impressed by the credentials and cop voice. "No, ma'am, not a problem, but I would like to find out more about your employees. Could you give me some information?"

"Yes, I can, but why does the FBI want to know about us? Are we under investigation for something? I think I'd better let you talk to Louis Sherwood. He's the

CEO, so you should be able to get everything you need from him. Please hold." The Muzak started up again, this time with The Scorpions' "Rock You Like A Hurricane." Baldwin gave out a little laugh. Whoever decided hard rock made melodious calming music was crazy.

It seemed as though he had been on hold for an hour, but it was probably more like five minutes when a voice came back on the line. "I'm Louis Sherwood. Is there something I can help you with, Agent Baldwin?"

"Yes, sir. I'd like to get some information about your traveling executives. I'm in the middle of an investigation and your company's name has come up in relation to the case. Would you be willing to give me some information?"

Sherwood didn't hesitate. "This is about the Southern Strangler, isn't it?"

"Yes, sir, that's the case I'm working on. You are familiar with it?" Silly question, he knew, anyone who owned a TV, lived next door to someone who owned a TV, drove a car with a radio, walked, slept or ate knew about the cases. The virtues of modern media.

"I am familiar with it, and I'm glad you've contacted me. I understand that three of the victims worked for our company in one capacity or another. I think that merits a sit-down discussion, don't you?"

Baldwin was pleased, anything that would shed light on any aspect of the case was important. "Absolutely, sir. When would you be available?"

"I'm free anytime for you. Are you here in town?"

"No, sir, I'm in North Carolina, but I was planning on coming back to Nashville today, if nothing keeps me here." Yeah, like another girl getting snatched.

"Back to Nashville? Do you have some interests here in town already?"

"Oh, sorry, I actually live in Nashville. I work out of the field office, handle national cases as needs be. I can be back in Nashville by late afternoon. Will you be available then?"

"I will be waiting for you. Do you need directions?"

Baldwin took down the information and thanked Sherwood. It felt good to do a little old-fashioned detective work rather than stand over dead girls. Now he needed to get the information about the poems from Taylor, and it was time to head back home. He figured he might as well rent a car and drive back instead of flying. Grimes was going to be here in Asheville for the time being anyway, finishing up with Christina Dale's autopsy and the other aspects of the investigation. Baldwin needed some time to think, and the four-hour drive to Nashville was the perfect opportunity.

He called Grimes and told him what he was planning on doing, and told him about the meeting with Louis Sherwood. Grimes thought that sounded great and asked for Baldwin to keep him filled in. Baldwin didn't mention the poems on Whitney Connolly's e-mail. He figured it would be better to have some kind of confirmation on them before he threw that little wrinkle into the mix.

They hung up and Baldwin called down to the front desk of the hotel and asked for them to secure a rental car for him. They told him it would be quicker for him to get it himself, the rental-car agency was on the same block, just on the opposite side of the building. He agreed and checked out of the room. Within ten minutes he had a car and was on his way home.

Thirty-Three

Taylor was sitting in front of Whitney's laptop computer, looking through the e-mail that had been piling up in the two days since Whitney's accident. She was distracted, worrying. Baldwin's case was completely out of control, but hopefully, these notes would be the key. She had to search through at least two hundred e-mails, some boring, some interesting, most completely irrelevant. She continued to scan and soon found the original six messages with the love poems. She sent the messages to the printer so Baldwin would have a hard copy.

She reached to close the laptop and saw that there was another e-mail from the same address that had been sending the poems. She'd missed one in her distracted state. This one was marked "Unread," which meant it had come in after Taylor and Quinn had left Whitney's house.

She opened the e-mail and saw another poem. She sent it to the printer. Knowing now that these were possibly copies of notes that had been left at the scene of the murders was very disconcerting. And Baldwin had not given her enough information about them for her to deduce anything. She decided it would be best to send the e-mails to Baldwin's e-mail address and let him look at them firsthand.

She started forwarding the messages and decided to send them to her home computer, as well. Ah hell, why not just take the whole computer with her? She could get out of there now, being in Whitney's house made her uncomfortable. It made more sense to do that anyway. God forbid, if Whitney continued to get these messages, they wouldn't have to come over to her house every time they wanted to check something out.

She looked for and found the case for the slim laptop, and unplugged the components and packed them into the carrying case. She rummaged through the desk and found a manila file folder. She slipped the printed copies into the folder, pausing briefly to read the latest install-ment, the one that had been sent after Whitney had died.

> *Mark but this Flea, and mark in this,*
> *How little that which thou deniest me is;*
> *It suck'd me first, and now sucks thee,*
> *And in this flea our two bloods mingled be.*

Taylor recognized that one. John Donne, a poem known as "The Flea." Easy enough, it had been a hit in high school. The whole sucking business had every guy in her English class beet red when their teacher, a comely young woman, had read the poem aloud. Well, Baldwin said the poems are some of the classics. Now they just needed to figure out what they meant to Whitney and the man who was sending them to her. Taylor pulled her cell phone out of its holster and dialed Baldwin's number. She got his voice mail and left a message for him to call her as soon as he got the call. That was the best she could do for now. She carried the laptop out to her truck, then went back in to make sure she hadn't left anything. Satisfied that she wouldn't need to make another return trip, she left, locking the door behind her and placing the key under the mat, just as it had been that first day when she and Quinn had come over.

"I need to let Quinn know I'm taking the laptop," she thought out loud. A neighbor walking her fluffy white lapdog gave her a funny look. Taylor just smiled and waved, then climbed into the truck, started it up and put it into gear. She'd call Quinn later, after she and Baldwin had gotten a chance to go over what was on the e-mails.

Baldwin was wending his way through East Tennessee, enjoying the view and drive as much as he could, considering the situation he found himself in. Six girls dead and he didn't have a suspect. Hopefully all that would change once he got to Nashville and talked to the CEO of Health Partners. Maybe when he heard from Taylor with the poems from Whitney Connolly's computer. His sixth sense was telling him that the two were related, he just needed to sit down and find out what that relationship was.

He'd left Asheville early, and had made good time. He was passing through Crossville on Interstate 40 when his cell phone rang. He was only an hour out of Nashville but he'd lost service a few times from the mountains to here, so he pulled over to the side of the road, happy to have a cell. When he looked at the display, he saw that it was Taylor calling.

"Hi, honey, how are—"

"Baldwin, I've been trying to reach you. Where are you?"

"I'm on 40 outside of Crossville. I rented a car and decided to head on back to Nashville for a couple of things. I'll be back in an hour if traffic holds. Why, what happened?"

"I went to Whitney Connolly's to get the e-mails. There was another e-mail, one that came in yesterday or this morning, after Quinn and I had left her house. If the e-mails and poems correlate to your poems, we may have trouble."

Baldwin gritted his teeth. Damn. It was very possible that another girl had been taken from Asheville, and no one had reported it. "What was the poem?"

"I actually recognized it, it's a few lines from 'The Flea.' John Donne. You know that one?"

"Actually, yes, I used to use it on girls all the time. Okay, I need you to do something for me. Do you have the poems in front of you right now?"

"Yeah, I just brought the whole laptop with me. In case there are other e-mails that come in from this address, I thought it would be best if we had the computer in front of us."

"Okay, I'm going to start driving again. Bear with me a second. If I lose the cell I'll call you right back." He started the engine and pulled out onto the highway. "Okay, I want you to read what each e-mail says, starting with the earliest one."

He could hear Taylor flipping through pages. The poems were going to match, he already knew that. He was starting to feel it, that connection that things were about to break all over the place. Taylor came back on the phone.

"The first one is dated a month ago. The content reads,

"A perfect woman, nobly planned,
To warn, to comfort and command;
And yet a Spirit still, and bright
With something of an angelic light.

"Uh-oh. There's a postscript here I didn't see before. This is the first time I've read them on paper, I didn't see it on the screen. 'This was at the crime scene.'" She paused. "Baldwin, she knew. She knew and she didn't come to us. Stupid reporter."

Baldwin's heart started pounding. "That's the same as the note found in Susan Palmer's bag, without the postscript, of course," he said quietly.

"All right, the next one came in two weeks ago. Here goes…

"A creature not too bright or good
For human nature's daily food
For transient sorrows, simple wiles
Praise, blame, love, kisses, tears and smiles.

"Here's the P.S. 'This one was from LA.'"

"That's Jeanette Lernier's. Shit. This guy was sending Whitney Connolly the same poems that he was leaving at each kidnapping scene. That second P.S. makes it sound like she hadn't figured it out, that he was giving her more to go on. Taylor, honey, you are the greatest. Please keep going."

"The next is from Sunday, right after we found Jessica.

"A sudden blow: the great wings beating still
Above the staggering girl, her thighs caressed
By his dark webs, her nape caught in his bill,
He holds her helpless breast upon his breast.

"The P.S. says 'Do you get it yet?'"

Baldwin was getting excited. "That's the poem they found with Jessica's things. Right on, Taylor, thank God you were there to find these. What's next?"

Taylor read him the next e-mail.

"How can those terrified vague fingers push,
The feathered glory from her loosening thighs?
How can anybody, laid in that white rush,
But feel the strange heart beating where it lies?

"'P.S. From your backyard.'"

"That's Shauna Davidson, no doubt about it. What else?"

"The next one reads,

"Being so caught up,
So mastered by the brute blood of the air,
Did she put on his knowledge with his power
Before the indifferent beak could let her drop?"

Taylor stopped for a moment. "Marni Fischer?"

"Yeah, that's right. No P.S.?"

"No, this one is just the poem. What's up with that?"

"I don't know. Either he felt he'd made his point or he got into a rush. What else do you have there?"

"The next one's dated two days ago. It goes:

> *"She half enclosed me with her arms*
> *She pressed me with a weak embrace;*
> *And bending back her head, looked up,*
> *And gazed upon my face.*
> *'Twas partly love, and partly fear,*
> *And partly 'twas a bashful art,*
> *That I might rather feel, than see,*
> *The swelling of her heart."*

Taylor could hear what sounded like paper being brushed against the phone. She envisioned Baldwin raking his hand through his hair.

"That's what we found at the motel room where Christina Dale was killed. But you said 'The Flea' came in last night?"

"I have to pull it up and double-check the time stamp, but it came in sometime after Quinn and I left Whitney's house yesterday evening. I take it you didn't have any missing persons reports when you left Asheville?"

"No, we didn't. But if this follows the pattern, he has taken another girl. Dammit, this guy's on overdrive. I better get the word to Grimes, but we can't be absolutely sure he struck in Asheville. Of course, he could have taken someone that no one's missed yet. Listen, I've got a meeting as soon as I get into town. I've got to talk to the CEO of the company that owns some of the hospitals where three of the girls were employed. It's called Health Partners, he's going to go over some of the—"

"What did you say?"

"I'm meeting with the CEO of Health Partners," he said, and he could hear Taylor's breath quicken. She spoke softly.

"Baldwin, Quinn Buckley's husband works for Health Partners. He's a big time VP. There has to be a connection there, that's got to be what Whitney Connolly found out. You don't think…"

"He's a vice president, you say? I bet he does some traveling. Let's get together before I go over there. Can you meet me at your office? I'll be there in less than thirty minutes."

"Hurry, Baldwin."

Thirty-Four

He flashed by the car with the FBI agent in it. How funny was that? Here the man was looking all over the Southeast for him, yet if he had looked to his left, just for that one moment, he would have seen the grinning visage of the man he was trying to find. Such a pity really, they just didn't have a clue what he was up to.

He'd been watching the tall man from the FBI. He'd seen him stand quietly over Christina's body, seething, wondering. He wouldn't need to wonder much more. It was nearly time.

He wrinkled his nose. The smell in the car was getting worse. He was going to have to give his car a bath. Clean out the trunk, too, that was for sure, get some fresh ice for the cooler. It was a good thing that he had tinted windows, the look on his face must have been enough to cause some stares. There was always the bag on the floorboards in the back seat. A relatively non-descript leather bag, it was the contents that would get the tongues wagging.

The man smiled. This was going too well. He only had one more to go, then it was time for his triumphant return to watch the fireworks from the safety of his own home. He just hoped she was getting the picture at last. He knew how smart she was. This would make everything right.

Thirty-Five

Taylor sat at her desk, tapping her fingers on the bleached wood. Where the hell was Baldwin? She had caught his excitement over the phone and had been trying to go through the case herself. She was lacking the details, and the frustration mounted. She wanted to be out there chasing the killer rather than sitting in her office. She knew she'd helped, but damn, it would be great to be out there, gun in hand, stalking the stalker.

Lincoln and Marcus came into Taylor's office, interrupting her fantasy of shooting the bastard between the eyes. She started and smiled at them. For at least an hour, she'd forgotten all about Betsy Garrison and the Rainman case. She tried to play it off.

"Hi, guys. Good timing. Did you catch me a rapist?"

"Would that it was so easy to woo me, lady, simply drop a bad man in her lap and call him rapist." Lincoln gave her a smile through his pidgin Shakespearean answer.

"I take it that's a no?"

"It's a no. The print you lifted belonged to Brian

Post. So that was a dead end. Marcus and I have been going through all the personnel files from the area, looking for a cop who lives in the general vicinity that would go to those stores and that gym. We also asked around about the gym, and there are a few guys that go there. Problem is, none of them match the description of the cop that the latest victim is giving. And we talked to Betsy, and she can tell us for sure that it isn't any of these guys. She's familiar enough with them that she really didn't think they were worth looking at any further."

Taylor nodded to the chairs in front of her desk, indicating that they should sit. They did and she leaned back in her own chair.

"Marcus, what do you think? Do you think it's a cop?"

"No, I don't. At least not one of Metro's. Now, it's possible that she got the uniform or the car wrong, that it belongs to a Williamson County cop or something like that. We don't have the right to go into their files as of yet. We did go through the victim's background a little bit. She has a collar for resisting arrest and a DUI. I'm just wondering if she's fingering the cop that arrested her during her DUI, whether consciously or subconsciously. She has a restraining order filed against a guy named Edward Hunt. Thought we'd have a chat with him, as well. See if maybe he's been hanging around. Maybe she's just seeing things. Rape's traumatic enough. Anyway, it would be nice to get the DNA back from the TBI, but I suppose that's not going to happen anytime soon."

"Well, sounds like you have a plan, then. Go bug the TBI, see if they can help. I'm going to be working with

Baldwin for the rest of the day, but I'll have my phone if you need me."

They both looked at her but shrugged. It was her prerogative if she wanted to work off the reservation for an afternoon. They went on their way and Taylor opened Whitney Connolly's laptop, clicking on the button that took her into the dead woman's e-mail. There was nothing new, so Taylor got out of the program and started trolling through files until one caught her eye. Whitney had a file marked "Notes" that was dated the day she died. It had last been accessed that very morning.

Taylor opened the folder and saw a jumble of remarks and annotations. Whitney took notes on the computer in modified shorthand that would make more sense to a teenager text messaging her best friend. It was garbled and words were shortened, but she saw the six poems in their entirety with the postscripts, and the letter Q appeared several times. There were a few QJB entries, which she assumed stood for Quinn and Jake Buckley. But the rest was too garbled for her to make sense of. She knew some journalists took notes in a proprietary way so no one could steal their work, and it was obvious that Whitney was one of them.

She closed that file and started going through others. They were almost all in her peculiar shorthand. Better to wait and let Baldwin or one of Whitney's workmates figure it out.

Just as she thought of him, Baldwin appeared in her doorway as if she'd conjured him up from the dark recesses of her mind. Her heart skipped a beat when she saw him. Taylor got out from behind the desk and gestured for him to come in and close the door. He did, and she put her arms around him, drawing him into a hug.

Baldwin gave Taylor a deep kiss, one that she returned almost gratefully. He could sense that something was off, something had been off for a few days now, but he thought he knew her well enough to know that she'd talk to him about it when she was ready. In the meantime, he needed to find out if there was another victim out there.

Taylor broke off the kiss and gave him a smile, running her hand along the back of his neck in a way that made him want to forget all about the case and take her right there on the table. But she stopped, smiled a knowing smile, then reached down and turned the laptop so it faced the guest seat. She pushed slightly on his chest and he flopped into the chair, and she pushed the laptop across the desk so he could have easy access to it.

He took a deep breath, steadying himself, then became all business. "This is Whitney Connolly's e-mail?"

"Yes, it is. I have been through the e-mails and tried to go through her notes file, but she uses some crazy sort of typing shorthand and I can't make heads or tails out of it. What I do know for sure is that Quinn Buckley's husband is the vice president of Health Partners, you said three victims worked at hospitals that were owned by Health Partners, and Whitney is receiving e-mails of poems from the crime scenes. Since you said no one knew about the notes, that means the killer has singled her out to make contact with. I haven't put in a request to have her car checked for sabotage, it seemed like she had a legitimate accident. But I can have them start an investigation into it if you want me to.

"Plus, I think we need to do a little history on Jake Buckley's traveling schedule, don't you?"

Baldwin was popping his fingers across the keyboard on the laptop. He bit his lip, thinking.

"So the last e-mail came in after Whitney's accident, right?"

"Yes, it did. You can look at the time stamp, but it was definitely after she was dead. Why, Baldwin, what are you thinking?"

"I'm thinking that the killer doesn't know that Whitney is dead. Which means he's not here in Nashville, because I assume there was a lot of coverage on Whitney's accident over the past few days."

"It's been a lot of feel-good stuff. Her history, her credentials, her journalistic life, that kind of stuff. Nothing about her and Quinn's kidnapping. Just very sweet, respectful stories. You would think that she was everyone in town's best friend. But yes, there has been a lot of it."

"And I bet none of it went national, huh?"

"Well, I don't know for sure. We can call the network and ask. Why?"

"It doesn't matter. I talked to Garrett on my way in. The geographical profile has Nashville as one of three central staging points—it's less than a day's drive from each crime scene. If the GP is accurate, and the killer is from Nashville and doesn't know that Whitney's dead, that would explain why he's still sending her e-mails. What we need to do is start getting a back-trace on this e-mail address, and I need to get over to Health Partners and talk to Louis Sherwood. Have you talked to Quinn yet?"

"No, I didn't want to put it all out there, not until we know more."

"Why don't you talk to her, see if you can get something. Don't fill her in, just see if she drops anything good. I'll meet you back at home after our meetings, okay?"

He leaned across the desk and gave her a kiss, a kiss that was full of promise, and started for the door. His cell rang before he could get out into the hallway. He checked the ID. It was Grimes.

"Baldwin, we've got a report of a body in Louisville, Kentucky."

"But we never had a missing persons report from Asheville, right?"

"No, and we're hopeful that perhaps this isn't related. But Louisville is one of the cities on the list that Health Partners is in, so I thought we better check it out."

"Yeah, but did he grab someone from Asheville and take her to Louisville, or snatch someone in Louisville?"

"I can't tell you that. You're going to have to figure that one out for me. Are you going to Louisville? Do you want me to meet you there?"

"Right now, I need to follow this trail here in Nashville. Let me work this out for you, because some of this information I'm guessing at. The geo profile indicates that Nashville may be a staging area. I think the killer may be based here. I believe he's been in contact with one of the local reporters. I've been waiting to go over all of this with you until I could get a positive confirmation. I wanted to make sure the poems that were at the scenes match the poems he was e-mailing the reporter. They do.

"Now, the story gets a little crazy here. The reporter, Whitney Connolly, was afraid for her twin sister, was trying to pass along a message to her. But she was killed in an accident before she divulged the information. We've found out that the sister's husband, Jake Buckley, is a vice president with Health Partners. So there is definitely something to this side of things, and we need to get to the bottom of it.

"The killer e-mailed another poem to Whitney Connolly's e-mail, one that doesn't match what we have found so far. There's a body in Louisville. Most likely, that's what the poem correlates to, but we won't know until we get some identification."

"I don't know, Baldwin, I just don't know. This case, it's gotten away from me. From all of us. Do you even know when he sends the poems? Is it when he takes them? Or when he kills them? Where's he sending them from? Does he have a laptop?"

"I don't know the answer to that one, Grimes. Did you check with the community hospital in Asheville to see if they have any employees unaccounted for?"

"I did, and they don't have anyone that hasn't shown up for work. There's not a lot else I can do unless we get a missing persons report."

"What about the colleges? There are several schools in Asheville. We know that Shauna Davidson didn't work for a Health Partners hospital but attended a class there. Maybe there are students who come in to do lab work or something."

"Baldwin…"

"I know, man, I'm grasping at straws. I'm just trying to think…"

"No, Baldwin, wait. I think I've got an idea. Student health centers, right? They probably wouldn't have any ability to do lab work. Maybe they send out."

"Grimes, that's a great idea. Start at UNC–Asheville, it's the school closest to the hospital. Double-check they don't have anyone missing, make some calls to the other schools, try to track this down. Then you can head out to Louisville. I'll do what I can here to find out what's going on."

Disappointment spilled from Grimes's mouth. "Oh. Okay. I'm waiting on some more information to come in from Louisville, but I'll check things out here. In the meantime, you'll let me know as soon as you hear something?"

"Will do. Go get the college checked out. I've got a feeling about that."

Thirty-Six

Grimes drove through the gates of the University of North Carolina at Asheville and was struck by the beauty of the campus. It seemed like a very nice place to spend four years of your life. He followed the entrance drive to a large board that had all of the buildings laid out in a map. He looked for the student health center, found it and drove over there.

He got out of the car and went into the quiet building. There was a reception area, and he asked a pretty, blond girl sitting behind the desk if he could speak to the head of the center. She told him to hold on and disappeared. While he waited, he thumbed through a brochure that extolled the virtues of the campus health system.

A few minutes later, a woman came out from a back room, black hair shot with gray, hard lines etched deep in her upper lip. "I'm sorry, sir, but this is a private health center for the students of the university and you have to leave."

He badged her, making sure she saw the large blue-and-white FBI card first and foremost. She was still mouthy.

"I suppose you have questions about that poor dead lamb that showed up here in town. Well, that wasn't one of our students and we didn't have anything to do with it. So I'd appreciate it if you left."

"Are you done, lady? 'Cause I've got a few questions and I'd appreciate it if you'd shut up and answer them."

The rudeness shocked her into silence, and Grimes took advantage of the quiet.

"I need to know if you ever send lab work or anything else to the Asheville Community Hospital."

The woman looked at him for a moment. "If there's something that needs to be done for a student we simply send the student there, to the hospital. They can do things we can't in a few cases. A very few cases. We do have a full-service health center here," she boasted.

"Give me an example. When's the last time you sent a student down to the hospital?"

"Well, we had to send one young lady down yesterday for a chest X-ray. Our machine is down. She's been ill and the doctor thought it would be a good idea to rule out pneumonia."

Grimes leaned into the woman's face. "Who is the girl you sent?"

"Now, I can't tell you that. That's private information. I would—"

"Lady, tell me who it was or I'm going to arrest you, so help me God. I don't have time for this crap from you. *Who?*"

The woman became indignant. "Well. You don't have to yell. Her name is Noelle Pazia. There, satisfied?"

"No. Tell me how I can get in touch with Noelle."

"Well, I suppose I could call her if you insist."

He put a hand on her elbow and propelled her toward the door to her tiny office. "Let's go make that call. I'm trying to make sure one of your students isn't in trouble."

The woman gave him a look that made him think of his daughter's pet rabbit, nose twitching in fear, and picked up the phone. She dialed an extension, asked for Noelle Pazia and held up a finger to indicate she had been put on hold.

"The campus operator is routing the call," she whispered, though there was no reason for her to keep her voice down. Grimes paced a few feet in either direction until the woman spoke again. "Is Noelle there? This is Nurse Brooks at the student health center. She isn't. When did you see her last? You know she's very ill, she needs to be in bed. She didn't? Oh my. Yes dear, thank you." She hung up the phone and gave Grimes a look he could not distinguish, whether it was anger or delight he would never know.

"She wasn't in her room. She didn't sleep there last night as far as her roommate can tell. I assume that means she went to stay with one of her male friends." The nurse sniffed self-righteously, obviously not approving of such outrageous behavior. "A lot of the girls here do that."

"You know that Noelle has a boyfriend?"

"Well, no, I don't, I just—"

"Call that number again, I need to talk to the roommate. Tell her to meet us, right now. Go on, dial the phone. Then take me to her dorm."

The woman started to sputter but picked up the phone. She got the roommate and told her to meet them downstairs in her dormitory. The second she hung up, Grimes got a hold of her arms and propelled her toward the door before she had a chance to speak. She was in his car a moment later and pointing him toward the residence halls. His heart was sinking with every moment, he had a bad feeling that Noelle Pazia wasn't staying in a boyfriend's room, but was lying on the side of a road in Louisville, Kentucky.

He got out of the car and made his way to the front entrance of the dorm. A very pretty redhead stood in the doorway, a multicolored scarf wrapped around her neck, ends trailing almost to her knees. She looked concerned, and as soon as he was within earshot he heard her ask, "Where's Noelle?"

"I don't know. I was hoping you could help me with that."

"I spent the night at my boyfriend's place." Another, more audible sniff came from the nurse and Grimes turned, pointing a finger at her, a warning not to interrupt.

"Go on," he prompted. The redhead complied. "He lives here in town, he's an artist. She wasn't here when I got in this morning, around eight. Her bed was made, but she always keeps her bed made, and she gets up early, so that didn't strike me as strange. I assumed she went to breakfast. But she hasn't been back in the room."

"When is the last time you saw her?"

"The last I saw of Noelle was yesterday morning. She was going to go to the health center again, get some more medicine and try to take it easy. She's got a heavy courseload this semester, so she was spending a lot of time studying, in groups and alone. She would have had her study group at the library. All I know to do is talk with them. Here's a list of their numbers, Noelle had it on the refrigerator door. Please, just tell me she's okay. Her father's going to flip if something happened to her. She's too good of a kid, straight, doesn't drink, doesn't even date, for God's sake. She's here to get her education."

Grimes gave the nurse a dirty look. See, it said, she wasn't with a boyfriend after all. He was ready to be out of her company. "Do me a favor, okay. Please go back to the health center. I'll contact you if I need anything."

"Gladly," the woman snorted and stalked off.

Grimes took the list from Noelle's roommate. He leaned against the hood of his car and opened his phone. The roommate took the cue and looked at the list, running her finger to the bottom, tapping on the last name. She'd start there.

Grimes got two voice mails before a young man with an Indian accent came on the line.

"This is Harish?" He spoke with an inflection on all of his words that made every statement sound like a question.

"This is Special Agent Grimes with the FBI. Have you seen Noelle Pazia today?"

"Noelle? No, I haven't? She left our study group last night? I didn't see her after the break? Is she okay?"

The last sentence was a real question and Grimes could hear the concern in the boy's voice.

"What time was this break last night?"

"I don't know, around nine-thirty? Noelle was sick, she looked terrible? We suggested she go home, but she said she would be okay to finish out the group? We took a break, she got a phone call and she left? That's the last I saw of her?"

"And that was around nine-thirty, you say. She had a call and she did what?"

"Well, Noelle was very polite? She didn't want to take the call in the library, especially in our study group, and so she took the call outside? She told whomever it was to hold on, and she walked out the side door? She had her backpack with her, when she didn't come back we just assumed she went on home to bed? It would have been the best thing for her, she was really looking awful?"

Grimes thanked him and hung up. Left out the side door to the library. Damn. He turned to the roommate.

"Do you have a recent picture of Noelle?"

She hung up her own cell phone and nodded. "Yes, in the room. Hold on and I'll go get it. You think she's gone, don't you?"

"I don't know, but I really need that picture. Thanks." The girl trotted toward the stairs and Grimes dialed Baldwin's number. He answered on the first ring. Grimes filled him in on the situation, including the fact that the missing girl had gone to the Asheville Community Hospital for chest X-rays because the school's machine was down. As he finished, the roommate came back with a picture.

Grimes stared into the soft brown eyes, thanked the roommate and took her cell phone number, promising to call her within the hour with information. He got into his car, prepared to drive out of the campus, but he saw the library on his right and slowed. The poem. Baldwin said there was a poem sent to the reporter in Nashville that indicated another girl had been taken. He decided to check the library. If it was there, they'd have one more set of confirmations that this was their guy. Man, he was getting sloppy. He should have thought about that earlier.

He parked and walked around to what he assumed was the side entrance that young Harish had mentioned Noelle went toward when she got her phone call. He scanned the ground, the doors, and saw nothing out of place. He noticed that there was a bulletin board next to the door, sheltered from the weather by a plastic covering. He walked toward it, searching through the wanted messages and For Sale notices. Tutoring, no he didn't need that. Didn't need a new yoga ball and mat, didn't need…yes, there it was. Under two colored pieces of paper he saw a stark white sheet pinned to the board. He pushed open the plastic, and with a pen he grabbed from his pocket he pushed aside all the surrounding paper. Sure enough. Damn if he hadn't posted this for all to see, right there on the bulletin board. Son of a bitch.

Grimes read the poem aloud.

"Mark but this Flea, and mark in this,
How little that which thou deniest me is;
It suck'd me first, and now sucks thee,
And in this flea our two bloods mingled be."

Shit. Another one. He looked around wildly, as if the killer would be sitting nearby, enjoying the show. There was no sign of anything amiss.

The fact that he'd been left behind was not lost on him.

Baldwin, the FBI's glory boy, off chasing his solid lead while Grimes the grunt stayed behind, trying to play catch-up yet again. At least he had found the newest poem.

A girl in a stocking cap walked by, grinning at the crazy man mumbling to himself. He flipped his hand in front of his face, hoping to dismiss her gaze. He took a bag out of his pocket, angled the pushpin out of the note and the corked bulletin board, and managed to get it into the bag without touching it. He held the note by the edges and put it in the bag after the pin. Maybe they'd get prints off this one, who knew. But it wouldn't stand to do anything less than try everything they could.

Grimes went back to the car and drove out of the campus and toward his hotel. He had laid the photo of Noelle Pazia on the front seat facing him. Noelle's eyes stared up at him, accusing, sad, lonely, and he feared for her. He'd know soon enough.

He opened his cell phone and punched in a number he knew by heart. A man answered the phone.

"It's me," Grimes said.

"Hey, Dad, what's up? Have something new for me?"

"I do. Just found out there's a girl missing from Asheville, name's Noelle Pazia. There's also been a body found in Louisville, Kentucky. I'm assuming it's her, you'll have to do the rest on your own."

"Thanks, Dad, I appreciate it. Gotta run. I can get this on the wire right away." The phone went dead.

That's just how my life is, Grimes thought. Screwed up the case by not getting the poems, wife gone for going on four months now, a spoiled daughter who never spoke to him unless she needed money, a son that used him because he could give insider information and bolster the boy's fledgling career as a news producer in New York. Baldwin would kill him if he knew where the leak was coming from. Well, fuck Mr. Perfect Profiler.

He pulled into the lot of the hotel and parked. Taking the picture of Noelle with him, he went to the front desk. The information should be in from the Louisville office. Maybe Perfect Boy Baldwin had sent some of his pro-filing guidance too.

"Do you have a fax for me? Grimes, FBI?"

The man behind the desk gave him a nasty look. "I do, sir, and I have to ask that you refrain from having this kind of material sent over our fax lines. It's just outrageous. I won't stand for it, and neither will my manager—"

"Shut up and give me the fax." Grimes was so far out of patience that he wanted to punch the mouthy brat. Maybe he could arrange for the nurse at the school and this man to have a date.

The man flounced around the side of the desk and disappeared into the back room. He came out a moment later with a manila folder in his hand. "There," he huffed dramatically. Grimes just gave him a smile and slid the folder under his arm. He walked over to the bar and ordered a scotch. It was drawn and poured, and he took a sip, trying to calm his heart. He didn't want to know if Noelle Pazia was dead. He didn't want to imagine those bottomless brown eyes dull and gray. But he didn't have a choice. He could hardly ask the bartender to compare the photos.

So he swallowed the liquid courage in a single gulp,

pulled out the picture Noelle's roommate had given him and set it on the bar. He poised the folder above the picture and opened it. The sight made him want to vomit.

There was no question. Noelle Pazia was dead.

He looked away from the file and caught the bartender's eye, signaling for another shot. The man slid the bottle to him, it was as if he decided it wasn't worth the time it would take to refill the glass again and again. Grimes nodded his thanks and poured himself a glass to the brim. His hands were shaking as he brought the liquor to his lips. He needed to call Baldwin, give him the confirmation. Before he had a chance, his phone rang.

The call didn't take long. As he hung up, staring in disbelief at the cell, all thoughts of calling Baldwin left him. He set the phone down on the oak-planked bar. He pulled out his credentials case, eyes lingering on his FBI shield. All the things it meant to him. Fidelity, loyalty, bravery. Ah, this fucking case.

All he wanted to do was suck down a few more drinks and float away.

Fuck the Southern Strangler.

Fuck Baldwin and the FBI while you're at it.

Fuck it all that seven girls had died at the hands of this maniac. The hand burglar. For fucking what?

Noelle stared up at him with those baby-brown eyes, and he heard her voice in his head. "You're drunk, Grimes. It's okay, you don't have to get so upset. These things happen. You know that. These things happen and there's nothing you can do about it, you just have to try and catch the man who did this to me. To all of us. Do you understand what I'm saying? You need to catch him and stop him, he's going to do this again."

The big brown eyes started to cry and Grimes slammed the folder closed. Jesus, he couldn't take this anymore.

What was this freak hoping to accomplish? And here he was sending the poems to a reporter. Did he want to get the story out on the news? Or did he just have the hots for this chick? Did he just want to impress her? Well, it was going to be pretty hard to impress her now, buddy. She's dead, and you don't even know it. You can come and fuck her and get off on all the wonderful things you did for her, you stupid son of a bitch. She's dead and cold, and all of these girls are dead and cold, and you can't have any of them anymore, you bastard.

Grimes was shouting, hysterical, flinging his arms around and becoming more incoherent by the minute. He'd chugged his way through more than half the bottle of scotch and was looking like he needed a good place to sleep it off. That's what the bartender saw, he had come over to try and slow him down. Grimes was crying and blubbering, spilling liquid from his glass on the bar and the seat next to him. His hand was on his gun, and when the bartender tried to get him to stop he swung out his arm. Crying, he told the man to tell Baldwin he was sorry. He put the gun to his temple and pulled the trigger.

Thirty-Seven

Baldwin beat the early-evening traffic out of town, heading south on I-65 to Franklin. He took the exit onto Highway 96, into the heart of downtown Franklin, passing picturesque row houses and the quaint downtown square. Precise choreography got him through the traffic circle, he came out the other side and found himself in front of Health Partners headquarters.

He parked and went inside. The cool air-conditioning gave him goose bumps. He introduced himself to the receptionist, who sat behind a clear glass desk, showing off young supple legs. He was expected. She gave him a charming smile that he returned, then rose and indicated a door to her left. Coming out from behind the desk, she brushed against him provocatively as she walked to the door. He smiled, the girl couldn't be more than eighteen. Nice to know he was still remotely attractive to the younger generation. Not attracted to, of course. With a woman like Taylor at home, he wasn't attracted to much else these days.

"Do you need anything?" she asked, and he shook his head.

"Too bad."

The girl pushed a combination of numbers on a keypad and the door unlocked with an audible click. He followed her through the door, down a spare hallway and into a larger, more comfortable waiting area. A tall black man with crinkly gray hair came out of an office and made his way to Baldwin. He stuck out a hand and introduced himself.

"Louis Sherwood. You're Agent Baldwin? Good to meet you. That will be all, Darlene, thank you." The girl shot her boss a look of annoyance and left them.

Sherwood ushered Baldwin into a spacious office decorated in dark mahogany. Just the kind of office you'd expect from a CEO. Tastefully decorated, expensively accented, yet understated enough to make it seem that Health Partners wasn't totally rolling in dough. A nice presentation, overall.

Sherwood motioned to a matching set of overstuffed brown leather chairs with brass nails running up the sides. Was there an office anywhere that didn't have this kind of chair? Baldwin took a seat, and Sherwood sat opposite him.

"Can I get you anything, Agent Baldwin? Coffee, tea?"

"No, thanks, I'm fine. Darlene already offered."

"So then, what is it that I can do for you?"

"Like I said on the phone, I'd like to ask about your traveling employees."

Sherwood leaned forward and started running a rake through a Zen garden. "Any in particular?"

Baldwin's antennae went up. "Are there any in particular that you think I should be looking at?"

"No, no. I just wondered if you'd narrowed it down. We've got quite a few travelers on our rosters, as you can imagine." Rake, rake, rake. Baldwin sensed the man was killing time.

"How about we narrow it down to your people who have traveled to the cities in question, the cities you've lost employees."

"What cities exactly would those be?"

Baldwin gave Sherwood a long, level gaze and spoke as clearly as he could. "I'd appreciate it if you'd drop the act and tell me what I need to know."

Sherwood leaned back in his chair, appraising. Baldwin just stared him down.

After a moment, Sherwood broke into a huge smile. "Just testing there, son. Wanted to make sure you was on the up-and-up, you know? Just can't ever tell with folks these days. Now, you want to know about our travelers. Mostly, we send the girls on the road. Our marketing team only has one gentleman."

"Jake Buckley?"

Sherwood's eyes popped open. "Why, yes, as a matter of fact. Jake is one of the finest men I've ever had the privilege to know. One of the finest."

"That's great. Does Jake Buckley cover your interests in Alabama, Louisiana, Mississippi, Georgia, Virginia and North Carolina? And has he been traveling in those specific areas recently? I'm aware that he was here in Nashville during some of that time. That's all I need to know." He sat back in his chair and waited.

Sherwood's mouth drew into a firm line. "And I don't

think it's wise to go around sullying the man's name, if you know what I mean. He has a lot of very powerful friends…but that's neither here nor there."

"Mr. Sherwood, you don't seem to understand. You're in an interesting position. Several of the killer's victims worked for your companies. The media hasn't seized upon the connection, but rest assured, they will."

Sherwood's eyes narrowed, and Baldwin could see the wheels spinning. He picked up a pen and started twirling it, breaking eye contact as soon as he started to speak. Baldwin prepared himself for the lies to come.

"Now, Agent Baldwin, you have to understand. We're a small company here, just trying to make the world a better place for some people that normally wouldn't have the chances we give them. Do you understand that, son? It breaks my heart that we've lost three employees to violent deaths, it surely does. But could Jake Buckley be involved in those deaths? There isn't a snowball's chance in hell of that, you mark my words."

He leaned in close, ready to impart a great secret. Baldwin stayed put. "Buckley hardly knows what to do with a live woman. I can't imagine he'd know what to do with a dead one."

Sherwood leaned back, guffawing. "Naw, good ole Jake couldn't have done this. He's too twitterpated by that wife of his. He can't afford to fuck things up. She's got the money, not him. God knows I'm not paying him enough to live on."

"How much *are* you paying him, Mr. Sherwood?" Baldwin felt pure disgust. Over the phone he sounded like a man seriously intent on helping with the investigation. Now it was obvious that he was just an ass.

"Aww, son, that's neither here nor there. Isn't much more than a couple hundred, give or take. How much they paying you FBI boys these days? Bet I could make you an offer that would blow your socks off. How 'bout it? Come work for me, personal security. I can make it worth your while."

This was a fruitless endeavor. The man wasn't going to tell him anything. If he were a bit more jaded, he would think Sherwood brought him in to gauge his knowledge of the cases and the company, but he dismissed that thought. No, this was just a guy who had some power being a jerk.

"That's awfully kind of you, Mr. Sherwood, but I'm happy with my current position. I suggest you think about cooperating with me. It won't take me long to procure a warrant for your records." He stood and stalked to the door.

Sherwood just laughed. "You get a warrant, and then I'll chat with you."

"Count on it." Baldwin grabbed the handle and threw the door open, then retraced his steps to the locked entrance that led to reception. He banged through it to find Darlene, smiling expectantly at him.

Seeing the fury on his face, she dropped the cutesy affectation and gave him a sympathetic smile. He realized she was older than he first thought, probably more like twenty-five.

"Sherwood being an ass again?" she asked with a sigh.

Baldwin nodded. "I don't know how you stand him."

"I don't. Here. I have something for you." She handed him a plain manila file folder. He opened it and read ITINERARY in boldface at the top. "Jake

Buckley" was directly underneath. A quick scan showed that Jake's travel had taken him all over the Southeast, confirming Baldwin's suspicions. No more wasting time, and no need to get that warrant.

Baldwin looked up to see a tear in Darlene's eye. But her voice was hard. "Nail him, if he did this. Nail him for me."

Baldwin nodded, not knowing exactly what to say. He had the impression that perhaps Jake Buckley did know what to do with a live girl after all.

He took her hand, squeezing it gently, and sincerely promised to do just that.

Baldwin was finally home. The weather had cooled off after the storms, so he'd showered and defrosted a container of Taylor's homemade vegetable beef soup. He settled in to wait for Taylor to come home. He was also waiting to hear from Grimes. The man should have called by now to let him know if there had been any reports of a missing girl in the Asheville area. He'd talked to the men on the ground in Louisville, and it was starting to seem like this may be a different killer. Though the girl they had found was a brunette that seemed to be in her late teens or early twenties, there was no visible cause of death, and she still had her hands. The Louisville police were desperately searching their databases and tip lines to see if anyone had reported a girl missing that fit the description of their Jane Doe, but there hadn't been so far. Maybe they were in luck. If Buckley was their killer, he seemed to be taking a break.

Baldwin went to the kitchen, pulled a Guinness out

of the refrigerator, popped the top and poured it into a glass, then walked back into the living room. He should call Grimes, check his status.

He dialed the number, and an unfamiliar voice came on the phone.

"Who is this?" the voice demanded.

"This is Special Agent John Baldwin with the Federal Bureau of Investigation. Now, who are you?"

"I'm the one wiping blood off this damn phone so I can answer it. Do you know a Jerry Grimes?"

Blood? Shit, what was happening? Had Grimes managed to get himself into an accident?

"Yes, I do. I'm working a case with him. Can I speak to him?"

"Um, I'm sorry, sir, but you're going to have to wait on that. I'm Detective Moss, Mike Moss, with the Asheville police. It seems your friend Grimes had a little accident with his gun. Shot himself in the head. I'm sorry, but he didn't make it."

Baldwin sat in silence for a moment. Accident. Blood. Gun. Head. None of the words added up, and he shook his head, trying to sort them out.

"Wait a minute. Are you saying Grimes shot himself, or was shot by someone else?" Baldwin was up off the couch. This was bad. Very, very bad.

"No, sir, he shot himself. We're in the bar of the hotel that Mr. Grimes was staying in. It's absolute pandemonium here. Apparently he'd been in the bar drinking for a couple of hours and just lost it. Started yelling and throwing his arms around, the gun went off right next to his right temple. I'm willing to bet that our M.E. will find a way to call it an accident, but I'll tell you for true, he shot himself. Now, are you coming up here to claim the body, or what?"

"Whoa, man, slow down. I need something from you first, then I'll decide what to do. Did Grimes have anything with him? Files, his briefcase? Anything?"

He could hear the man asking the question to the room. He came back on the line.

"Yeah, there's a file that was sitting on the bar next to him, a manila folder with what looks like crime scene photos. And there was a picture on the bar, a real pretty little thing. Oh…" He got silent for a few moments. "The picture of the girl on the bar is definitely the same girl from the crime scene photos. There's also a plastic bag in the file, looks like it's got a note and a pushpin in it."

"Read me the note, please."

Baldwin listened as the man recited the first few lines of "The Flea." Dammit, Grimes.

"Tell me, does the picture have an identification with it? Is there a name or anything?"

"Yeah, there's a picture here, looks like an official school photo, you know, with the border along the bottom? Ah…damn, man, she's a student here in town. Goes to UNC–Asheville. There's a hand-written name on the back of the photo. Noelle Pazia, 2004. Damn, guess I have a dead body on my hands. Where do you think he left her?"

Baldwin realized the officer thought Grimes had committed the murder, then killed himself. "Whoa, no, Grimes didn't kill her. I believe that's the identity of a body found in Louisville, Kentucky. You're looking at the crime scene photos that were sent to Grimes from the Louisville police. We're operating under the assumption that the murder was perpetrated by the Southern Strangler. Which means I need to get the Louisville team up to speed on this. I need you to fax that information you've got in front of you to me immediately. Send it to this number—615-555-9897. And where are they taking Grimes?"

"He was declared here at the scene. Been transported to our M.E. Is there a family that we need to notify?"

"I'm going to call my boss. His name is Garrett Woods. He'll call you and get everything worked out. Damn. Grimes was a good man. You take care of him, okay?"

"Will do, sir."

They hung up and Baldwin sank into the sofa. Shit. What the hell had happened? He knew Grimes was tense and not holding up great. This was his fault, if he had stayed there maybe he would have been able to stop his suicide. He heard the phone ring and the fax tones kick in. He went into the office and watched as the photo of Noelle Pazia scrolled out of the fax machine. He looked in her eyes and for a moment thought he understood what Grimes had done. He'd been there himself once, too. But this girl, she was so full of innocence and hope and it spilled out of her eyes like a waterfall of goodness. And he was just looking at a fax, he couldn't imagine what the real thing looked like.

Not strangled, her hands weren't cut off. If it were the Strangler, he'd taken some kind of pity on this girl and hadn't ravaged her like the others. Baldwin didn't totally understand, but he could see that she was just so innocent that she might have just turned the killer off. Maybe that was it. He'd already taken her, but when he saw her he couldn't go through with it. Hell, he'd never know. These killers did what they wanted no matter what. Profiling them was almost a joke, you just never knew what they were going to do or say anymore.

Okay, man, pull yourself together. He needed to focus, there was a lot that needed to get done. He started making a list as he dialed the number for the field office in Louisville. A woman answered the phone and he asked to speak to the SAIC.

"That's me, Special Agent in Charge Eleanor Walker. How can I help you?"

Baldwin identified himself. "I've got an ID for you on your brunette. Her name's Noelle Pazia and she's a student at UNC–Asheville. He took her and no one missed her right away. The killing is being attributed to the Southern Strangler, though the information I'm getting doesn't match up with his MO. Am I correct in that information?"

"That's the information we have. The fact that the girl is from Asheville would tell me that it's the Strangler, but the absence of violence disturbed me, too. We've got an initial cause of death from the medical examiner up here—looks like she suffocated. High levels of histamine in her system, petechial hemorrhaging—he's calling it SAA, sudden asphyxic asthma. She had a fatal, massive asthma attack. We'll get as much evidence as we can gather, get it to Quantico ASAP."

An asthma attack. Now, that was interesting. Maybe she died before he could kill her. That would explain why her body wasn't interfered with.

"I appreciate that, Agent Walker. Right now, all I know is what you know. I'm working a lead here in Nashville and I've just been informed that we've lost an agent. I'm kind of up to my ears right now."

"Please tell me it wasn't Jerry Grimes?"

"You know him?"

"I do. There's been some rumors flying this afternoon. I talked with him earlier, sent him the crime scene photos of our Jane Doe, now ID'd as Noelle Pazia. He sounded drunk. Did he have an accident?"

Baldwin wasn't about to divulge the nature of Grimes's "accident." "You could say that. Things are a bit uncertain right now."

"Damn shame. Hate to lose one of the good guys."

Baldwin deflated. Grimes's death was going to haunt him.

"You're right. He was one of the good guys."

"In the meantime, I wish there was more information that you could give me, Agent Baldwin. We've got our own missing girl, and this one *has* been missed. Ivy Tanner Clark. Her father is Tanner Clark, the horse magnate. And he's making a fuss so loud I'm surprised you haven't heard it down there in Nashville."

Baldwin sat down hard. Shit. "Okay, there's something you need to do. We've just realized that the killer is leaving poems when he kidnaps a girl. You need to look in Ivy Clark's car, go through her personal effects. See if he's left a note."

"I haven't seen that information in the files." She sounded pissed, and Baldwin decided to head her off at the pass.

"We haven't been holding back, we've only known

about the poems for a couple of days. Do me a favor and get on it, see if there is one, okay? Get back to me as soon as you know." He rattled off his cell phone number and clicked off his phone.

He ran his hands through his hair and made the call he'd been dreading. He dialed his boss's number, heart in his throat. Garrett was not going to be happy with this call.

He answered on the first ring.

"I know already," he barked. "You didn't see it coming?"

"Well, maybe I did, but I certainly didn't think it was going to come down to this."

Garrett's voice softened. "You're going to have to let it go. I should have requested Grimes be pulled from the case sooner than I did."

"Sooner. What do you mean, sooner?"

"I talked to Grimes a couple of hours ago. Told him to drop everything and get his ass to D.C. They convened a disciplinary hearing in his honor."

"A disciplinary hearing?" He thought for a moment. "Oh, you've got to be kidding me."

"Nope. I did a little checking. Turns out Grimes has been doing a little off-the-record chatting with a certain news producer for one of the cable networks in New York. The producer was his son. Grimes was the leak. We talked to the kid, he denied talking to his dad at all. Refuses to release the name of his source for the information. But a quick check of Grimes's phone records refuted his claim. They've been talking regularly for the entire duration of the case."

"My, you've been busy."

"Yeah, and for what? A dead agent? Grimes wasn't going to be part of the FBI anymore regardless. So this one is on me, Baldwin. There's more than just this, in case you're wondering. His whole life was falling apart. With Grimes's death, there are several open issues that don't have to be addressed. That's all you need to know about that. Just keep moving forward. Don't look back."

Baldwin filled him in on the Jake Buckley scenario. Garrett concurred that they needed to have a conversation with Mr. Buckley, and fast. As they were hanging up, Garrett stopped him.

"Keep on it, Baldwin. You're getting close."

Thirty-Eight

Taylor had just hung up the phone with Quinn Buckley when Lincoln and Marcus appeared in her office door.

"What's up?" she asked.

Lincoln came in and sat down heavily. Marcus lounged in the doorway. "We've got good news and bad news. Just got out of the Tennessee Bureau of Investigation offices. The DNA sample from Lucy Johnson's rape doesn't match the earlier exemplars from the Rainman cases. The sample from her doesn't match any known offender in the system, either." Lincoln flipped open a file folder and consulted his notes.

"We talked with the man Lucy has the restraining order against, Edward Hunt? He is a former cop, retired from Metro last year, went to work for a top-dog security firm here in town. Runs their entire operation, makes a ton more than he did on Metro's payroll. Anyway, he and Lucy used to be an item, but he broke up with her. Seems Miss Lucy is quite the psycho, at least in his opinion."

Marcus chimed in. "From what Hunt says, they'd had a pretty rough time of it from the get-go. He wanted to break it off, she was desperate to keep him around. Long story short, she cornered him in a bar off Old Hickory, they had a few drinks, he went home with her and they had a farewell fling. Officially broke up, he actually started seeing someone new. According to Hunt, Lucy started stalking him, wouldn't leave him alone. He filed a restraining order against her, she responded by filing a TRO of her own. It's a bunch of crap, basically. Lucy came forward and said she'd been raped, Betsy answered the call. Lucy managed to make it seem like it was the Rainman. There's been enough info in the news that she was very convincing."

Marcus finally came in the office and sat down, looking discouraged. "Who knows whose DNA she had in her system. Hunt gladly volunteered a DNA sample, we've taken it and gotten it to the TBI. It's in the works. We've been chasing a phantom."

Lincoln tossed the file to Taylor. "I think you should bust her for filing a false report. Hunt seems like a stand-up guy, just wants Lucy to leave him alone. We're ready to go talk to her, confront her with Hunt's statement. If you want us to get a warrant sworn out against her, we will."

"Do it," Taylor said, furious. "She wasted countless man-hours for her own personal vendetta. You guys have been off chasing your tails because of her story, not to mention all the time and effort Betsy's crew put in. Jesus, and the TBI…yeah, go haul her ass in. We don't need this kind of crap. Maybe that will take some of the media attention off the 'mystery' victim as well. They can make hay out of this Lucy, for all I care."

"Will do, LT." Lincoln gave her a smile. "How's the Strangler coming along?"

She groaned. "It's coming. I'm on my way to meet Agent Baldwin right now."

Marcus leaned back in his chair. "You know, Taylor, about 'Agent Baldwin'?" He used his fingers to make quotation marks as he said the name. "You don't have to do that, you know. No one's going to care…"

She shot him a look, and he didn't finish his sentence, just grinned and got out of the chair, clearing his throat. "C'mon, Lincoln, we need to go get a warrant for Lucy Johnson."

Taylor stopped him. "Hey, you guys put together a statement for the press once she's under arrest so they know we're moving forward. They'll be staking out night court anyway, it'd serve her right to get filmed while she's being booked."

They left, Lincoln whistling a ditty, Marcus with his head held high. They'd done a good job ferreting out Lucy Johnson's bullshit, and they knew it.

Taylor watched their backs, running a hand through her hair. Agent Baldwin. She was utterly transparent. So much for that. She stood, gathering her papers. Time to get out of here. She left the office and exited the building, stopping on the stairwell to light a cigarette. As she stowed the lighter in her pocket, she saw Fitz ambling up to her.

"LT, glad I caught you."

"What's up, Fitz? I'm on my way out."

"I'll walk you to your car." He stepped in beside her. "Just got finished talking with Julia Page. Word on the street is that Terrence Norton is taking over the drug trade for the entire east side, but it's going to take more than a few conversations with informants to get the whole story. We're going to need a full-blown investigation, undercovers, the whole works. It's not something that I can get cleared up overnight, unfortunately."

They reached her truck and Taylor leaned against it, smoking the last of her Camel, thinking.

"Fitz, let's get this out of our hands. Talk to Julia, tell her we need to turn the whole thing over to the TBI. Homicide can't be responsible for running a drug sting. Let them take the lead, if we need to task out of Metro I'll have them talk to Price. Interagency cooperation, and all that bullshit. That sound good to you?"

"Sounds great to me. We'll have to deal with Terrence Norton on our own side of the fence soon enough."

She patted him on the arm. "I'm going home, work on some more stuff with the Strangler. Oh, by the way, Marcus and Lincoln—"

"Yeah, I know. No connection to the real Rainman. Wish we could have tied that up in a nice tidy bow for Betsy. We still waiting on her DNA results?"

"Yes, I haven't gotten word back whether it's a match or not."

"If I hear something I'll give you a call. Try and get some rest, we'll tackle it again tomorrow." He gave her a pat on the rump, a wink, and moseyed away.

Thirty-Nine

Baldwin was moving like a whirling dervish through the house. He had a cell phone to one ear, a portable house phone to the other, the desktop computer was on, his laptop was open and buzzing and the laptop that belonged to Whitney Connolly sat in a place of honor in the middle of the slate coffee table.

A new message was blinking on the screen, from the same address as the other poetic e-mails.

He heard Taylor come through the door but barely looked up, just gave her an absent "Hi" and went back to the computer screen. She came over to see what he was reading.

She read the words aloud.

> *"Thou know'st that this cannot be said*
> *A sin, nor shame, nor loss of maidenhead;*
> *Yet this enjoys before it woo,*
> *And pamper'd swells with one blood made of two;*
> *And this, alas! is more than we would do."*

Baldwin sat down hard in the leather chair, flipping the hair back from his forehead. "Just came in. It's been a bit of a rough afternoon."

"Let me get you something to eat, then you can fill me in. I'm starved, so I assume you are, as well."

"Yeah, I am. I already put some soup on. You had some of that vegetable beef in the freezer, it should be about ready."

She brushed her lips against his forehead then left the room, headed for the kitchen. He heard her rustling around and was struck by the normality of it. He belonged here. With Taylor. It was time to start thinking seriously about getting the hell away from the FBI.

A bloodcurdling scream coincided with the crash of china. He leaped from the couch and bolted to the kitchen.

"What, what is it?" he yelled.

Taylor was backed into the corner between the refrigerator and the wall, her right hand on her gun, the left holding the holster in place so she could unsheathe the weapon smoothly. He looked around wildly, trying to find the intruder. Taylor was white faced, eyes wide. As he took a couple of breaths, he realized that no one was in the kitchen.

"Someone outside?" he whispered, his own hand reaching for his weapon.

"Huge. Spider. Sink." Taylor hissed the words, teeth clenched.

Baldwin's eyebrows rose a full inch, and he burst out laughing. "What were you planning to do, shoot it?"

"Just. Kill. It." Taylor's hands had dropped to her sides, her eyes shooting daggers at him for laughing.

"What would you do if I wasn't here?" He went to

the back door, where a week's worth of newspapers were stacked neatly in a large basket, ready for recycling. He picked up a section, folded it in half and made his way back to the kitchen.

"I'd evacuate."

Biting his lip so he wouldn't laugh again, he looked at Taylor. "Evacuate?"

"Yeah. Go get Sam or someone. I don't like spiders."

"I've noticed. It's in the sink?"

She nodded. "Dropped right down out of the damn sky, landed on the plate I was taking out of the cabinet. I threw the plate at the sink. Christ, would you quit dilly-dallying and kill the damn thing?"

He held up his hands, the newspaper crackling in his left. "Okay, okay. In the sink, you say?"

"You're going to need something bigger than that flimsy piece of newspaper. I'm not kidding, it's a freakin' monster."

Baldwin sidled to the sink and looked in. "Damn!"

"Told you!"

Among the broken shards of a white dinner plate was the largest spider Baldwin had seen outside the Caribbean. They had banana spiders there the size of your hand, but this thing was running a close second. The body of the spider was the size of a small plum, the legs thick and hairy.

"I think you stunned it. It's not moving. You realize this is some entomologist's wet dream, right here. I've never seen anything like it."

"Just mush the stupid thing. Then clean out the sink, I don't want to see any trace of it. Jesus, I hate spiders."

Deciding his love wasn't wrong about the newspaper, he went to the back door and picked up a size eleven tennis shoe. "This oughta do it." He smashed the shoe into the sink, crushing the beast, and the remainder of the plate. "Eugh, that's gross. Okay, it's definitely dead."

He turned back to Taylor, who was still frozen in the corner. He was overwhelmed. Seeing her scared, vulnerable was just too much for him. He spoke before he could stop to think. "Baby, I want to be around to kill all your spiders. Forever. Starting right now. Will you—"

The phone rang, startling them both. Taylor was staring at Baldwin, but the words dried up in his throat. The moment was gone.

Finally breaking their gaze, he smiled and went to the other room, still carrying the remains of the very dead spider on his shoe.

Taylor only half heard Baldwin talking as she left the kitchen, working her way toward the back of the house. She pulled her 9mm out of its holster and ran it along the palm of her hand, as if she could pick up her gun and solve the ills of the world. There, that was better. She was still tough. Still ready to take on the world. Amazing that in the course of a few days she'd felt so out of control, enough that a spider rattled her to the point of no return. She imagined that must be what Baldwin felt, chasing after a phantom. What was he saying, there in the kitchen? From a man to a woman, the words *Will you* can only go a few ways, especially following the word *forever.* Interesting.

She stepped into the office, secured her weapon in

the gun safe, which she always left unlocked; there was no one to keep the guns from, other than her and Baldwin. She heard phones simultaneously hang up and stuck her head out into the living room.

"What's going on?"

Baldwin collapsed in a ball on the sofa. "Are you fully recovered from your trauma?" he teased.

"Yes. I'll have the exterminator out here first thing. They must have forgotten a spot last time." Baldwin was avoiding her eyes, trying not to smile. "Yeah, yeah, so I have them come spray once a month. I don't like bugs. And we'll have to order something in for dinner, 'cause I'm not going back in there until that mess is cleaned up. Now, what's going on?"

He ran his hands through his hair. "To start with, Grimes committed suicide."

"Are you joking?"

"No. He's been riding the edge on this case. Missing the poems really made him topple. Garrett was looking into the leak for me. Turns out Grimes's oldest son is a news producer in New York. That's how the media's been so on top of the game all along. Grimes was giving everything to his son. I should have seen this coming. I did see it coming. I left him behind in North Carolina because he was becoming a liability to the case, and it must have caught up with him. I feel terrible about it."

"I bet you do. But you know you can't blame yourself, Baldwin. This is a big case. He should have pulled himself from it."

"He tried. I told him it was okay, to ride it out. My fault. But there's nothing I can do about it now. I'll talk to his family, try to help, but…" His voice trailed off. There were so many other avenues he could have taken with Grimes. This one would stay with him for a while.

"Anyway, before he did it he ID'd the girl they found in Louisville as Noelle Pazia, from Asheville. The preliminary autopsy showed she died of an acute asthma attack. I'm betting he took her and she died along the way, before he had a chance to kill her. If that tracks, he would be furious that he couldn't kill her himself and would search for a suitable replacement immediately. I think he found one, we have a new girl missing. Ivy Clark from Louisville. The SAIC in Louisville just called me to let me know they've found a poem in Ivy Clark's car. So it's been a bit of an afternoon."

"Any word on Jake Buckley?"

"I interviewed his boss. Complete dickhead. Claims there's no way Buckley could have possibly been involved. He was totally uncooperative. But the secretary or receptionist or whatever she was, snuck his itinerary to me."

"Let me guess. Mr. Buckley has been through Huntsville, Baton Rouge, Jackson, Nashville, Noble, Roanoke and Asheville during his travels."

He looked at her, amazed. She smiled.

"I talked to Quinn Buckley for a moment. Told her we wanted Jake's opinion on the case since the victims had a connection to Health Partners. There's more. He is supposed to be in Louisville, and expected to make his way back to Nashville today or tomorrow. Quinn told me he doesn't keep to the schedule sometimes. I don't know, Baldwin, you need to go have a sit-down with this guy, and do it quick. I think Quinn's probably going to kill him. She's been trying to get in touch with him to let him know about Whitney, and she hasn't been able to nail him down. That sounds about right, doesn't it? He doesn't know that Whitney's dead. I think this may be your guy."

"By any chance did Quinn give you his vehicle?"

"Of course. Big shock, he's driving a BMW 740iL, silver, with Vanderbilt plates. Here's the number." She handed a slip of paper to Baldwin. "Shall I have a Be on the Lookout put out for our friend?"

"Do it, Taylor. And mark the BOLO armed and dangerous. He may have Ivy Clark in the car with him. You saw the new e-mail on Whitney's laptop? It's the rest of the stanza from 'The Flea.'" He recited from memory:

> *"Thou know'st that this cannot be said*
> *A sin, nor shame, nor loss of maidenhead;*
> *Yet this enjoys before it woo,*
> *And pamper'd swells with one blood made of two;*
> *And this, alas! is more than we would do.*

"I don't know what the symbolism means to him. That's the biggest problem, poetry, especially this type of romantic eighteenth-century work, is totally subjective. I can think 'The Flea' is about making love while another man may think it's about smashing an insect. You know how that is. So I don't even want to try to get into his psyche based on his poems of choice. But I promise you this, he wants Whitney to have these messages. I just wonder if the story was meant to *be* Whitney."

Taylor ran her hand along the back of Baldwin's neck. "Let me call in the BOLO. You need to try and relax for a few minutes."

"Maybe you could help me with that?"

"Maybe I can."

Forty

Taylor was lying on a warm, sunny beach, her long legs spread in front of her on a plastic chaise lounge. She shielded her eyes against the sun, watching the waves crest and break, tranquillity permeating her bones. There was no more to worry about. She was on a bona fide vacation with Baldwin at her side. She turned her head to take in his form, and instead was greeted by a sight that made her jump. Identical-twin midgets, both in blue double-breasted blazers and snowy-white ascots, stood at her right hand, leering. One held a silver tray with an old-fashioned rotary telephone. The phone rang, and Taylor shooed them away.

"I'm not taking calls today, boys." She started to roll over, get some sun on her back, but the midget with the phone stepped closer, shoving the tray at her. The phone continued to jangle incessantly, and Taylor finally reached out a hand…

She came awake, realizing that it *was* her phone ringing. She groaned and rolled over, picking up the receiver with a grunted hello. She reached a hand out to find Baldwin, but his side of the bed was empty. She focused her attention back on the phone. A chirpy voice rang out into the bedroom.

"Lieutenant, this is Metro Dispatch. I was asked to inform you that we have a possible home invasion in progress that your presence is requested at."

"Is anyone dead?"

"No, ma'am, the message I was given—"

"Then go away, Dispatch. If no one's dead, they don't need me."

"Lieutenant, Officer Parks is on the scene and requesting your company. He mentioned there might be a 216 involved that you would be interested in."

Shit. That got her attention. Bob Parks was a good friend, and if he thought there was a rape involved in the home invasion that she'd be interested in, and if she was being called off the books, that could only mean one thing. The Rainman.

Taylor was out of the bed, trying to balance the phone between her neck and ear as she struggled into a pair of jeans. She realized the TV was on—sure enough, the identical-twin midgets in blue blazers and ascots were parading across the screen in a ridiculous late-night infomercial. No wonder she had been dreaming about them. But hey, maybe their investment opportunities could make her millions and she could quit this crazy job.

"Where's the scene, Dispatch?"

"Off Old Hickory Boulevard across the street from Harpeth Hills Golf Course. A gated community called Middleton. Are you familiar with the area?"

"Got it, Dispatch. Tell them I'm on my way. Raise

Lincoln Ross and Marcus Wade for me, too, get them out there. I can be on-site in ten minutes."

She hung up the phone, buttoned her jeans, yanked on her cowboy boots and tucked in her T-shirt. Crossing to the dresser, she snapped her holster onto her hip, glanced into the mirror and smirked. This better be worth dragging her ass out of bed at two in the morning.

Baldwin was on the couch, half asleep, piles of paper scattered across the cushions and floor. Taylor gave him a quick kiss on the forehead, told him where she was headed and let herself out of the house into the dark. A soft drizzle misted through her driveway. Shit.

She got in her truck and slapped a red light on the dash. Speeding through Bellevue, she hit Old Hickory within five minutes, tearing up the deserted road, the stone guardrail flashing dark gray as she sped past. She passed the steeplechase course and the golf course, saw the stone entrance to Middleton a moment too late. A patrol car with emergency lights rotating sat at the entrance as she blew past. Braking carefully so she wouldn't skid on the wet asphalt, she made a quick U-turn and turned left into the community. The patrol officer held out a hand, stopping her. She put the window down and waved. The patrol turned friendly.

"Hey, Lieutenant."

"Good morning. Where's the scene?"

"Drive to the end of the road, then turn right. You can't miss it, there's a bunch of us down there. Why're you here?"

She ignored the question, gunning the truck and waving out the window as she drove through the big steel gates. The brick houses loomed like silent giants as she drove past. Porch lights spilled golden illumination into the street. She could see the flashing blue and white lights ahead of her. She followed the road to the end, parked behind the crime scene van, and made her way through the crowd to the tape that designated the crime scene control area. She saw Bob Parks standing in a puddle of light from a lamppost and went to him.

"Bob," she whispered in his ear, making him jump. He turned and gave her an uncharacteristically grim nod.

"Good, you're here," he said. "I thought you'd want to see this." He gestured toward the house, a stately two-story with white harled brick.

"What's happening? Dispatch said you had a home invasion with a possible rape?"

"Yup—911 got a call from a kid inside the house. Kid heard noises from downstairs and came down. Saw his mom wrestling with a man in a mask. Guy had slipped in through the back French doors, grabbed the woman as she slept on the couch. Kid's a smart little cuss, he ran right back to his room, locked the door and called 911. Patrol got here within a few minutes, but the guy had already done his thing and left."

"Did he rape her?"

"Yep. She's very shaken, but she did manage to tell us that he had a knife to her throat. It was all pretty fast."

"And you think it was the Rainman?"

"Well, it is raining. Plus the MO sounded right. I know you've been dealing with the case, thought you should be here at the scene."

"The kid all right?"

"Yeah, he's fine. Shook up, but he may have saved his mom's life, you know?"

"Thanks for the heads-up. I don't know how much I can do, but I'm glad you called. Lincoln and Marcus should be here soon. We'll talk to the vic, see if she remembers anything that could help. We'll have to get her to the hospital so they can do a PERK and check her out. Do you have guys searching around here?"

"We do, got the dogs, too. Vic said he took off out the back door when he was finished, right as the sirens were within hearing distance. There're heavy woods out there that back into the farm. That abuts to the parking lot of Christ Presbyterian."

Taylor stared off toward the north. "Did you get patrols in their parking lot? He may have parked there, then come in on foot."

"Yep. We're on that. We don't have anything yet. Like I said, just thought you'd want to know what was happening."

Taylor touched his arm. "I appreciate it, Bob. You did good to call me. Go on and do what you need to, I'll just wait for Lincoln and Marcus and get into the house in a minute."

With a nod, Parks went off toward the house. Taylor took in the scene. There was a large crowd of people assembled, watching the drama unfold. Women in bathrobes and men in sweatpants stood in knots, necks craning to see whatever they could. Taylor was reminded of an evening when she was in her teens and a neighbor's house caught fire. It seemed the whole neighborhood had gathered in the street to watch the conflagration envelop the home. People were drawn to tragedy like moths to a flame.

Years of training unconsciously kicked in, and she

looked at each face in turn. No one seemed out of place. Tired countenances, lit with anguish, but all looking appropriately rumpled from being wakened in the middle of the night by sirens. She shook her head and turned toward the noise of another engine making its way down the road toward them.

Lincoln Ross pulled up in his assigned vehicle. They weren't supposed to bring personal cars to a crime scene, and he had grabbed an unmarked and made his way to the west side of town. Marcus was riding shotgun. What good boys, she thought. As she started toward them, a shadow caught her eye. She looked to the right, could have sworn she saw someone moving along the side of the house. Lincoln got out of the car and she silently got his attention, motioning with her head toward the house next door. She started that way slowly, not wanting to look as if she was chasing anything in the gloom, but intent on finding out what had caught her eye.

Lincoln and Marcus joined her and they formed a flying V, walking slowly and carefully toward the darkened edge of the house. Lincoln whispered in her ear.

"What'd you see?"

"I don't know," she whispered back. "Looked like a person standing on the side of the house. I just saw a quick shadow move. Might've been my imagination."

"Might've not," Marcus growled. He unsnapped his holster, and Lincoln and Taylor followed suit.

They were ten feet from the house. On top of the musky scent of soaked grass, Taylor thought she could smell a hint of gasoline. She stopped midstalk and turned to Lincoln. "Smell that?"

"No. I don't smell anything."

"Oil," Marcus said. "Smells like a garage."

They shared a look of horror, having the same thought at once. Was someone trying to set this house on fire? Caution thrown to the wind, Taylor took off in a sprint. As she turned the corner of the house, she barely caught a glimpse of a shoe dangling off a retaining wall.

"There he is!" she shouted, racing to the wall. She missed grabbing the ankle that belonged to the shoe by a fraction of a second. "Dammit, he's gone over the retaining wall. Parks!" she yelled. "Parks, get your freakin' dogs over here! He went over the wall!"

With that, she took a running jump, pulling herself over the wall in one clean leap. She landed hard on the other side, breath knocked out for a moment. She could hear rustling and muttered cursing. Lincoln and Marcus came over the side.

"You okay, LT?" Marcus hauled her to her feet.

"Yeah, yeah, let's go. He went through there." She pointed into the dark woods. Lincoln snapped on a Maglite, Marcus followed with his. They could hear someone making his way quickly through the brush. Dogs were barking, people were screaming. Taylor took off after the noise.

Branches scraped her face, and she put up an arm to ward off their blows. The shadowy figure they were chasing couldn't be more than forty yards in front of them. The going was rough. Marcus tripped on a branch and his Maglite disappeared, making Lincoln's one beam the only light they had. Then suddenly, the forest cleared and they were racing through the field that led behind the farm. Taylor could see the man they were chasing, he was getting winded, slowing up. She was gaining on him, could hear a dog to her right making tracks toward them. She didn't want to be mistaken for the perp by the dog; he wouldn't be discriminating when he started to bite.

She pushed herself a little harder, long legs stretching out, running as hard as she could. The man was five feet away now, three… She left the ground and had her arms around him, taking him down from behind. He fought and kicked, lashing out, screaming at her. Lincoln was right behind her and grabbed on to the man's leg, fighting him, trying to get a hand on his arms. The man turned ever so slightly in Taylor's arms, and suddenly she saw stars. The impact of his fist snapped her head back and she almost let go. Suddenly Marcus was there, he and Lincoln had him. They rolled him over, snapped on the cuffs. She finally thought to breathe, realizing it hurt everywhere she could feel.

The German shepherd was three feet away, on point, barking furiously at the suspect. The cacophony of shouts and barks nearly drowned out the suspect's screams.

"Get off me, you pigs! I didn't do anything. Get the fuck off me." The man was only able to squirm under Lincoln and Marcus' combined weight.

The dog's handler appeared, calling him off. The German shepherd barked a few more times, then stood at attention, droplets of rain gathering on his whiskers, whining. Four more men came into view, and Lincoln rolled to the right, giving them access. Marcus got to his feet, dragging the man with him. The officers were all screaming different commands, pushing the suspect around. Taylor rolled onto her butt and sat, catching her breath.

"I'm telling you I didn't do anything. False arrest, false arrest. Let me go!"

"That him?" she asked, the roar quieting at her commanding question. "Did we get the son of a bitch?"

The man was practically being strip-searched, with affirmative answers coming from all involved.

"Got a ski mask here."

"Got the knife."

"He's got rope in this pocket. Shut up, you crazy motherfucker. We've got your ass."

Taylor rose to her feet. She strode to the man, who was still struggling. He stopped when he saw her, smiling a crazy smile. Her eye hurt, her head hurt, her legs were tired. But it looked like she had her man.

There were several flashlights trained on him, giving plenty of light for an initial assessment. She gave him a once-over. He was wearing black cargo pants and a black T-shirt. He was thin and wiry, with ropy muscles snaking along his forearms. He was wearing black combat boots.

"Quite the little ninja, aren't you? What's your name?"

"Fuck you."

"Nice. Any ID on him?"

A few more pats, then a laugh. "He's got his wallet in his pants pocket. What a frickin' idiot." The officer passed Lincoln the brown leather wallet. He opened it and extracted the man's driver's license.

"Smart move, Norville. Folks, I'd like you to meet

Norville Turner. Norville, meet the people who are responsible for making your life a living hell from here on out." He looked at Taylor, shaking his head in the gloom. "Brings his wallet along. Brilliant."

"I didn't do nothin'. You got nothin' on me, pigs." Turner started struggling again and was quickly subdued.

Taylor got eye level with him. Stared into his eyes, searching. Realized that they'd taken him down for good. She wrinkled her nose. He smelled like dirty oil. "Shut up, Norville. Your fly's open, you dumb ass."

He lunged and before she could jerk away, he spat at her. "Stupid cunt. What the fuck're you doing? I didn't do nothin'."

Taylor wiped at her face, furious. His captors started in on him again, but she stood her ground, waiting. When all the struggling and yelling finally stopped, she smiled back at him. Then she hauled back her right arm and landed as hard a blow as she could right into his jaw. His head snapped back and his knees buckled. The officers around her whooped and laughed. Lincoln came to one side, Marcus to her other.

"When he wakes up, tell the fucker he's under arrest." Shaking her hand, her ponytail streaming down her back, she turned and walked away.

Taylor crashed back through the woods with Lincoln and Marcus in tow. Her head was throbbing and she was having trouble seeing out of her right eye. She felt wonderful.

Returning to the scene, they saw complete pandemonium at hand. More patrol cars had piled into the street, an ambulance was parked catty-corner to the driveway of the victim's house, lights flashing merrily in the night. The ubiquitous news vans had arrived. Taylor checked her watch, it was nearly 5:00 a.m. The newsies would be able to give live shots on the early-morning broadcasts.

"Lincoln, Marcus, get on the horn with Price, tell him what just went down. I want to check in with the victim, see how she's holding up. You'll need to get the suspect down to booking, then make up a six-pack for me. We'll want to see if the victim can ID him. Maybe the mask slipped. Either way, he'll need to be processed. Make sure it all goes smoothly for me, okay?"

"Gotcha, boss. I'll call ahead and have a photo array put together. I'm sure we can find five mug shots similar to this hosebag." Marcus took her by the arm, turning her toward him so he could get a better view. "You're gonna have one helluva shiner in a couple of hours."

Taylor used gentle fingers to explore her face. Wincing, she decided she didn't want to see what she looked like anytime soon. "Yeah, well, all in the line of duty, you know?"

Lincoln appeared at her side, offering a chemical ice pack he'd lifted from the back of the ambulance. "Here you go. You want me to stick around?"

"No, you two go handle downtown. I'm all right here. Thanks, though." She nodded at them in dismissal and started toward the house, holding the ice pack over her eye, trying not to jar her head. It had been a while since she'd taken one in the face, and she'd forgotten how much it hurt.

Brian Post was exiting the house as she reached the front door.

"Hey there, good to see ya, LT. Heard you took the bastard down all by yourself."

Taylor dropped the ice pack from her face. Post whistled long and hard.

"Wow, that's some shiner. You okay?"

"I couldn't be better. How's our vic?"

"You need a towel?" He eyed her dripping hair dubiously.

"No, it's letting up."

"Okay. Let me take you in." They started toward the door, Post chattering away. The adrenaline had consumed them all. In a few hours they'd crash, but for now they were all on speed.

"When we got the call, it was all I could do to keep Betsy in the bed. She wanted to come charging down here, deal with the vic herself. I practically had to handcuff her to get her to stay."

"That's my girl." Taylor gave him a crooked smile. "I wouldn't expect anything less out of her. She's a ballsy broad."

The inside of the house was lit up like a Christmas tree, every light in the house glared. Ignoring the setting, Taylor went directly to a small brunette wrapped in a white sheet. Good, she thought. Standard protocol for a rape victim, wrap her up and make sure she didn't contaminate the evidence, or lose any by changing before they got her to the hospital and took all the samples for the PERK, the physical evidence recovery kit.

The woman looked up at Taylor, eyes glazed. "Who're you?"

"I'm Lieutenant Taylor Jackson. I wanted to check

on you before we take you downtown to Baptist. Are you okay?"

"I'm Nancy. Nancy Oldman. I'm…well, I'm not okay, but I will be. The officer over there said that you might have caught him? The man who…who raped me?" The woman's small pointed chin lifted a fraction, her strength not completely sapped.

"We did have an altercation with a man outside your property line. Can you tell me anything about the man who attacked you?"

Nancy sniffed hard, tears welling up in her eyes. Just as quickly, they were gone. "I didn't see his face. He had a black ski mask on. But he stank. Smelled like gasoline, or something. He was quick, just grabbed me, threw me down and it was over so fast, I just don't know what to tell you. It seemed like an eternity but I know it couldn't have been that long. I mean…" She was babbling but stopped and drew in a deep breath. "You're hurt. Are you okay?"

Taylor stooped to get to eye level. "I'm fine. Nancy, we're going to need you for this. Are you willing to testify against the man who did this once we have him officially in custody?"

The chin came up another fraction of an inch. "Yes. I'll testify."

"Good girl. I'm going to let you get to the hospital here with Detective Post. You've done great, Nancy. I'll talk to you soon, okay?" Taylor patted her awkwardly on the knee, the sheet rustling under her hand.

She smiled at Post then left the house. She needed a hot bath and some Advil, take some of the sting away from her bruised face. But first, she had to run the gauntlet.

As she got to the end of the driveway, the din started. Reporters fought in a rugby scrum to get to her. She stopped, held up her hands. The lights flared in her eyes and she was blinded for a second. She heard a gasp from one of the women; she couldn't see which one it came from but surmised that she must look like hell. She ran her hand through her hair, trying to get it in some semblance of order. A leaf fell out and she almost laughed out loud. The wild woman of Borneo speaks to the press.

"I have a brief statement," she said and the crowd hushed.

"We have taken into custody a male Caucasian who was apprehended running away from the scene of this home invasion. It is possible that he was the perpetrator of this crime. I'm sure the department spokesman will have plenty more information for you later this morning. Thank you." She turned and started toward her truck. The cries followed her.

"Lieutenant, was this the work of the Rainman?"

"Have you finally caught the serial rapist?"

"Has he been taken to night court?"

"Did he hit you, Lieutenant?"

That one she decided to answer. She turned back to the reporters and tried to wink, but her eye wasn't working properly. "At the very least, he will be charged with assaulting an officer." She gave them a smile, then got into the truck and headed for home. All in a night's work.

Forty-One

"Dear God, Elle, you have to stop. I need to get on the road and get home. My wife's going to kill me if I don't make it back soon." In response, the brunette just smiled and slid lower down his body. He felt the warmth of her mouth, and the dark head started bobbing up and down, harder and more rhythmically, in his lap. He lost himself for the moment. Why not get off one more time before he headed back into the frigid world he called a family? He couldn't remember the last time his wife had been in the position Elle was in. The brief thought of Quinn on her knees was enough to push him over the edge. Elle jerked back in response, giving him a dirty look.

"Sorry, Elle, I lost track. I apologize," he said to her back as she went to the bathroom to wash out her mouth. Women, he thought, can't do anything right with them.

He zipped his pants and stood, stretching to nearly six foot four. He glanced in the mirror and saw that his sandy-blond hair was mussed. He ran his fingers through it to smooth it down and caught the sadness in his eyes. He couldn't identify the exact moment that being in a hotel room with a virtual stranger was a better alternative to being at home with his wife and their two kids, but somewhere, somehow, that had become the norm. He'd finish a trip but not want to go home. He would find himself lingering over the end of a presentation with a sales rep here, or accepting a dinner invitation from a marketing department head there, and his serial promiscuity had begun.

It was fun for a while. It was nice to have a woman fawn all over him, even if he was the boss and deep down he knew what they were looking for. But after Quinn had discovered the proverbial lipstick on his collar, except it was on a pair of boxer shorts, any hope of reconciling with his wife left him. They stayed in the same house, raised their children, but didn't speak a word to each other than what was necessary for civility or pretense.

He wished he could undo things, make it right with his wife. If he could just go back to that moment that things went south. Quinn had shared a secret that had floored him. He had not reacted well, and she had simply shut him down. He tried to get her to see reason, that he was only surprised, not repelled, but she was having nothing of it. So his enforced exile had begun, and before he could stop it, it was too late. His marriage was done.

His companion came out of the bathroom and struggled back into her skintight clothes. She slid a zipper up her left side, fluffed out her hair and stood looking at him expectantly. He started to say something to her, anything, but he couldn't get the words out. He was just too damn tired. He'd been on the road for weeks, traveling all over the Southeast, and dammit, he wanted to go home to his wife.

Elle stood there a moment longer and realized her ephemeral lover was not going to profess true love and offer to sweep her off her feet and into his BMW-clad wheels. She stomped haughtily from the room and he breathed a sigh of relief. Oh well. She wasn't the right type anyway. There would be others. In the meantime, he had time to catch a shower, load up the car, have a beer or two in the hotel bar, then make his way back to Nashville.

The BMW stood in the shadows, out of the soda vapor lights that dominated the parking lot of the hotel. Without the keys it was harder, but it was not a huge problem. Checking to make sure no one was watching, he slipped open the driver's-side door and pulled the latch for the trunk. He walked quickly to the back of the car and lifted the trunk lid open silently. The cavernous space yawned at him and he smiled. Plenty of room.

He pulled up the carpeting and exposed a small hole meant for a spare tire. The spare was gone, he had taken it out months before to make room for all of the accumulating crap that accompanied him on his road trips. It made the perfect hiding spot. He placed the bag in the hole lovingly, then placed the carpet back over the spot. With a last look around, he walked to the edge of the parking lot where he'd left the girl. He reached down for her, amazed, as always, at how much they weighed when they were dead. It seemed they were as light as a feather when they were in his arms, but after they stopped breathing they became as heavy as lead. He swung the girl up and over his shoulder and staggered the last few feet to the trunk of the car. With a heave, he flopped her into the trunk, watching with a smile as her hair fanned itself perfectly around her pale face. He couldn't have done that if he tried. It was faultless.

There. Now it was time to go home.

Forty-Two

Baldwin ran his fingers through his hair and made the ends stick up like quills on a hedgehog. He'd been up all night, unable to get any restful sleep. Grimes, a faceless killer, dead bodies had swarmed through his troubled dreams. He'd finally roused himself at 3:00 a.m., after Taylor had left in a rush, and powered up his laptop. He went through his notes again and again, trying to make all the details fit into a pretty little package.

The transportation of the dead girls was bothering him. There were a few tight time frames in Buckley's schedule. Mapping it out, it was clear that he must have skipped some flights, driven instead. Of course, itineraries change, flights are missed, rental cars lost. He'd put in a request for all of the rental cars Buckley had used to be worked over by forensic teams, but that could be a mute gesture. The feds would be working that today.

He got into the shower, stood under the stream of water and made a mental note that he needed to change the filter on the showerhead. The thought stopped him. In the middle of all of this death and mayhem, he was worrying about water pressure.

He let the water run a few moments longer, then snapped off the faucets and stepped out from behind the plastic curtain. He wanted a new house with a shower and tub that were separate, but he wasn't sure how to approach Taylor about it. He knew how much she loved their house, the cabin sanctuary that she had created for herself, and then him, to live in. But it was a small place for two people, and what happened if they got married and had kids? They would need a bigger house for that anyway, unless they wanted a child living in a hammock in the loft, strung above Taylor's precious pool table. He laughed to himself at the image. All he knew was that he wanted to spend the rest of his life with her, and give her anything she wanted. Kids, house, dogs or cats, it was hers. He just prayed that she would feel the same and want to let him give her the world. Taylor was a strong woman, but he could not believe that she would not want to be with him exclusively forever. Well, he would have to tackle first things first, and a marriage proposal was top on the list. He had already bought the ring, it was this damn case that had interrupted the events that he had planned. He'd almost managed it in the kitchen last night. She'd circled him warily for the rest of the evening, as if he was a bomb about to explode. He laughed and vowed to himself that the minute they caught this bastard, he was asking her to marry him. The thought gave him new resolve, and he dressed quickly and walked back to the study.

Jake Buckley was looking more and more like a plausible suspect in this case. A BOLO had been issued for the man's BMW, the airports had been faxed pictures of him in case he tried to hop a plane; train and bus stations were circulating pictures among the ticket agents, yet he was nowhere to be found. Nor had any trace of Ivy Clark been discovered. He checked his watch, it was almost noon. Seven girls dead and one missing. He shook his head. It was just too much sometimes. He understood that. But Grimes had not, and Baldwin was sorry about that. There wasn't much Baldwin could do when a fellow agent was on that track, despite Garrett's admonishments. He still thought he should have seen it coming. Regardless, he couldn't get himself into a funk over it now. There was too much to be done.

Baldwin went back to tracking Buckley's exact timeline and whereabouts to see if Buckley was in the specific area when the girls were kidnapped. As vice president of Marketing and New Development for Health Partners, Jake Buckley traveled a great deal, checking on new properties, making sure the established hospitals were running properly, making adjustments in staff and provisions for the hospitals that were under way but not totally established yet. A lot of responsibility lay on the man's shoulders.

The first thing Baldwin had done was simply match his schedule to the timeline of deaths and kidnappings. Jake Buckley had been in every one of the cities that the girls were missing from as they went missing, and was at each town where the bodies had been dumped on the day they'd been found. The timeline matched. He'd driven his own vehicle to many of the meetings, but in some cases he'd flown. That's why Baldwin had put in the call about the rental cars. It was a long shot, but everything needed to be checked out.

He had started to pull the files together when the phone rang. He looked at the caller ID and saw it was Taylor. He answered the phone with a smile in his tired voice.

"Hi, honey."

"Hey there. You making any progress?"

"Not really. I was just finishing the timeline to see if Buckley's actual travel matched with the kidnappings and murders. They do, to a tee. Everything okay with you?"

"We've finally had a break in the Rainman case. The call I got last night? He broke into a woman's house and raped her. But we caught him." He heard the pride in her voice.

"What happened with that victim you were interviewing?"

"Oh, that's right. I forgot to tell you about that last night. I can safely say she was just a woman scorned. She'd basically made the entire story up to get back at a former boyfriend. There was enough information in the paper for her to make some pretty educated guesses as to how to make herself look like a victim of the Rainman, but the DNA came back and didn't match the other cases. We arrested her for making a false report. In the meantime, this asshole went off for another night of jollies. We took him down leaving the scene. It was great."

"Tough girl. Only you would describe a takedown as great," he teased.

"Anyway, that's not why I called. Fox News is getting ready to do a one-on-one interview with Tanner Clark and one of Ivy's friends. I thought you might want to see it."

"I do." Baldwin got up and started rummaging for the television remote. "Where did you hide the remote for the TV in the office?"

Taylor laughed. "Yeah, I hid the remote. I never watch TV in the office. Sorry about that."

"Okay, okay. Had to ask. When will you be home?"

"Hopefully soon, barring any bizarre happenings. Brian Post has the rapist and is questioning him now. You'll be there?"

"I'm planning on it unless something breaks. I'll make you something nice to eat."

"That's so sweet of you. Here you are, in the middle of this big bad ugly case, offering to make little ole me dinner. Whatever happened to that big tough cop I fell in love with?"

"Hush up. We'll talk when you get home."

"Yes, sir. By the way, you might want to put an ice pack in the freezer for me. The son of a bitch tagged me when we were chasing him, I look like half a raccoon."

"Are you okay?"

"I'm fine, sweetie. I haven't felt this good in weeks."

"All right then. I love you." Baldwin waited for the love-you-bye response that Taylor always gave then hung up the phone. He'd have to scramble to come up with something great to make for her. The woman loved food, though her metabolism was filled with jet fuel. She could eat anything and never gain a pound.

Baldwin found the remote hidden behind a fern on the bookcase and laughed. He swore Taylor moved it around and hid it just to make him crazy. He pushed the power button, and when the picture came up put in the satellite number for Fox News.

He was just in time. The pre-interview information was being given and the anchor, a sandy-haired man with round glasses, was giving some last-minute details.

"It's believed that Ivy Tanner Clark could be the eighth victim of the vicious serial killer known as the Southern Strangler. Ivy has been missing for twenty-four hours now and we have her father and best friend linked by satellite from Louisville, Kentucky, to give us some more information. Mr. Clark, can you hear me okay?"

The screen split, and the image of an attractive, silver-haired man with Ray-Ban Orb sunglasses came onto the screen. The lenses of the sunglasses were polarized, and they looked dark yellow under the studio lights. He looked more like a Hollywood actor than a grieving father. The man had his faded jean-clad legs crossed, an ankle across the opposite thigh, and Tony Lama brown suede cowboy boots peeked out from the overlong jeans. His shirt was snowy-white linen and his tanned body rippled beneath it. The man oozed sex and money, he was a perfect example of Ralph Lauren's vision for the horsey set. Watching the silent show, Baldwin understood how Tanner Clark came to be known as the don of the horseracing world.

"I can hear you fine." The man's voice was booming, commanding, and the anchor smiled. It would be a strong interview.

"Mr. Clark," the anchor continued, "we understand that you believe your daughter has been taken by the Southern Strangler. Can you tell us what information you have been given that has led you to draw this conclusion?"

"My little girl is missing, and I want to plead with whoever took her to please let me have her back. I'll be posting a hundred-thousand-dollar reward for any information leading to her safe return. She's such a sweet girl, she never hurt anyone. Please, please, just let her go." His head dropped into his hand and his shoulders started to shake. A small arm appeared from his left and the camera pulled back to show a young girl comforting Clark. The alleged best friend, of course.

The girl looked young, younger than Ivy Clark's age of twenty-one, but the cameras could be deceiving when it came to youth. She could have been twelve or thirty as far as Baldwin knew. The way she touched Tanner Clark made him wonder if there wasn't something more between Ivy's best friend and Ivy's megamillionaire father. A montage of pictures filled the screen while the man broke down. Ivy on a horse, Ivy in a ball gown, Ivy in jeans and boots and a tiny pink tank top with a young man who looked suspiciously like Prince William.

The anchor wasn't about to lose the shot of the grieving father, but he had gotten to dead air and needed to keep the interview rolling. "Miss Simone, is that right?"

"Yes, I'm Serene Simone." She had a slight accent that Baldwin wanted to say was French but he could not be absolutely sure. "I am Ivy's best friend. She is dear to me and I want to echo Mr. Clark's sentiment. We just want Ivy back home safe and sound."

"Can you tell us a little more about Ivy, please, Miss Simone?"

As she began to speak, the montage started again. Ivy Clark was a stunningly beautiful young girl who looked like she could have a good time. She was smiling in all of the pictures, and Baldwin could see the sparkle of a small diamond in her right nostril. A photo of her in an open-backed dress showed a couple of tattoos on her shoulder, and another shot of her from the back showed some sort of tattoo on her lower back. Baldwin pulled the missing persons report to the front of the file and read a bit more. Chinese symbol on the inside of her right ankle, a small dragon on her bikini line, a rose on the top of her foot, a small butterfly on her right shoulder blade and more Chinese symbols on her lower back. They should not have any trouble identifying the body if the tattoos were intact.

He looked at the screen again, muting out the honeyed words of Serene Simone and concentrating on Ivy's face. The mischievous grin and the sparkle in her eyes got to him the most. This girl was so alive, too alive to possibly be dead. But Baldwin knew that was probably exactly what she was. Dead and gone, like all the others. They needed to catch Buckley. Damn, why hadn't they gotten any more information on him?

The time for the segment was up; the anchor wrapped the interview quickly. "I'm sorry to have to cut you off, but we are out of time. Let's see that emergency number again, producers. If you have any information on the whereabouts of Ivy Tanner Clark, missing from Louisville, Kentucky, please call this number. We'll see you after the break."

The screen filled with an 800 number, one that Baldwin recognized as the FBI tip line. The number had generated hundreds of calls with leads that were going nowhere. It was time to make a change, to make something happen.

A hundred thousand dollars might help. Of course,

it might hurt, too, because they'd be inundated with tipsters dolling out bogus information.

Baldwin looked down at the files in front of him. He went through the list again, covering Jake Buckley's travel schedule for the past two months. The man had been on a junket, and had been in thirty cities in the past month. But the cities they needed to see him in figured prominently. Huntsville, Alabama; Baton Rouge, Louisiana; Jackson, Mississippi; back to Nashville. Then on to Noble, Georgia; Roanoke, Virginia; Asheville, North Carolina, then Louisville. He was scheduled for a break back in Nashville that would last for a week. Maybe he was done killing, maybe he wasn't, but he was coming home, and home was where they'd hopefully find him.

He was due back in Nashville last night. He had not arrived home, so the BOLO, Be on the Lookout, for his car had been issued, yet no one had reported seeing the car anywhere between Nashville and Louisville. It was time for Baldwin to talk with Quinn Buckley. He needed to get a better sense of who they were dealing with.

Forty-Three

He dug in the dirt like a carefree child, singing softly to himself under his breath.

"One little, two little, three little Indians…four little, five little, six little Indians… Don't have the seventh or the eighth little Indian…but that's okaaaaay for now!"

He spread the rich, loamy soil into the holes, then dusted off his hands and broke open a package of seeds he'd gotten at the local hardware store. Sprinkling the minute buds of life, he started to laugh. Pushing up daisies, literally. Really, he could be so funny sometimes.

He stood, brushing the dirt from his knees, and reached for a gentle misting hose. He started the water and stepped back to admire his newly sown garden. How very lovely.

Forty-Four

Quinn Buckley was starting to get worried. Jake was due home and had not shown up, the FBI was looking for him, a nationwide alert had gone out about his car, and nothing was happening. She was sitting alone, in her empty kitchen, nursing a cup of tea and a broken heart. She had not been able to reach her brother for several days, and she had not been able to make plans for her sister's burial. The children had gone to play at a friend's house. She barely remembered telling them that they could, but there was a terse note from Gabrielle telling her that the kids were down the street on a play date. The big house was silent and brooding, and she felt like she was losing her mind.

She knew there was no way Jake Buckley had killed all those girls. Jake may be many things, a poltroon, an adulterer, a bad husband, yes, he was all of those. But he was not a killer, and when she got the phone call from John Baldwin at the FBI she had readily agreed to have him come out and sit with her, to talk about some of the details about Jake Buckley that he had not been able to ascertain. Maybe she was just lonely and needed to have someone sit with her, hold her hand and tell her they understood.

She wandered into the study, the one room in the house that she felt she could call her own. Perhaps a book would cheer her up. She entered the room and took in a deep breath. Standing in the middle of the room was Reese, her little brother. She jumped and let out a startled cry. He just looked at her with unfathomably sad eyes.

"Jesus, Reese, you scared me to death. When did you sneak in here? I didn't even hear the doorbell. Oh, it's good to see you. When did you get back?"

She went to him and enfolded him in a hug. Reese was tall; like Jake he was nearly six foot four in his stocking feet. He had black curly hair, a rogue's smile, dark blue eyes and a dimple in his chin. His jaw was broad, his nose chiseled, and Quinn couldn't help but give him an admiring glance. He was just so handsome. And so very young. She was filled with pride for a brief moment then shook it off.

"Sweetheart, I tried to reach you for days, but I could never get through."

"I'm sorry, Quinn. I told you we'd be out of touch. It was amazing. Really amazing. I learned so much. I got in late last night and heard your message on my machine this morning. Why did you need to reach me?"

Quinn did not know how to approach the subject. She knew Whitney and Reese were not close by any means. But they were related, after all, that had to count for something. She took his hand and led him to the closest chair, a huge leather swayback with studded nails going up the sides. She sat him down and in turn took a seat on a velvet ottoman facing him. She took both of his hands in hers and looked him straight in his gorgeous eyes.

"Sweetheart, Whitney has been in an accident. She was killed. It happened, well, she was on her way here, to the house. I didn't know if anyone else had gotten through to your team down there, that someone from home had told one of the doctors you were with. I wanted to tell you myself."

There was no reaction from Reese, and Quinn's heart sank. He couldn't hate her, not that much. Reese looked up at her, his eyes troubled.

Quinn squeezed his hands tighter. "I know, honey, I know. It's awful. There's more. The police have taken Whitney's laptop. Apparently she's been involved, somehow, with this horrible man that has been killing these girls all over the Southeast. I didn't know if you'd heard about that, either, though it's been national news and in all the papers. I thought you might have heard something about it. Reese? Reese?"

Reese was staring, unblinking, his face drained of all color. A single tear built up in the corner of his eye and dribbled down his cheek unchecked. He shook his head, unbelieving. Quinn nattered on, trying to fill the uncomfortable silence.

"I mean, I can't understand it. Whitney, involved with this killer? I don't know how that's possible, and the police aren't giving me a lot of information. I'm sure she was planning on doing some sort of story on it, and she was trying to reach me the day before—" Her voice broke, and she had to gather herself before she continued. "The day before she died. Oh, Reese, what are we going to do?"

Reese finally met Quinn's eyes, gently removing his hands from hers. "So she didn't know?"

"She didn't know what, sweetheart?"

Reese stood up and walked to the bookcase. He reached out a slender finger and traced the spine of an intricately carved book. "All that work," he murmured to himself.

Quinn heard but didn't understand what he said.

"What, sweetheart? I didn't hear you. Are you okay?"

He turned to her, a small smile on his face and a glistening in his eyes. "All my work. She didn't know." He started to laugh, and Quinn was unsure what to do. Grief took all forms, and though she knew Reese was not terribly fond of his other sister, she thought that laughter was hardly the best emotional avenue for him to take at the news of her death.

"Now, Reese Connolly, I don't know what's wrong with you. I've just told you your sister is dead and you laugh. What is wrong with you?"

He was laughing harder now, tears streaming down his face. He stepped over to Quinn, took her in a brief yet forceful hug, and then, still laughing, disappeared from the room. Quinn heard the laughter fade away, then heard the front door slam. A throaty engine turned over and he tore off down the driveway.

She sank into the chair he had been sitting in before his bizarre reaction to his sister's death had drawn him to stand. What the hell was that about? Quinn shook her head. It was beyond her. She knew that there was no way he could know the truth, but maybe she was mistaken. Maybe Reese had been fooling them all along.

The doorbell rang, and she took a deep breath, got out of the chair and went to the door. She opened it to find both Taylor Jackson and a man she assumed was the FBI agent she'd spoken to standing on her doorstep. Taylor was sporting a black eye and a tight smile. The FBI agent just looked worried.

"Come in, come in, please." She beckoned to the foyer and watched them closely while they came in the door. Something was going on. Hell, what else could be happening? The police had confiscated Whitney's computer. They were searching for her husband. Her little brother had laughed when he found out his sister was dead. Her life was quietly disintegrating, and she didn't know how to stop it.

Taylor and Baldwin settled themselves in the library, watching Quinn flutter about like a feather caught in a breeze. She finally sat across from them and took a deep breath.

"Please, tell me what's going on. What's the real reason the FBI is looking for my husband?"

Baldwin leaned forward, hands on his knees. "Mrs. Buckley, we have reason to believe that your husband has been involved in several crimes we've been investigating over the past few weeks."

Quinn threw back her head and laughed. "Let me guess. You think Jake is the Southern Strangler. Please, Mr. Baldwin, let me assure you, Jake is no more the Strangler than I am. It's just not something that could possibly happen. He's not capable of killing. Sticking his dick into any female that comes within twenty feet of him, absolutely. But killing? No."

Baldwin wasn't deterred. "Mrs. Buckley, you don't seem to understand. Your husband has been in the exact areas that the girls have gone missing from, and the exact spots where their bodies were recovered. That in and of itself is compelling evidence against him. Have you heard from your husband today?"

"No, I haven't, but that means nothing. Jake goes for days without checking in. I have no idea where he is half the time…" Her voice trailed off. She stared out the window for a moment. "You're serious, aren't you? That's why you took Whitney's computer. You think Jake's been sending her these messages, these poems. But why in the world would he do that? Jake doesn't send poetry to anyone." She broke off, her voice catching. "At least, not anymore."

Her eyes widened. "That son of a bitch. He was sleeping with Whitney, wasn't he? He was sending her love poems, like he used to do with… Dear God, is nothing sacred? That would make sense. My perfect husband fucking my equally perfect sister. Isn't that just a riot?"

Baldwin tucked that morsel of information into his mind and tried to get the interview back on track. "Mrs. Buckley, I know how hard this must be for you. You've lost your sister, and your husband, well, we don't know where he is, or what he's been doing for the past few weeks. I'd like your permission to take a few articles of Mr. Buckley's personal items with me. We'd like to run some tests, see if we can't match—"

Quinn came to life, fire spilling from her eyes. "Are

you out of your mind? Do you actually think I'm going to march upstairs and give you anything that might implicate my husband in a crime? You get a warrant, Mr. Baldwin. I won't help you frame my husband for something he didn't do."

Taylor stepped in. "Quinn, you and I both know that the best thing you could do would be to let us take some things to the lab, to rule Jake out as a suspect. It would make everyone's life easier if you'd just cooperate with us now. Think about it, Quinn. There have been seven girls murdered. An eighth is missing. Your husband has dropped off the grid. Your sister died trying to warn you that you were in danger. It all fits. Help us now. Help us help him."

Quinn shook her head, a sob escaping from her throat. "Absolutely not. No. Now, I'd appreciate it if you'd leave." She stood, arms crossed against her chest. Her eyes were strangely bright, tears of frustration trying to break free glistening in the corners.

Baldwin and Taylor stood, as well. As they walked into the hallway, they heard soft mewing sounds coming from behind the door. Quinn noticed the noise, too, and stalked into the marble-floored hallway. Gabrielle, her Italian student-cum-nanny, head in her hands, was weeping softly. Quinn softened for a moment.

"Gabrielle, it's all right. Everything will be okay. *Sarà tutto il di destra, cara. Non si preoccupi.*"

Gabrielle raised her head and glared at Quinn.

"Non, it ees not going to be all right. You have no idea. None. There ees no way Signor Buckley has done these things. I know." She began crying harder and a torrent of Italian flowed from her mouth. *"Sto facendo l'amore con il Signor Buckley per parecchi mesi. Siamo nell'amore. Non significo danno a voi. È il mio amante. È il vostro difetto, Signora Buckley. Non è di destra voi non lo ama come."*

Gabrielle stood straighter, and Taylor recognized immediately the stance. A woman in love. Not like Quinn Buckley, resigned but proud. This young girl was madly in love with her employer, and had seen fit to let her employer's wife know it.

Taylor looked at Quinn. She seemed to have shrunk three inches, her arms wrapped even tighter around her slim frame.

"Quinn, what did she just say?" Taylor asked, a note of concern in her voice. Woman to woman. That might be the trick.

Quinn was still in a visual standoff with her young nanny. She finally took a breath and began to speak, her eyes never leaving Gabrielle.

"She says that she and Jake are having an affair. That they are in love. That it's my fault, that I don't love him enough. Is that about right, Gabrielle? I don't love my husband enough, so you felt the need to step in and love him for me? Get out of my house, *voi poco squaldrina. VOI SORCA!"*

Gabrielle's eyes widened, and Taylor realized Quinn must have called her some sort of terrible name in Italian. The girl cried out, whipped her long hair about her body and ran from the room.

Quinn collapsed in a heap on an antique chair that didn't look like it could hold her weight. She looked so small, so fragile, that Taylor couldn't resist reaching out, giving Quinn what she hoped was a comforting touch on the shoulder. Quinn stiffened. Taylor removed her hand.

"I'm sorry, Quinn. Sorry that things have to be like this for you. Are you sure there's nothing else you want to tell us?" Taylor's voice was low, coaxing, as if Quinn were a startled cat she was trying to get out from under a couch. Quinn didn't move for a moment, then sighed heavily. All the fight went out of her.

"Let's go back in the library. I'll help you any way that I can."

The three filed back into the library. Taylor and Baldwin resumed their positions on the couch, watching Quinn wander around the room. They didn't interrupt when she finally started to speak.

"Jake and I have been having problems for some time now. It's been a couple of years, actually. We had a fight, a horrible, terrible fight on a Sunday evening two months ago. Jake was getting ready for another business trip—you know he travels constantly for his job. I wanted him to stay home, to pick me over Health Partners just once. That's when he admitted he'd been cheating on me. He'd taken up with some intern that he'd met, a marketing company he works with. The affair was brief, only a couple of days, but it was like he'd decided then and there that he didn't want to be with me anymore. I didn't know what to do. What woman is ever prepared to go through the realization that her husband doesn't love her anymore? I did the only thing I knew to do. I had separation papers drawn up. I showed them to him last Monday night. That's why I wasn't answering the phone when Whitney called. I was telling my husband that he can kiss me, his kids, his house and my money goodbye. He stormed out of here, and I haven't seen him since."

Baldwin tapped his fingers on the arm of the couch. "He was having an affair with an intern? Do you know if this was here in town or out on the road?"

"I'd like to think Jake had the common sense to keep his philandering at a distance." She stopped for a moment, thinking. "Of course, I was wrong about that. Gabrielle and Whitney, right under my nose. My God, I am such a bloody idiot!"

"Of course you aren't. These things happen," he comforted. "I'm sorry to have to put you through this, Mrs. Buckley. But the affair, the intern. Do you know…?"

"I believe it was New Orleans, during Mardi Gras, something like that."

"Did he mention a name?"

"Oh, it was something French. Started with a J."

"Jeanette Lernier?" Baldwin asked.

Quinn waved a hand. "It could have been. I didn't stick around to hear all the gory details." She paused, processing. "Wait a minute. You knew her name off the top of your head. You already knew he'd been with her. How did you—I don't want to know." She stopped talking, defeated, a hand over her eyes.

Baldwin's and Taylor's eyes met. Quinn needed to know. Baldwin took a deep breath. "Jeanette Lernier was the second victim of the Southern Strangler."

Quinn's hand dropped and her eyes flew open. Comprehension dawned at last.

"Jesus," she muttered.

They were running out of time. Taylor cleared her

throat. "Jake hasn't called home this week? No word from him at all?"

"No, Lieutenant, not a peep." She laughed shrilly. "Maybe I didn't handle things well. I should have told him the truth from day one, when we first met."

Baldwin spoke softly. "Tell the truth about what, Mrs. Buckley?"

She glanced at him for a moment, cool, appraising, then turned away. "The truth about what happened to Whitney and me when we were children. About what a farce our lives were. You remember," she accused Taylor. "You probably know the whole story already, being a cop."

All three of them jumped when Taylor's phone rang. She was tempted to let it ring but knew she had to answer. "I'm so sorry. Please, let me just take this call. I don't know the whole story, Quinn. Police reports and court transcripts only tell half of it. I'd like to hear your side. Excuse me for a moment."

She glanced at the caller ID. It was Fitz. She picked up the phone and stepped out of the room. "Jackson here." As he spoke, she couldn't believe what she heard.

Hanging up, she went back into the library. Baldwin and Quinn were quiet, subdued. Taylor took a deep breath before she spoke. This news was going to tear a rift through Quinn's life so large that it would most likely be irreparable.

"Quinn, please. I have some news about Jake."

Quinn didn't look at her, just sank gracefully into a chair, hands clasped in her lap. She was holding on so tight her knuckles were white. "Go ahead. This day can't get any worse."

"Quinn, Jake's been arrested. His car was pulled over on I-65, heading south to Nashville from Kentucky. He had…" Her voice wavered for an instant, then gained strength. "He had a body in the trunk of his car. We believe that it's Ivy Tanner Clark, the girl who went missing from Louisville yesterday."

Baldwin stood, ready to pepper her with questions, but she held up a hand. "Jake's being transported to the Criminal Justice Center downtown. Special Agent Baldwin and I are needed down there right away. We have to interrogate him after he's booked. Do you understand what I'm saying, Quinn?"

Quinn's lips were stretched taut, a bloodless line across her crestfallen face. She shook her head once. "Do I need to get him a lawyer?"

"That's his right. Or he can waive that right and talk to us. Why don't we go on downtown, you can sort it out there."

"No." Quinn's voice was the strongest they'd heard all afternoon. "No, Goddammit. Let him rot. If he did this, I'm not helping him." She fled the room and Taylor could hear her footsteps thudding up the stairs. She shrugged and turned to Baldwin.

"We should go. I want to have a few moments alone with Mr. Buckley."

Forty-Five

Taylor and Baldwin rolled into the CJC in high spirits. After a hellacious few days, the Strangler seemed to have fallen into their laps, a product of solid police work and a little bit of luck. Not to mention the possible resolution of the Rainman case. Taylor was giddy with achievement; her name was going to be linked with the capture of two nationally known criminals. Not that she needed a career boost, but her level of satisfaction with her job rose appreciably when things were going her way.

They made their way down the hall to the Homicide office, chatting. Turning the corner, they found Fitz, Lincoln, Marcus and Captain Price waiting. They didn't look happy.

"What's wrong with you guys? You look like the party's over before it's even begun. Where's Buckley?" Taylor peered out of the office toward the interrogation rooms. The lights were on in one. Jake Buckley, the Southern Strangler, would be behind that door. A wave of excitement rolled through her.

Price answered Taylor, looking glum. "He lawyered up. Won't say a thing, just keeps repeating the word. Lawyer, lawyer, lawyer. He, uh, needs a phone to make the call, but we haven't found a phone that works yet."

"Smart move, Cap. Why don't you let Baldwin and I give it a go, see if he decides to play with us. We have some background on him from his wife. Let's see if his guilt about her will let him open up."

"That's what we were waiting on. Go for it. But if he asks again, we'll have to let him call his lawyer. Actually, I wouldn't be surprised to see one wander through the door any second. You were with the wife, right? Wouldn't she be calling one for him right about now?"

Baldwin shook his head. "I don't think Quinn Buckley's going to be doing much of anything in the way of helping her husband right now. She's one very upset lady."

"Okay then, give it a whirl. The body was taken to the M.E.'s office. 'Torn to shreds' was the phrase the arresting officer used."

"Torn to shreds?" Taylor turned to look at Price.

"Apparently she'd been stabbed, her throat cut, couple of visible broken bones. Torn up."

"And the hands?" Baldwin asked.

"Intact. Looked like a frenzied killing, maybe he got interrupted before he could finish, decided to dump the body in the trunk and get out of Dodge. I don't know. And there's more good news. There was also a bag found in the wheel well under the trunk liner. A whole murder kit. Rope, tape, a military-type K-Bar knife, scalpels…crime scene techs are sorting it all right now. There's forensic evidence galore in that bag. Oh, and look at this."

Price handed Taylor a green file folder. Baldwin looked over her shoulder while she flipped through it. The first photo was of Ivy Clark's mutilated body, stowed in the trunk of the car. Leafing through the file, Taylor stopped at a photo of an overnight bag. An innocuous black leather bag, full to the brim with death.

Price smiled grimly. "Found everything in here. But that's not the best part. Look at the close-up."

She flipped to the next picture. There was a very distinct monogram embossed into the leather with the initials J-W-B in gold. Taylor shook her head in amazement.

"His own personally monogrammed murder kit. How convenient. Okay, let me at him. See what I can shake out." She looked at Baldwin. "Ready?"

"As I'll ever be."

"Then let's do it."

Price motioned toward the interrogation-room door. "We'll be on the other side, watching. Good luck."

Taylor opened the door and strode into the room. It was relatively small, just enough space for a table and four chairs. The walls were an institutional shade of robin's-egg blue, marred only by a mirror. She gave Price and the team a few moments to get themselves situated as Baldwin took one of the chairs opposite a haggard-looking man. Taylor eyed him, he was about her age, mid thirties, but his disheveled appearance added a decade to his rugged good looks. His beard was growing in, his hair was tousled. He had a small drop of blood at the corner of his mouth. Taylor figured that would be the best way to get him to open up. She glanced at Baldwin, who gave her a nod. She was the lead right now. He'd back her up if and when necessary.

Jake Buckley watched her as she entered, pure hatred in his eyes. He didn't look as defeated as he had just moments before. Taylor tsk-tsked, stepped out of the room, then came back in with a tissue box. She offered one to him, a conciliatory gesture. He took it and pressed it to his mouth.

"Looks like you got roughed up a bit out there, Mr. Buckley. I'm so sorry about that. I'm hoping this is just a huge misunderstanding, that none of our men actually meant to hurt you. Regardless, that wasn't very professional of them, and I'll have a word with the arresting officer, make sure it's noted in his file. Would that suit you, sir?"

He met her eyes and a bit of arrogance crept into his gaze. The term *sir* had put him back in control. He had money and power, and by God he was going to be treated with respect. A subservient woman to interrogate him was just the ticket. Taylor was playing him perfectly.

She leaned against the wall, arms crossed, smiling. "Now, Mr. Buckley, can I get you anything? Coffee, maybe? Soda? Maybe some ice to put on that cut? Looks like it might be swelling up just a little bit."

Buckley eyed her. "Coffee. Black, two sugars. The ice won't be necessary. Looks like you could use some yourself."

Taylor ignored the jibe about her black eye. "No problem, Mr. Buckley. Let me go get that for you." She smiled again, nonthreatening, a buddy, not a cop.

Stepping out into the hallway, Lincoln met her, a mug of coffee in his hand. She winked at him, then stepped back into the room.

She handed him the coffee, then sat in the chair opposite him, next to Baldwin but distancing herself by sliding the chair a few feet to the side, so the table wasn't between her and Buckley. "Here you are, Mr. Buckley. I sure am sorry we had to put you out like this. I'd understand if you didn't want to talk to me, but I'd love to hear your side of the story, how that lip got cut. Was it one of the patrol officers?"

Buckley snarled at her. "Don't think I don't know what you're about there, little lady. You're trying to get me to confess to something I don't know anything about. All I know is I got pulled over, dragged from my car, assaulted by one of Metro's finest and brought here. What the hell do you people think you're doing? I swear I'm going to make sure every single one of you is fired." He glowered at her, hostile and demanding. Taylor could see this man as a killer, and the thought made her blood run cold. She almost dropped the act, nearly spit out what she was actually thinking about the bastard, but she held her tongue and simply nodded and crossed her legs.

"I understand completely, Mr. Buckley. I can't apologize enough, for the whole department. We are truly sorry we inconvenienced you. I'm sure you understand, we have just one little problem to clear up and then we'll do our best to get you out of here. Get you home to Mrs. Buckley. Quinn, isn't it? I'm sure she's worried sick about you right now, sir, what with you being on the news and everything tonight. She's probably sitting at home right now, crying her eyes out because she doesn't know what's happening. Would you like to call her?"

"I'm on the news? Why the hell is that?"

Taylor chose to stall him. "Tell me, Mr. Buckley. Your wife mentioned that you like poetry."

"What the hell are you talking about?"

"Oh, I think you know. Love poems. She mentioned you used to send them to her, way back when. Are you still in that habit now, Mr. Buckley?"

"What difference does that make? So I send my wife love notes. Doesn't make me any different than the next guy."

"And when you send them to your wife's sister? Does that make you any different?"

"Send poems to Whitney? What exactly are you accusing me of, Detective?"

"It's Lieutenant. And I'm asking if you were having an affair with your wife's sister. Identical-twin sister, at that, who happens to be very, very dead."

Jake Buckley opened and closed his mouth, took a breath and spoke, menace in his voice. "I don't know anything about Whitney's death. I'll have your badge for this, Lieutenant. I may not be a lawyer, but I know slander when I see it. Is that what you've been telling my wife? That I cheated on her with her own sister? What do you think I am, some kind of monster?"

"Perhaps you are."

"And perhaps I'd like to know what you meant by me being on the news."

It was time to get to it. Taylor raised her hands, palms up, entreating him for calm. "Well, Mr. Buckley. Sir, I'm sure you understand that we've been looking for you for a couple of days now. And there's that little technicality we've been dealing with. Sir, how do you explain the girl in the trunk of your car?"

Buckley's eyes widened and his bullying veneer dropped for an instant. "What girl? What the hell are you talking about?"

"How about the bag with the knives, rope and tape...your tool kit, full of bloody evidence?"

Buckley shifted in his chair. "I don't have the faintest idea what you're talking about."

Taylor stood now, ready to hit her stride. She paced the room. "Let me guess, no one mentioned that you had a dead girl in the trunk of your BMW, Mr. Buckley? A girl named Ivy Tanner Clark? You met her in Louisville? It's okay, Mr. Buckley. I understand how these things work." She sidled up to him. "You meet a girl, maybe get a little friendly with her. Maybe things get a little rough, and suddenly, *BAM!* She's dead, and you don't know what to do. So you stash her in the trunk of your car and drive toward home, figuring you'd find a good place to dump her along the way. Is that how it happened, Mr. Buckley? Isn't that what you've been doing here for the past couple of months? Meeting a girl here or there, sweet-talking her to go somewhere with you? Getting a little frisky, okay, maybe a lot frisky, and she somehow accidentally ends up dead?" Taylor stopped pacing and planted herself two feet from Buckley. He reared back in his chair as if he'd been hit.

"No. No, no, no, that's impossible, that's not right. I never killed any girls. I have no idea—"

Taylor interrupted him, all the sweetness and light gone from her voice. "Oh yes, yes, yes, Mr. Buckley, that's just what you've been up to. Your happy little road trip throughout the Southeast? Picking up girls, murdering them, transporting their bodies. Or has that little tidbit slipped your mind? What about their hands, Mr. Buckley?" Taylor was two inches from Buckley's face now, each word biting and cutting as well as a knife. He looked terrified.

"What do you do with their hands, Jake? Do you mind if I call you Jake? Do you tell them your name before you kill them, Jake? Were you just trying to get yourself a little bit of ass and it went awry? You found out how much you liked it, didn't you? You liked forcing them, liked choking the life out of them. And then you administered the coup de grâce, didn't you, Jake? You cut off their hands, took one with you to throw down at the next dead body, the next mutilated girl. Isn't that how it went, Jake?"

Her voice was sharp, loud, and Buckley flinched away from her, shaking his head, a low keening sound escaping his throat. "No, no, no, no, *NO!* No, I didn't do any of those things. I didn't, I swear it! I may be a jerk, but I'm not a killer. I didn't kill anyone. Christ, you have to listen to me. Lawyer. I want my lawyer. Right now!" he roared, eyes white with panic.

Taylor turned tail and walked out of the room. Baldwin followed suit. They left Jake Buckley blubbering like a baby in the interrogation room and joined the rest of the homicide team.

They met her in the hall, all four men grinning. "Nice performance, Lieutenant." Price congratulated her. "You scared him so shitless he forgot to ask for a lawyer until the very end. Well done, girl."

"Thank you, thank you. But we have to get him to say something other than 'No, I didn't do it.' Baldwin?"

Baldwin was staring at the floor, lost in thought.

"Baldwin?"

He met her eyes. "Something's not right about him."

"Well, we know that. Your average guy doesn't like to kill his dates at the end of the evening," she said.

"No, it's something more. He was really cocky with you when you let him think he was in control. But the second you turned on him, he cowered like a beaten dog. This killer wouldn't do that. The notes he's sending, the sensational nature of the crime—I think he'd be bragging about it. I don't think he'd let you get under his skin like that."

"C'mon, Mr. Fed, give the girl some credit. She can waltz back in there and he'll tell her anything she wants to hear." Fitz wasn't quite growling at Baldwin, but he definitely was pushing things.

"He just might. But I don't know if it's him. We need to get some of the forensics together, get his DNA. We can compel a DNA sample from him now, right?"

Taylor nodded.

"Then let's do that. We can try to match it against the semen taken from Christina Dale's crime scene. I just can't get my head around him as the killer. Not the way he backed off when Taylor got in his face. An accomplice, maybe. Hell, I don't know. Let's get some proof."

Fitz stared at Baldwin as if he were an alien. "Baldwin, the man had Ivy Clark all laid out in the trunk of his car. He was speeding back to Nashville to get rid of the body. He had the bag of tools right there in the car with him, his own damn initials stamped on it. What the hell more do you need?" He raised a beefy paw. "Naw, don't answer that. I'll go get the sample, have it run over to be tested." He disappeared into the hallway.

Baldwin turned to Taylor, whose smile had faded. It had felt right. "Let Buckley stew for a little bit. I want to go over the file on Whitney and Quinn."

Forty-Six

Baldwin set up shop in the conference room across the hall from Jake Buckley's interrogation room. The files from Quinn and Whitney's kidnapping were spread before him. He buzzed through them, absorbing all the information. The story was all too familiar.

Whitney and Quinn were bright, bubbly twelve-year-olds when they went missing. They'd been playing that day, innocent and pure, two sisters enjoying an afternoon of free time after school, no responsibilities other than make-believe and fun. They were both towheaded, blue-eyed and happy. All this Baldwin gleaned from the photos of the girls that accompanied the files. Photos from before the kidnapping.

The after shots, pictures taken when the girls were recovered and taken to police headquarters while their parents were notified, told a different story. Their eyes were troubled, no smiles, just blank stares. Both girls had been beaten, eyes blackened, and Quinn had a split lip. The only way he could tell them apart was the small white label affixed to the bottom of each photo designating each girl. There was a shot of Whitney staring into the camera as if she hadn't realized her picture was being taken. There was no innocence in the gaze, she had the eyes of a woman twice her age that had seen a lifetime of abuse. What three days could do to a child was overwhelming.

They'd been riding their bikes that day. They'd ridden down a garden path they'd discovered that led from the back edge of their parents' estate. The path traversed a wooded area and opened onto a grassy clearing, which bordered the west edge of Belle Meade Boulevard. It was hidden from the road by a long line of crepe myrtle trees. Whitney's bicycle had gotten a flat. Instead of making their way back through the woods, they'd decided to go the long way, to push their bikes along the boulevard, back to their house.

He flipped the page and stared at the photo of their kidnapper. The file identified him as Nathan Chase, a thirty-seven-year-old construction worker, more often out of a job than in one. He had approached the girls, offering them some ice cream, a treat to cool them down on a hot summer day, and a ride back to their house so they didn't have to push their bikes.

In the time of innocence, before Amber Alerts and children being schooled day in and day out about the horrors lurking behind every stranger's shadow, the girls had accepted. They were on the Boulevard after all. They wheeled their bikes to his truck. After Quinn's bike was safely in the back and she was climbing into the cab, he'd grabbed Whitney, shoved her in behind Quinn and taken off, leaving Whitney's flat-wheeled bicycle behind. And then they were gone. Disappeared. Vanished.

But their story had a happy ending. Three days later, the girls appeared on Charlotte Avenue, disheveled, dirty, bloody, but alive. A Good Samaritan had seen them stumbling toward home and called the police.

It was Whitney who had explained how Chase had gotten drunk, had passed out, that the girls had seen an opportunity and had made a successful break for freedom.

It was Whitney who had identified Chase and his truck. She gave detailed descriptions of his home, a tiny, dirty two-bedroom bungalow off of Charlotte Avenue. The girls had only been five miles from home for the duration of their captivity. Quinn never volunteered any information, had only nodded in confirmation as Whitney told their story. PTSD, post-traumatic stress disorder, was Quinn's biggest problem. She'd suffered such a shock that she'd been mute for weeks after the kidnapping, the file said. Whitney, having told the story, given all the information she could remember, had sat quietly waiting for her parents to take her home. The stronger of the twins.

The police had followed the directions Whitney gave them and found Nathan Chase alone in his living room, sucking on a Budweiser, watching a movie on television. He'd just smiled as they'd cuffed him, refused to confirm or deny the charges against him.

He'd been tried and convicted on the strength of Whitney's testimony, Quinn refused to come to court, wouldn't take the stand, but the jury decided in only two hours that Nathan Chase was guilty as hell. He'd been sentenced to thirty years, a decent amount of time and punishment for a kidnapper in the early 1980s, and was serving out the remainder of his time at Riverbend, a maximum-security prison that had opened in 1989. He spent his days watching television, reading, working in the library and being a model prisoner.

Baldwin sat back in his chair, rubbing his eyes. Nathan Chase. What kind of man kidnaps two little girls, beats them, but lets them get away? Then sits in his house, drinking a beer and waiting for the cops to come a-calling?

Baldwin leafed through the pages again. There was no sign of the sheets that mentioned the sexual assault. The girls' reports were of multiple beatings and sleepless nights. They said he'd talked to them, told them stories, tried to entertain them. The odds that they weren't assaulted were so slim that Baldwin finally sought Taylor out. She was in her office, sipping a Diet Coke and reading a case file.

"Whatcha up to?" Baldwin lounged in her doorway, drinking in her beauty. She should look frazzled and tired, it was the middle of the night, they'd been working for so many hours Baldwin had lost count. But she sat serenely at her desk, eyes wide and clear, looking like she'd just gotten up from a refreshing twelve hours in the bed. Except for the black eye. It gave her a rakish air. He briefly imagined her in his bed and smiled. She caught the look and laughed, closing the file in front of her.

"Lincoln just brought me up to speed on our Rainman suspect. Norville Turner. He works at the precinct filling station, doing mechanical work on the squad cars. Apparently, there's no great psychosis behind his pattern. He's a cop buff, couldn't get on the force. He failed his entrance exams at the Academy four times, so he's spent all this time trying to get back at us. Thought that setting up his crimes in a bizarre pattern would make him look mysterious. He's just an everyday rapist. The good news is, he admitted to the rapes, which is an excellent first step. Now we have to do all the fun stuff, matching the DNA and all, but it looks like we got our man."

"That's great news, hon."

"Yeah, I'm just happy it's over. What are you doing?"

"Trying to figure out why Quinn and Whitney's file doesn't mention anything about the sexual assault."

"It doesn't? That's strange. There's no documentation on it?"

"Not a thing. Their hospital records don't have a record of a rape kit being performed on either of the girls."

"Well, that can't be right. Chase went to jail after he was found guilty of kidnapping and sexual assault. I've seen those pages myself. There must be a part of the file that's missing." She started rooting around her desk, didn't find anything of use, then went out into the Homicide office. She looked through the papers on Fitz's desk and found a slim file labeled Connolly.

"Here's something. Looks like Fitz didn't grab all the files. Let's see." She opened the file and scanned. "Says here that only one of the girls was assaulted. That's the reason it's not in the hospital reports, it wasn't reported the night they found them. It came a few weeks later. Hmm. Now that's funny. It doesn't say which girl was raped. Huh." She handed the file to Baldwin. "That's a little bizarre, isn't it? The girls' personal physician made this report, but he doesn't identify which girl it happened to. Granted, this was twenty years ago. It's still strange, don't you think?"

They went back into Taylor's office. Baldwin sat in the visitor's chair and propped his feet up on her desk. "Didn't you say there were rumors about the girls after they transferred in to Father Ryan?"

"Well sure, there were rumors," Taylor answered him, rubbing her temple. "But it was all just that, rumors. They came in as freshmen my sophomore year, and I didn't know too much about them. They were attending Harpeth Hall before, and I think I remember someone saying they'd taken a year off, then came over to Ryan. I know their mom was pregnant while all of this was going on, that I do remember. They had a little brother, what's his name again? Oh yeah, Reese. Reese Connolly. Quinn said he's a doctor, doing his residency at Vanderbilt."

Baldwin raised an eyebrow at her. "The timing's right, don't you think? They take a year off, and suddenly they have a little brother?"

Taylor was taken aback. "You think that one of them got pregnant by Nathan Chase? And had Reese, then their parents covered it up? Man, that's screwed up. They were only twelve. But it begs the question. Which one would it have been?"

"That's something we may want to find out. In the meantime, I want to see if Nathan Chase has had any visitors lately. I have a feeling what happened to Quinn and Whitney twenty years ago may be linked to what's happening today. Remember Quinn said she should have told Jake the truth from the beginning? You think she was trying to confess that she'd had a child and he rejected her?"

"Lord, Baldwin, you're just grasping at straws now. There's nothing in the evidence that leads that way."

"Maybe not, but I want to get a list of Nathan Chase's visitors anyway. We'll do that in the morning. In the meantime, let's go home. I'm too tired to think anymore tonight. Anything new on Whitney's computer?"

Baldwin had dropped the laptop off in Taylor's office earlier.

"No, nothing since we arrested Jake Buckley."

"Maybe that's a sign. Let's get out of here."

Taylor nodded, so they gathered up their things, straightened up her desk and left the Homicide office. Five minutes after they left, the light began blinking on Whitney Connolly's laptop, informing one and all that she had new mail.

Forty-Seven

Baldwin's phone rang at six in the morning, rousing him from the best sleep he'd had in weeks. He'd gone to bed without the report of another missing girl floating through his brain, without wondering what new horror awaited him when he opened his eyes. He slept dreamlessly, snuggled beside Taylor in the warm bed, knowing that he was close to cracking this case.

Though he'd been a bit circumspect about Jake Buckley's culpability in the series of murders, the talk he and Taylor had gone through on their way home abated his concerns. Taylor's theory was a strong one. Quinn Buckley had told the truth to her husband about what happened when she and her twin sister were kidnapped. That they had been raped, had borne a child in secret, that the news was too much for Buckley to take. Already a promiscuous, bullying man, he'd gone over the edge, making his regular travel a cover for murder. A bit thin, but plausible. Today was the day they'd put it all together. The DNA would confirm everything.

The phone call would derail every theory they had.

"Baldwin," he answered, yawning.

"It's Garrett. Why are you sleeping so late?"

"It's 6:00 a.m. Central time, Garrett. You're an hour ahead of me, remember?"

"I do remember. You need to get up. We have a problem."

Baldwin groaned and rolled over, realizing Taylor wasn't lying beside him. Where had she gotten off to? He sat on the edge of the bed, running his fingers through his hair, dreading the answer to his next question.

"What's the problem, Garrett?"

"The DNA sample you submitted for Jake Buckley doesn't match the Strangler. He's still out there."

Baldwin was wide awake now. "Aw, man, damn. Shit." He threw out a few more expletives, enough to get Taylor back in the room, eyes questioning what was wrong. He held up a hand, stopping her question.

"But Buckley had Ivy Clark in the trunk of his car. Are you saying that he really didn't know she was there, like he claims?"

"I can't tell you that, Baldwin. I'd talk to him again, but without a DNA match, you're going to have to figure something else out. He definitely isn't a match to the DNA found at the Dale crime scene, that much we know for sure. I can't say he didn't murder those girls, but it seems likely that he's not your man."

"All right. Let me get on this. I'll need to talk to Buckley again. Shit, Garrett, I knew something wasn't right about this."

"As usual, your intuition pays off. Always trust it,

Baldwin. Now get out there and find us the real killer before he hits again."

Baldwin clicked off the phone and flopped back onto the bed. Taylor eyed him, concerned. "What's wrong?"

"You're never going to believe this. The DNA from Buckley doesn't match the Strangler's vics. Come on, let's go to your office. We're going to need some help on this one."

Half the day was gone by the time they had gotten Buckley back from the sheriff, interrogated him again, nailed down his timeline, then sent his sorry ass home. Taylor didn't think he'd be all that welcome when he showed up at Quinn's door, but didn't feel sorry for him in the least. The man was a horse's ass, and she was sorry that they had no charges they could press against him, just for being a jerk.

He'd left threatening to sue, and Taylor waved to him as he left, wondering how quickly the suit would appear.

She glanced at the corner of her desk where Whitney Connolly's laptop had taken its place of honor. The e-mail light was blinking.

Holding her breath, she opened the cover and booted up the system. Whitney's e-mail was practically empty compared to the other times she'd checked. There was one new message, flagged in red, and Taylor's heart began to race when she saw the address. IM1855195C@yahoo.com. It was him, it was the Strangler. And the time code was from the previous evening. Shit, that meant…

"Baldwin!" she yelled. He was right outside her door, stuck his head in as quickly as her shout ended.

"What? What's wrong?"

She turned the laptop around so the screen faced him. He saw it immediately, rushed into the room and double clicked to open the message. There was yet another poem. He read it aloud.

> *"Cruel and sudden, hast thou since*
> *Purpled thy nail in blood of innocence?*
> *Wherein could this flea guilty be,*
> *Except in that drop which it suck'd from thee?*
> *Yet thou triumph'st, and say'st that thou*
> *Find'st not thyself nor me the weaker now.*
> *'Tis true; then learn how false fears be;*
> *Just so much honour, when thou yield'st to me,*
> *Will waste, as this flea's death took life from thee.*

"The rest of 'The Flea.' And there's more. It says, 'I AM FINISHED.'" He sat down in the chair, white faced. "Son of a bitch. Son of a bitch!" He ran his hands through his hair, shoulders slumped.

Taylor went to him, speaking softly. "He's still out there, Baldwin. I don't care if he says he's finished. He's not. Someone like that will never just stop what he's been doing. Never. We have to find him, Baldwin. We have to find him now." She set a hand on the back of his neck and squeezed. He reached up and took her hand, grateful for her touch. He gathered himself as if a great decision had been made.

"Okay. Okay, let's do it. This is just further confirmation that someone was setting up Jake Buckley. Someone who would know his schedule, his habits." He was back on his feet and pacing the small room. "Where's the information from Nathan Chase? I made a request for his visitors' log. And we need Lincoln to do the back trace on the e-mail address. Maybe something will hit this time. We deserve a break." He took a deep breath, composure regained, and picked up the phone. Taylor smiled at him and stepped out to see Lincoln.

She found him on the computer at his desk, trolling through some area of cyberspace that she wasn't familiar with. He threw up his hands as she walked up, yelling, "Score!"

"Playing games on company time again, Lincoln?" He turned, his smile wide, eyes shining. "Not that kind of game. The more esoteric version. I had a link set up to Whitney Connolly's address, put a worm in her system that would enable me to see where any message she received came from. I got him, Taylor. I know where your Yahoo guy sent his last e-mail."

Forty-Eight

Taylor, Baldwin and Lincoln stood outside a coffee shop named Bongo Java, right off the campus of Belmont University. The shop was teeming with people, bohemian students, yuppies in suits, grunge rockers with tattoos and black fingernail polish. It was one of those places that transcended class, didn't care what your background was or who you were trying to be. It served coffee, had a great Internet café and was one of the most popular places in town precisely because it was so ordinary.

They'd secured a quick warrant to smooth their path. As they entered, Taylor took a deep breath, savoring the rich scent of coffee. A latte wouldn't go amiss right now.

They went to the counter and ordered drinks. Baldwin paid, winking. The Bureau would be buying today, a semicelebratory drink for getting on the correct path at last. Taylor and Lincoln withdrew their badges and asked to see the manager. The owner of the shop came out from the back room instead, ready to help Nashville's finest with anything they might need.

While Lincoln talked, explaining what they needed, Taylor looked around. Notices about bands playing, apartments for rent, an upcoming writers' night all crowded into a small but organized corkboard. The realization hit her that the Strangler had probably stood right where she was standing, and a chill crept down her spine. They were close, she could feel it. A visceral reaction to the presence of evil. He could be here at this very moment. She glanced around. That one, with the semi-Mohawk and pierced nostril. Her gaze slid away when the punk gave her the finger. Anarchy, baby. Or him, the mild-mannered-looking man sitting by himself with his briefcase open, staring out the window as if his world had just ended? Perhaps the owner himself, a potbellied man easing into his fifties, looking somber while he talked to Baldwin. Evil took many faces, many of them benign. It just wasn't always apparent.

Lincoln was sitting at a computer docking station, fingers flying, running a program he'd written through the hard drive of the computer. He looked over at her and made an okay sign. He'd found the right computer, found the tracks of their killer in cyberspace.

But the fact that the message had been sent the night before meant that countless people could have used the computer since the Strangler had sat there, typing out his message. Prints weren't an option. There was no other way to trace him. They'd found his last vessel of communication, but couldn't do anything about it.

Taylor went back to the owner, interrupting his conversation with Baldwin. "Is there anyone in here that you recognize from last night?"

Baldwin nodded at her. "That's what we were talking

about. He doesn't see anyone that was here last night other than their regulars. They had a poetry reading, an open-mike night, and there were about fifty people gathered around. He didn't notice anyone unusual."

"I did." A small voice peeped up, right below Baldwin's elbow. A pixie dressed in a long flowing peasant skirt and a vivid rainbow scarf practically had to raise her hand to get their attention. She was tiny, under five feet tall, and beautifully delicate. She gave them a winning smile when they looked down to see her.

"I mean, I saw someone in here last night, working on the computer, during the reading. I was people watching, you know? You get all kinds, they're great fodder for work. I'm an artist," she stated proudly. Taylor bit back a grin, the girl was so tiny, so garishly dressed that Taylor liked her immediately. She'd always admired people who could express themselves in such ways.

"Wow, what happened to you?" the girl asked Taylor. "You're looking pretty beat up." She eyed Taylor. "I don't even know if I could mix the right colors to paint that bruise. Does it hurt?"

Taylor smiled. "It's nothing to be concerned about, but thanks for asking. We need to know what you saw last night."

"Yes, ma'am, what did you see?" Baldwin asked, hands clenched in anticipation.

Suddenly the center of attention, the girl stood a little straighter and cleared her throat. "There was a man on the computer last night. I took notice because he was just so damn handsome. I thought about going over and introducing myself, but as soon as I got up the courage, he logged off and left. I was bummed. You don't often get to see such beauty in a man. I would have loved to have him sit for me."

Taylor felt her heart quicken, just an extra beat per second. "What did he look like...what's your name again?" she asked.

"I'm Isabella. I'm in here most every night. Days, too, sometimes. Depends on how the craft is going, if the Muse is with me or not."

"So, Isabella, what did he look like?" Baldwin wanted to get things back on track.

"He was about six-four, almost as big as you. Muscled, too, he had on this black cashmere T-shirt that looked like it was painted on him. Saw every muscle, and he was cut, too. A regular Adonis. Black hair, wavy, kinda long. And these blue eyes. I've never seen such a shade of blue. I would have to mix my own colors to get it just right, it's not something that comes from a box, you know?" She shook her head, eyebrows knitting. "Well, I'm being stupid, I sketched him."

She opened a portfolio and riffled through a few pages. "Here, this is him. Amazing, isn't he?"

Taylor took the page from her eagerly. She and Baldwin each held a corner, staring at the perfect jaw, the chiseled nose, full lips that made the face almost feminine. Taylor was taken aback; surely this angel couldn't be their killer. Their eyes met and she realized Baldwin was thinking the same thing. He gave her a little nod.

"Isabella, may we hold on to this?" he asked.

The waif looked sad for an instant, then nodded.

"Well, of course, of course you can have it. But is there any chance I could get it back once you're finished with it? It was the best of the lot." She blushed furiously. "I did a few," she admitted.

Taylor reached out and shook the girl's hand. "I promise we'll get it back to you. You may not want it, but we'll get it back." She gave Isabella a card. "Thank you, Isabella. This is going to be a huge help."

"Can I ask you what he did that has you so interested in him? I mean, was he sending bomb threats or something?" Her eyes went a little dreamy at the thought of a dangerous man in an eye-catching package.

Taylor shook her head. "Just do me a favor. If you see him again, run away. Then call me."

They left her staring after them, trying to figure out what he could have possibly done that was so awful the police were after him. She gave a shrug and turned back to her coffee.

Forty-Nine

Taylor and Baldwin pulled up to the gate in front of Quinn Buckley's house. They'd called to make sure she'd see them, surprised when Jake Buckley answered the phone. He had adamantly refused to let them come to his house until Quinn picked up the phone and told him it was her house and he didn't have a say anymore. He'd hung up in a huff, and Quinn had told them to come. Taylor reached out the window to press the button, but the gate swung open before her hand reached the box. She glanced at Baldwin. Obviously Quinn had been watching for them.

Taylor drove up to the house where Quinn was waiting on the front step. They got out of the car and mounted the steps, meeting her at the top.

"You said it was important. About Whitney. What is it?" she asked without greeting them. There were black circles under her eyes, her hair was slicked back into a ponytail and her nose was red. She'd been crying recently. Taylor's heart went out to her, she barely looked like the same put-together woman she'd come to expect.

"It is about Whitney. We have a sketch we'd like to show you. A witness saw this man on a computer at the same time we received a message on Whitney's e-mail. Can we go inside?"

Quinn looked startled, then shrugged. She turned and led the way into the house.

The activity was obvious. Jake Buckley's luggage was sitting in the foyer. Buckley himself was standing at the foot of the stairs, defiant. Taylor just nodded to him, Baldwin ignored him completely. He was no longer a person of interest to them.

But Buckley wasn't going to let them pass without a fight.

"Hey, you two. When do I get my car back? I need some transportation, you know."

Taylor rounded on him. "You'll get it back when we're finished with it, Mr. Buckley. There is a great deal of evidence in that car, and we need to process it. You'll get a call in a few weeks, I'd assume."

"A few weeks? Jesus, lady, you don't have the right—"

Taylor pointed a finger at him. "I have all the right in the world. I'm conducting an investigation, in case you've forgotten. A dead girl was found in your car, Mr. Buckley. How about a little respect for her, huh?"

She turned away from him, furious. What a complete asshole, she heard from her shoulder. She stifled a laugh. Baldwin had spoken so only she could hear, but it took all her wherewithal not to giggle. She agreed completely.

They followed Quinn to the library. She ushered them in, gestured to the sofa and shut the doors behind them. They could still hear Buckley blustering in the hallway.

Quinn settled herself on her leather chair and shook her head. "He's completely come undone over this. I filed for divorce this morning. Kicked his ass out. He just won't leave."

Taylor leaned forward. "I can take care of that if you want."

"We'll see. Now, what do you want to show me? A picture of someone?"

Baldwin drew the picture out of his briefcase and handed it to Quinn. "Do you recognize this man? We believe he may have been the one sending the poems to your sister."

Quinn took the picture with a steady hand, but gasped aloud when she looked at it. She dropped the paper as if she'd been burned. Her face drained of color and her hand flew to cover her mouth.

"What is it, Quinn? Do you recognize him?" Taylor retrieved the sketch from the floor at Quinn's feet. She had begun crying, softly at first, then the emotion building so fast that the words were choked off by her sobs. She was speaking, but neither Taylor nor Baldwin could understand her.

"Quinn, please, you have to calm down. Take a deep breath, good girl, that's the way." Baldwin's voice was low, soothing, and he took Quinn's hand. "Try again. Tell me who this is."

She took a few more snuffling breaths, then swallowed hard and looked Baldwin straight in the eye. "It's Reese."

Taylor stood. "Wait, you mean that's Reese Connolly? Your little brother?"

Quinn nodded. The two words she'd spoken had aged her twenty years. Her mouth opened and closed a few times as if she was trying to find the right words. Taylor stood still, not wanting to interrupt. Quinn finally began to speak.

"I don't understand. What in the world was he thinking? Why would he be sending Whitney poems like that? You don't think he had anything to do with this? It's impossible, he's been out of the country. There's no way that Reese… Oh my God!"

She stood and looked ready to bolt. Baldwin stood as well, the three of them making a stiff triangle, waiting to see who moved next. Quinn was the first. She crumpled in a graceful heap.

"Shit, she's fainted. Baldwin, do something."

Baldwin looked at her, helpless. "What do you want me to do? She fainted dead away."

"Well, wake her up. You're a doctor, do what doctors do. We need to get her to tell us where Reese is. Surely she knows, he's her brother after all."

"I'm a psychiatrist, Taylor, not an internist." He knelt down, but Quinn's eyes were already fluttering, and her hand raised up limply, looking for support. Baldwin grabbed it, feeling her pulse at the same time. It was just a good old southern belle faint. He helped her back up, onto the sofa.

Taylor went in search of something cool to drink. She came back with a bottle of Evian water she'd found in the cavernous refrigerator. Quinn was looking better but she gave her the water anyway, eyeing her like she was a bomb about to go off. Taylor hated that kind of weakness, the notion of it made her nervous.

Quinn took a few sips of water and leaned back into the cushions of the sofa, looking utterly forlorn. She was mumbling to herself, saying the name over and over. Reese, Reese, Reese.

Taylor stared at Baldwin and he sat down next to Quinn. "Quinn, I need you to tell me where Reese is. Where does he live?"

Quinn rattled off an address. Taylor grabbed her phone and walked to the other side of the room. She dialed in to her office. Fitz picked up the phone.

"Fitz, I've got an address on the Strangler. Name's Reese Connolly... That's right, their little brother. Listen, you need to get over there right now. With any luck... Yes, I'll meet you there. Okay then. Suit up, too, this guy's dangerous." She hung up and walked back to Quinn and Baldwin. She raised her eyebrows at him, saying, okay, let's go, we got an address, it's time to roll. But he shook her off. Quinn was talking to him, the words coming out in a torrent.

"It makes sense to me now. Reese would know about the poems. Jake, when we first started dating, used to send me little notes. He'd put them in the mailbox, leave them in the refrigerator. He was hopelessly romantic back then. Reese would know all about them, he lived with us until he started college. We married right after he moved into the dorms. You know he was an exceptional child. Brilliant, started college when he was only fifteen. He's only twenty-one now and into his residency at Vanderbilt. I'm so proud of him. There's no way he could be killing these girls. Sending the poems, that I can see, not understand, but he'd know. And he could do that with his laptop. But the killings, he's been in Guatemala. There's no way." She was babbling, and Baldwin tried to guide her through it.

"Is there any way to confirm that?"

"Well, certainly. I can just call one of the doctors he was with. Hold on a moment, let me get the number. I couldn't reach them while they were in the field, that's why Reese didn't know about Whitney, but they returned yesterday… You'll see, Reese wasn't involved." She opened the drawer of a writing desk and pulled out a brown leather dayrunner. She flipped to a page, ran her finger down to an entry, then with her other hand dialed the number into the phone. It took a moment to get the connection, then she began speaking.

"Jim Ogelsby, how are you?" The gracious greeting was accompanied by a smile. "Did you have a wonderful mission trip? You did? That's amazing. I want to hear all about it. No, I just have a quick question for you. How did Reese do? What? He didn't? He…are you sure? Okay then, thanks, Jim. No, we'll have to catch up later. See you soon."

She hung up the phone, eyes wide. "Jim says Reese didn't accompany them on the trip. He told them he couldn't get the required shots, that he was allergic to something in them. He lied." The wonder in her voice was painful. "He lied to me, about everything. How could he do that? Oh dear God, he was here all the time."

Taylor nodded. "Would Reese know about Jake's travel? Where he is at any given time?"

"Of course. I always send a copy of Jake's itinerary to both Whitney and Reese. Jake's secretary compiles it once a month and I just get in the habit of sending it out to them." A look of horror dawned on her face. "You think Reese was trying to set Jake up, don't you?"

Baldwin nodded. "It's possible. Did Reese know about the problems you and Jake were having?"

Quinn thought hard for a minute. "I always try to keep that private, but I'm sure I've let little things slip here and there. Of course, they're both men, and men sometimes understand each other and what they're doing outside of the house."

"Did Reese dislike Jake?" Baldwin asked.

That stopped her for a moment. "Dislike Jake? I honestly don't know. He always seemed respectful and courteous. They weren't that close."

Baldwin nodded, then caught Taylor's eye. "Quinn, we have to go now. We need to see if we can find Reese. Please, lock your doors behind us. You'll be perfectly safe here at the house. Just don't go out until we call, okay?"

Quinn sat, hands in her lap. She was so still, Taylor thought she must be holding her breath. She finally looked up at them. "I'll do whatever you say. Please, don't hurt him. He doesn't know, he couldn't know. This is all just a huge misunderstanding. Please, when you find him, let me be the first to talk to him."

"What doesn't he know, Quinn?" Taylor walked back to the couch and knelt in front of Quinn. She took one of Quinn's hands in her own. "What doesn't he know?" she repeated.

Quinn looked at the ceiling, drawing in a breath. She whispered the words. "He doesn't know that he's not our brother."

Fifty

"There's no one at his house." Fitz's disembodied voice was yelling out of Taylor's speakerphone as she and Baldwin broke all the traffic laws and speed limits getting to Reese's house. "We've cleared the scene. He got away."

"Put out a BOLO for him and his car. He's in the wind again, and we can't take a chance that he's going after another girl." She clicked off the speaker and glanced over at Baldwin, who was talking into his cell phone and making notes as quickly as he could.

"Okay, thanks. That's what I needed." He hung up and returned Taylor's gaze, eyes deadly serious. "Nathan Chase has had one visitor. Only one. It was a male who came to visit him nearly five years ago. Care to guess who that someone is?"

"Reese Connolly."

"That's right. Now it all makes sense. If Quinn had just told us in the beginning that Reese wasn't her and Whitney's little brother, but a son, that would have made life a little easier."

"Baldwin, I don't think she's told too many people about it. Obviously, she didn't even think Reese knew. But he figured it out, didn't he?"

"He must have. Visiting his father in jail. Man, that's…wait a minute. Head back to the office. I want to check something out." They arrived at the CJC in five minutes. Taylor parked on the street and they bounded through the back door, right into her office. Whitney Connolly's laptop was still open on Taylor's desk, an inanimate object that held all the answers they'd been seeking, if only they'd known where to look.

Baldwin pulled up the e-mail folder, then went to the white board in Taylor's office, writing the address down.

IM1855195C

He started teasing the letters and numbers apart, the white board quickly filling up with symbols that made no sense to Taylor. Baldwin looked positively blissful, a mad Sam Nash of the profiling world. He finally stood back and let her see the finished product.

I/ M/ 1/8/ 5/ 5/ 1/9/ 5/ C
IM/18/5/5/19/C
I'm 18 5 5 19 5 C
I'm R E E S E C
I'm Reese Connolly

Baldwin's face was triumphant, as if he'd just solved the most intricate key to the world's most obscure riddle.

"How'd you do that?" she asked, not exactly stroking his ego but knowing he wanted to show it off.

"At first I thought it was Nathan Chase's prisoner number, but that didn't match up. It's a simple code, correlating to the letters of the alphabet. R is the eighteenth letter, E is the fifth. S the nineteenth. After that it was pretty clear."

Taylor stared at the board for the longest time, then stood, took the pen from Baldwin and wrote her own answer below his. The words chilled them both.

I AM REESE CHASE.

"His father's son. That's what all this is about, isn't it, Baldwin?"

Baldwin was staring at the board, nodding. "I think it is."

Fifty-One

Quinn Buckley was lying on the sofa in her library. She hadn't moved since the police had left, simply stretched her feet to the right and her arms to the left and had gone horizontal with the minimum amount of effort. She was numb. Her sister was dead. Her husband was gone. And her son was wanted for murder.

For so many years, Whitney and their parents had fought about it. Whitney was willing to take on the responsibility, to call Reese her own. She wasn't afraid of the scandal. She wasn't afraid of anything. But their parents had decided.

The word had gone out. Eliza Connolly had been blessed with a late-in-life pregnancy. A wondrous miracle, and weren't they so deserving, after what the whole family had been through. Why, Peter Connolly had comforted his wife in the only way a man truly knows how to comfort a woman who's grieving, and look at the result. A son to call their own. Of course, Eliza had the baby a couple of months prematurely, but no one quibbled about that. It just wouldn't be the right thing to do, now, would it?

Reese Connolly had come into the world the object of wonder and innuendo, but never, never to his face. The child was brilliant, precocious, so beautiful with his Raphael black curls and his cherub mouth. The eyes that took in everything, let nothing slip him by. No, there was nothing Reese didn't excel at.

Quinn shifted slightly. Her life's punishment was her inability to be brave at the appropriate times. She should have kicked Jake out the minute he yelled at her when she tried telling him the truth. When he cheated on her the first time. The tenth. The twentieth. She lost count. She should have stood up to her parents like Whitney had. Insisted that Reese get the recognition of his own heritage when he was old enough to understand. No, she'd never had the strength her sister possessed in abundance. It had driven them apart—Quinn, her compatriot, her fellow victim, siding silently with the grown-ups, refusing to admit what had really happened.

Yes, she cosseted Reese while Whitney shunned him. She tried, as she got older, to make up for some of the things she'd neglected to help him with in his past. That's why she took him in when their parents died. She could be his mother now, not that he'd be allowed to see that. She made sure he ate well, got to school, paid for his college education as well as medical school. Reese had gotten his own share of the inheritance, but she didn't want him to be troubled with the financials. He didn't need her coddling anymore. He was all man now.

A man wanted for murder. Dear God, where had she

gone wrong with him? She laughed softly to herself. Where hadn't she gone wrong with Reese?

The phone rang. She tried to ignore it, but its shrill insistence finally drove her to get up, drag herself four feet away and pick up the receiver. When she reached it, the noise ceased and no one acknowledged her greeting.

She realized it was dark outside. She'd been lying on the couch for hours. A thought crossed her mind. The twins. Did Jake have them? He must, she hadn't heard a peep from them all afternoon. She didn't remember telling him he could take their children with him when he took off this afternoon. She figured she'd best call his cell phone, insist he bring them home.

She dialed the number, surprised when he answered after only one ring. She tried to be courteous. "Jake, I'd appreciate it if you brought the children back for the night. I don't know where you're staying but they have their own needs, their own beds to sleep in…. What? You don't have them? Did you drop them off somewhere? Oh my God, Jake, where are they?"

She was wailing, running through the house calling their names. There was no sign of either child.

The phone rang again. She rushed to it, thinking it was Jake, telling her he was kidding, just punishing her for kicking him out. It wasn't.

The voice on the other end of the phone was so soft, so low, she could barely hear it. Even months later, she'd swear she hadn't really known what was said.

"Meet me in the clearing. Come see your children die."

Fifty-Two

Taylor and Baldwin were sifting through Reese Connolly's life. His small two-bedroom bungalow in West End was simple, clean and held few clues as to the nature of the killer who lived within its walls. A dig was going on in the backyard. Marcus had spotted freshly turned earth, and further investigation showed six perfect mounds, one laid out next to another with flawless symmetry. The first grave held a decomposing woman's hand. Very carefully, the remainder of the mini graves were being excavated.

Taylor's cell rang, and she sighed as she stopped, reaching for the phone, clicking it on. Even the most mundane task was exhausting. She wasn't prepared for what she heard when she answered.

Quinn Buckley was hysterical, screaming into the phone. Taylor tried to calm her, to no avail. She gleaned only a few tidbits of information from the call—that Quinn's children were missing, and that Quinn had been instructed to go to the spot they'd been playing the day she and her sister were kidnapped. Taylor remembered from Quinn and Whitney's file that it was behind their parents' old place, out on Belle Meade Boulevard.

The homicide team split up. Taylor and Baldwin headed to the park. The drive took only ten minutes. Reese's West End home was easily accessible to the main roads and they sailed through the dark night without trouble.

Taylor and Baldwin were tense and alarmed. Not speaking, each attuned to the other, they got themselves emotionally prepared. When children were involved, sometimes the results could be heartbreakingly bad. They had both seen the tumult that came into play with domestic violence. If what Quinn said was true, they would need to focus as much of their energies as possible to get the children out safely.

They pulled onto Belle Meade Boulevard, Taylor counting down the addresses until they located the home that had belonged to the Connollys when the girls were children. They pulled into the entrance, struck by the house in front of them. Quinn had mentioned the house had sold recently but was unoccupied. A stroke of luck, the new tenants weren't there to contend with.

Taylor backed out, then pulled to the side of the Boulevard, right down the street from Quinn's, and cut off the lights on her car. The moon was full, making the shadowy world before them shimmer. She and Baldwin jumped the fence and carefully made their way up to the house. There were two cars before them in the circular drive.

Taylor recognized the bottle-green classic Jaguar that had been parked in Quinn's driveway. The other car she wasn't familiar with, a black soft-top Jeep Wrangler. She radioed in the plates. The car was registered to Reese Connolly.

It was time, then. All the leads, the missteps, the death over the past two weeks would be decided in this last moment. Reese Connolly's last stand against the world. And he was doing it with two innocents at his side.

Taylor and Baldwin crept around the side of the house, silent in the darkness. Surprise was their only chance to help Quinn and her children. Reese didn't know they would be here, ready to take him into custody. Or worse, if warranted.

"How do you want to do this?" Taylor asked, eyes adjusting to the darkness. The moon was giving off enough light to help them.

"Let's take it slow, go through the woods. With any luck, Quinn was overreacting. Let's get in there, see what there is to see. Maybe nothing will have to be done."

Taylor's hand slid the familiar route to her Glock, stationed at the ready on her hip. She unsnapped the holster strap, heard a corresponding snick from Baldwin, two feet to her right. She signaled to him in the shadows, motioning for him to go ahead. She broke out a flashlight, covered the edge with her free hand so they wouldn't be seen and moved through the gloom into the backyard of the house.

"Through there," Baldwin whispered, pointing to a small opening in the woods. "That should be the path to the clearing."

They crept along the path, swatting branches and spiderwebs from their faces. After about fifty yards, the path grew wider. They could see the clearing just ahead.

Careful to make no noise, Taylor slid from behind the cover of the trees, Baldwin right on her heels. She could already hear sobbing, pleading and the strong voice of the man who'd claimed eight lives.

"Quit blubbering, Quinn, it makes your face all puffy. You want to look beautiful for the cameras tomorrow, don't you? You'll want to be the fresh and pretty mom next door, keening and wailing in your reserved way, sorry about the death of your children and only brother. Oh, but that's not right, is it? I'm not your brother after all. Just a poor kid who no one thought could handle the truth. You and Whitney let them, Quinn. You let them perpetrate the lie." There was a shuffling and a thin, high-pitched squeal came out of the darkness. One of the children had cried out and been muffled.

Quinn's voice was choked with emotion. "Reese, you don't understand. You can't possibly understand. We were twelve years old, Reese. Twelve. Our innocence stripped away on a couch that stank of beer and sweat. Please, Reese, my children have nothing to do with this. You and I have many things to talk about, to work through. I'll help you every way I can. I'll get you out of the country so you don't have to stand trial. But please, Reese, let my children go. They're innocent in all of this, they shouldn't be punished for the sins of their mother."

Quinn was pleading now. With her voice for cover, Taylor stepped even closer, lodging herself against a young tree for support, her gun drawn and ready. She risked a glimpse around the tree. Quinn was approximately forty feet from her, she could see her clearly in the moonlight. Reese, though, was out of sight, a disembodied voice ringing out through the night. She couldn't see the children, either. Shit, it was a blind shot. Not a thing she could do. Not yet.

Quinn continued trying to talk Reese into handing over the children. She must have started moving, because Reese's voice rang out, clear and cold.

"Don't move another inch, Quinn. This knife I have against sweet little Jake Junior's throat could slip, and he'll go down fast if you come any closer."

Quinn raised her hands in submission and took a few steps back. Taylor realized that from Quinn's angle, she could see Reese, had a clear view of him. Could see the knife pressed to her child's throat.

Quinn gave up trying to negotiate for her children's lives, settling instead on trying to get answers from Reese. Good girl, Taylor thought. Keep him talking, let us get him surrounded and cut off. She sent the mental message to Quinn, praying that the woman could feel her presence.

Baldwin caught Taylor's eye. He held up a hand, fingers splayed. Five minutes, he was saying. Give me five minutes to get into place, then we'll take him. She nodded and watched Baldwin creep away. If Quinn could keep him occupied for five more minutes.

Taylor tuned herself back into the conversation Quinn and Reese were having.

"Reese, please honey, tell me why. Why did you kill all those girls? What made you go crazy like that?"

"I AM NOT CRAZY!" he roared, and one of the children gave a whimpering yell. "Shut up, you little shit. Shut up or I'll kill you, you hear me? Quinn, that kind of talk is going to get your babies killed. But I'll answer your question. I did it for my mother."

"Reese, you don't—"

He interrupted her. "Don't tell me what I don't know. I know, all right? I've known since I was fourteen. Old enough to understand, I think. Mommy got raped and had a baby. I knew all about the birds and bees by then, Quinn. All you had to do, all any of you had to do was tell me the truth. We wouldn't be here now. But you didn't. You hid it away, ashamed of me, ashamed of what had happened.

"I read Whitney's diary the day your parents were killed. That's when I realized, finally understood. She was so strong, wanted so badly to let the world know I was her son. Even though she never admitted it, I knew. I could tell as she looked at me. As I got older, she started pulling away. She didn't want to have to admit how wrong she'd been. But I would have forgiven her, Quinn. I would have forgiven my mother anything."

Taylor inched around the trees, trying to get into a position where she could see Reese. She moved deliberately, stalking from one tree to the next. After two minutes, she could almost touch Quinn, she was so close. Three more minutes.

Reese continued his diatribe. "I did the next best thing. If Mommy wouldn't acknowledge me, maybe Daddy would. And he did. You remember Daddy, don't you, Quinn? Nathan Chase? I'm sure he remembers you fondly. No, don't get me wrong, I'm not saying that it was right, what he did." His voice broke for a moment. "I'm not saying what I did was right, either. But it had to be. I had to help my mother." His voice grew stronger.

"It was the best idea. Something that would get Whitney's attention. Something that would make her a star. You knew how much she wanted to be a national-network reporter. You know the pains she went to, making herself perfect. She just needed that one story that would break her out of the pack. I gave her that."

Quinn's breathing grew shallow. "You're telling me you killed eight girls to help Whitney get a story? That's what all this is about?"

"Seven. One little bitch died on me. It was a wonderful idea. Something that would get national attention. Especially moving the bodies from state to state, and leaving a hand behind. I knew that would get the right people involved, would dramatize everything. I thought it was fitting, seeing as my real mother never laid hands on me, never held me in her arms as her son. I didn't have the stomach for it at first, but as I went on, I got used to it."

The vomit, Taylor thought. At the first crime scene. He'd been so scared and nervous he'd thrown up. That explained the hesitation marks on Susan Palmer's arm, as well. If only he had stopped then.

But Reese was bragging now. Any hope of him being sane was gone.

"I got good at it. Even started enjoying myself. And it got your stupid husband out of the way, too. I set him up so good." Reese sounded like a child at that moment. A child wanting a pat on the head for his good behavior.

"I did it all for her, Quinn. I knew, deep down, that if I helped her, she'd love me again, like she did when we were kids. I'm her son, dammit. Now she's gone, too, and all my hard work was for nothing. For nothing!" His cry echoed throughout the dark emptiness, and Taylor took that moment to step out of the shadows, gun leveled at the sound of Reese's voice. The minute she was behind Quinn, she could see him, silhouetted against the night sky. She could see Baldwin, as well, inching up to Reese's left. They were in position, would be able to stop him.

Quinn had been silent for the past few moments. She spoke again, her voice clear and strong, as if a decision had been reached deep within her soul. "Give me my children, Reese. I will make sure that you don't see a jail. That you'll go free. I'm sorry it had to be this way. I'm sorry you felt compelled to kill to get our attention. I assure you, you have it now. You've been bad, Reese, a very bad boy. But I can get you out of this. Just let the twins go and I'll help you."

Quinn began moving toward Reese. Taylor caught a glimpse of something in Quinn's hand out of the corner of her eye. Oh hell, that was just what she needed. Quinn wanted to play hero. She had found a weapon and brought it to the standoff with Reese. She continued to walk toward Reese. Taylor needed to stop this before it went any further. Taylor stepped out in full view behind Quinn and Reese saw her for the first time. He panicked.

"Quinn, who the hell is that? Did you call the cops? I told you not to call the cops. I wanted to talk to you. Now look what you've done. You've given me no choice."

Taylor heard the blade whisk and shouted at Reese.

"Put that knife down! Put it down, Reese! There's no way out of this for you unless you put the knife down and let the kids go. After you do that, we can talk. Put it down, now, Reese." She edged closer to Quinn. "Don't move, Quinn. Stay right where you are. Let us handle this."

She stepped carefully, slowly, advancing on Reese's position. He looked startled, confused, and suddenly heard Baldwin's voice from behind him.

"You're covered on all sides, Reese. Drop the knife and we can walk you out of here alive."

Quinn, ignoring Taylor's instructions, kept talking and moving forward slowly, trying desperately to save her children. "Reese, you can't do that. You can't kill your own brother. Reese, listen to me. Jake Junior is your brother. Jillian is your sister. Do you understand what I'm saying? They're your brother and sister, Reese. You can't kill them." The light shone briefly in Quinn's eyes, tears pouring down her face. "Please, Reese. Please."

Reese was growing more and more agitated. Taylor could see the edge of the knife tip disappear, and a thin trickle of blood ran down Jake Junior's neck. Jillian started to wail. The sight was too much for Quinn.

She bolted, covering the last twenty feet in scant seconds. Taylor tried to grab her, but she was too quick, like a deer startled from the brush. The gun was out in plain view now, leveled at Reese.

"Quinn, don't!" she screamed, but it was too late. Quinn stopped a few feet short of Reese, took aim and pulled the trigger. Reese was down before Taylor's voice faded from her throat. The children ran to their mother, throwing their arms around her legs.

Taylor rushed for Reese. He lay quietly on the ground, a hole in his upper chest, blood spilling out like a fountain. Taylor could see that he was losing blood too quickly, they weren't going to be able to save him if help didn't get here soon. She keyed her radio, called for a bus to rush a shooting victim.

Baldwin was feeling around Reese's body, making sure he had no other weapons he could use. Baldwin pocketed the knife Reese had been holding and nodded to Taylor, he was clean. He kept his weapon trained on Reese, though it looked like there was little chance that it was necessary.

Taylor turned back to Quinn, who was still holding the gun at chest level. "Give me the gun, now, Quinn. Let me have it, that's right. Good girl." Quinn looked at Taylor as if she were a stranger. The gun was limp in her hand, and she didn't fight when Taylor lifted it gently from her. Once she no longer had the gun, Quinn broke down. She wrapped her arms around her children, crying with relief. Taylor stood, pulled the clip from the gun and emptied the bullets into her hand. She shoved them in her pocket and put the gun in the small of her back, tucking it into her jeans.

Quinn pulled herself together and spoke to her children. "Stand with that lady for a minute. I need to talk to your uncle." The children obeyed, too terrified to do anything but, and sidled close to Taylor's legs. Taylor absently patted them on the head, watching Quinn.

Quinn came closer, standing over Reese for a moment, waiting for him to meet her eyes. He finally managed to focus on her. She looked to Taylor and Baldwin for guidance.

"Don't touch him, Quinn. You hit him in the chest,

his lung's already collapsed. I don't know if he's going to make it."

"I just need to talk to him for a moment." There were tears coursing down her cheeks. She knelt beside Reese, her voice quiet but determined.

"Reese, I am your mother. I am so sorry. You're right, we should have told you."

Reese's voice was wheezy, full of pain. "No, you're wrong. It was Whitney. Whitney was my mother." He coughed and a bubble of blood appeared on his lips. He was badly hurt.

Quinn shook her head. "No, that's not right. It was me. They kept us both in seclusion after the kidnapping, but *I* was the one who was pregnant."

Reese tried to speak again, groaning with the effort. "But…Nathan…told me…told me he raped Whitney… not…you."

"Oh, Reese. We were identical twins. He didn't know who was who. We never told him."

The faint wail of sirens reached their ears, growing steadily louder. Taylor murmured to the children to stay put and went to Quinn.

"You have to step back now, Quinn. We need to make room for them to work on Reese." Taylor could see the waxiness of his skin, the light fading from his eyes as he struggled for breath. Funny, neither she nor Baldwin had made an effort to help him. She supposed that was fitting.

Quinn was down on the ground, smoothing Reese's hair back, murmuring to him. The blood was flowing steady and strong from the wound in his chest, and Taylor could see the sheen of sweat on his upper lip. He was whispering back to Quinn, over and over, repeating the same two words. "I'm sorry. I'm sorry."

The sirens cut through the night. The ambulance pulled to the road and the EMTs rushed through the clearing. Taylor pulled Quinn back.

"We need to give them room to work on him, Quinn. Hold it right here for a moment."

Quinn looked at Taylor. "Will they be able to save him?"

Baldwin stepped into the light, laying a hand on Quinn's arm. "Let's let them work, Quinn. You're going to need to step over here with me."

Baldwin signaled to the patrol officer that had joined the ambulance. "Please take Mrs. Buckley to your car. She needs to sit down." The man marched her smartly away.

Taylor raised an eyebrow. "Are we going to have to charge her?"

"She just shot a man. I think there will be enough to claim some kind of self-defense, but we need her clear of the scene."

Quinn was put into a patrol car, eyes down. Baldwin signaled to another patrol, the children needed to be attended to, as well. Neither was badly hurt, just shaken. Jake Junior had a thin line of blood along his collar. One of the EMTs came to them, looking them over. They were going to be just fine. They were seated in the car with their mother, who gathered them in her arms and buried her face in their shoulders. Baldwin studied them for a moment. They would remember this night forever, he was sure of that. He turned back to the focus of the night.

The EMTs were lifting Reese onto the stretcher, ready to take him to the hospital. Taylor went to them.

"Is he going to be all right?"

The EMTs' hands were slick with Reese's blood. "Yeah, we should be able to get him to the hospital without too much trouble. Another inch and he wouldn't make it. Lucky son of a bitch."

"Then hold on just a moment." She pulled her cuffs out of her back pocket, reaching for Reese's arm. He was groaning and cursing, incoherent with pain and weak from blood loss. She snapped the cuff around his wrist, then affixed the other end to the stretcher rail.

"He's under arrest. Don't let that cuff off of him, do you understand?"

The EMT started to protest. "But we can't—"

"Don't even think about arguing with me. A patrol will ride with you for security. I'll meet you at the hospital. Now go."

She walked the few steps back to Baldwin, a smile on her face.

"We got him."

Fifty-Three

Taylor and Baldwin were seated on the back deck, drinking ice-cold beer from the bottle. Reese Connolly was being arraigned today.

The past week had gone by in a blur. Reese had made it to the hospital, and after several touch-and-go hours, the doctors had repaired the damage and declared that he would live. Taylor felt such immense satisfaction at the declaration. The bastard would pay for his crimes, would be brought to trial and judged. Reese's instincts had been right, he was a national story, one his aunt would have been desperate to cover. As it was, in death Whitney Connolly had gained the fame and notoriety she'd always craved.

Quinn kept insisting Reese was so consumed with hatred and misguided loyalty that he wasn't in his right mind when he committed the atrocious murders that paralyzed the Southeast for the summer. The D.A. had decided not to seek an indictment against her. She had hired the best criminal attorney in Nashville and was fervently seeking support for an insanity defense for her eldest son.

Baldwin had spent a long afternoon at Riverbend prison, visiting with Nathan Chase, trying to find if there were any missing pieces to fill in. Nathan happily admitted to his past crimes and showed genuine pride in his son's accomplishments, as he'd referred to Reese's murderous spree.

For his part, Reese was seeking sympathy from all quarters, doing his damnedest to make sure all involved knew he wasn't culpable for his crimes. At the hospital, after his surgery, he had explained in detail what he had done. How he had shadowed Jake Buckley, watched him cuckold Quinn again and again. Had decided that Jake would be the perfect fall guy for the crimes.

Reese had admitted that he had started running out of time, had started killing the girls on the road instead of taking the time to get them back to their homes. Blood evidence had been found in a roadside rest stop just forty miles south of Roanoke. The blood matched Marni Fischer. Baldwin had been correct about Noelle Pazia's asthma attack. She'd died in the trunk of the car, and his fury at finding her dead drove him to new lengths of horror with Ivy Clark.

There is no such thing as killing for the right reason. But in his mind, Reese was doing just that. He was reaching out in the only way he knew how, trying to get the approval and nurturing he thought he'd been denied for so long. Ironically, it was Quinn who met all those needs, something he never recognized.

His lawyer, a shrewd and experienced man, was

making it quite clear to anyone that would listen that Baldwin had coerced a confession out of his client while the man was still under the influence of narcotic drugs from the surgery. He was making a play to get the whole case dropped on the technicality. It was turning into one of the most impressive three-ring circuses that Nashville had ever seen.

Baldwin was quiet, basking in the late-summer sun. The days were cooling, the evenings bringing a chill to the air. Fall would be here soon.

"Taylor," he said softly. She looked at him, eyes smiling.

"I talked to Garrett this morning. Told him that I was resigning."

Taylor turned to him, putting a hand up to shield her eyes from the glare of the sun. "Are you kidding me?"

He shook his head. "No, I'm not kidding. I want to strike out on my own, get away from the Bureau. Maybe start my own firm, consulting. You could come work with me."

"I'm not ready to leave Metro, Baldwin, you know that."

"Then you could confer with me on some of the consultancies. Regardless, it's done. I'm mailing the papers in the morning. I want to be here, Taylor. With you."

He stood and went to her, hands on her arms, head bent to touch her forehead.

"I'm tired of this life. Tired of watching these crimes, waiting for the next killer to surface. I want more. I want to be with you. Today, tomorrow. Forever.

I want you to be my wife." He took her left hand in his and she felt something hard slide down her fourth finger. She looked at her hand, astounded by the sparkling diamond.

Taylor was stunned. Not so much by the proposal, but by the emotion she was feeling. Wife. The word was so foreign to her. It wasn't something she had really thought about, not seriously. She knew Baldwin loved her, and she him. But the idea of spending the rest of her life with him wasn't something she'd let herself think about.

They faced such danger every day. Evil spread like a cancer through their lives, binding them to the darkness. Marriage seemed like such a hopeful proposition. Happiness wasn't a luxury she'd thought she could afford.

"Baldwin, I…I don't know what to say."

The look on his face broke her heart. "I don't mean that I'm saying no. I just hadn't thought about it. Not seriously. I…Baldwin, I hate the thought of losing you. I'm scared that if we do get married, I might lose you."

"Taylor, that's crazy thinking. I'm not going anywhere. No one is going to come between us. I'll keep you safe. I'll keep us both safe."

She felt tears prick the corner of her eyes. Baldwin was standing back a few feet now, looking at her as if she might explode. The naked vulnerability on his face overwhelmed her. He took it as a sign that she was refusing, started to leave, to go into the house. Taylor caught his arms. She grasped his hand, brought it to her lips. The tears were coming now, trickling down her cheeks. She swiped a hand across her cheek, smiled through the haze that was clouding her eyes. She pulled him close, drawing him back down to her. She brushed his lips with hers.

"No, please don't. Please, don't go."

She took a deep breath.

"Yes."

ACKNOWLEDGEMENTS

The process of writing *All the Pretty Girls* was without a doubt a group effort. There are many people who graciously gave their time and expertise to help me get the details straight. I would like to send my deepest thanks to the following:

My extraordinary editor, Linda McFall of MIRA Books, and all of the MIRA team, especially Margaret Marbury and Dianne Moggy. A very special thank-you to Tara Kelly for designing the perfect cover.

My incredible agent Scott Miller, of Trident Media Group, for taking a chance on a unknown, and Holly Henderson Root, for all her help and editorial advice.

Detective David Achord of the Metro Nashville Homicide Department was an invaluable resource for the law enforcement details in the book. Not only did he allow me to ride along with him, he read, edited, gave ideas and information, encouraged me to keep on track and was always there for a question, chat or dinner. In the process, he's become a great friend and I am very thankful to have him on my side.

Officer Carl Stocks of the Metro Nashville Police Department took me on a midnight-shift ride-along that changed my life. He showed me that the horrors we write and read about are very real and I have great respect for his abilities and dedication to getting it right.

The Metro Nashville Homicide Department gave me complete support and continues to handle even the most mundane questions. Detective Mike Mann helped me understand the mind-set a homicide detective must have to keep sane and shared in ghost stories. Dr Michael Tabor, the Forensic Dentist for the state of Tennessee, was a font of detail and information and my respect and awe for his efforts following the September 11 attacks is everlasting. Kris Rinearson of Forensic Medical and the Medical Examiner's Officer for Tennessee provided long-standing insights.

Nashville is a wonderful city to write about. Though I try my best to keep things accurate, poetic licence is sometimes needed. All mistakes, exaggerations, opinions and interpretations are mine alone.

The support and encouragement of friends and family were vital for both motivation and sanity. Many thanks to the Bodacious Music City Wordsmiths – Janet, Mary, Rai, Cecelia, Peggy, my Dutch uncle Del Tinsley and my wonderful critique partner, J.B. Thompson. This story couldn't have been told without your input! Joan Huston caught all the little errors and a couple of big ones. Linda Whaley is there for me always.

John Sandford inspired me to write and Stuart Woods gave me the rules. John Connolly taught me about faith, grace and pitch-prefect prose. Lee Childs, my ITW mentor, is just one big class act and M.J. Rose is always ready with a quip or a shoulder. Fellow authors Tasha Alexander, Brett Battles, Jason Pinter, Rob Gregory-Browne, Toni Causey, Kristy Kiernan and all the Killer Year folks have created a support net that is indispensable. My fellow Murderati bloggers keep me honest.

All my buddies at the Bellevue Post Office, who constantly cheer me on and treat every package with care.

My amazing parents, who constantly remind me that I can do whatever I set my mind to, and my brothers, who've always stood behind me. Jade the cat listened attentively whenever I needed a sounding board and amazed me with her ability to park her butt on each page of the manuscript as it printed.

Finally, to Randy. Your love, fortitude, patience, indulgence, sacrifice and faith in me keep me going. You are the keeper of my soul.